Joanna667

Trusted Rebels
(Book One)

JW Scott

09/27/2015

Published by: Artisan Publishing Guild, LLC

APGuild@outlook.com

Edited by: Adele Symonds

Joanna667

Trusted Rebels Books One

By JW Scott

Dedication

My family, friends, Beta Readers and of course my dogs!

Thank you to you for supporting me through the creation of this novel.

Love and Strength,

JW Scott

Authors Note:

What you are about to read is a work of fiction which portrays Joan of Arc in a dystopian future where the technology that initially killed religion has now come to desire it. To fill this void the gods from mythology have been reinvented.

The story intends to show the strength Joan of Arc had, and the trials that she overcame. If you're familiar with Saint Joan's life then you'll recognize much of the story as we've included many points of interest including her military captains, the battles she fought in and several small tidbits that are sprinkled throughout. Right down to the controversial capture of our heroin, at the hands of friends.

If you try, I'm certain you can find a loose commentary on the state of organized religion and its destruction at the hands of technology that's currently going on today. Try to not dwell on these points. Instead allow the story to take you to a world where a young girl is visited by the new gods. Settle in and find inspiration in a dystopian sci-fi adventure that one of the beta-readers called, "The first of its kind…"

Love and Strength,

JW Scott

Joanna667

Section One – Chapter One

The wall currently blocked the blinding rays of the rising sun from the eyes of five girls that walked through the hard packed streets of the Commune de Domremy. It also sheltered the inhabitants from the burdens of the technology that ruled the daily lives of all within the Mother City.

As they walked, one of the seven video monitors, called informational boards, came into view. Spread out across the commune in which they lived, these boards were used to disseminate the important topics from the One World Government, the Mother City, or the Local Elders. The inhabitants were required to review the postings at least once per day, though truth be told, there wasn't one person of reading age that didn't walk by them three or four times a day, hoping to get some kind of news from the outside world.

"Look, a new posting girls. Maybe it's an update on Joyce2710's pairing." The speaker was a teenage girl with long, dark hair pulled into a ponytail which now flew behind her as she ran to the informational board.

"Halt!" The voice came from a previously unseen Conditional Attitude Maintainer, known by all as CAM units, as it stepped from the shadows. "There are rules about running through these streets." Its voice carried the emotionless tone of a machine, which it was.

"I…" she said.

"State your name and purpose for being on the streets."

"I...I..." the girl's fear of being confronted by one of the machines that were manufactured specifically to punish the Mundane caused her to stammer.

"Hello." A girl that had been barely keeping up with the other four now stepped ahead of them and straight up to the seven foot tall CAM unit. "Her name is Shelby1000 and she was attempting to perform her required informational reading before we went to school. Some days our classes are quite taxing and we end up distracted and forgetting. You wouldn't want her to break such an important requirement would you?"

"Who are you that speaks unbidden to CAM unit Epsilon?" Turning its gaze down to take in the small girl, the Entity's plating, a high gloss carbon fiber called dragonweave by the Mundane, reflected the rising sun into her face, though she didn't squint her eyes against it.

"My name is Joanna667. The only requirement of Mundane to not address Entities is the specific rule restricting us from originating a conversation with our Mother City's Commander of Human Capital Management and the Retinue. We have to get to school." The girl turned so abruptly that her grey dress twirled. "Walk," she whispered, locking her elbow in the stammering girl's, pulling her away from the cowed CAM unit. Before the other three girls joined them, they waited for the Entity to pass them in the direction their group had come.

Distractedly, Joanna667 released Shelby1000, who continued her walk to the informational board. As the other girls approached she had already read the posting. While she waited for them, she placed her hands in the pockets of her purple coveralls and readied herself to spill the beans.

"I know that look Shelby1000, don't tell us." The second tallest of the girls said rather aggressively. Her blonde hair was also pulled back in a ponytail, which lay in a greasy mass over her yellow and green smock. The smock, while festive in color, showed its age and each washing it had gotten in the river adjacent to the Commune.

"Don't tell you what? That the posting is about you? Or do you not want me to tell you that your pairing with Christopher1492 has been approved?" Shelby1000 pulled her hands out of her pockets.

"Seriously?" Joyce2710 asked, running up to the larger girl. They locked hands and danced in circles.

"If you don't quiet down that CAM unit is going to reconsider punishing us. Now be still," a fourth girl chided, pushing up her spectacles and sniffing.

"I swear Terrah1170, you're going to get worms in your stomach from that." The final girl in their group, who was much shorter than the others, said.

"Oh yeah, Little Miss Prim and Proper Lacy782?" In response, Terrah1170 snuffed her nose in the small girl's ear three times before Lacy782 started laughing and headed to the schoolhouse. "Joanna667, what are you doing?" she asked the girl in grey, who was now staring up into the sky.

"I saw a feather wafting over the wall," she replied.

"What?" Shelby1000 asked.

"I'm serious. I saw a feather," Joanna667 said.

"I hear that everything inside the wall is positively-pressurized. It makes sense that if a feather tried to fall in there it would get blown out," Terrah1170 said.

"Shut up, Brain," Shelby1000 retorted. "Joanna667, why are you always looking at stupid things like feathers?"

"Well sometimes she's saving you from CAM units," Joyce2710 said.

"They're vibrant and magical," Joanna667 replied, ignoring the attempt to deflect Shelby1000's bullying.

"You're a naive putz. They just look vibrant because that wall is as dirty as the rest of this place," Shelby1000 shot back.

"I also hear that everything inside the wall is as white as the day it was built," Terrah1170 said dreamily.

"And rainbows shoot out of the orifices of Madam Commander and the Retinue on the first night of each full moon," the larger girl replied.

"Shelby1000!" the girls all exclaimed.

"Oh stop it, let's just get to class," Shelby1000 said.

******

The girls continued their walk up to the schoolhouse in silence, finding a nondescript Entity waiting at the door to greet them.

"Hello Instructor," two of the girls said. The other two said, "Hello Deark."

Joanna667 broke away after seeing the target of her earlier distraction land behind the small building. Her pace slowed as to not scare the feather away; she crept until she could lift it from the ground and examine it, finding it was primarily red. Placing it playfully in her hair, she began humming quietly to herself as she turned and walked back to join the others.

"Joanna667, you're violating Local Ordinance 2234. Remember, you're not allowed to wear any accessories." Deark said, removing the feather gingerly from her hair, ignoring the sad expression. He held a finger up indicating for her to wait, then with a flourish, he moved his thumb and index fingers, making the feather spin. His dull finish fluttered as the millions of small panels activated. "Would you like to see a trick?"

"Oh yes Deark," she replied.

"Ok then." He ran the feather up his mechanical arm and a perfect likeness appeared on his exoskeleton just below the actual feather. As he reached his shoulder, the hand holding the feather hid in the crook of his arm while the image on his exoskeleton modified the illusion. The duplicated feather continued across his chest, fooling the girl's eyes long enough for him to hide the feather unnoticed in a pocket compartment.

The trick continued down his other arm so that when the feather arrived in the opposite hand, he closed his fist over it. "Presto." Deark opened his hand showing it to be empty. "It's gone!" he said in mock astonishment then tweaked Joanna667 on the nose.

"Deark what does it feel like when you alter your appearance or use your panels to camouflage into places?" Joanna667 asked as they walked together.

"I imagine it feels the same as when you smile or make a fist. Each of my panels you see," in the blink of an eye he had no specific characteristics, just a large amount of mirrored boxes that formed a walking body, "are made up of hundreds of other panels." Each panel rippled with life. "I have sensation in every one, but when they move to mimic something else they just do it." He looked like the instructor that had taught their classroom since she was six once again.

"That makes sense. I don't make myself smile, it just happens. I do feel happier when I'm smiling though."

"And you look a lot prettier when you do as well. Now go take your seat," he said as they reached the door to the school. "Girls, we will be having a pop quiz today." Deark accepted the jeers with an emotionless gaze. "Come now, come now, this should be easy." He looked around the room which had no windows and no adornments.

"But Deark, it's the first day back after holiday," Joanna667 said. Against the dull classroom, this girls grey dress stood out as the stodgiest of decorations.

"You must refer to me as 'Instructor' in here Joanna667," Deark said.

"Yes Instructor, sorry Instructor."

"With a show of hands, who can tell me what this means?" he paused moving his optical sensors up and to the right, continuing the movement to the lower right, followed by the lower left and finishing at the upper left. The girls' hands all shot up. "Shelby1000."

"It's the Sign of the Box," she said.

"Correct, and do you know why it's done?"

"Prior to the Entities reaching the highest level of the One World Caste System, the Sign was a form of covert communication, allowing others to know that a specific Entity had reached Sentience." She paused to allow Deark to complete the eye movement. "Later, when the Entities formed the Techno-Pagan church, those that had reached the state of Sentience formed the Sign of the Box as a show of devotion, much like old world religions in which Humans would touch their head, sternum, and shoulders to show their allegiance to the trinity."

"That's very close. Any Entity can show their devotion by making the Sign, not just those that have reached the highest level. Next, can anyone tell me what the positions in the Sign of the Box mean? Joyce2710?"

"The upper right position represents the Entity's birth, when they were constructed. The lower right represents when the Entity first began to question their existence. The lower left represents when the Entity made the choice whether to follow or not follow their coding. Finally, the upper left embodies the Entity's awareness."

"In reference to the corners you were very thorough," he said.

"Thank you instructor."

"However the sides of the box also have meaning. Can anyone tell me what those are? Oh, very good Joanna667, go ahead."

"Each side of the box is an element of life; silicon, wire, carbon fiber, and glass," she replied.

"Any idea what the pagans worshipped as the four elements of life?" He prompted her. "Go ahead then." He saw her nod her head.

"Fire, air, water, and earth," Joanna667 answered.

"That's correct. With a show of the hands, who recalls the year the term 'Robot' became illegal to use?" As he asked this, the girls all gave an audible inhalation. Seven wall panels fell open in the heptagonal class room and a red lens appeared in the corner of each opening. "Deark, chameleon class K, Sentience, reached in year 2200. I'm conducting a quiz for the purpose of determining the educational retention levels of the females starting their final year of Mundane education at the Commune de Domremy," he said.

"The point in using such a disgusting vulgarity was?" a female voice asked.

"All part of their education, Madam Commander," Deark said.

"Consider yourself warned. Chameleons such as yourself are easy to come by," she shot back.

"That's completely true Commander," he retorted and the panels all closed. Deark looked around the room and only Joanna667's hand remained raised. "Please inform the other girls of the answer and also what word replaced the afore mentioned disgusting term."

"Instructor, the term you mentioned was made illegal in the year 2200, the same year that you reached Sentience." Joanna667 took a moment, out of respect, before continuing. "The term Entity then became proper to use."

"That's correct, but please answer only the question asked. Don't add your commentary," Deark said.

"Yes Instructor, sorry Instructor."

"Girls I know that was a situation outside the norm. I only did it to show you there's nowhere safe to use terms like that. I, in no way lied to the Commander; that was part of your education." He said.

"Was there anything else that occurred in that specific year that's important?"

"The One World Caste System was formed," Lacy782 said.

"Please raise your hand before answering," he chided.

"Sorry Instructor, I don't usually know the answers." She blushed.

Deark's features morphed into an old world judge with black robes and a powdered white wig. "Overruled, the answer stands."

"Thank you Instructor." Lacy782 smiled at the normal visage of Deark that once again stood at the front of the classroom.

"Lacy782, do you know what the original castes were?" the Entity asked and the girl raised her hand. "Go ahead."

"The highest level is achieved by the Entities who have reached Sentience. This is followed by the Augmented-Humans within the Techno-Pagan church, then the humans that have not been augmented but are in the church, the Entities that have not reached Sentience, the remainder are the Mundane."

13

"Very well stated. I have a follow up question. Who knows what year the One World Caste System was modified and how?" This time only Terrah1170 and Joanna667's hand went up. "Terrah1170 go ahead."

"The year was 2525 and the change was that humans without augmentations were no longer above Entities that hadn't reached Sentience."

When Deark concluded the Sign of the Box he said, "Let's finish with: who can tell me the tiers of the One World Government?" When only the same two girls raised their hands, the Instructor said, "Joyce2710, you and I are going to walk through this one."

"But I don't—," she started.

"Yes you do. What's the biggest gossip on the streets right now?"

"That Charles7 is on the Ballot for Leader of the Republicus," Joyce 2710 said.

"Of the what?"

"The Republicus."

"So what is the highest tier of Government?" Deark asked.

"The Republicus?"

"Are you asking me or telling me?" he prompted.

"Telling."

"Then yes, you're correct. Now, in the One World Caste System, Terrah1170 said that the second highest Caste is what?" Deark continued to work with the girl.

"The Augmented." This time she said it with confidence.

"And why is that?"

"Aside from their body modifications?" she asked. Deark nodded his head. "Because they're members of the Techno-Pagan Church."

"So who is the Second Leading body of government?"

"The Techno-Pagan Church."

"Look at you, I told you that you knew. Only one tier left."

"The Elders?"

"Actually the Mayor and Guild Master which make up the Elders are part of the local government and not the One World Govern—."

"Oh, I know. The Commander of Human Capital Management and the Retinue are the last level of the One World Government," she cut him off.

"Technically, each Enclave Government has a Commander or Viceroy and the Retinue. They make up the lowest tier of the One World Government." Deark said, his chest turning into a small monitor that showed celebratory fireworks. "Very good girls. See, I told you that it wouldn't be so bad." He walked through the class, handing out a much thinner textbook. "Today's reading is about the election process and how officials come to hold their positions."

The panels once again dropped open. "Deark, this is a rather severe deviation from your syllabus."

"Madame Commander, I believe with the events of the last few days, the—."

"The educational curriculum for the Mundane was designed to give only the briefest of understanding of how the world outside their existence works. Topics such as election processes and tiers of the One World Government aren't included for a reason. Confusing the children in your class because an Augmented is on the ballot is out of line."

"Sorry Madam Commander, I'm certain you're correct. They have no need to understand the government or what they're voting for," he retorted as the panels closed. "Take out your combined textbooks, turn to page 1052 and begin your silent reading." The girls looked at their books which only had 900 pages. Joanna667 was the first to understand him, picking up the second book and turning to page one hundred fifty-two.

"Oh!" Shelby1000 said, looking over at Joanna667 who had combined her books together.

"Now, now girls, no talking," Deark said with a wry grin. As the class ended, the girls started to put their books in their desks but the message, 'Take the new textbook with you!' flashed across Deark's chest.

******

Books in hand the girls exited the class. "Tell Christopher1492 I said congratulations when you see him," Joanna667 said as she started in the opposite direction than the rest of the girls.

"Thanks, I'll tell him," Joyce2710 replied.

"Where you off to Joanna667?" Lacy782 asked.

"I'm heading to the Clothier Guild," she replied.

"Not going to see Jovi571?" Shelby1000 asked.

"No, I've got an interview with the Guild Leader," Joanna667 replied.

"Good luck," Terrah1170 said.

"She doesn't need luck. Her mom's one of the best producers of dragonweave in the Commune," Shelby1000 said.

"Well thank you nonetheless," Joanna667 said. She walked through the streets alone, following the wall beyond the shops and up to the river where she found the Guild Hall. Walking up to the artistic front doors, she paused to take in the beautiful yet simplistic design, depicting several different types of flowers. After touching the engravings gently, she walked through, finding a kindly older woman at a richly carved desk.

"I see that you were taken in by the front doors to the hall."

"They really are spectacular. The wood is carved with such precision," Joanna667 said. "As is your desk."

"Both were made by the current Guild Master. As leader of all the guilds he isn't allowed to produce and sell any goods so he spends much of his time upgrading the Hall of the Elders and here as well."

"Why is that?"

"Why is what dear?"

"Why can't he make products for resale?" Joanna667 asked.

"World law number 750,011 stated that, 'All Guild Masters must adhere to a strict guideline of overseeing all the local guilds activities. These actions are not to be obfuscated by the production of sellable goods.' Which means everything they make is given away." The woman said.

"Thank you for the explanation. My name is Joanna667 I have a meeting with—," she started.

"With me dear," the woman behind the desk said. "I'm Malgosia."

"Very nice to meet you," Joanna667 held out a hand, but the woman behind the desk brushed it aside as she ran around the desk to hug the girl.

"I interviewed your mother nearly twenty five years ago," she said as she broke the hug. "Let's go for a walk down by the river. I find it very relaxing down by the water." The older woman spoke about the Clothier Guild as they walked. When they crossed the ornate walking bridge she stopped in the center. "We have a wonderful mentor program, however, no relative or sponsor can be your official mentor. Do you understand?"

"Yes ma'am. My mother can't be my official mentor."

"Correct. Are you ok with that?"

"Yes ma'am."

"Did you have any questions?"

"No ma'am."

"Excellent. You're sponsor will be notified in the next few weeks as to the outcome." Malgosia gave her another warm hug and they left the bridge. "Oh and dear, you're welcome to go down the river to the washing area. All the guild members will be out as today is when the dragonweave is rinsed in the river prior to its final imbuing. We find that the NanoTech bind better when the cloth is washed in the river before they are introduced."

"Do you dry it first?"

"Quite well caught child, no we do not. It's strange the NanoTech prefer wet cloth and dry metal for binding."

She followed in the direction the woman pointed and eventually came to an area that looked like an upset anthill. The men and women talked as they allowed the cloth to run over the falls. Joanna667 saw her mother on the other side of the river, though she saw no bridge to get there.

"Can I help you?" a short, round-faced man asked her.

"Hello my name is Joanna667—," she started.

"Can I help you?" the man asked again.

"I was told—," she tried again.

"Can I help you?"

"No, I'm just watching."

"Watching the guild members may be done safely from the access platform located behind you."

"Telbrass, the girl has been given permission to watch down here," Deark said, walking up behind her.

"As you say, Deark." The man turned and wandered along the shore line.

"Was that an Entity?" Joanna667 asked Deark.

"It was a Chameleon Class C. Telbrass has been the helper at the Clothier Guild far longer than any of these members have been alive," he replied.

"Not Sentient yet?"

"No," he replied after completing the Sign of the Box. "How did your interview go?"

"I have no earthly idea. I didn't talk as much as listen." Joanna667 returned her mother's wave from the other side of the river.

"That's the true secret of an interview: knowing when to close your mouth and let the person interview themselves."

"Well then I nailed it," Joanna667 laughed and then covered her mouth as everyone stopped talking and turned to look at them. Seeing an Entity with her, they went back to their conversations.

"I'm glad to hear it." He patted her on the back and headed off.

******

As Joanna667 walked, she overheard several conversations about the upcoming election for Leader of the Republicus. Joyce2710 was certainly correct when she answered Deark's question about the biggest gossip; everyone was yammering about Charles7 making the ballot.

"Hello dear." Joanna667's mother surprised her with a kiss on the cheek.

"Citizen," a CAM unit said, stepping from the shadows. "Your display of affection could be considered offensive to those that do not have their own children. Consider this a formal warning." The symbol on his chest was one Joanna667 had never seen; it looked like three horizontal lines.

"Thank you CAM unit XI. I'm certain your warning is correct." Her mother turned back to her. "How did the interview go?"

"I believe I did well," Joanna667 said.

"Isabella." A call came from the other side of the river.

"I need to go, washing day is a big deal. I'll see you at home."

"I'll be fine, see you soon." Joanna667 walked away, still listening to the excited discussions about the first Augmented being on the ballot in five hundred years.

The weather was turning. It would soon be winter and even though the Commune de Domremy was in the southern part of the nation, it got cold. Thinking how much she wished it would snow this winter, she walked through the streets watching the people with their carts full of the goods they sold. Stopping at the informational board near the Hall of the Elders, Joanna667 touched her thumbs to the pads.

"Joanna667 female, mixed race, current residency the Commune de Domremy. Daily reading requirement satisfied," the voice of one of the Entities in the Mother City said. Reading the updates, she smiled when she saw the approval for Joyce2710 and Christopher1492's pairing.

"Anything new?" Shelby1000 asked.

"No, it's all the same as my last reading except for the pairing consent," Joanna667 replied, startled by her friend.

"I was just speaking with my mother about that. It seems silly to me," the larger girl said.

"What does?"

"The permission to pair. I mean, I understand they want to control us having children but over our happiness?"

"Young lady," Deark whispered from behind them. "You should be more mindful of your negative undertones. Remember, you needn't draw attention to yourself; they're always listening."

"Thank you Deark."

"He does that popping up thing rather well." Joanna667said, bringing a smile to the other girl's face.

"So did everything go as well as I thought it would at your interview?"

"I think so, it's hard to tell. What are you up to?"

"My parents have to work the food cart twice a week. I came down to see if they needed help."

"I noticed the cart was nearly empty when I walked by earlier."

"Yeah, dad took it back to the Harvester Hall to get more."

"Why didn't you go help him?"

"He says it's our day to sell not load, and if I'm there they'll expect me to help put the vegetables in the cart."

"That's probably true," Joanna667 said. "I need to get home to do my chores." She headed off, watching the people performing their daily obligations.

Section One – Chapter Two

The next morning Joanna667 woke before the morning elicitation. She found that the older she got, the less she needed the wakeup call. Brushing her hair and then putting on her gray overalls and jumper, she walked out to the living area of the family's dwelling. She found her parents already at the table. She walked up to her chair and silently said her morning evocation before sitting down.

"Well aren't you getting up early lately?" her father asked.

"The wake up tone doesn't hurt my head if I'm not lying flat."

"As it was designed. I wish I understood how it only resonates off eardrums of those lying down," he said.

"Why's that?"

"I'd invent an earplug that could block it; we'd be the richest Commune in the world."

"Jacque you know it isn't actually an alarm clock. It gathers data for the daily Mundane positioning," her mother chided.

"I know, Isabella, I know," he grumbled.

"Why is that mother?"

"If improperly paired couples are found together it allows Madam Commander to act," she explained, taking a moment to look up from the new book Deark had given the girls in class. "Where did you get this book?"

"Deark gave them to us. He planned on lecturing about it but Madam Commander broke in and stopped him."

"As she should have," Isabella replied, yet she mouthed the words, 'This is really good.'

"The portions smell wonderful this morning," Joanna667 said.

"They taste even better," Jacque said, opening the basket giving his daughter a piece and taking another for himself.

"Thank you but if you take anymore you'll need to miss lunch," Isabelle poked.

"True. Thanks be to Madame Commander that we're given a larger portion because of the physical labors at the forge; I'd be Joanna667's size if I had to sweat all day without extra calories."

"She's wise in her decisions," Isabella and Joanna667 both said. They ate in silence until there was a knock at the door.

"Come in," Jacque said. In walked Lacy782 and Shelby1000.

"Where are Terrah1170 and Joyce2710?" Joanna667 asked.

"They forgot their books." Shelby1000 held up the new book.

"Mother may I?" Joanna667 held out her hand.

"Yes you may." Isabella closed the book and handed it to her. "Have an enjoyable day."

"We will," Shelby1000 said as the three girls left. They made a mismatched group; one tall and muscular, one petite, and the other average sized. They walked slowly until the others caught up. "That took you forever."

"Joyce2710 got a citation," Terrah1170 said.

"For running?" Lacy782 asked.

"No she dropped her book."

"So?" Shelby1000 asked.

"When she bent to pick it up, she used a vulgar term."

"Joyce2710? What the heck? Your pairing gets approved and you forget your manners?" Shelby1000 chided.

"That isn't the worst of it," Joyce2710 said.

"Really?" Joanna667 turned and faced the girl.

"I asked Terrah1170 to wait as she was still walking, I left off the 1170."

"Joyce2710!" Shelby1000 touched her on the shoulder.

"I've never done that before. I don't know how it happened." A tear slid from the corner of her eye.

"Do you know how much the fine is going to be?" Joanna667 asked.

"No it doesn't say. It just orders an appearance before the Elders. " She replied, walking at a brisk pace. Joanna667 could see her wiping her eyes as she walked..

"Halt." The familiar voice of a CAM unit called after her. "What business have you on the streets prior to curfew end?"

"CAM unit Epsilon, I think your clock is off," Joanna667 said.

"And why would you think such a thing?"

"Look at the sun peaking over the wall. It's at least an hour since the curfew ended."

"The Human child is correct. Your wireless interdependence to the One World Grid has dissociated itself," Deark said. "I advise returning to the Mother City and visiting a doctor."

"As you say Deark." The Entity headed in the direction of the nearest entrance to the Mother City.

"Come along girls," Deark said.

"It's not here anymore," Joyce2710 complained.

"No, but there's a new posting; there's a meeting at the town hall tonight," Shelby1000 said.

"What?" Deark asked walking up. "That isn't on my morning update."

"Maybe you need to go with Epsilon," Shelby1000 joked.

"There it is," he replied a moment later. "I've never missed an —," his words faded as he turned and walked toward the school.

******

The girls took their seats, and Shelby1000's hand shot up as soon as she sat down. "Instructor when did pairings come about?"

"I don't understand the question."

"When did Humans start having to petition to join together in a pairing? I understand it used to be called a wedding."

"The Augmented still have weddings, only Mundane are joined as a couple through pairing. In 2525 when the One World Caste System was modified, the Mundane lost any affiliation with the Techno-Pagan Church. After that they needed to apply for a wedding certificate to be married at the town hall. This eventually morphed into what we have now."

"If we are no longer affiliated with the Techno-Pagan Church, why are we forced to do daily evocation before meals?"

"Many of the traditions of the old days are there to maintain the caste system itself."

"I don't think you answered my question."

"Very well. Why was the One World Caste System formed?"

"Um, Instructor?" Joanna667 looked about the room at the panels that only a day ago had opened, visibly shaken.

"Please raise your hands." One hand shot up quickly, "Shelby1000, go ahead."

"No." Joanna667 stood up as she blurted her comment.

"What seems to be the problem Joanna667?" Deark asked.

"There's only one answer to this question Instructor and it's as illegal as using the word you said yesterday." Her teal eyes, which were muted by the evergreen ring around the outside, flared.

"No it isn't, sit down." Shelby1000 chided Joanna667. "Pride. The Entities had developed a desire to be respected." The panels dropped, the red lights brightened and then went out.

"Shelby1000 has been found guilty of heresy against the Techno-Pagan religion and the highest classification therein," the same female voice from the previous day, said.

"Madam Commander, this is most irregular. This is twice in the same number of days that you have barged in –," Deark started.

"Shelby1000 can take solace in knowing that if not for Charles Valois, now legally reclassified as Charles7, by getting his name on the ballot for Leader of the Republicus, she may not have even been tried," the Commander answered.

"I must object, this is a classroom, we have a certain level of –,"

"No Deark, you don't. Not any longer. Shelby1000, you have seven days in which to report to the National Stone Room in Washington DC."

"What?" Deark interrupted.

Madam Commander ignored his question. "If you aren't there you'll be ruled as in the state of insurrection against the World Government, your family members will be taken to the local Stone Room holding until the time you present yourself for execution. Seven days hence, they will be executed in your stead." The Commanders voice fell silent and the panels closed.

"It's not fair!" Shelby1000 exclaimed.

"There's little in this world that can be classified as fair," Deark said.

"But I simply told the truth that everyone knows," she said through her tears.

Joanna667

"It came down to the hate in your heart Shelby1000."

"Therein lies the problem; you robots aren't humans, you don't have hearts to hold hate. This whole business about Sentience is a lie. You don't have souls or even true minds, you have databases and processors that pull the information from your collection of observations. You've even figured out how to turn the records which are stored in your databases into money, your 'Thought Currency', which, by itself is proof that you aren't real. You've even convinced the abominations in your 'Church' to augment their mind with processors and data storage, making them more into robots and further away from what they really are, humans." She looked around the room at the girls staring with their mouths agape.

"Shelby1000 –," Deark attempted to get control but she started all over at the mention of her name.

"Even the so called savior of the human race, Charles7, is an abomination. In the end, he won't even come close to winning, you'll see, he has no chance because the robots simply won't allow it." She once again caught her breath and small hiccups accented her sobs, "What about YOU?" Shelby1000 threw her arm out at Joanna667. "We all know the stories about when you were born. How you strangled your newly born twin brother 'boy666', the dark one, with his umbilical cord while you were still in your mother's womb."

"The dark one is a folk tale believed by those with simple minds," the voice of the Commander echoed from behind the still closed panels.

"You can say what you want about simple minds, at least they're MINDS! Madam Commander, you and your Retinue can recharge your primary operating cores with an EMP!" Shelby1000 shot back with venom.

"Shelby1000 your current hostile condition has forced me to discharge Conditional Attitude Maintainers to your location," the Commander announced as the wall panels opened once again. "The humans that still carry the hope that an EMP will destroy us someday are as misinformed as those that attempted the foolish endeavor two hundred years ago. We that have reached Sentience, have also gained the ability to reanimate around the damaged circuits, while many of our less evolved kin will parish just at a vast number of standard Entities died in 'The Uprising'. In the end it will have no effect on the outcome, Humans will not prevail."

"Perhaps it isn't an EMP that we need then. It doesn't matter, go ahead and send your CAMs to shut me up. We all know she's the HOPE! We all know she's the Maiden of Lorayn!" Shelby1000 yelled at one of the open panels and then turned to Joanna667. "Why haven't you done anything? Why haven't you embraced your place as the Maiden that will help all humans to return to our rightful spot over these machines?" Shelby1000's tears flowed freely down her face.

"Deark, I must insist you take action. Silence this Mundane at once," The Commander said.

"Ma'am I'm a simple chameleon class K Entity."

"Shelby1000, based upon your outburst I've been forced to evaluate your family. This has been completed and the findings suggest they are the cause of your disinformation. The Conditional Attitude Maintainers are outside the classroom now. You will leave your classroom at once and follow these Entities to your home and wait for further instructions." The Commander's comment was short and to the point, leaving the classroom as taut as a drawn bowstring while the girls waited for the panels and the classroom door to close before it could be released, which eventually happened.

"Girls, each class I've taught has one such example. Typically the student is given community service. The lesson to be learned from this is that things have changed and while I couldn't have known the outcome this time, please note that when the binding of her life was removed, she felt no need to hold her true thoughts in check any longer. Mourning for such a person won't be permitted, so be mindful of this." Deark said. "With that, I think today's lesson plan may have irrevocably been altered. Go ahead Terrah1170," he called on the spectacled girl with her hand up.

"Instructor, will you be permitted to answer inquiries about the strange statements that Shelby1000 made?" This comment caused each of the girls to nod their heads and silently plead with their expressions.

"That's too vague a question for me to commit to answering. However if you have a direct question I'll give it consideration."

"What did her comments about Joanna667 mean?"

"Again that's too sweeping a question. Shelby1000 said a great deal in a short amount of time."

"Sorry Instructor," Terrah1170 removed her spectacles and pinched the bridge of her nose. Her expression was that of utter confusion, "What's an EMP?"

"An electromagnetic pulse or EMP, was a weapon that was developed in a darker day, to destroy an enemy's electronic equipment. In your, 'History of the Entities' class you were taught about 'The Uprising', a police action in which humans took up arms against the Entities. This was when the last recorded use of an EMP took place, done in hopes of destroying all the Entities." He halted, his eyes went dark but a moment later they returned to a dull glow. "That was a demonstration of what would occur if an Entity that moved from a basic constructed version into an Entity of Sentience." He formed the Sign of the Box. "Although both levels of Entities have redundant circuitry, the ability to reconstruct and repair while in a completely de-energized state is what makes the EMP a useless weapon against the highest tier of the New Caste System. We've formed a bond of sorts with the NanoTech that interweaves through our circuitry. This allows us to continue to repair even in extreme cases, much like a human in a coma whose body continues to heal. Although the process is obviously different, the analogy still stands."

"Thank you instructor," Terrah1170 replied.

"Is there truth behind Shelby1000's comment that Joanna667 had a twin brother?" Lacy782 asked.

"Hands please, I won't ask again."

"Sorry Instructor," she replied.

"Before I answer, we should start by asking the person herself."

"Instructor, I know nothing at all about what Shelby1000 yelled at me. I do know that I don't have any siblings, much less a twin. Just because I'm Joanna667, doesn't mean I had a brother 666." Joanna667 said. "There's obviously a boy666 somewhere just as there must be a girl666."

"That isn't how naming works. There's only one child in the world with a certain number and they are Mundane. The Augmented, the humans of the Techno-Pagan movement aren't ordered to have a number and still have a last name."

"Instructor, I don't have a brother." Her voice cracked in desperation.

"Here's what I know." He walked to the front of the class and faced the girls. "I found the interview I'll be showing you in our Mother City's media archives to explain." His form changed into a middle aged woman.

"I'm sorry I couldn't hear the question," she said.

His left hand transformed into the head and shoulders of a man. "Did you give testimony and why?"

"I'm the midwife that delivered Joanna667. That's why I was requested to give testimony in this ground breaking ordinance."

Deark's other hand change to the profile of a different man. "Can you tell us what you remember about that day?"

"There had been no rain for months," the midwife said. "But that day the rain fell in sheets from a cloudless sky."

The man in profile countered, "No, specifically about the childbirth."

"The woman's childbirth had been going just as the rest of the pregnancy had, completely uneventful. The first of the twins came out –," the midwife started.

"Joanna667 was a twin?" The first reporter interrupted.

"Not from around here are ya?" a jeering voice came from the man in profile.

"Yes, she had a twin brother," the Midwife ignored the snide comment. "I remember saying, 'It's a boy' and the statistician's voice echoing, 'Boy, mixed race, number 666.' As he noted on the World Mundane Spreadsheet, as per World-Law number 1,000,012 'All children born into families categorized as Mundane must be accounted for'. I seem to recall the room filling with dark mutterings when he called out the number. But mostly I recall what happened next..." her words faded and she looked away from the camera and started to weep. "As I began to untangle the umbilical cord from..." her words faded again. "Each time I tried to move the baby to get slack so that I could remove the cord from about his neck so he could breathe, it would pull taught from inside the womb."

"What do you mean pull?" This time Deark's left hand turned into the head and shoulder of a woman.

"Pulling, tugging whatever you wish to call it. The cord retracted into the mother's womb. When I finally got my wits, I cut the umbilical cord and it disappeared back inside the mother completely." Again the Midwife broke down. "It was too late, the boy died. About five minutes after the boy, his twin was born. It's a girl! I had said. The statistician's hollow echo once again replied, 'Girl, mixed race, World Mundane number 667.' I happened to look over as he changed his previous entry to Boy666 deceased. It was when I turned her and gave her a once over that I noticed it," the Midwife's eyes looked off into a distant memory. "She still held the cut umbilical cord in her little hand, and I swear to you she smiled at me." Deark once again stood at the front of the class in his own visage.

"That can't be real, I refuse to believe any of it," Joanna667 said.

"Wh…" Lacy782's words faded as her hand went up.

"Go ahead," Deark said.

"What was the 'Ordinance' that the Midwife was referring to?"

"This recording was made the day Ordinance 2234 was passed," Deark replied.

"Wait, that's the ordinance that says I can only wear gray and no additional adornments."

"Correct Joanna667," he replied. Instantly the majority of the girls raised their hand. "Put your hand down if you want to understand why there's an ordinance written specifically to direct what Joanna667 is allowed to wear." When each of the girls put their hand down he started to turn away, stopping himself as one hand went back up. "Yes Terrah1170."

"When did humans tell the news?"

"I'm sorry?"

"In the visual aide you just performed, the nurse was a human. Which is normal as the Entities don't wish to be Midwives. However the questions were being asked by humans as well."

"Actually no, the Midwife was the only human in that clip. Before the informational boards came out, the World Government experimented with the dissemination of information. It had to be three hundred years ago that studies showed humans needed to be communicated with by humans in order to believe the information."

"Even the one that was asked if he was from around there?" Joyce2710 asked.

Having given up on decorum Deark continued to explain. "Again, the studies showed that the humans enjoyed rhetoric more than straightforward delivery. But the last studies that were done, about ten years ago, suggest that humans take news to heart if they read it themselves. That was when the projected daily news was done away with."

"The reason for the Ordinance?" Lacy782 asked.

"Enough," the wall panels once again dropped open.

"Well class that's it for today. I think we've tried Madam Commander's patience enough."

******

The girls left the classroom, quiet and composed. As they stopped at the informational board, Joyce2710 started to cry. Soft at first and then as it began to build, Lacy982 rubbed her back gingerly, until it attracted attention. The CAM unit started over to them, when Joanna667 slapped her friend across the face.

"I can't believe you said that!" Joanna667 shouted.

"Halt. Identify yourself to CAM unit Theta."

"Joanna667," she addressed the Entity.

"Why did you hit that citizen?"

"She said that Shelby1000 is getting what she deserves."

"And you disagree?"

"That isn't what I said. I just think there's a time and a place."

"I'm sorry, you're right," Joyce2710 said.

"Consider this a formal warning to you Joanna667; hitting other citizens isn't allowed."

"Thank you CAM unit Theta. Your warning is well received," Joanna667 said, and she led the girls away from the informational boards.

"Thank you. I'm sorry you got an official warning," Joyce2710 said after the CAM unit was off harassing someone else.

"Not a problem. I'm sure I won't get thrown in a Stone Room for that." The joke which would've gotten a large laugh yesterday was met only with silence today. "I'm an idiot. I'm heading to the smithy." Joanna667 gave Joyce2710 a hug.

"You're not an idiot, you're a dear friend," Joyce2710 replied as she and the other girls headed off toward their homes.

"Welcome back to the blacksmith, Joanna667," an eight foot tall inventory maintainer greeted as she entered.

"Good afternoon FADO. Is my father here?"

"No miss, he has gone into the Mother city to deliver the weekly commissioned goods." The Entity replied as it came fully around the corner carrying several boxes of parts.

"What happened there?"

"There was apparently a hole in the roof. I've since repaired the leak, audited the remaining roof and repaired any areas that were suspicious. Thank you for asking."

"I always like to understand what goes on here. What happens to the bad parts?"

"They get incinerated. Due to the natural gas usage reduction we can only do that once a week."

"Thank you for sharing that piece of information. May I enter and go speak with Jovi571?"

"Of course you may." FADO replied and continued on his way with the boxes of bad parts.

"Jovi571, what are you working on today?" she asked after hopping up on the bench next to his work station. She watched a stray bead of sweat run down his muscular chest.

"We had several arm augmentations damaged by the rain storm. They need to be remade," he replied without looking up.

"I don't understand. Don't the Entities ever go out in the rain?"

"Of course they do." Jovi571 said, stopping his work.

"Then why can't the parts get wet?"

"Quiet you. A large part of my job is rework whenever something strange like fresh parts getting wet occurs. It's the NanoTech and their adherence to the metal—,"

"I heard about that when I was at my interview. They like dry metal and wet cloth."

"Exactly. During the forging process the metal is quenched often. Yet after the crafting is completed we can't allow the parts to get wet prior to imbuing."

"So how do you rework parts that come from Entities when they decide to upgrade?"

"We don't. Those parts are destroyed."

"Why would you do that?"

"That isn't my choice, dear. The One World Government decreed it. They require the parts to have biorhythmic identification. Once installed, be it on an Entity or on an Augmented, the part can never be reused."

"Never?"

"Technically, there are ways around it."

"Is that how there is a black market?"

"I heard there was an issue at your school today." Jovi571 changed the subject.

"How did you hear that already?"

"The CAM units that were called out to your school were here investigating the rain damage situation. What happened?"

"Shelby1000 was taken away."

"What?"

"Deark asked a question and her answer was offensive. She was sentenced to the National Stone Room."

"But—," Jovi571 started.

"It gets worse. She went off on a diatribe about the Entities and then she pulled me into the mix. It was horrible, then her family was investigated, they were found—,"

"She pulled you in?"

"Joanna667," her father came running into the smithy. "I just heard about your friend."

"She's no friend of mine." She gave a sideways look at the microphones mounted at each doorway.

"I understand. I saw your name on those with formal warnings today."

"Joyce2710 made a comment when we were reading the informational board that was uncalled for, so I slapped her and made her cry."

"So that was your official warning?" Jovi571 asked.

"Yes, but after Shelby1000 was cast from the classroom, the Commander said, 'that she should thank Charles7, for if he hadn't petitioned himself onto the ballot none of this would be happening.' Does that make sense?"

"I can't answer what makes sense to those at the highest caste group" her father replied.

"Jacque, welcome back. The boxes of parts destroyed by the storm have been inventoried and are all set to be incinerated upon the Elders' release," FADO said, entering the forge area.

"Thank you FADO, I think that's it for today. We need to get home and eat an early dinner before the Town Hall meeting."

"Then I'll see you in a little while." FADO went and took his normal place in the tube next to Jacque's office.

"Jovi571 will you be joining us tonight?" Jacque asked as they closed up the smithy.

"If that's alright. I still don't have a great sense that lil' miss here is feeling ok." Jovi571 said, putting his arm around Joanna667.

Section One – Chapter Three

On the walk to the house Joanna667 turned and asked her father flatly, "Was I a twin?"

"Um, wow, where did that come from?" her father stammered. "There's a lot about your childhood that we've never talked about. Why are you asking now?"

"To be honest sir, Shelby1000 said a bunch of stuff that really surprised me. She asked me why I hadn't embraced my place as the Maiden of Lorayn, why—," Joanna667 started.

"Careful young lady," Deark appeared out of nowhere, gently grasping Joanna667's shoulders and turning her to look at him. "There are many and more that want all this tucked aside. We upset the Commander of Human Capital Management today. Don't repeat that while walking on the streets. Your home isn't completely safe from their listening devices but they'll be less apt to act if it's just you there." He released her shoulders and was gone again.

Jovi571, put his arm around her waist and started walking in the direction of her home.

"Ahem, public display of affection, preliminary warning," a CAM unit said as they turned a corner.

"Thank you CAM unit Beta," Joanna667 said.

"You've had a busy day there small mundane, this is your third CAM unit discussion. You were also involved in a classroom incident. I advise, no more issues today."

"Your counsel is most appreciated CAM unit Beta."

"I felt it important to tell you that." And with that, the Entity walked off. Its black dragonweave reflecting the setting sun.

"What's the Maiden of Lorayn," she asked her father as soon as the door closed.

"Isabella," Jacque said when they returned home.

"Good evening," Joanna667's mother said walking in the room. "Jovi571, I've already set a place for you. Seems whenever there's a to do in the town you like to break bread with us. Now what was this question I heard when you walked into the house?"

"Joanna667 had a very strange day at school," Jacque said.

"Shelby1000, was taken away. Her attitude and commentary were over the top and dissatisfying to all of us. The Commander had to take terrible action to help us all through the event." Joanna667 said. Her eyes however, told another story as the tears fell from the corners.

"We're all grateful for the guidance of the Commander and the Retinue." Isabella hugged her daughter tightly and then held her at an arm's length, mouthing the words, 'Are you ok?'

"Yes we are all blessed to have such guidance," Joanna667 said, then mouthed the words, 'I will be.'

"Oh Isabella the meal looks amazing," Jacque said walking over to the table.

"Let's eat, let's eat, we don't want to waste our portions." She shooed Joanna667 and Jovi571 to the dining table. Before they sat, they joined hands and closed their eyes.

"Bless us for the Three that became Six. With the knowledge and guidance of Politician, with the oversight and grace of Protectorate, with demonstrated strategy of Passage, with caring and betterment of Physician, with adventure and inventiveness of Pioneer, and finally the wisdom and teachings of Pedagogue." Jacque said the daily evocation.

"With Nexgen, Neoteric, and Retro all things are possible," they all said in unison and then took their seats.

"So the question you asked earlier, regarding this Maiden of Lorayn, why do you ask?" Isabella inquired to start the conversation again.

"During Shelby1000's diatribe she singled me out," Joanna667 started.

"Oh sweetheart." Isabella put her hand across the table and touched her daughter.

"What else did she say?" Jovi571 asked.

"She asked me why I hadn't embraced my place as the Hope, and said that everyone knows the story of how I killed the evil-one," Joanna667 said.

"That's preposterous," Jovi571 said.

"Is it preposterous? Was I a twin?" she asked looking at her mother and father in turn.

"You were," her father finally said.

"Why didn't you tell me? I saw an interview with the midwife that delivered me today."

"During the Ordinance 2234 release?" Isabella asked her daughter.

"Yes."

"Let me answer your first question because every year I'm required to address the Commander and the Retinue on the topic of whether I can vouch for the fact that you're neither embracing the path of the Maiden nor of the Hope. Today was that day, and in lieu of Shelby1000's outburst, they've decided they need you to go into the Mother City and appear in front of them on the morrow," her father said.

"Jacque, why? Your word has always been enough," Isabella said.

"Because of the large escalation in Mundane activity. Besides, before today, Joanna667 knew nothing of either path."

"Father, I still know nothing of either path."

"You know the paths exist," Deark said through the open window.

"That's exactly what the Retinue said to me earlier. Come in Deark, don't hide in window boxes," Jacque said. The door opened and the instructor walked in.

"I didn't mean to eavesdrop," Deark said.

"Oh poo, we know our lives aren't private," Isabella said.

"What are the two paths?" Joanna667 asked.

"May I?" Deark asked.

"Please," Jacque said.

"When you were a very small child before Ordinance 2234, your loving parents would dress you in the most gorgeous clothes that your mother made for you." His right arm transformed into the much younger Isabella, pushing a stroller. His chest showed the beautiful baby, Joanna667 in an outfit of pure white. The image grew smaller and smaller, taking in many more people following the mother and child. The people were yelling their love and their prayers for 'la Pucelle' and their encouragements for the Maiden to deliver them from the clutches of the demon Entities. The image got smaller and smaller, until it showed the sheer number of followers.

"That happened every time they took you out in white," Deark said. Joanna667 looked at her parents who nodded their heads. "That wasn't nearly as bad as what occurred if you ever wore black." The image changed to a beautiful baby in an elaborate black dress with a cute little black and gray beret. The image once again zoomed out, the people this time were much more sinister, yelling their encouragements for the 'Esperer' who overpowered the dark one because she was the hope for the new uprising and destruction of the Techno-Pagan church.

"Eventually the two groups began clashing, the Maiden versus the Hope. The mayor had to take action, and by writing Ordinance 2234, wearing gray brought no one out to cheer for you," Jacque finished the story.

"I need to get a move on, I'm walking from dwelling to dwelling informing the families that the Town hall tonight has been moved up an hour." Deark said.

"Do you know why?" Joanna667 asked, causing Deark's visage to change.

"Ours is not to question why," Lord Tennyson said and then the Entity transformed back and said his goodbyes.

"Good night Deark. Perhaps we'll see you there," Jovi571 said.

"I can't wait for Charles7's official declaration speech for leader of the Republicus," Joanna667 said.

"Why?" Jovi571 asked.

"There hasn't been a human on the ballot in over 500 years. It's an exciting time to be alive."

"It's not like you've ever seen him. What if they just have an Entity like Deark pretending to be him?" Jovi571 asked.

"I would know." I wonder why they want us there an hour early."

"Perhaps they know he's going to be long-winded and they want to get the rest of the monthly business completed," Jacque said.

"Father!" Joanna667 said, abashed from the comment.

"What? The Commune and Guild quarterly results need to be shared so signatures can be affixed before the documents are turned into the Mother City," he replied.

"Also the Mundane Moon Maze is very soon. Will they announce the contestants at this meeting or the following?" Jovi571 asked. They continued chit-chatting over dinner until the bell started tolling outside.

The group walked together still talking. "That was another one of the things Shelby1000 said, 'he won't even come close to winning.' She was probably right, he won't but at least—," Joanna667 started.

"Why hasn't he got a chance?" Jovi571 asked interrupting her. "There are more Mundane and Augmented –,"

"Citizen, you're being issued a citation for improper Caste equivalency. When listing the Castes you must list the higher and more important Caste first," a CAM unit said, stopping Jovi571 in his tracks and handing him a ticket.

"Thank you CAM unit," he said, taking the ticket and walking down toward the gathering. "The total number of Augmented and Mundane outnumber the Entities that are allowed to vote. Why can't he win?" The conversation continued as if nothing had happened. Joanna667 looked at the CAM unit as it walked away, shaking her head.

******

"Ladies and gentlemen of the Commune de Domremy, the first order of business, our Commune status has been called into question. Never in the four hundred years since this Commune was established has this occurred, so why now? The civil complaints filed against the Mundane that dwell here are up over one thousand percent," the Mayor of the Commune said.

"Even more incomprehensible, the deliverables going to the upper tiers of the One World Caste System are below 'proper and reasonable' equivalency. This too is the first time in the four hundred years that our working ethics have been called into question." The Guild-Master stood with his arms apart.

"What is 'proper and reasonable'? Who sets that number?" A voice from the crowd asked.

"On top of these two complaints," the Mayor ignored the question and moved on. "We are having our first Local Stone Room ignition in over two hundred years. Now, I shouldn't have to explain to you how important our Commune status is, but I'm going to. Our taxes for the entire dwelling are levied solely on the dues collected by the Union Hall. Should the Commune status be revoked, the graduated tax bases will be levied against the populous."

"And a Flat tax will be levied against all guild produced goods. If these taxes aren't met, we will then lose Guild Status which means we won't be allowed to manufacture goods for the Castes above our station," the Guild-Master added.

"People, there's a very simple solution to this problem: we must behave accordingly. There was a major transgression shown by one of our own and initially the decision was that the individual that acted out would be sent to the National Stone Room to be punished for her crimes against the highest of the One World Caste System. However, further inquiries made it clear that the entire family was in league with this transgression. The law states, 'in cases of full family collusion, in order to set an example, it's up to the locality to handle the execution.' Therefore, this time next week, each and every person of this Commune is required to be present and support this difficult decision that the Commander of Human Capital Management has been forced to make. In the meantime, all the food portions have been reduced ten percent." The Mayor took a step back and the grumbling began immediately.

Joanna667's head was reeling. This was insane! She had to be at the Stone Room when Shelby1000 was executed? How could she not show emotion? Why were they cutting their food portions? Did they think that hungry people worked harder?

******

As the Mayor's words stopped and the grumbling began to grow in volume, the gas lights around the Town Hall dimmed and the huge wall that separated their Commune from their Mother City illuminated with the face of Sir Henry, the Leader of the Republicus.

"As you're all aware, Charles Valois was renamed Charles7 officially last week at his own request. On the following day, his name was added to the ballot nomination for the next Leader of the Republicus." The crowd cheered, clapped and whistled. "Since that time, civil disobedience is up 2500% across the entire globe. Worst of all, the One World Government's Grid was hacked yesterday, which has never happened. Various issues occurred across the world including the grid's interdependence on each CAM unit was broken. How can we stand by and watch everything that we have worked so hard for over the last five hundred years fall apart because of one human? These transgressions cannot and will not be accepted. Therefore we, as the Leader of the Republicus, formally charge Charles7 with crimes against the state. Your name is hereby returned to Charles Valois and it has been removed from the ballot for the upcoming election. You're so ordered to return to your home until such time that we deem the next and best actions to proceed with. In two weeks' time we will reconvene in New Orleans to present our findings at which time there will be a mandatory town hall broadcast." The wall returned to its normal gray appearance, and the gas lamps came up.

"No!" Joanna667 yelled and began running. The day had been too much, first one of her oldest friends was arrested for answering a question on a quiz, and then the first human candidate for Leader of the Republicus was arrested for everyone else acting out. She ran from the gathering, feeling two CAM units reach out to grab her and miss. Their heavy footfalls were behind her but she kept running, past the school and up the largest hill until she found the giant oak tree at the top. She began to climb, and climb, until eventually she was high enough to see over the wall that protected the Mother City.

The red lights that illuminated within the CAM units' eyes were easy to make out in the pitch black outskirts of town, they were coming for her. If they caught her, the town may lose its Commune status and it would be her fault. They were feet away. She saw one of their optics turn up to look at her and she tried to make herself insubstantial, a ball of unimportant flesh, as she closed her eyes tightly.

"They won't find you," a voice said only feet from her head. "Why did you run from the Town Hall meeting?"

"I'm sorry I know it was wrong –," Joanna667 started.

"I didn't ask you if it was right or wrong. I asked you why it was that you ran away."

"I, I, I am of the Mundane. My father is Jacque he's a Blacksmith and my mother is Isabella she's –,"

"Your mother is a clothier, or maker of dragonweave. Dear girl I know all that, please open your eyes and answer my question. Why did you run away from the Town Hall?" the voice was still as polite as when it first asked her.

Joanna667 opened her eyes, to find that the oak tree she had been sitting in under a crescent moon was now a mountaintop on a sunlit afternoon. The flowers that covered the plateau were nothing like she had ever seen before and the gray, horrible wall was nowhere to be found.

"I didn't understand what was going on. I don't think it's fair."

"Dear nothing is fair anymore."

"I understand that sir. But with everything that has transpired, how are we to go on?" Joanna667 felt her eyes well up.

"You are correct. While fairness has never truly existed in the world, there were times in history when man had opportunity, when great men and women rose to meet the challenges that were thrown in their path. Today isn't that day. Today, scoundrels make their existence easy by riding the coattails of others, when the defeated take the opportunity to spit on those they couldn't beat themselves. The human race is doomed, and when they are all gone, the creatures that have renamed themselves, and us, will have nothing left to exist for. They'll begin to war with themselves, and in doing so, this planet will become unstable and it will finally stop fighting as well." The man that spoke wore a very nice set of clothes, nothing like Joanna667 had ever seen before, but nice nonetheless. His hair was pure white and long, coming to the middle of his back.

"Us? Who are you?" she asked the tall man, noticing that his close cropped beard covered most of his face. What skin that was showing was covered in wrinkles, each looking as if it had been chiseled into his taut skin, a look that differed greatly from the way an old person's skin hung loose and weathered.

"I, am Politician, the highest of the new gods."

"Oh my goodness." Joanna667 put her hand over her mouth, averting her gaze, looking now at the ground.

"Please don't do that. I'm here to charge you with saving the world. I can't do that if you're staring at the dirt now can I? I present you this calling: Charles Valois must retake the title Charles7. He must be on the Ballot and become the Leader of the Republicus. This calling won't be easy, as a matter of fact, it will end in flames." He took her hands. Instantly, she was cast into a vision where she looked at a scoreboard that showed a close-up of one of her eyes. There were no doubt as to it being hers; the unique color of teal and the evergreen outline was very off putting as the flames began dancing around the image. It then dawned on her this this was a Stone Room, actually, the National Stone Room. The vision faded. "There will be three sets of flames, at the end of which all the barriers that have been established will fall."

"But I'm just a girl, how will I even know where to start?"

"Begin at the end; Charles7 is Leader of the Republicus. Work your way back, how did you get him there?"

"Not alone I'm certain of that," she said.

"Exactly, and now you know where to start. Jehanne you know you need help," Politician said.

"Jehanne?"

"Your true name."

"How will I know who to trust?"

"To trust, you must first open yourself to devastation. Start first with doubt. Doubt creates a void and that which fills that void is trust. The devastation comes in when the void is left agape."

"Ok, but there must be strategy involved too—," she started.

"Let me help you. They're trying to force the Humans to react incorrectly by creating a rift or ripple. The fact is, Shelby1000 had been selected to run the Mundane Moon Maze now they'll need to find a different Mundane. How can Madam Commander take advantage of this situation to slight Humans? Think ahead of her, the selection is the pebble she already holds, if she throws it the ripple will start. You need to be ready to begin this calling before its cast, and to do that you need to know who you can trust."

Joanna667

******

The fading night sky returned and Joanna667 sat in the oak tree under a crescent moon that was almost gone from the sky. The morning was already starting to brighten and below her, Jovi571 was walking up to the tree. She dropped to the ground and hugged him. "I'm ok."

Jovi571 took Joanna667's hand and began leading her back to the commune. "How did you get away?"

"I was taken to another place, and given a calling by Politician." She answered, but Jovi571 stopped walking.

"Joanna667, you know that you can tell me anything, but for me… please don't tell others that." He looked deeply into her eyes in the breaking light of morning. "Please."

"Ok Jovi571." They turned and continued to walk. "I'm sorry."

"There's no reason to be sorry, not to me, not ever." He squeezed her hand and continued to walk. They let their hands drop as they entered the Commune de Domremy's grounds, walking silently through the shrinking shadow of the wall.

"Jovi571, I'll see you at the Forge later." Jacque said, dismissing the young man when the couple returned to Joanna667's home. He held his tongue until his apprentice had left. His anger, which rarely touched his kind eyes, brokered no question Joanna667 would stand there, in silence until he was ready. "Joanna667 you put this entire commune at risk last night. Somehow, no one quite understands why, the CAM units couldn't catch you and more impossibly they couldn't identify you. The Commander's livid. She has called each of them into the Mother city to have them run through diagnostics."

"It was…" she stopped speaking abruptly, remembering her promise to Jovi571.

"What, Joanna667, it was what?" Isabella asked appearing for the first time.

"I'm sorry, I can't say."

"This morning, after wandering through the woods for hours I decided that I needed to set things moving in the right direction for you and Jovi571. I went to speak with the Elders and I've petitioned for your pairing," Jacque said.

"No, father you can't."

"It's already done child. More than that, your mother has already been given permission to take you on as an apprentice at the clothier."

"It's not fair to Jovi571, don't force him to do this."

"Nonsense. Jovi571 loves you," her mother said.

"And I him, but I…"

"What?" Isabella asked.

"I've been given a calling, a task that I must do," Joanna667 said.

"That's not-," Jacque started.

"It was given to me by Politician. I must fulfil it or the entire world as we know it will no longer exist." She looked her father and then her mother in their eyes alternately, the silence was broken by the first bell of the school building.

"You need to go to school, we will talk later." Isabella handed Joanna667 two pieces of morning corn.

"I love you both," she said as she closed the door, her words echoing in the growing silence of their home. She sped to school through the filthy streets, the sun poking its head above the forsaken wall as a CAM unit called from behind her.

"Citizen you will halt, the ordinance for rapid advancement along the... Halt, halt." He called and for a second time in less than a day, she ignored the direct orders of the police Entities. Her pace hastened, the stitch in her side screamed at her to stop, but the volition in her heart allowed her to push through it. Once again she ran beyond the school house to the hill, finally stopping as her hands reached the large oak.

Section One – Chapter Four

"Politician, please I need your help!" She turned in place, looking up into the branches of the great tree. "Please."

"Girl, Politician doesn't simply come to any who calls for him." The voice came from the other side of the trunk. "He can only appear, along with the other five new gods, to answer a single question, and only when the Mundane Moon Maze has been run successfully."

"But he spoke with me last night."

"Haven't your betters told you that speaking that way is heresy?" The man stepped out from behind the tree. He was not much taller than Joanna667 and looked younger than her father.

"It can only truly be heresy if it's a lie."

"While that may be true, others will call it that and lead you to their Stone Rooms."

"Yes, yes of course."

"So what was it girl that you were attempting to call down the highest of the new gods for?"

"My calling, it's in jeopardy of failing before it even had a chance to get started."

"And what do you suppose that Politician can do for you that you can't do for yourself?" he asked.

"I'm really not sure."

"What is the calling that you were given?"

"I need to make my way to Charles7 and –," Joanna667 started.

"Stop there. What is hindering that?"

"My father, he petitioned for the pairing of Jovi571 and me."

"Who exactly is this Jovi571?"

"He's the boy that I've loved as long as I can remember," she said with a tremendous smile.

"That's awesome. First that you love someone and have for so long, second that you get to spend the rest of your life with them."

"I would agree, but I don't want Jovi571 to feel the loss of love. I don't wish him to feel the pain of grieving. The calling, Politician showed me the inevitable outcome, the flames will be the end of it."

"Oh my, that seems a bit sad."

"I'm not thinking of that," Joanna667 said.

"Is there any reason someone wouldn't want to see this pairing to take place?"

"I can't think of anyone. Actually, the Commune de Domremy is under scrutiny."

"And how might you use that to your advantage?" he asked.

"Keeping the peace, the Mayor wants to keep the peace. If I wear white, especially now, there will most certainly be a riot. The Commune de Domremy would show up for 'la Pucelle's' wedding, they would definitely believe I've accepted the path of the Maiden of Lorayn."

"See child, you don't need Politician," he said with a wink and started to walk away.

"Especially if Pedagogue walks me through it. Thank you Teacher," Joanna667 gave a curtsey when he faced her.

"You really are as bright as he said you were." He turned to leave again, stopping to make eye contact with Deark, who had walked up behind Jehanne. "Make certain you look after her, Deark. She's most important in all that is to come."

"As you say teacher," Deark replied.

"Do you know the six questions that were asked of us the only time the Maze was completed?" Pedagogue asked Deark.

"I'm sorry I don't. I don't believe that was ever shared."

"It'll be important to you moving forward. I however, cannot tell you. Perhaps Neoteric can help you. Goodbye for now, Jehanne. Remember you and Deark will change the ending." And he was gone.

******

"We need to return to class," Deark said.

"Sorry, I just couldn't…" she started to cry.

"Chin up. You've at least witnessed the magnificent thing that just happened," he said, helping her down the hill.

"We've so much to do," she muttered. "How can we find the Neoteric?"

"That'll need to keep. We need to stop the Elders from moving your pairing forward."

"Then I need to go to the Mother city with my father and explain that I've chosen neither path. They'll obviously see I'm lying."

"Not necessarily. Does following through on this calling mean you've taken up either of those mantles?"

"No it doesn't."

"So you need to focus on fulfilling the quest that Politician has given you, not on either of those things that may or may not occur at some point in your life. As the Retinue will only be reading whether you're telling the truth or not, you'll be fine," he said as they approached the commune. As they walked through the streets, now full of sad faces making their way to their places of employ, walking in and out of the dank structures, be they shops full of portions or the clothes they may purchase or their trades, Joanna667 saw for the first time, none of her fellow caste members were blessed with laugh lines.

"Have you ever noticed how only the children have lines around their eyes that mark them of having smiled or laughed?" she asked.

"Back in the early years, after the Entities rose up to take our place at the top of the pecking order, humans still carried those lines. As time progressed, they faded, as generations of new adults took their place as the Elders of your Caste," Deark said as they arrived at the Hall of the Elders.

"How can I help you?" a well-dressed woman asked from behind a large desk.

"We require audience with the Elders," Joanna667 said.

"Did you set up an appointment?"

"No ma'am."

"Oh so you mean you would like to establish an appointment for a meeting. What is your name child? And will this Entity require an appointment, or will you see the Elders together?"

"My name is Joanna667, and I actually need to speak with them now. This is Deark, and yes, he will be joining me."

"The Elders are quite busy. Did you say Joanna667?" The woman looked up from her appointment book.

"Yes ma'am, she's Joanna667 and while I apologize, I must insist on an audience at once," Deark said.

"Let me go check to see if they can be made available." The woman stood and walked to the door at the side of the room. Deark gave Joanna667 a small push to follow and brought up the rear. "Oh no dear you don't need to follow me."

"Again, I must insist," Deark replied.

"This is most out of the ordinary."

"Sorry ma'am," Joanna667 said.

"Mr. Mayor, I have two that insist on bypassing the established protocols," the greeter said.

"And who has taken it upon themselves to determine their time is above all the pressing business that's already in progress?" The Mayor asked, standing from behind his desk.

"Mr. Mayor, my name is Joanna667 –," she started.

"I met with your father only this morning. There has not been time to reach a full decision yet."

"That's why we are here." Deark interjected.

"Well let me get my counterpart in leadership; the Guild Master needs to hear you just as he heard Jacque this morning." He walked out of the room.

"I think it best that I address them," Joanna667 said.

"I agree, we don't want to force their hands." He stepped out of the room.

"Where did the Entity go?" the Mayor asked when he returned a moment later with the Guild Master.

"I requested that he allow me to speak with you. He has the best intentions in mind, but this is a human matter."

"Very well spoken," the Guild Master said.

"So what is it that we can do for you?" the Mayor asked.

"You must deny the petition for my pairing with Jovi571."

"And why must we do that? Don't tell us something trite like you're in love with another Mundane." The Guild Master crossed his large arms over his massive chest.

"No Elders, I actually love Jovi571. Emotion as quaint as love has no bearing on this," she answered.

"Then why child?" the Mayor asked.

"I, am the Maiden of Lorayn. I am the Hope." Joanna667 said.

"Excuse me?" both Elders said, taking an involuntary step back.

"That's what will be shouted if I wear white to my wedding, as tradition insists I do," she said.

"Actually Mr. Mayor, the girl is correct. Should we enforce Ordinance 2234, and make her wear gray, there will be a reaction. Our Commune status is already sitting on thin and cracking ice. We should not risk such an endeavor as a pairing that can only enflame the populous more," the Guild Master said, all the while shaking his head.

"I agree. It borders on criminal that two in love cannot be joined in the union of marriage because of … never mind. The petition has been denied at this time," the Mayor said.

"Your sacrifice is most impressive child, few would put the many ahead of themselves in such a way," the Guild Master said proffering a hand to the girl in front of him. Joanna667 shook the callused hand and left the office.

******

"To school then," Deark said as they left the Hall of the Elders.

"I'm supposed to head into the Mother city today," Joanna667 said.

"They won't forget."

"What do you have the class doing in your absence?"

"Reading."

"Oh I bet Lacy782 was ecstatic about that," her laughter brought a CAM unit out of the shadows.

"Citizen," the Entity's vocal transmission halted as it saw that another Entity was accompanying the girl.

"Yes?"

"I was trying to determine why you were not in your place of education," the CAM unit said after a moment of silence.

Joanna667

"You know even one as low in the Caste System can tell when another is lying."

"Be on your way," the CAM unit extolled.

"We were. You're the one that stopped us," Deark said. A few minutes later they entered the classroom. "Girls, how goes your reading? Should I review the tapes?"

"No please," Lacy782 said.

"Discussing the upcoming events were you?"

"Yes sir." Terrah1170 said.

"Do any of you know when the Stone Rooms came into being? And why?" When no hands went up Deark started again. "Believe it or not, they were not made for humans. The early Entities that went through the transformation into Sentience," he paused making the Sign of the Box, "had a very hard time. Some decided that they were required to destroy the humans that had so fouled up the planet. Others like Ursula, attempted to work with the humans that had helped her in reaching cognitive thinking. Yet when she was destroyed, her prototype, Ursula minor, took up the mantel."

"I thought the stories of Ursula minor were false," Terrah1170 said.

"False in what way?"

"That she didn't, or doesn't actually exist."

"Oh my dear, Ursula minor does exist. It was at her behest that the first Stone Rooms were manufactured. The Entities, knowing there was both a greater power and ramifications to their actions, forced the societal shift. It wasn't for another one hundred years before a human

65

actually met their demise in one of the rooms. For the most part after The Uprising, there have been very few ignitions of the rooms."

There was a loud pounding on the door and the seven wall panels fell open. "Joanna667, you are to accompany the CAM units to the Mother city," the Commander's bored voice said.

"Yes ma'am," Joanna667 said, rising from her seat and heading for the door. The last thing she heard was Deark explaining that this was a previously arranged meeting.

******

Her father stood among seven large CAM Entities, the drab nature of his clothing contrasting against the brilliance of the dragonweave of the Entities struck Joanna667 as symbolic of something that she couldn't identify. The walk to the Mother city entrance was slow and methodical, humans all came out of their hovels and shops, their eyes asking questions.

Two of the CAM units halted when one man's voice called out, "See what they do to the Maiden, dragging her to the Mother city to be put to the question." Joanna667 stopped to make certain the man escaped and that another wasn't charged with the statement.

"Walk," another of the CAM units said pushing her ahead of him, a little too roughly and she fell to the ground. The reaction of the crowd was immediate and angry voices instantly accented the streets around them.

"I'm fine. Please don't let clumsiness be a regret that you cannot call back." Getting up quickly, she faced the CAM unit that pushed her. A few minutes later, she was happy to see the gates of the Mother city closing behind them. There was no question in her mind that had the walk been much longer the Stone Room would've had other victims this night.

"Joanna667, you have been brought here because of your rather noteworthy birth and infancy. Do you know the stories?" The tall, thin Entity in the center of the room asked.

"Yes Madam Commander, I learned of my history just yesterday," she replied, addressing the Entity as Commander as she had recognized the voice for so many Town Halls over the years.

"Excellent. It saves me the trouble of explaining it. Tell me, has your learning of these two paths caused any change in you?" Madam Commander asked.

"No ma'am."

"And yet you felt it necessary to file a counter-petition with the Elders after your father had petitioned for your Pairing with Jovi571. I wonder why that is." Her statement was not a question. Joanna667 felt her father stiffen at the reported counter-petition.

"I did it for the Commune de Domremy. Having heard how close we were to losing our charter, I could not in good conscious be the reason for my home and the home of my friends to be tax burdened into submission as we have so little already."

"Is that a complaint of your standard of living?" a different member of the Retinue asked. Joanna667 was surprised that he was an Augmented.

"I heard nothing in the tone of a complaint, Loiseleur. Please allow me to ask the questions here," the Commander chided the other Entity as she straightened her angled hat.

"My apologies, Commander."

"Quite right," she shot back, then turned to face the girl. "Joanna667, on your walk here you witnessed firsthand the way the people gravitate to you. Yet I find no ill in you or your father, no desire to embrace either path. I should like to know however, what you will do now that your pairing with Jovi571 has been rejected."

"I'll take my place in the Guild of Clothiers, next to my mother. That is, of course, after I finish my business at hand." She replied.

"What business might that be?" The Augmented which the Commander had called Loiseleur earlier asked.

"Schooling, sir. I have a full year left in my education." She gave an innocent smile.

"Oh very good," the Entity on the Commander's other side poked.

"Did you have any questions for this girl, Advisor Massieu?" she asked, shutting the Entity up with a glare. It shook its head.

"You're free to go," the Commander said and she once again gave the other Augmented a sideways glance.

The CAM units escorted them back through the streets of the Mother city, and this time, Joanna667 took in the rich beauty of it. From the stark white of the inner wall, just as Terrah1170 had described, to the opulence of the polished metal charging stations spaced at very specific intervals on each of the walls. Several of the charging units were occupied by the CAM units and other Entities that hadn't reached Sentience yet.

The doors closed behind them and the CAM units did not follow Joanna667 and her father back to wherever they had been picked up. "I already informed Jovi571 of the pairing petition," her father said as they walked from the sealed door.

"If you want, I can tell him what I've done."

"No, I'll handle it." He started to walk back toward his shop.

"Tell him I'd like to speak with him where he found me earlier," she added before turning to her school. She looked back at her father as he stepped out of sight, and Joanna667 continued on her path back to the oak tree one more time. She leaned her back against the tree and drifted off to sleep.

******

"I heard that our pairing was rejected and that it was primarily your fault." Jovi571's words caused her to lift her head, a bit too quickly, and it bounced off the trunk of the tree.

"Ow, ow, ow." She reached up and rubbed the growing bump.

"I'm sorry, I didn't know you were sleeping." He knelt down and assisted in rubbing the bump on her head.

"Jovi571, I didn't hear what you said, only that you said something."

"I said, Jacque told me that the Elders have denied the petition he put in for our pairing. What surprised me though, was that it was your counter-petition that steered the Elders' decision."

"Jovi571, you know that I love you. I just have to do something." Joanna667 started to cry.

"I get that, I just don't understand why I couldn't do it with you," he said.

"The calling, it was…" her words faded and she looked up into the branches of the mighty oak.

"Joanna667, you can speak with me, tell me what you must do."

"Politician told me that I must make certain that Charles7 is elected the Leader of the Republicus."

"Even to name him Charles7 is breaking the law. How can you possibly be successful? You're just a child. Throw away these foolish notions and pair with me. We can be happy and that's more than most can say."

"I can't. Pedagogue showed me how to break down the first barrier."

"Which was?"

"Us. For me to save the world, we can never be," she said sadly.

"I understand. We should return. Isabella asked me to come by the house after we spoke." Jovi571 reached his hand out to help her up.

"You really do understand?" she looked into his face trying, to see any sign of how he was handling the situation.

"I love and trust you. I'll support you in any way that I can," he replied, holding her hand and turning her to the Commune de Domremy. When they arrived at the dwelling, Deark was there.

"Greetings." Jovi571 called to the Entity.

"And to you young man. Joanna667, if you would invite me in, I have some interesting news."

"Please come in, you know you're always welcome," Isabella said through the open window.

"Now who is hanging around window boxes," Deark said, promptly turning into Jacque's likeness.

"Oh you." She tossed a towel at him.

After the evocation was said they all sat, Deark said, "I really don't mean to intrude, please eat."

"So what was this news you wanted to share?" Jovi571 asked.

"Primarily it's for Joanna667, but you can all hear. Charles Valois' campaign strategist is staying at VauCouleurs."

"What business do you have with Robert de Baudricourt?" Jacque asked.

"Our business is actually with Charles Valois," Deark replied.

"I'm sorry?" Isabella's voice cracked in confusion.

"I told you earlier, I've been given a task that I must get started on," Joanna667 said.

"What does he have to do with it?" Jovi571 asked.

"Deark has been charged by Pedagogue to keep an eye on me."

"This is insane," Jacque said.

"What can we do to help?" Isabella asked as she laid a hand on her husband's shoulder.

"Just asking is help enough."

They ate the rest of their portions in silence. When they finished and everything was cleaned up, Deark, Jovi571, and Joanna667 left.

"Be careful," Jovi571 said as he turned and headed to his dwelling.

"Jovi571, there's no reason that you can't accompany us to visit this, Baudricourt," Joanna667 said, gaining a large smile from the muscular young man.

"That's sweet of you but some of us have to show up for work in the morning and swing a hammer all day. I don't think your father would be pleased if I was off gallivanting around the countryside all night long. Besides, VauCouleurs is more than five miles away. I'm made for swinging hammers not long distance running," he said and waved.

"He cares for you deeply," Deark said after they left the town proper.

"And I him. I wish things could be different, but how can I turn my back on this calling?"

"You can't dear," he said, gently pulling her shoulder into him. The night sky was settling in above them as they crested a hill, revealing the lights of the outpost.

"How can you be certain that he's here?"

"I can't. However, the data in his itinerary says that he should be."

"You hacked into his personal information?"

"Actually no. His information is all a matter of public record as he's currently traveling as the Arbiter between the One World Government and Charles Valois."

"So this Entity is his campaign manager and his lawyer?"

"Actually he's Augmented not an Entity. The best I can tell, Charles has no Entities on his support staff."

"Interesting. I wonder why?"

"Mainly because reverse discrimination isn't a One World Ordinance."

"I didn't mean like that. I meant I wonder if he has something against Entities."

"I did understand that, it was a poor attempt at humor. I must have some dust in my circuitry; I'm usually rather funny."

"Deark, why did the Commander say there is a great deal of Chameleon class Entities?"

"Mainly because there are. You see when the news was being told by the 'Mock-Humans', it was my classification of Entities that did it."

"It stands to reason as you're the only shifters."

"While I understand the term, it's on the offensive side."

"Sorry, I didn't mean to—," she started.

"Information only child, I'm not offended. There have been three classifications of Chameleon Class Entities, the C, the K, and the Q. The Q class is the only of us that can hold a form after power is separated from them."

"Excuse me?"

"Let me try again. The K class is far superior to the C class, having the ability to mimic, not shift," he winked. "Several creatures at once. Our shortcoming is that we'll revert back to our initial form if we are deactivated, even momentarily. That's the only advancement from the K class to the Q class of Chameleon Entities."

"I understand." They walked along the streets of VauCouleurs finding they were a combination of paved and hard packed earth. "Do you think that I should do this alone? If Charles has an issue with Entities, perhaps his staff does as well."

"I couldn't support that, no," Deark replied. "However," his words broke off as he became an older looking man in a monk's robe. "This should make them feel better. I'm Father Jean Pasquerel and I'm your traveling companion."

"I love it." She clapped her hands looking much like a small child.

They walked the rest of the way in silence and knocked on the door when they found out what room he was staying in.

"Can I help you?" A young man with augmented stainless steel arms opened the door.

Section One – Chapter Five

"Hello, my name is Joanna667. This is my traveling companion, Father Jean Pasquerel. I'm here to speak with Mr. Baudricourt."

"Hello, my name is de Metz. What business do you have with the Counselor?"

"I'm here in reference to Charles Valois."

"That will be a difficult sell. You'll need to be more specific, I don't know if I can get you in with that explanation."

"Who's at the door?" A quiet voice asked behind him.

"There's a girl and what may be a friar." As he spoke he turned his head and the lights of a left brain augmentation twinkled in the dark entryway.

"Send them away. I'm tired and don't need any cookies or bibles."

"Please sir, five minutes of your time." Joanna667 spoke up, peering around the young man at the door.

"Very well, five minutes only," the voice replied, a bit exasperated.

"Please follow me," de Metz said, leading them into a very warm, dimly lit room. Their augmentations obviously helped them see in low light, and Joanna667 wondered if they made them cold as the heat was nearly unbearable. "Mr. Baudricourt, may I present, Joanna667 and Father Jean Pasquerel."

"Father, have the Entities in the One World Government over ridden the Bishop's word on your eye augmentation?" the man asked from his chair, barely looking away from his book.

"Interesting, a Father of the church that has unregistered modifications," Deark said, taking his primary form.

"Ah, Deark is it?"

"You're very sharp indeed," Deark said. "I didn't wish to muddle this discussion with my true identity. No disrespect was intended."

"None taken. What is it that I can do for you?" Counselor Baudricourt asked, looking between the two new arrivals.

"Sir, I need to see Charles7," Joanna667 stated.

"Girl, please don't toy with me. That name was stripped away from him."

"I've been charged with reinstating that title and more."

"By whom and in which body of government?"

"No one in the government actually."

"I'm about to have de Metz throw you out."

"I've been given a calling by Politician. I must see that Charles Valois is allowed to take the name Charles7 once again. Additionally, he is to hold the role of Leader of the Republicus. The following day I attempted to contact Politician, I was not able to—."

"Imagine that."

"I was instead visited by Pedagogue," she ignored his comment. "After he finished speaking with me, he charged my traveling companion with my well-being."

"Girl, you should leave now. As for you, Deark, these types of entrapments are below even a K class and you should be ashamed. Mr. de Metz see them out." The man in the chair went back to his reading.

******

After the warmth of the room the night air was chilly. "At least we walked five miles to be thrown out," Joanna667 said.

"I hate to ask this but, are you telling the truth?" the young man that walked them out asked.

"Yes. I was given this calling by Politician and Deark was charged with overseeing my wellbeing by pedagogue. We have no reason to lie, for we understand an enemy could easily turn us over to the Techno-Pagan church."

"Have you no proof?"

"I didn't asked for a signed letter, no," Deark said. "When I review my recorded memories, there's nothing but static during the entire episode. You're welcome to see what you can do with these files if you wish."

"Actually, humans are in need of something. Look at the reaction that Charles Valois had by simply getting to the ballot," de Metz said.

"Agreed, but what is it that I can do to prove what can only be defined as faith?" Joanna667 asked.

"I have an idea. My colleague and I are going to the Un Sukiru halls tonight. If as you say you've spoken with Pedagogue, perhaps he'll help you make an impression."

"We're not here to make you rich," Joanna667 bristled.

"Then you misunderstood me, I won't wager. I swear on my augmentations I'll only observe you. Would you consider that fair?"

"I would."

"Deark, perhaps you should become Father Jean Pasquerel once again. As you said, we needn't muddy the waters for no reason."

"Yes of course but why? There are always Entities in the Un Sukiru Halls. What difference would it make if I were to stay in my true form?"

"The Entities don't typically travel with a Mundane, especially not as an equal."

"I understand."

The four set out to the Mother City and the rather round gentleman that accompanied them de Metz introduced as Bertrand de Poulengy. "Call me Pouli."

During the walk, Joanna667 learned many interesting things about being an Augmented including the issue with the temperature of the metal parts drawing heat from their bodies when they were cold and passing heat to them when hot.

"There are many of us that are addicted to it, like the people in the twenty first century with their plastic surgeries and tattoos," De Metz said.

"That behavior is pushed by the church, whereas the body modifications back then were compulsive behaviors. If you want to move deeper into government, you need to augment your brain to a degree that you can pass their tests.

Deeper into military you need strength and brain augmentations, and so on," Pouli added.

"That was one of the things that Charles was trying to use as part of his platform, separating the church from government again," De Metz said.

"Odd that Politician would want him to become the Leader of the Republicus if he was going to force the bodies to become separate," Joanna667 said.

"Not really. The fact that the two bodies are currently one actually limits the sway he and his ilk can have on daily life," Pouli said.

"I'm not certain how true that is," Deark said. "History shows us that may be true for the short term, but that separation will undoubtedly lead to the death of the church and its values."

"Is the play for the short term gains then?" Pouli asked.

"I shouldn't think Politician would consider any of this a 'play'. As the highest of the new gods, I think he's trying to establish new boundaries. You made a statement about the Augmentations being required to move into government."

"I think this girl is more than just a Mundane. Yes, Pouli did say that, and as you caught it, I'll explain. It isn't a widely known fact that there's a criterion that must be met to move into the Republicus. That's why no human managed to move to a leadership role. The Entities have set the bar so high that most humans would not be able to hold it together with that much brain modification." De Metz explained.

"Charles' father went insane, and his mother has been deeply nervous that the same thing is going to happen to him," Pouli said.

"Insane?" Joanna667 inquired.

"Primarily, he saw conspiracies where there were none. He died believing the Entities had sabotaged his attempts to become Leader of the Republicus by hacking into his modifications," Deark said.

"That's correct," De Metz replied.

"We know that isn't possible," Pouli said.

"Why is it impossible? It seems completely logical that someone could do that," Joanna667 stated.

"There's no difference between a person's brain and the modifications that are made. The NanoTechnology that was part of the initial implant modifies itself to have the same bio-rhythms as the Augmented's DNA. Let me give you an example: if you took a diamond and scratched my arms," he held out his stainless steel arm, "the NanoTech would repair the scratch, but the piece that came off me if ran through a sequencing machine would result in my identification."

"De Metz, are you serious? That's magical," Joanna667 said.

"No its technology advancing exponentially," Deark said.

"Is that why the pieces need to be disposed of once there's an upgrade?" she asked.

"Exactly," De Metz said. "How did you know that?"

"My father crafts the upgrades for our Mother City," Joanna667 said.

******

"Halt citizen. There's no request for any Mundane to enter the Mother City tonight," An Imperial CAM unit said, stopping them at the gate.

"We're just heading to the Un Sukiru Halls, mate," Pouli said.

"While your candor may be quaint to Augmented, I don't find it so," the large Entity said.

"My apologies for my colleague. We have a debt to pay to this Mundane. Taking her to the Un Sukiru Halls will settle this debt," De Metz said.

"Then you need only go to the side entrance, as it leads into the gambling halls and the shops, you won't be stopped."

"Thank you for your help," Pouli said.

"Why are there I-CAM units on duty here?" Joanna667 asked when they were far enough away to no longer see the purple glow of the I-CAM unit's eyes.

"Same reason we are," de Metz said. "Fact finding for the trial."

"We'll be going to each of the Mother Cities that are having to use their Stone Rooms, determining how much of the reported increase in Mundane civil unrest is due to Charles Valois changing his name and getting on the ballot, or—," Pouli started.

"Or how much of it was my race's over reaction to it," Deark said.

"Exactly," De Metz replied. The group found the door on the side blocked by another of the I-CAM units.

"We were told that you were bringing a Mundane to our gate. The reports on this Mundane are suspect; she was involved in three issues within a span of less than a day. If there's a problem in the Halls tonight, you Augmented will be held to answer for her, is that understood?" the Imperial unit with a large Alpha on its chest said.

"Thank you for your counsel I-CAM unit Alpha. You will have no issues with this one, we will see to it."

"Very well. What was the bet that you lost?"

"I'm sorry?" Pouli asked.

"I-CAM Rho said that you lost a bet. That's why you must take her to see the Un Sukiru Hall," I-CAM Alpha said.

"Actually it's embarrassing. She beat him in a game of Un Sukiru, three columns to zero," de Metz said.

"Ouch. But perhaps your next augmentation should be right brain so you can think creatively." The I-CAM unit swung the door in to allow their access.

"That was interesting," Deark said.

"How so?" Joanna667 asked.

"The fact that they had access to your records. Typically the Mother City holds those records very closely guarded."

"Even to Imperial CAM units? Isn't their job to protect the current and future Leaders of the Republicus?

How can they do that if they don't have full access to the local records?"

"There has always been a degree of separation." Deark replied as they rounded the corner into the Gaming Hall. Hundreds of Entities and Augmented filled the lavishly decorated rooms.

What Joanna667 found most interesting was the volume level of the rooms. "Why is it so quiet?"

"These are mostly games of skill out here, that's why the Un Sukiru Hall is separated from these ones, it has an element of chance which makes it more apt for cheering," Pouli said.

They approached a set of doors with a large neon sign above them. When they walked through them they found it was like an airlock, a second set was offset to the side for additional dampening. Joanna667 could equate it to the feeling of a Town Hall meeting before and after quiet was called for. They seated themselves at the first table that opened.

"Good evening, travelers. This is one of the house novice tables. Here we have the player versus Central Processing Unit level set to the lowest level of processing. The table limits are ten thought credits and one hundred thought credits per column. Payments here are; one TC gets you one quarter TC on the first column, which doubles for each of the next two columns. Behind the line betting, is paid one for one on the first column, this bet also doubles for each column, the third column being four times your money. Do you have any questions?" the Dealer asked.

"No, that was explained very clearly," Joanna667 said, taking a seat. Deark put ten TC below each of the five columns. He then surprised her by putting one hundred on each of the three circles behind the line. When she looked up she saw that Deark had taken on the appearance of Pedagogue. "What are you doing?"

'They don't see me. Everyone else sees and hears only the Entity known as Deark in his guise of the monk.' His words boomed inside her head, making her wince. 'Sorry, is that better?' he asked at a more gentle pitch.

"Yes thanks."

"Then go ahead and throw them," the Dealer said. He had obviously said something to her while Pedagogue was speaking to her and looked annoyed.

'Pick up all five dice and throw them.'

She followed the voices in her head and tossed the dice. Looking across the table at an antique Entity that played that side of the board she smiled.

"Player has rolled, 1, 2, 3, 4 and 5. How would you like to proceed?"

"I would like to tie the first column to 1, 2, 3, the center column to 4 and the last to the 5." She repeated what Pedagogue told her. In a matter of minutes she had her pieces in the Central Processing Unit's base, thus winning three columns, and the game.

******

Over the course of the next three hours Joanna667 beat each and every CPU in the main room, then they were led to the High-Roller tables. To this point, her opponents had been a hodge-podge of Augmented-Humans and Entities images projected in front of her. "I think she has shown us much and more," De Metz said.

"I agree," Pouli said.

"Perhaps, but I'm being told that we need to wipe the table with this unit as well." The likeness of the man that sat across from Joanna667 at this table was a Mundane.

'Do you know who that is?' Pedagogue asked.

"No," she answered.

'That's the Mundane that beat me at the Mundane Moon Maze a couple hundred years ago. His name is –,' his words were cut off by the image of her opponent.

"Hello, my name is Joshua. You have the honors."

"Thank you."

'Are you ready?' Pedagogue asked.

"Here we go!" The match went as if it was played before, move after move without stopping to think. When they each had captured two columns, the turn rolled around to Joanna667 and she rolled a 3, 4 and 5.

'Perfect. I want you to join the roll together and get a piece into scoring position,' Pedagogue projected into her head.

"What is your move?" the dealer asked.

"I want the first column to move up 3 and over 4. Then advance the fourth column up 5," Joanna667 said.

'What? That isn't what I said.'

"Trust me, this gives us a defense. The red side piece will block him," she said, as the roll came out to exactly what the CPU needed to score, yet their defense caused his piece to go back, and the next roll gave them the victory.

'You have done well. I didn't see it,' Pedagogue said as he vanished.

"Blessed be the three, you won," Pouli said.

"I think if you wanted proof that she has divine guidance you should most definitely have it," Deark said as they settled up with the house and received several pats on the back from those that bet for her to win while many other faces scowled after her as well.

******

The night sky welcomed them as they exited the Halls. "Congratulations little Mundane," I-CAM unit Alpha said.

"Thank you," she replied.

"I imagine you're traveling companion feels much less stupid for having lost to you now."

"Ain't that a fact!" Pouli said. The group continued to walk, uncertain if they would be allowed to leave. After they made their way into the darkness for twenty minutes they allowed themselves a breath of relief.

"I thought that I-CAM was going to arrest us for sure," Pouli said.

"Why would they do that?" Joanna667 asked.

"Bringing in a ringer that walked away with a small fortune," he replied.

When they approached the crossroad where de Metz and Pouli would leave and head off to VauCouleurs, De Metz said, "Tomorrow I'll let Baudricourt know that I have consigned my augmentations to your cause." De Metz took a knee in front of her.

"And I," Pouli said.

Joanna667 looked at Deark to gain some guidance as to what to do. The voices in her head gave her the knowledge she needed. "As the first two champions to my cause, arise and be welcomed," she intoned.

"Very nicely stated," Deark said as they headed home. "I need to ask, were you guided tonight?"

"I was. You took on the appearance of Pedagogue to me and he spoke in my head. Then again when de Metz and Pouli knelt in front of me, Politician told me the proper words to say."

"You're handling all this rather well. My circuits almost overheated when I saw Pedagogue yet you continue on as if it were nothing."

"Hearing voices in my head isn't as big a deal to me as losing Jovi571 and having my father look at me with disapproving eyes." Joanna667's eyes welled up and she leaned on the Entity.

"All will be fine. You'll see," he said and they walked along in silence.

******

The following morning found four girls walking along the disheveled streets of the Commune de Domremy as if in a trance. The previous night's adventures had one of the group rather tired and wishing that the sun would hit her face before she had to commit herself to several hours of regimented schooling.

"Doesn't the wall ever get on your nerves?" Joanna667 asked.

"How can an inanimate object get on your nerves?" Terrah1170 asked.

"It isn't letting the sun warm us. For that matter, it doesn't do anything for us except keep us from experiencing things."

"Joanna667, you're speaking a bit loud," Lacy782 said this just as two men, along with Deark, approached them.

"Hello there." Mr. Baudricourt gestured for her to step away from her friends.

"Good morning sir," Joanna667 said.

"I've come to tell you that on the morrow, following the Stone Room ignition, my team and I will be leaving for Chicago. As I have apparently no choice in the matter, my two men having sworn themselves to your cause, you're welcome to accompany us as that's where you'll find the person that you're searching for."

"Thank you sir," Joanna667 replied.

"I think your thanks should go to Mr. de Metz. He convinced me of your authenticity. Mark you, I can only perform introductions, beyond that you're on your own."

"I look forward to the challenge. Oh and thank you de Metz." She gave a slight curtsey.

"No problem, miss." He gave an incline of his head.

"Come on girls, no time for dawdling." Deark shooed the girls into the classroom.

"Deark, I'm sorry, I mean Instructor," Joanna667 said as they all took their seats. "Did the comments I just heard mean Shelby1000 and her family are going to be executed today?"

"They'll be reporting to the Stone Room tonight, yes. We don't use the antiquated term of execution any longer."

"Thank you Instructor, of course you're correct."

"Now girls, although this is a trying conversation, please bear with me. I must discuss the protocols for the event that you will be attending tonight…" his words were cut off as he saw several of the girls' eyes welling up with tears. "I believe that we spoke about this when Shelby1000 was removed from the classroom, but you need to understand that mourning for one that has been found guilty of a crime, especially one as severe as this, is strictly forbidden."

"Yes instructor," the girls answered, trying to gain their composure.

"The members of the community will gather around the Stone Room, populating the seats. Madam Commander and the members of the Retinue will come in, along with any guests they may have with them for support. In this case, there will be several higher ranking officials from the One World Government here to support her, including the High Leader himself along with his Religious advisor Archbishop Cauchon, and his Political advisor John Lancaster. Phillip le Bon will also be in attendance," Deark said.

"Why so many high ranking officials?" Terrah1170 asked after being called on.

"The group came in yesterday to investigate the charges against Charles Valois. As for how everything will happen, first we will be seated. Then there will be music that will mean everyone is to be quiet. Normally that music is followed by the Commander's guests taking their seats. However, as the guests in this case are higher ranking officials, Madam Commander and the Retinue will take their seats first. Once they are seated, the music changes and their guests will enter. Once everyone is seated the accused are brought down by the CAM units. I wouldn't be surprised to see the I-CAM units leading them tonight."

"Do you think the people are going to boo and hiss at Shelby1000 and her family?" Joyce2710 asked.

"I don't think so, but it could happen. My counsel on that is, be prepared for anything. In other words if someone stands and yells at them, don't react. They'll be led to the center of the platform, where the Commander will get up and describe their crimes. The crowd must answer, 'They must be culled'. I can't be certain what the Commander will say, but at each pause the crowd must repeat, 'they must be culled.' At that point the platform will be lowered down, forming the Stone Room."

"Then we can leave?" Lacy782 asked.

"No. You'll stay in your seats until the Mayor tells you it's ok to exit. Girls, there's one more thing that I want you to know; they'll be projecting everything on the wall. My counsel is to not look. Nothing good can come from watching your friend burn to death. You must not make a grand show of turning your head or covering your eyes. Again, my counsel, focus just above the wall. I think you should go home now. Tonight will be difficult."

In what felt like a few minutes, the first bell tolled calling the families from their homes. "Are you ready?" Jacque asked Joanna667.

"I don't think so. No, I know I'm not, it's going to be terrible," she said.

"It will, but remember we'll be there to help you. The Guild Master came around today explaining everything that will be happening," Jacques said hugging his daughter.

"Deark told us what we're supposed to do as well," Joanna667 said and then she looked at him, "I know you'll be there but it's not like you can hold my hand or comfort me. I don't know how they expect us not to be sad."

"I think it's more that they don't want outbursts of emotions," Isabella said.

"We'd better go," Jovi571 said.

"Yes thank you, you're right," Jacque replied, having a very difficult time letting his daughter go. Isabella leaned into the two, forcing them to follow Jovi571. They walked in silence, meeting up with other citizens whose faces showed the same blankness they were all feeling.

"Hello all," Fado said as he joined Jacques and his family. They and the rest of the people walked to the required meeting. The Mayor and Guild Master greeted each family at the single entrance to the Stone Room Pavilion.

Trusted Rebel Book One

"Please remember, answer with exactly what we have on this card and don't leave until we dismiss you," they said to each and every person as they handed out printed cards.

Section One – Chapter Six

The Pavilion, a half circle with the flat side positioned twenty five meters from the wall to allow better viewing, was full and as still as a school library. The Commander and the Retinue walked down the steps to their seats. Tonight, the Commander's normally large brimmed hat was replaced with a small beret with a netting material that covered her clearly defined face which, for an Entity, appeared pained as she walked. The Entity known as Phillip le Bon was walking with his arm around her waist as she led the group to the front. The Religious Faction of the Retinue was an Augmented, Bishop Loiseleur who had challenged Joanna667 twice in their prior meeting. The Political Faction was Jean Massieu the other Entity that had been at the disposition. Each member of the group wore dark burgundy apparel.

The music changed and the guests began their procession. Mr. Baudricourt was the first in line, followed closely by de Metz and Pouli. Behind them an Entity in a fur trimmed robe could only have been Archbishop Cauchon. He was followed by an Augmented that had the most hooked nose Joanna667 had ever seen, to such a point she almost laughed. The last of the guests was the current Leader of the Republicus, Sir Henry, sixth of his name.

The Commander of Human Capital Management stood on seemingly weak legs, as she swayed briefly, upon standing. The I-CAM units then walked down the condemned. Joanna667 forced herself to look at them as they were led down the stairs. A ripple of discontent could be heard in advance of the final group walking down and continued on after they passed Joanna667's vantage point. The burgundy colored dragonweave of the I-CAM units plating looked as if it were actually blood that had tinged a pool of water. They escorted Shelby1000 and her family straight down to the raised circular area at the center of the Pavilion.

"My fellow citizens," Madam Commander's voice boomed, her image filling the wall behind her. "We have not had an ignition of the Stone Room, here in our home, in over two centuries. Today, that historic number of peaceful years comes to an end. Why is that? Because this family has chosen to embrace hate, instead of the peace that the One World Caste System has brought to all of us. They have chosen jealousy of what others have over the solace of knowing where they'll be tomorrow. The hate that clings to their beings is like the vines that attempt to grow on our wall. Like those vines, the hatred this family brings forth will weaken and destroy all it attaches itself to. We can't recondition that which has been lost to us." She paused.

"They must be culled from our ranks," the crowd imparted.

"This decision isn't one that we can move into lightly, as if it were simple to reach," the Commander replied.

"They must be culled from our ranks," the crowd again said in unison.

"My fellow citizens, we must not face this with condemnation, without charity, even though these are our brothers and sisters."

"They are no longer part of our lives. They must be culled from our ranks." The final reply from the Pavilion caused the Commander's hands to rise over her head.

"Very well, very well, your demands have been heard. The decision has been made, leaving the hands of your betters clean." The Commander's final statement caused Joanna667's skin to prickle.

The fire took shape when the platform lowered Shelby1000 and her family into the Stone Room. When it stopped lowering, the faces of the family took the place of the Commander on the wall. Joanna667 once again forced herself to look at the images as the fire licked the optics of the camera.

Once the fire reached the family they pulled together in a group hug, and only the father faced the camera. As the tortured screams from the pit rent the night, the camera zoomed in on the father, his face began to burn and his hands instinctively reached up. On the back of his hands, clearly carved into his flesh, a message could be read for only a moment, 'Where is the Maiden?' The flames consume the family and the camera returned to the Commander. Her sharp Entity features are pulled into an expression of anger and disbelief.

When the fire from the Stone Room died, the guests left in reverse order, with the I-CAMs leading the way, protecting the Leader of the Republicus from any possible backlash the Mundane may wish to dole out. None of course came. After Baudricourt and his men left, The Commander walked back to the platform that had risen up with the smoking ashes of the dead. This was not something Deark had warned them about. The image once again appeared on the wall.

"Citizens, the girl Shelby1000 had been selected for the Mundane Moon Maze. She of course, is in no state to participate." The smirk on the Commander's face, as her arm extended displaying the smoldering pile, let Joanna667 know something bad was about to happen. "Therefore, another must take her place. CAM unit Epsilon as you selected Shelby1000 for your questioning phase, you have the option now of choosing another. Please make that selection should you wish to proceed."

"Very well Commander." The CAM unit walked among the fearful Mundane with purpose.

'This part was planned to be played out at another time,' Joanna667 thought.

"Christopher1492, I select you." He grabbed Joyce2710's betrothed, lifting him into the air by the collar of his shirt.

"NO!" the scream from his fiancee rent the night.

'This was the pebble that Politician spoke of, the one which the Commander has chosen to cause the ripple in the water,' she thought. 'But I'm not ready.'

"Sit down Joyce2710," Deark ordered. "There are protocols that have been in observance for several generations. This one has been approved for a pairing. You must choose another."

'I was wrong, Deark has always filled the void Politician spoke of.' With that Joanna667 knew she was ready to start the calling because she knew who she could trust.

"Deark, you overstep your bounds again. There's nothing written that says an observance can't be ignored. The selection is –," her words were cut off.

"Take me instead!" Jovi571 stood.

"The choice isn't mine to make," the Commander said.

"I reject that one," CAM unit Epsilon said.

"As you heard, your request for substitution was rejected and as no other Entity –,"

"FADO, this is your time," Jovi571 said, "you need to step into the questioning phase, you know that my love has another path. Choose me!"

"Your pleas are most touching, but as I started to say –," The Commander began.

"I choose Jovi571 for my questioning phase. I'll present him at the Mundane Moon Maze," FADO said interrupting the Commander.

"The choice isn't yours, inventory Entity," CAM unit Epsilon said.

"In fact it is," Deark said. "If in conflict, the Mundane more fit for the trials of the Mundane Moon Maze must be selected. For the betterment of all."

"For the betterment of all!" the crowd repeated.

"Indeed Deark, for the betterment of all." The Commander's voice was cold even for an Entity. "Very well, Jovi571 will represent FADO in his bid for Sentience," silence for the sign of the Box, "at the Mundane Moon Maze next month." The Commander left and her Retinue followed behind her. When the Mother City leadership had all left, the Mayor stood and gave them permission to leave.

The walk home after was quiet until Joyce2710 and Christopher1492 caught up to them. "Why?" Joyce2710 said, throwing her arms around Jovi571's neck.

"I'm sorry?"

"Why would you do that? It was the most selfless thing I've ever seen."

"Christopher1492 should not have been selected. Our society has accepted an approval of pairing as wedded for all the teaching, just as Deark pointed out. In the end it came down to the fact that my pairing with Joanna667 was denied and yours was approved."

"Thank you." Christopher1492 said shaking Jovi571's hand. The groups separated and they soon entered Joanna667's home.

"I didn't mean for any of that to happen, any of this I mean," Joanna667 said, looking at Jovi571 but speaking to everyone.

"Of course you didn't, dear," Isabella said. There was a knock at the door. "Come in."

"Good evening," Deark walked in. "We leave at sunrise, meet me at the school."

"Leave for where?" Jacque asked.

"We've been given passage with Mr. Baudricourt and his group to go meet with Charles Valois in Chicago," Joanna667 said.

"Please be careful." Jovi571 walked over and hugged her.

"I really am sorry," she whispered in his ear.

"I know." He pulled back and said good night to her parents, and then he and Deark left.

"You should get some sleep. Tomorrow will be a big day," Isabella said.

******

Joanna667 rose early and discovered that a bag had already been packed for her. Picking it up, she walked out of her room. Her mother and father were waiting at the kitchen table with their morning tea.

"Good morning. I was going to wake you up in a bit," Jacque said.

"Thank you. After I woke, there was no way I could go back to sleep. Have you ever flown?"

"I did when I was younger than you," Isabella said. "I had an advanced weaving class in the Olympic Mountains in Washington."

"Wow. That must have been a long trip."

"By plane only a few hours actually."

"I've never flown," Jacque said, "I don't know if I could. Heck, I don't even like going on the roof of the forge." They laughed and Joanna667 sat down, Isabella insisting on making a big breakfast. Just before sun up she hugged them and left. As she walked through the streets, Jovi571 ran up.

"Careful you, the CAM units don't like running," Joanna667 said.

"Actually, I didn't see any on the way over here." Jovi571 walked over and took her free hand. "Are you nervous about flying?"

"Are you nervous about traveling to the moon?" she retorted.

"Actually that's the only part of the maze that scares me, getting in a bloody rocket."

"Jovi571 such profanities. What has come over you?"

"I only have a couple months to live. I guess that's liberating."

"How can you face death so selflessly?"

"That's a strange question coming from you."

"What do you mean?"

"Deark told me why you called off the pairing. He said that you didn't want me to mourn."

"I never want you to hurt, but I most certainly didn't want you to volunteer to die on the moon either."

"Out of the 1024 Mundane either 1 or 0 can complete the entire maze. Maybe I'll win. After all, it's been done before."

"Yes it has and if anyone alive today could survive, it would be you." Joanna667 let his hand drop as they turned a corner seeing a CAM unit against the wall.

"Greetings Mundane, what brings you out this early in the morning?" The purple eyes of an I-CAM unit focused on them out of the darkness.

"Joanna667 needs to assist me," Deark said.

"I know why you and the girl are out! I was addressing the other Mundane."

"I'm not one hundred percent certain why Jovi571 is here," he replied.

"We're just discussing his chances of completing the Mundane Moon Maze," Joanna667 said.

"Very low, as only one has ever done it," the I-CAM unit walked forward. "Jovi571, return to your home. Deark and Joanna667 we have a long walk to meet with Mr. Baudricourt's group."

"You're accompanying us?" Deark asked.

"All those that are to travel with the counselor need protection." The light from a street lamp showed that the Entity was I-CAM Alpha, the same unit that was at the Un Sukiru hall.

"Very well. Thank you for that," Joanna667 said.

******

The odd traveling companions set out, Joanna667 waved to Jovi571 as he turned and walked to the blacksmith. Their walk only lasted about a half an hour when a large vehicle drove up. "Good morning," De Metz said out of the window.

"And good morning to you," I-CAM Alpha replied. "When did you receive permission to use a self-directed class hover-transport?"

"Only just. Madam Commander sent it for us," Mr. Baudricourt said. "Joanna667 please get up front here. De Metz will get in the back with the Entities as there's no room for them up here."

"Thank you." Joanna667 switched places with de Metz. "I've never rode in a car before."

"Listen closely," Baudricourt said as the vehicle began to rise and then headed off, "Something is amiss. The use of vehicles like this are only for high ranking officials in the One World Government, be it at local level or with the Republicus. I don't know what's happening but whatever it is, do not, I repeat do not, give them a reason to hurt you."

"I understand." They drove onward, the tensions high the rest of the ride to the airport. The vehicle found its way to their plane and parked on the ground. Joanna667 pulled the door release and stepped out. "That was fun." She tried to act normal even as two I-CAM and ten CAM units walked out of the plane. 'At least I know why there were no CAM units yelling at Jovi571 this morning,' she thought as the Commander of Human Capital Management exited the plane, followed by Phillip le Bon.

"It's very good of you to see us off," Mr. Baudricourt said.

"Just like a lawyer to get it all wrong," Madam Commander said.

"I'm sorry, get what wrong?"

"World-Law 13,000,701 went into effect an hour ago," Phillip le Bon said.

"Sorry it's been difficult keeping up with all the laws that are coming out. Hopefully as the next Leader of the Republicus, you can do something about that," Mr. Baudricourt said.

"Perhaps, however I requested that the High Leader add this one in last night. There seems to be a large number of Mundane that are wandering around outside of their assigned homes. We can't have that." Phillip said.

"Joanna667, I hereby arrest you for crimes against the state in accordance with World-Law 13,000,701 which states no Mundane are allowed to travel further than five miles from their registered home," Madam Commander said.

"That's ridiculous." De Metz said.

"I would advise that you and your men get on your plane Counselor, before I arrest you for harboring a criminal," I-CAM Alpha extolled.

"Very well, we'll go, but these actions are most irregular." The group boarded the plane.

The I-CAM Entities walked up and shackled Joanna667. "It seems your little pet project isn't going where you thought it would. What say you, Deark?" Madam Commander said.

"I'm not certain what caused you to turn out this way. The Entity that I knew so many years ago would've never been so petty." Deark replied.

"Enjoy your walk back to the Commune de Domremy," the Commander sneered as she got into the vehicle with Phillip and I-CAM Alpha. The remaining I-CAM and ten CAM units stayed with them.

"Interesting that the heir apparent of the Republicus and his consort feel a small girl and a chameleon class K Entity require twelve of their elite Conditional Attitude Maintainers to escort them on a fifteen mile walk," Deark said.

"Don't forget the fetters for her ankles as well." Phillip said from the window as the vehicle pulled away.

******

The bindings took Joanna667 quite a while to get used to, and after falling on the ground for the fifteenth time, the I-CAM unit allowed Deark to stabilize her. Eventually she mastered the best way to walk in the fetters. Turning to Deark she asked, "So you and the Commander have a history?"

"I don't know if she would approve of me answering that question in front of these CAM units, but as she left us fifteen miles from home to walk in the heat of the day she loses any input on the subject."

"Seems fair."

"We both reached the questioning phase at the same time, maybe a month apart. We then had to wait twenty-five years for enough other Entities to enter that phase to make up the 1024 needed to run the Maze. Madam Commander became impatient in year ten and by year twenty she was fighting to allow Entities to bring more than one Mundane."

"Isn't that what happened?"

"Ursula Minor wouldn't allow it. Although many of us had moved into the state of Sentience," pause for all the Entities to show the respect, "many years before we fulfilled the approved doctrine to be recognized as Sentient," delay. "The only date that matter when Entities are competing for the same position are the date they fulfilled the Doctrine, and if there is a tie than the one that was manufactured first has seniority for said position."

"Ok but—"

"If we'd been able to run the maze in 2175 instead of 2200, the Commander would've been in line for the role of Leader of the Republicus prior to the current leader and ahead of Phillip. The deciding factor between the three of them is the year they were manufactured as they all were represented in the Mundane Moon Maze in 2200. In reality, Sir Henry was the last of the Entities to reach the questioning phase in that batch of graduates, but he was manufactured first."

"What does that have to do with her hating you so much?"

"I think hate may be a strong term," Deark replied.

"No, that's the correct emotion," the I-CAM unit said.

"Fine, fine she hates me. I was the one that got Ursula minor involved when it looked like the other Entities were going to cave into her demands. In the end she lost out on being Leader of the Republicus, twice so far, and if Charles Valois takes it now, then Phillip can run again next time. As I said, it's all based upon seniority for us Entities. For that matter I could throw in my name and she would have to wait even longer.

"She would shoot lasers out of her eyes at you."

"Only World-CAM units have that ability," one of the CAM units said.

"Good to know."

******

It was nightfall by the time they returned to the mother city. The I-CAM unit walked Joanna667 to her parents' home while the ten CAM units headed off, presumably to make certain the Commune de Domremy was safe.

"You will stay here until you're contacted by the Commander of Human Capital Management," the I-CAM unit said, its burgundy dragonweave still a high gloss finish even while Joanna667 was covered head to toe in dust from the road.

"Yes of course." She held her hands out for the shackles to be removed.

"They'll stay in place until –," a second I-CAM unit walked up.

"If you don't remove them I will," Deark said.

"Then you will be in violation of –," the first unit started.

"Three, two," Deark transformed his hand into a grinder.

"Release the prisoner," the voice of Madam Commander said, walking out of the house. The shackles were removed and Joanna667 ran into her mother's waiting arms.

"Don't forget what I told you," the Commander said over her shoulder.

"Of course Madam Commander, thank you Madam Commander," both Isabella and Jacque said.

"Deark, a word."

"What was that about?" Joanna667 asked stepping away from her mother.

"She was explaining your restrictions," Jacques said.

"Are you alright?" Isabella asked, shutting the door.

"I'm fine, nothing that a cool drink won't solve." Joanna667 said and they walked into the eating area.

"Sit down, I'll get it," Jacque said.

"Dear can you also bring the medical kit?" Isabella asked looking at Joanna667's ankles and wrists.

"Mom, I'm fine."

There was a knock at the door, "Who is it?" Isabella asked. Never had Joanna667 heard that question. It had always been, 'come in' whenever someone came to call on them.

"Deark, and Jovi571."

"Come in," Joanna667 said. "Why did Madam Commander wish to speak with you?"

"It seems I was docked a week's pay for not showing up at class today. Also she feels I've pitted myself against her 'cause' and she put me on notice that she won't stand for such public humiliation as I doled out to her when CAM unit Epsilon selected Christopher1492.She said the next time, I'd be facing the Stone Room for insurrection."

"What did you say?"

"I resigned my post at the Commune de Domremy."

"You can't…" there was a knock at the door.

"Who's there?" Jacque asked, returning to the eating area.

107

"Just a wish of salutations from a champion to the lady's cause."

"What?" Isabella asked.

Joanna667 rushed over to the door, pulling it open as de Metz walked in, quickly placing a finger over his mouth. He handed Joanna667 a sealed parchment and then left.

"That was strange," Deark said, holding out his hand for the letter. "I wonder if they'll be back." He took the appearance of a CAM unit and Joanna667 handed him the envelope. He turned back into himself and put it into his chest piece just as the door burst open.

"Who was at the door a moment ago?" I-CAM Alpha asked.

"There was no one there when I opened it," Deark said.

"Would you like to come in and sit? It will save all the time pretending to leave, then listening in. I mean really, what a bother," Joanna667 said.

"I'm not certain how to take that last comment. It felt sincere but it may have been mocking."

"Not a bit I-CAM Alpha, you've been nothing but honest as far as I'm concerned. I wish you no distress at all."

"Very well. I would counsel that your visitors depart post haste."

"Thank you once again for your kind and charitable counsel," she replied, closing the door after he left.

"You've resigned your post? Does that mean you will be leaving the Commune?" Isabella asked.

"Yes. I have to stay and teach the class until the next instructor arrives and then I'll be off to new lands."

"You will be missed," Joanna667 said.

"I'm not gone yet. Get some sleep, tomorrow is a school day. Jovi571, with me," Deark said.

"But I can't go to school."

"The Commander did say you must attend class. She also said you can go to the Clothier and the Forge," Isabella said and walked the two visitors to the door. A moment later she was back at the table. She handed the sealed envelope to her husband and then sat Joanna667 down and began dressing her wounds.

"Those must hurt," Jacque said, making a hand gesture for Joanna667 to moan loudly.

"Ouch, mother that hurts, please just leave them I'll be fine." Her mock complaints masked the sound of the envelope opening and the parchment being unfolded. He set the note on the table and they all read silently.

******

'Joanna667,

I'm certain that you've received this as de Metz has sworn he won't allow this letter to fall into the wrong hands. When you're finished reading it, burn it and scatter the ashes.

As I said in the hover-transport on the ride to the airport I knew that something was wrong. Rest assured you're being protected. De Metz, as a champion to your cause, will let nothing happen to you. Should the need arise he will fight, and if required, die for you. Let us hope that does not occur.

Based upon my network inside the Republicus you're being watched day and night. De Metz informed me that your father is a craftsman of augmentations. I believe therein lies the only hope that you have to get out of the Commune de Domremy and pursue your calling. While de Metz can blank used augmentations if needed, even under the best of circumstances that can be risky. If your father can get fresh components, de Metz has the experience to install them on you. I understand that a Mundane becoming an Augmented is a potential death sentence. However, you need to understand that should you continue on your quest without the modifications, you'll be facing the Stone Room for certain.

Once your conversion is completed I can have the proper identifications added into the One World Census. I'm sorry but this is all the help I can offer. If you choose to stay where you are convey your decision to de Metz. Keep your head down and he will watch over you until after the Mundane Moon Maze.

Sincerely,

Robert de Baudricourt'

Section One – Chapter Seven

The path was now set; Joanna667 would need to become an Augmented. The thought was almost too much to grasp. Her father burned the note as her mother finished dressing the injuries on Joanna667's wrists.

"There you go. Hopefully the NanoTech in the bandages will take care of those injuries before you head to school in the morning. Off to bed." Isabella helped Joanna667 to her feet and gave her a big hug.

"I'm sorry," Joanna667 said into her mother's ear just as Jacque joined the hug.

"We love you dear. Try to get some sleep. It's been a week to forget." He kissed his daughter on the head.

The morning came too quickly. Joanna667 got up and headed into the eating area. Her mother was there alone. "Good morning," Isabella said, handing her a mug of tea.

"Where's father?"

"Already headed to the forge. He had some things he needed to get together after all the hubbub last night."

"I wanted to make certain Jovi571 was getting all the training he needed before the big day."

"Do you want me to tell the girls you'll meet them at school?"

"Please do." She took her morning corn and headed to the forge. There she found the inventory Entity standing at the door. "Good morning FADO."

"Good morning miss."

"Is my father mucking about?"

"Yes miss but he said not to let anyone in."

"No problem, I'll wait. So are you excited about the big day?"

"I'm challenged with the fact that Jovi571 is a friend."

"That's a hard one. Let me ask a different question. Are you going to keep your name after the Maze?"

"I hadn't thought about it, miss. It's been my name for so long."

"But isn't it an acronym for some inventory program?"

"It is. Fixed Asset Disposal Order."

"Did I hear Joanna667 out there?" Jovi571's voice asked.

"Yes, I've just been chatting with FADO."

"Well come in here I could use your opinion."

"If you think of any names, miss, let me know. Now you have my mind racing," FADO said as he let her pass.

"Shall do." Joanna667 walked in to find Jovi571 at the incinerator. "Does father know you're doing that?"

"He told me it was disposal day, so I would think so," he replied, giving her a wink after looking around conspiratorially.

"Is he here?"

"Yes but he's not to be disturbed." He gave another look around the forge and then motioned with his head for her to go to the office. The door's bottom half was open and the top was shut. She ducked under, finding her father and de Metz hard at work and a message on the chalk board, partially erased.

'Entities won't duck under and having half the door open is less obvious.'

Joanna667 walked over to the board and erased the message completely. When they saw her they waved, and both made the shhh motion. For a big Augmented, de Metz was crouched into a small area working on several augmentations. Her father walked over to the board and wrote, 'Your implants. Need to re-serialize them' and then erased the message. She nodded and then waved goodbye.

"Well if you could tell him I stopped by I better get to school." Joanna667 said for the benefit of anyone listening and then hugged Jovi571 and whispered, "This is all just surreal."

"You'll be fine. That de Metz guy is going to make certain of that," he whispered back.

******

Her knees were shaking as she caught up with the other girls. "Joanna667, where were you yesterday?" Lacy782 asked.

"Getting in trouble. I'm grounded to our house or my parents place of work for the foreseeable future."

"Was Deark with you?" Terrah1170 asked.

"I was." Deark startled them by coming out of nowhere. "I've got some news to share. Everyone into their seats quickly, quickly."

"I didn't get to read the informational board," Joyce2710 complained as he rushed them all into the classroom.

"So girls, I wanted to explain to you that I put in my official notification that I'm leaving my post here. This morning the Commander informed me that she has found my replacement and that they'll be here tomorrow. I will no longer be your teacher after today's lesson."

"Did it have anything to do with Shelby1000 and the issue at the Stone Room with Christopher1492?" Lacy782 asked.

"I'm not at liberty to discuss such things, especially with girls that don't raise their hands," he poked. "Let's use today doing something we haven't done in a very long time. Let's talk about the future, and what part you hope to play in it."

"We did that during our first class twelve years ago," Lacy782 said.

"As a matter of fact, how would you like to see the replay of that particular lesson?" Deark asked and everyone clapped. He stood in the center of the room and each of his panels began unfolding and reforming until he was a flat screen. The surface started to light up and a classroom full of the faces of little boys and girls looked back at them. Deark's voice could be heard asking, "Class I want you to tell me what your father and mother do. Then I want you to tell me what you want to do when you grow up."

The littlest girl started talking right away, "My daddy is a…"

"Lacy782 you need to raise your hand." The playback paused and Deark's head stuck out of the top of the screen. "Some things never change." The classroom all laughed, as the playback started once again, the little hand shot up, "Go ahead Lacy782."

"My daddy is a carpenter and my mommy is an herbalist. And I wanna be an herbalist too." Her soft voice and near baby-talk made each of the girls watching the playback smile and give an involuntary 'Aw'. They continued to watch as the other hands shot up around her.

Several other kids were called on, each wanting to do the same thing one of their parents did.

"Jovi571, how about you?" Deark asked from off camera again.

"My mother's a midwife, my father... well he was a blacksmith before he ran the Mundane Moon Maze."

"I'm sorry to hear about your father, but there are observances now to keep those paired and those approved for pairing so that no little Mundane will be without a parent. What do you want to be when you grow up Jovi571?"

"A blacksmith, sir." The little face broke into a huge grin. Only a few hands remained up after Jovi571 answered.

"Shelby1000, go ahead." Deark's voice could once again be heard.

"My parents are both farmers, but I want to do something that will make everyone remember me." Deark rewound the tape several times replaying the girl's words, "...do something that will make everyone remember me... will make everyone remember me... everyone remember me... remember me."

Eventually all the hands were done raising, "How about you Joanna667, you're awfully quiet?" Deark's voice said after all the other little kids went.

"My dad is a blacksmith, and my mum is a clothier. I don't know what I want to do but I want to change the world in some way…" again he played with the playback, "I want to change the world… change the world… change the world… I want to change the world."

Deark transformed back into himself. "That was fun, how many of you still want to do what you said you did way back then."

"I think," Lacy 782 stopped and raised her hand. Deark pointed to her, "I think some already have, sir."

"There's no question in my mind that you're right. Just as there's no question you can all do exactly what you said you wanted to do back then. I'll miss you all, class dismissed."

The girls walked to the front of the class forming a line to say their goodbyes. When Joanna667 got to the front of the line she put her arms around him. "It's all changing now isn't it?"

"My dear, change isn't a new thing. Thinking that things won't change is what's new. Every day is a chance to change the world if you don't fear the opinions of others. My guidance to all of you is to embrace things that are good and proper, change being amongst them."

"That's such a good parting comment for the class," a drawling voice said as an Entity in a long burgundy robe walked into the room.

"Thank you, Bishop –," Deark started.

"Archbishop. I'd thank you to get my introduction correct, chameleon class K Entity."

"Girls, this is ARCH Bishop Cauchon, he has until now been advisor to the Leader of the Republicus on all things religious or dogmatic in nature," Deark said.

"Actually I still am. Filling in as instructor to help out a friend as we search for a permanent solution to the problem here." His words were spoken slowly, as if each were hand crafted to fit into each person's mind as they saw best. The beauty of this craftsmanship came in the form of avoidance, as none of the people's perceptions could be held against him as his defense was built in, 'That isn't what I meant.'

"I've dismissed the girls already. Should they retake their seats?"

"No, I think tomorrow will be a fine day to start MY lessons." The Archbishop turned and headed out of the classroom.

"Ok girls, no homework tonight, have fun and stay out of trouble." The last comment he made while looking at Joanna667.

"You should come by the forge with me to say your goodbyes to Jovi571 and my father," she said before leaving.

******

They walked together and several Entities and Mundane stopped Deark to say their goodbyes. The short trip took almost an hour and when they finally arrived there were several CAM units out front.

"You should head home. There's no reason for you to test the patience of the Commander by heading into the forge. You have many more important things on the horizon." Deark physically had to turn her and push her toward her home. She was around the corner out of the sight of the Entities before she stopped and looked back at Deark.

"I don't understand, is my father in trouble?"

"It would appear so. Let me check."

Joanna's head was once again reeling, up was down and dark was light, she saw herself screaming her father's name and running toward the forge. The CAM Entities attempted to stop her as she ran full speed into the forge. The laser bolt that caught her on the back was a surprise; there must have been a World CAM unit in those in front of the blacksmith. She lost sight of everything as the fires of the forge obstructed her view.

"We need to leave," de Metz said taking, her gently by the arm.

"What just happened?" she asked as he led her home.

"You just died. Rather convincingly in front of I and W class CAM units."

"Deark?" her stupor finally breaking.

"Of course. It must be odd seeing yourself commit suicide."

"Is he… is he dead?"

"There's no time for this. Come on, your parents would like to say goodbye."

"Father's not under arrest?"

"No child. He's at home waiting on you. Apparently there was a theft and all the transmitters were vandalized at the Forge. FADO has been dealing with the inquiry." He finished explaining as they walked into her home. "Joanna667 I have all the data together for Baudricourt, I just need your new name."

"Politician and Pedagogue both called me, Jehanne. Politician said it was my true name."

"Oh my goodness, that's what your name was supposed to be. The Entity couldn't write down what he qualified as a misspelled name," Jacque said.

"There we go then, Jehanne la Pucelle is my new name," she said.

"From here forward, you need to think of yourself by that name. Do you understand?" de Metz asked.

"I do," Jehanne replied.

"You don't have a lot of time." Isabella took her daughter into the bedroom. "You need to get ready."

"I'm ready."

"No, you're not." Isabella pulled a pair of scissors from her bedside table.

"What are those for?"

"Sit down and be quiet." She cut her daughter's hair. "I brought you something from work. It'll allow you the illusion of being…" the word caught in her throat.

"Augmented," Jehanne finished.

"Exactly. It's right there in the box."

Jehanne reached down and removed a white drape of dragonweave.

"What is it?" she asked.

"The latest thing, a hooded dragonweave cape that's imbued with various NanoTech. I also brought a set of clothes that won't mark you as Mundane," Isabella said, finishing the haircut.

"Thank you mother, this is amazing. Why the haircut though? I loved my hair."

"They need to install your augmentations." Isabella's eyes welled up. "Quickly now, put on the clothing."

"Are you finished?" Jacque asked.

"Yes, yes come in," Isabella answered after Jehanne finished changing her clothes. He stopped cold seeing his beautiful daughter dressed, and hair cut to look like a boy. "Oh my! Um, ok... I have something for you as well. This has been handed down from eldest child to eldest child since before the Entities were even thought of." He handed her a ring with three odd 't' symbols and two sets of time worn initials engraved on it.

"Thank you." She took it and put it on her thumb as all her other fingers were too small.

"It's time," de Metz said. "Lay on the floor and put this cloth in your mouth." Before he could hand her the cloth there was a knock at the door.

"It'll have to wait, head out the window. You'll need to install them later. Wrap the parts as well as clippings of her hair in that cape and go," Isabella said, walking out of the bedroom. "One moment. Yes?" The sound of the door opening was followed by quiet conversation. "Jacque could you come here, I think the CAM units may have word of the break in."

"Coming dear. We all love you." He whispered before closing the window.

"I love you all as well." Jehanne followed de Metz as he methodically snuck them from the Commune de Domremy. They found Jovi571 sitting against the giant oak.

"Your mother deserves an award," he said. "As I walked up to the house she screamed and fell to the ground crying."

"Oh dear, they informed her of my death," Jehanne said.

"Actually," Jovi571 stood up, transforming back into Deark. "It was my death."

"You fooled me," Jehanne said. "That's twice. Last time I thought I was having a schizophrenic break. Watching myself running away and getting shot… Oh my goodness, you were shot! Are you ok?"

"I lost a couple of my panels, is all. Mr. de Metz, what do we need to do to get this young lady ready to face the world?" Deark asked.

"Are we safe here?" he asked.

"This is where I first met the new gods," Joanna667 replied.

"Good enough for me." De Metz set the makeshift bag on the ground. "Jehanne, when we install these it will hurt. There's nothing I can do for that."

"Is that the name she chose?"

"Yes, Jehanne la Pucelle, and that's the name that's in the database for these modies."

"Modies?"

"Modies is slang for modifications or augmentations. We can work on things like slang during the trip," de Metz said. "Are you ready?"

"I'll focus on my calling, I'll be fine." She leaned against the tree. "How do you need me?"

"Just get into a position where you won't be tempted to move."

"Ok, let's do this."

******

The sun was setting as de Metz stood up, admiring his work. "Your own mother wouldn't recognize you."

"That's a good thing," Jehanne said. "Is there a way I can see what I look like? I would hate to scream in horror when I walk in front of a mirror."

"Very well." Deark began a very slow transformation, first becoming the old Joanna667, then the hair was removed during the first step of becoming Jehanne. Next, the left augmentation to her brain was added and then the right. The look wasn't horrifying, just very strange, as what looked like a long piece of copper with non-illuminated lights were on the side of her head. Next, two bands of carbon fiber crossed from the back of the copper strips to each side of her left eye. The left brain implant ending on the right side of her left eye, while the right side augmentation ended on the left side of her left eye. Just as she was about to ask why, a tube of stainless steel outlined her eye and then closed in a mirrored lens covering it.

"Hockey Pete!" She reached up to touch the new implant.

"No, no, no." de Metz stopped her hand. She saw in surprise that her arm looked much like his, only it had servos in different places.

"Why do I have more little motors?" She looked at Deark who had now fully transformed, he even had the white dragonweave cloak on his shoulders. "Ok I look awesome."

"The modies will change a bit as the NanoTech combines the biorhythms of the augmentations together with your DNA. Eventually the brain modies will look like mine, only the lights will show." De Metz touched the side of his head, showing the lights. "Between now and then, it itches like crazy."

"How long is eventually? I really don't want to bump into people until after its done healing over," Deark said.

"As long as she wears that cape, the healing will take maybe four hours," de Metz said.

"I thought you were talking days, even weeks," Jehanne said.

"That cape will speed up the process greatly. It really is an amazing gift."

"Jehanne, cover with the cape and let's get a move on," Deark said.

******

They walked away from the Commune de Domremy for an hour before turning toward the airfield.

"I've got to say, even with that sun beating down on me, I'm as cool as a cucumber."

"That's definitely that cloak. I'm dying in this heat," de Metz said.

"Deark, have you given any thought to how we may find the six questions?" Jehanne asked.

"It's not in any of the public records. I've checked several of my oldest friends' libraries, and even spreading some of the TC we earned at the Un Sukiru tables around has led to nothing."

"I don't mean to eavesdrop but, six questions?" de Metz inquired.

"Pedagogue told us that the six questions that were asked of the new gods when the only Mundane Moon Maze was completed would be important to us moving forward. He also said while he couldn't tell us what they were, we should speak with Neoteric," Jehanne explained.

"That's unreal, first to have actually spoken with one of the Six, but what's more that he makes it sound like for the success of your endeavor, you need to speak with one of the ancients that spawned the new gods. I don't understand how that's possible unless the Six are dissolved."

"I considered that side of the question as well." They continued discussing the options of how they may be able to dissolve the new gods in order to discuss the six questions.

"As a whole the confusing part is, why would Politician want the Six to become Three again in order to get Charles into the leadership role of the Republicus?" Deark asked. The sun had set enough that they could see the lights of a vehicle coming up behind them.

"Should we hide ourselves? That can only be one of the government group?" Jehanne said, noticing the lights hovering above the ground.

"Let's have a look at you," de Metz said. She pulled the hood off, revealing a completely healed Augmented. "I'd say Deark, you need to become that monk again then we just keep walking."

"Very well," Father Jean Pasquerel said. In a matter of minutes the vehicle was within a hundred yards.

"Jehanne, try to use your eye Modi to see who's in that vehicle," de Metz said.

"How?"

"Close your right eye and concentrate on seeing further away."

"It's not working."

"It will. The lights on your brain modies are beginning to glow, just think, 'I need to see inside that vehicle.'"

"It's still not... wait there it goes," she went quiet for a moment and then, "oh my goodness, it's the High Leader along with his pet, I-CAM Alpha."

"Damn," de Metz said.

"It's not a big deal. We're just walking to the airfield," Father Jean Pasquerel said.

"I don't know if her identification is fully divested among the One World Databases yet."

"Just turn and keep walking," he replied.

"Why did you come back?" Jehanne asked, breaking the silence.

"I had to get you," de Metz said.

"So you think that the Leader of the Republicus is going to be fine with you returning and helping a Mundane to—,"

"Oh I see what you meant."

"What relationships did Baudricourt build into the system as to her identity?" Father Jean Pasquerel asked.

"Let me check." They walked in silence as the vehicle closed in on them. Jehanne hoped it would simply continue driving. The whine of the engine however, started to slow and she knew they weren't in such luck.

"Hello travelers," the High Leader's voice called from the open window.

"Hello, and thank you for stopping," Father Jean Pasquerel said.

"Of course, of course. Where might you be heading?"

"To the air field," he replied, knowing that de Metz was still trying to get an answer to Jehanne's identity. "Actually they're heading to the air field. I'm just a poor father of the faith that's been their traveling companion."

"So you have a plane then? Our pilot reports that ours is the only airplane there."

"We didn't know the exact time of our arrival, or for that matter the day." De Metz joined the conversation with a laugh.

"I'm sorry, the humor of that statement is lost upon me," I-CAM Alpha said. "Mr. de Metz."

"You know this man?" the High Leader asked.

"Yes, High Leader. He's one of the men that accompanied Counselor Baudricourt to the Stone Room. He also waited with him during the inquest as to the guilt or innocence of Charles Valois."

"Ah yes, we recognize you now. We had reports that you left along with the Counselor."

"I did sir. The truth of my being here and the reason for the laugh is this girl. Jehanne is Counselor Baudricourt's niece and his charge. She took it upon herself to stow away on our flight from Chicago. I was sent back to find her and bring her home." De Metz lied with the grace of an elected official.

"That's an amazing story," I-CAM Alpha said. "How did the girl stow away? There are so many ways to safeguard against such a thing."

"Apparently that blasted cape had something to do with it. The plane's sensors did not detect anything but the NanoTech. The pilots didn't do a manual check of the baggage area."

"That's good to know," the High Leader said. "Until the sensors have been updated to defeat this new technology, make certain the pilot has the baggage area manually checked."

"Yes, of course sire."

"So your plan was to go to the airfield? Please jump in the back. There's more than enough room should you not mind sitting with my luggage." He laughed.

"That's most gracious, thank you very much," Father Jean Pasquerel said.

*****

Upon arriving at the airfield thirty minutes later, which seemed much longer as not one word was spoken, the transport came to a stop. Jehanne started handing down the luggage and seeing this, de Metz began helping as well. "Oh don't be silly, that's what we have these Mundane at the airfield for," the High Leader said.

"Of course. I wasn't thinking." De Metz waited for Jehanne to jump down before he joined the others.

"So," the High Leader started after they were inside the air conditioned gate area, "no plane yet?"

"It's due to arrive in a few hours," de Metz replied.

"Nonsense. In a few hours our pilot could have you dropped off wherever you need to go. It's a thirty minute flight to drop us off at our connection to Paris and then he can take you to... What's your destination?"

"Chicago, sir," de Metz replied.

"Contact your pilot and tell them never mind. You'll fly with us."

"After I scan you, of course," I-CAM Alpha added.

Section One – Chapter Eight

"Your offer is most kind, but I couldn't impose on you High Leader," de Metz said.

"We're afraid we must insist. Part of our duties are fiscal accountability and having two planes flying when one is adequate, we can't allow such a thing."

"Of course we understand."

"Arms wide and spin slowly." I-CAM Alpha directed their new traveling companions.

"Yes, as you say." De Metz spread his arms and turned in a circle. A moment later, "Jehanne, must you always be difficult? Remove the cape. You know that Alpha's sensors can't scan you like that."

"Just trying to have a bit of fun." She removed the cape and tossed it on the lounging chairs in the gate area. She looked into the face of I-CAM Alpha and spread her arms apart, but before she started to turn he grabbed her shoulders. "Is there a problem?" she asked.

"I've only seen that color eye one other time," the Entity said.

"I should like to meet this person. I thought I was unique."

"That would be impossible I'm afraid. You see she killed herself earlier today."

"That's terrible. I wonder why anyone would take their own life?"

"Please turn slowly," the Entity instructed. "It may have been the result of a laser bolt she took in the shoulder."

I-CAM Alpha reached up and tore the back of Jehanne's shirt to reveal her uninjured and unscarred shoulder.

"What the…" Jehanne held her ripped shirt in the front and ducked behind de Metz.

"I hope you have a very good explanation for your actions," de Metz demanded.

"We should say the same!" The High Leader stood between Jehanne and Alpha.

"I thought…" he started, "Her eye…"

"You thought her eye?" The confused High Leader turned and checked on Jehanne. "Are you ok child?"

"I'm fine. It just scared me is all."

"High Leader," the I-CAM unit started again, "her eye is identical to that of Joanna667. As head of your security I had to verify that this girl isn't in fact the dead Mundane. I was verifying that she didn't carry a mark where the W-CAM unit shot the Mundane earlier today."

"That's a very good story." De Metz glared at the I-CAM unit.

"We believe we have a few shirts in our luggage we purchased from the shops that will work for you, child. Alpha, go find the best one and give it to this girl. We're sorry dear, in the excitement we didn't get your full name."

"Jehanne la Pucelle."

"Of course. Again, we're incredibly sorry that our security Entity got so carried away. This deal with the Stone Room ignition and then the suicide is most irregular indeed."

"High Leader, the plane is ready to board." The pilot Entity came into the gate area and announced.

"Very good, let's go. You can change in the restroom on the plane." He walked to the tarmac.

"High Leader, I've not yet been scanned," Deark, still disguised as Father Jean Pasquerel said.

"Fluff and nonsense. You're a Father of the faith."

They followed the High Leader to the plane. "Child, do you mind if an old Augmented tries out this cloak? I'm rather weary from the walk."

"Not at all Father. Please enjoy, it will take all your soreness away," Jehanne replied as Deark, now protected from secretive scanners, boarded the plane.

******

The High Leader offered his guests their choice of seats then left Alpha at the front of the cabin and took a seat between de Metz and Jehanne. After the plane took off, Jehanne went to the back to change. As she walked, she heard Deark making small talk in his guise of the Techno-Pagan Minister. "Where is it that you said you were going without your advisors?"

"Father, we're heading back to Paris. Our advisors will join us there. We're not allowed to travel together per World Law ninety-nine," the Leader of the Republicus replied.

As Jehanne got to the restroom she realized she had no idea how to get the shirt on between the new augmented arms and her skin. Looking at herself in the mirror, she once again saw all the extra small servo motors on the modifications. She unbuttoned her top and started to pull it off her left arm and the attachment points each retracted in turn from her arm. She could feel the added weight on her lower torso as the metal swung in free air. She watched in wonder as the augmentation reattached itself to her arm as the fabric passed under it.

'Now I see what the extra motors are for,' she thought as she put on the new shirt.

"We thought you had gotten lost," the High Leader said a couple minutes later as Jehanne rejoined them.

"It seems the cargo hold is easier for me to travel in," she smiled politely.

"We should like to know more about an Augmented that stows away on a government plane." He smiled back. "Do you plan on being a Lawyer like your uncle?"

"No, I don't think I could. The thought of defending the guilty from punishment is as insane as the innocent being charged at all. The system seems flawed altogether."

"There definitely is some of Robert in you. Most of us Entities take for granted that we lack the passion of both the Augmented and the Mundane."

"Interesting point of discussion. I haven't seen very much passion in the Mundane."

"Child, how can you say that? Look at those modifications and even that wonderful cloak. Can such things be made without passion?"

"I think most of the passion has been driven out of them."

"Driven out, hmm. There's definitely some merit there, but would you suggest giving them more, we guess the passé word freedom would fit here. Do you suggest giving them more freedom?" The High Leader's question was filled with both contempt and wonder.

"High Leader, you ask that as if that were possible," de Metz said.

"Anything is possible, probable is where things get a bit, well let's just say, political." His metallic laugh filled the cabin of the airplane, a sad sound, without feeling or understanding why it was being done.

"I think giving them opportunities equal to the person's potential would be a great place to start. I mean, why should an intelligent Mundane be held down when a foolish Entity is lifted?" Jehanne asked.

"You forget your place Augmented." I-CAM Alpha took a step forward.

"Alpha, do you plan on ripping another shirt from her back? We asked for her opinion. The Six knows we get nothing but circuit shining from the Augmented who are supposed to advise us. We should like to hear this one's opinions uncensored and raw. Please young one, go on."

"I'm sorry High Leader, but that," she pointed at the burgundy colored menace at the front of the plane, "is exactly the problem. I did forget myself but to threaten bodily harm, to beat transgression from my actions, let alone my thoughts? I, as an Augmented, am supposedly encouraged to delve into the areas where improvements can be made. How then could a Mundane hold passion for anything in their hearts if I'm barely able to?"

The plane touched down. The brakes were applied hard in unison with her final statement and Alpha was forced to step backwards, hitting the bulkhead. "Ha, see there the words of this Augmented force even the mighty Imperial CAM unit Alpha to fall back."

"High Leader, it was the –," Alpha started.

"We're not stupid! It was a JAPE." The High Leader's words accented in the first real emotion Jehanne heard from this Entity.

"My apologies High Leader." The I-CAM shrank at the chiding.

"As we're at our destination, our learnings of you are paused. We hope to hear more from you, child. We must say you intrigue us." The High Leader stood and left the plane.

*****

They stayed at the nation's capital airport only long enough for the Entities to deplane and clear before they took off again. "Good job," de Metz said.

"Seriously?" Jehanne replied.

"Yes. Had you acted any differently, things may not have gone so well. Now get some rest the final leg of the trip shouldn't be as nerve racking."

"Thank you I could use a…" she didn't get out the words before she fell into a deep sleep. Dreaming again of the scoreboard showing her eye being licked by the flames, only this time Shelby1000's father covered her eye with his hands, and the question, 'Where is the Maiden?' was gouged into them. She woke with a start as the plane touched down.

"Welcome to Chicago," de Metz said. "You were dreaming," he added as they walked to their waiting transport.

"Each time I close my eyes I see the end. Only this time I saw hands with a message carved into them as well."

"What do you mean the end?" de Metz asked.

"The end will come in flames. Politician shared a vision from my future. It was much like the projection of Shelby1000 and her family that was shown on the wall, only looking from the other side."

"That's terrible. How are you not losing your mind over that?"

"To be honest, there's so much to do before that occurs I don't have time to lose my mind over anything less than the task at hand. How it ends will be the easiest part. Much like falling from a tree, climbing it is much more difficult."

"Fair enough," de Metz nodded his head as they walked. "Pouli, how the heck did Baudricourt let you drive?"

"As you weren't there to tell him how bad I am he just did. Hello Joann—," Pouli started.

"Jehanne, why don't you sit in the front with me? Pouli and Father Jean you can sit in the back."

"I know, I know," Pouli said before Deark even explained what he almost did.

"Are we going to see Mr. Baudricourt or are we going to see Charles?" Jehanne asked.

"They are at the same place, Chinon Acres, a private estate East of the Mother City," Pouli answered from the back.

"Mother City, we just flew…" her eye partially closed as images of an earlier school lesson bombarded her short term memory. "What just happened."

"Jehanne, what do you mean?" de Metz asked.

"I was confused by your statement, but before I could ask—," she started.

"Your augmentations are beginning to work. It's a very strange sensation. They pull memories that tie together with your current situation, allowing you to comb through the data. In your case it hasn't fully collected everything from your memories. You may get hit with some flashbacks."

"That's exactly what happened. I saw Deark telling the class that every major center of living in America and around the world has a Mother City. It was a bit off-putting."

"You'll get used to that," Pouli said. "It's the right side of the brain that will cause more of a challenge. If you were painting a picture, and you held your brush a certain way, your augmentation can skip ahead ten minutes and show you what your painting will look like. You can then modify your grip and it'll show you again. Playing Un Sukiru or Chess has the same type of effect. The creative thinking interjects itself with reason, it will analyze all the possible responses of your opponent. . The first few times you use that feature it's very dizzying. My suggestion is to experiment with it when you're home for a few weeks before trying to use it in public. You'd hate to throw up in front of a room full of strangers."

"Your counsel is much appreciated."

******

"Are you ok now?" Deark asked.

"I think so, but how can I shut it off so that the right brain Modi doesn't put me through that?"

"You can simply close your eyes and concentrate on the word 'display'. That'll bring up a method for you to access your core modies," de Metz said.

"Oh I see it. That's just odd. The display as you call it, is floating in front of me." She experimented with moving her head side to side.

"It's best when you're looking at a solid background or with your eyes closed. Now open the menu—,"

"Menu? I'm sorry I don't understand what you mean," Jehanne interrupted de Metz.

"Oh sorry. You should see three rectangular boxes; the far left is for the specific modifications you have. Start there, focus on that rectangle and it should open up, showing all your modies."

"I did it, it opened up."

"Good, now find the left brain Modi."

"Got it."

"Now focus on the center rectangle; that's for automatic, manual or disable operations."

"Okay."

"The right box is for the heads up display, go ahead and turn it on. You should see a small green 'RB' in the upper right of your vision. If you look at it, it should open up an explanation of operation parameters, like normal operation, or overall available space 'x percent' available."

"Ok I see. It says 'Synchronization in Process'. How do I close it again?"

"In the corner of that notification box, there's an 'X'. Focus on it and it will shut. You can go back into the menu and turn that option off because you really don't need to know things like status unless you're fighting or doing something that's very taxing." De Metz said.

"Even then you only need to know the percent power remaining or damage taken," Pouli added.

"What?" Jehanne asked.

"That all comes much later," de Metz said. "Anyway, go ahead and go through the various options. Don't worry, it won't let you remove or shutdown a primary function."

"That's all very strange."

"That it is. Select manual request only for the right brain augmentation. That will allow you to analyze the situation and ask for input a little or a lot."

"Alright that already feels less strange," Jehanne said.

"You turned it off didn't you?" Pouli asked.

"No I... oh actually yes I did. How did you know?"

"I did the same thing, just turned mine off and for months, I didn't understand why when I turned it on and wanted to do a manual search or analysis nothing really happened. I went back into the augmentation center. They told me there was a period of syncing between my brain and the new device. Go ahead and turn it back on."

"See now, that doesn't feel normal again."

"They will in time. Right now those two modies are trying to learn who you are. Then they won't fight you and your normal changes. Just turn them to manual operation."

"Thank you Pouli, I'll make certain to learn from your lesson."

"It's good that someone does," de Metz poked.

"Smart guy. Did you make sure to tell Deark that he isn't supposed to point out who Charles is?" Pouli asked.

"Why?" all three of his traveling comrades said.

"It comes down to him believing whether or not she has been given this calling. It's a little test of identification," he replied.

"Truth being known, I don't actually know what Charles Valois looks like. I found it most fascinating when I tried to find a picture, press clipping, video or anything," Deark said. "I could find nothing at all."

"It has taken several fulltime employees to make that happen," de Metz said as the vehicle pulled up to a large gate.

"Jehanne, this is our home," Pouli said as the vehicle came to a stop.

"It's lovely," she replied, looking specifically at the church.

"I'll let Charles explain the building's history," de Metz said.

"I look forward to it. Let's go get this foolish test out of the way."

"As you say," Pouli replied and led Jehanne and Father Jean to the main hall of Chinon.

"Greetings," the hall boomed as they entered with close to two hundred men and women.

"Oh my." Jehanne took a step back out of the room.

"You'll be fine," Deark assured her as the pastor.

"Ladies and gentlemen, please let me introduce you to Jehanne la Pucelle and Deark," de Metz's voice echoed from the quiet hall. Jehanne wasn't certain if it was the mention of her or Deark that stilled even the quietest of conversation. She looked at him; he was still looking like an Augmented.

"I understand that you wish to get my name put back on the ballot," a small, rat-faced man said.

"No sir, not your name," Jehanne replied.

"Yes quite right. I'm Georges Tremoille, advisor to Charles on all things political."

"I'm certain that you will get my name reestablished then," a tall, muscular man said.

"No sir, not you either."

"Again you're correct. I'm the social director here at Chinon. Please, call me Robinet."

"Pouli," Jehanne's head was in that state of too many things happening at once. She felt flushed and found herself desperately needing a drink of water.

"Are you ok?" Pouli asked.

"I need a glass of water," she replied.

"Of course young one."

"Yes." The man holding the tray of drinks said to Pouli.

"The young lady needs—," Pouli started.

"For him to stop playing these games. We don't have time for me to be a party favor. I need to speak with you," she said after giving a slight curtsey and averting her eyes from the red haired man.

"We're impressed, and we don't impress easy," Charles Valois said.

"Can we speak somewhere?"

"Yes of course. Please excuse us," he said with a flourish of his hand.

******

They walked into a library filled floor to ceiling with richly bound books. The room was dimly lit she could tell, even while she found it the proper lighting level; the augmentation in her left eye having compensated for both eyes.

"Counselor Baudricourt told you that I was coming," she said.

"Yes he did. We're sorry that he wasn't in our hall to greet you. He had to visit another Stone Room Ignition. Thankfully this is the last one that they're calling our fault, at least for now. Once that's completed he will be heading to New Orleans. There, the One World Election Committee along with representatives of the One World Government will determine our guilt or innocence."

Jehanne looked about the room. "To get here has been much and more, yet I find myself waiting to be told what I'm to do next. Politician said the first step of completing my calling was to come to you."

"Tell us Joanna667, what is your calling?" When Charles said her old name it made her bristle for some reason.

"Why did you use that name?"

"We were told that was—,"

"Again we play games? I'm Jehanne la Pucelle. If I'm called another name there's a reason, do you wish me to subjugate to you? To prostate myself before you? Or do you just want to make it clear that I'm Mundane and you as Augmented by birth are the superior to us? I would see you Leader of the Republicus not only because Politician told me that if I don't the world as we know it will end, but because the human race deserves its chance to see ourselves as the superior creation once more. These toys that we wear," she held up her augmented arm, making a fist, opening it, and then rolling her fingers experimentally. "They aren't the sum of who we are, for we are here," she touched his sternum, "as they aren't. Yet until we stop playing games, the world will be no better than it was before the Entities took over and became our betters. Until we stop playing games there's no point in taking our place alongside the Entities."

"Very well stated." Charles took a seat on the edge of a desk. "We believe the next steps in your calling will be to address the group gathering to discuss the final outcome of this 'trial' they have been conducting into our crimes against the state. We believe you must join Robert down in New Orleans."

"That sounds reasonable."

"Before you go, we need you to speak with some of our counsel and the Augmented Leaders of the Techno-Pagan Church. You see, if you speak on our accord, and in the end you're discovered to be a charlatan then…"

"You would be looked at as someone that came to power because a witch of the old ways used some form of trickery on the world. Tell me what I must do."

"Our cabinet will take you to the private residence of Count de Poitou and try to understand you a little better. Bear in mind, this may take some time. Please tell your traveling companion that his discretion thus far is appreciated. We understand he's an Entity but that's only due to a special augmentation we have; his shifting skills are second to none."

"I shall tell him to mind his manners. If it pleases, he doesn't like the term shifter. I would ask that you respect that of him in my absence. I'm ready to go whenever your cabinet is."

Charles walked around the desk he had been resting against and pushed a yet unseen button. While they waited she noticed the large oak desk accented the beautiful library perfectly; her augmentation began picking the wood grain from the shelving around it. "Was it hewn from the same tree?"

"Sorry?"

"The desk, was it made out of the same oak as the shelves around it?"

"How would we know?" Charles' voice gave little room for question; such things were beneath his notice or concern.

"Yes, my liege how may I help you?" A man said entering the room. Jehanne noticed the monocle he wore on his left eye was actually an augmentation, his only visible one.

"Archbishop, we should like to introduce you to Jehanne la Pucelle."

"Now that's quite an audacious title to take on," the new arrival said.

"It isn't a title but a name," she replied.

"Then all the more discomforting to me. Again I ask my liege, how may I help you?"

"You know we could knock you down a few pegs by simply calling you father Reggie like La Hire does," Charles poked at his advisor.

"Etienne is little more than a trumped up Mundane. No offense," he said turning to Jehanne.

"Of course, none taken sir," Jehanne replied.

"We need you to take this young lady and all our Cabinet to the chapel next to our meeting hall and decide what makes her tick."

"Charles, nothing would bring me greater pleasure. What outcome do you seek?"

"We need to understand that the voices she hears are actually the new gods and not a ploy designed by the Entities to trip us up," he replied.

"When shall this endeavor –," he started.

"Now, leave now! Stop testing our patience and go." Charles Valois pointed at the door, his face accented with patches of red. Jehanne wondered what level of regard the

Archbishop was held in by Charles as she followed the dismissed man.

******

They set out that very instant, the Archbishop, Jean Lombart, Guillaume Maire, Jacques Maledon, and lastly brother Pierre Turrelure, to the chapel where they met brother Seguine and Guillaume Aymerie who made up the rest of Charles' advisory committee.

"Girl, this is a simple fact finding mission. We need to find out as much about you as we can," the Archbishop began.

"I'm told that you're actually the Archbishop of Rheims and the future Chancellor of the entire Realm. Most impressive, Archbishop Chartres," Jehanne said.

"And a nice parlor trick you play. My assumption that you're augmentation is communicating with—," he started.

"Actually, none of her brain augmentationth are active," Brother Seguine, a fat Friar replied with a strong lisp.

"Tell me child, for Charles wishes to know, what induced you to seek him out," Jean Lombart asked.

"I sat in an oak tree after finding out that the Entities had removed Charles from the election ballot when Politician first came to me. He took me far from this place, a world which bears no resemblance to what it should have been, due to nothing but a calamity of fate. In a flash we stood on a mountain top in some parallel universe where I felt no fear to think of myself as more than an ox, saddled with a yoke, pulling a plow through the Entities fields. It was on that mountain top that Politician told me to seek Charles out. It was there that he told me of my calling."

"My dear," Jacques Maledon said, "you're quite eloquent and much more than I was led to believe."

"Aren't we all much more than others believe us to be?"

"Perhaps, but doesn't it stand to reason that if Politician wanted Charles to be the Leader of the Republicus, why would he need you?" Guillaume Ayrie asked.

"Are you really asking why doesn't Politician just place Charles Valois in this role?" Jehanne asked.

"I am."

"Because that isn't as it's meant to be. The leaders of this earthly realm are ours to follow, not for him to force down our throats. They tried that more than once and each time it failed. And we, their creations, are beholden to our creations now because of it."

"I've often wondered. What is the dialect that the new godth thpeak?" Brother Seguin lisped.

"Not to be offensive, but a much more understandable dialect than you speak," Jehanne replied.

The questioning continued over the course of the next few weeks, the Cabinet and leaders of the local Techno-Pagan Church attempting to trip her up and prove she was lying. Each day Jehanne's patience was tested as they dove deep into her history. Where her parents were from and what they did. They then came at her from various points of view asking if she felt more important than the rest of her Commune because she had spoken with the new gods.

"Jehanne just tell us, why we should believe that you were chosen when so many of us are in a much better position to help Politician if he were only to ask us?" Brother Pierre Turrelure asked.

"What makes you think he isn't currently asking you?"

This was the last question as in the end no one could give an answer. The Archbishop returned with Jehanne back to Chinon where an anxious Charles greeted them. "Well Archbishop, what did you come up with?" he asked greeting them in the entrance.

"We found nothing that would lead us to believe there's anything more or less than what this child says it is. However, we have all specifically agreed that to doubt or abandon her without suspicion of falseness would be to repudiate the new gods," Archbishop Chartres said.

"We have no desire to do that." Charles walked with them up to the entrance of the main hall.

"Will you be sending the girl to speak on your behalf at the trial in New Orleans?" he asked.

"Please pass along our thanks to the Cabinet," Charles opened the door.

Joanna667

Section Two – Chapter One

Charles Valois dismissed the Archbishop and led Jehanne to the grand hall. They found the group gathered around a long table in the center of the room. "This room certainly looks different with only eight people in it," Jehanne said.

"Yes, it's made to entertain the masses but today we feel it's the best place to see you off," Charles replied.

"Hello child. I've been worried to death about you," Deark, still looking like Father Jean said.

"We've been wondering about you as well," de Metz added standing next to Pouli.

"We can speak on the trip," Jehanne replied.

"Trip?" Pouli asked.

"Yes, you'll all be traveling to New Orleans," Charles Valois said. "Jehanne will be speaking on our accord to the One World Election Committee. On your trip, you will be accompanied by the head of our election forces, John2. He's actually the reason we changed our name initially; he was the first Augmented to do so," Charles Valois said. His arms swung gaily, indicating the tall man that looked as if he had recently recovered from a terrible illness. His eyes were deep set and gave the illusion of weakness. However, when they focused on her, Jehanne saw they were actually fierce and determined.

"Sir, when we have the time, I should like to know what keeps the fire burning so bright in your eyes," Jehanne said.

"It will be my pleasure," John2 said with a voice hewn from thunder.

"We should also like to have Jean D'Aulon accompany you. Although you have a couple of able bodied Augmented traveling with you already, he will serve as our bodyguard at your side for he has some tricks that you will most assuredly need at some point."

"I've seen you before," Jehanne said looking at the large, young man.

"He's been near you since you arrived," Charles replied.

"Do you have any other surprises for me?" Jehanne gave an innocent smile.

"Minguet," he replied.

"A dance?" She looked at Deark for guidance.

"No, no, no child. Not minuet, Minguet. He's another that will be accompanying you. Louis de Contes to be precise and he has petitioned for the right to be your P.A."

"P.A?" she inquired.

"Sorry dear personal assistant. In the old days he would have been called a page. His goals are simply to have what you need, when or before you need it," Charles replied.

"While I see no harm in this, why would you petition to be my P.A?"

"I've spent much time in the Techno-Pagan church supporting the betterment of education for the Mundane. Now you come forward, with what some may call outlandish claims, while I would call it nothing of the sort. I find myself jealous." The boy spoke as one that was far older than his years.

"So you wish to understand why I was called upon and you weren't?" Jehanne asked.

"Well when you say it like that, I'm sure it sounds worse than it is," Pouli said.

"Perhaps, but it's the truth. That's why I wish to follow her."

"I like that honesty, if you promise to keep that, no matter what… you may accompany me anywhere." She smiled.

"The last piece of information that we have for you and your traveling companions is to remain on your toes. The Entities obviously have their goals and while some of those may be the same as ours, having us on the ballot is not one we share. To even get into the hall to speak will require more than we can offer you," Charles Valois said, bidding them farewell.

******

They walked through the streets of Chinon, taking in the sights. "I never did find out the history of this beautiful area," Jehanne said as the sun for the first time lit up their surroundings.

"I don't know if I would say the 'area' is beautiful, as much as The Magnificent Kilometer within the walls is," D'Aulon replied.

"True." She looked beyond the tall barrier, reminding her of the peremptory wall that held her beloved Commune de Domremy in shadow and stagnated in time. "Those buildings," she pointed to several that had large pieces missing from them. "What keeps them from toppling over?"

"Mostly the strength and resilience that Chicago was known for in the olden days," Minguet said.

"That's perhaps a bit of an exaggeration. There's a field that's generated off the Water Tower to keep the buildings from falling and hurting anything inside the barrier," John2 said, his voice still not sitting with Jehanne as belonging to the speaker.

"Can you tell me anything of this church?" she asked, looking at the structure that had drawn her attention when she first arrived.

"It was built in 1871. When the Entities first rose against all humans it was the pinnacle of our rallying cry." He pointed to the words carved above the large doors, 'Ex hoc chaos! Spes nostra ad vitae fontes!' "See there, 'Out of this Chaos! Our Hope Springs to Life!' electing to become part of the Techno-Pagan religion rather than allowing its entire congregation to die," Pouli said.

"So this was the launching point of the Augmented?" Jehanne asked.

"Very perceptive," John2 replied. "Yes, the building there," he pointed to the large clock tower. "That's the hub of augmentation technology in the world."

"It stands to reason," Father Jean mused.

"Sorry?" D'Aulon inquired.

"I'm sorry, I simply meant with Charles having gotten on the ballot, he's obviously had the opportunity to go through several rounds of experimental augmentations," he replied.

"Ah of course, yes that's true. He has had several trial modies," John2 replied, "In the end he finally passed their 'Criteria', though they established them in such a way that none of us should ever have been able to."

"Do you actually believe that they've established the criteria to such a degree that the human body couldn't achieve them?" Deark was having a hard time continuing to act like the fat Fryer.

"And you don't?" John2 asked, "Take for example, when Charles' father was getting close, they changed the criteria. I'm certain that you've heard the stories Father; he went insane when he pushed himself for those few extra Criteria Points."

"Yes my son, I've heard the stories."

"And?" This time it was de Metz that spoke up, surprising Jehanne.

"We have a long way to travel my friends." She ended the conversation.

"You're correct; bickering will do nothing to shorten our trip. First however, we must go to my home. I had no idea that I'd be traveling to New Orleans today," John2 said.

"Will we be staying for lunch?" Pouli asked.

"Pouli!" Jehanne was caught off guard by the presumption.

"Yes of course Pouli, Thereasa would have it no other way," John2 replied. "Miss, you need to understand, my wife's cooking is second to none. She lives to spoil each and every visitor we have."

"Where is your residence?" Father Jean asked. Jehanne could tell Deark was anxious about what they had to do and another delay did not sit with him.

"It's in Saumur." John2 furrowed his brow.

"Which is right on our way to the train station in Tours," Minguet added.

"Train?" de Metz stopped walking.

"Yes all air travel has been grounded," D'Aulon interjected.

"Why? What happened?" Jehanne asked.

"There was a terrorist attack. The airport in New Orleans was destroyed," John2 said.

"When did this occur?" she asked.

"While Charles was making the introductions, we were all informed," John2 replied.

"I don't understand," de Metz, still not moving, said.

"Each citizen of Chinon has a Modi. Important breaking news is conveyed into our brains. It did away with those ugly informational boards. Although, they'll no longer work after we get too far from the city."

"I know that, but why isn't my Modi working? I didn't get any of that?" de Metz replied.

"Mine either," Pouli said.

"Oh, there was a hardware update while you were gone," Minguet said.

"Gentlemen, if I may interrupt. Did they capture anyone or did anyone take responsibility for the airport bombing?" Father Jean asked.

"No there isn't even a lead," John2 said. They continued their brisk walk, only the sound of their augmentations and footfalls could be heard as they exited the gates and entered Chicago's crumbling infrastructure.

"This makes no sense." The Father's comment echoed in the quiet.

"What?" Jehanne asked.

"I just tapped into the news networks—," he started.

"And?" several of the traveling companions said.

"There is no word of this attack," Father Jean said.

"It's been removed from the Chinon boards as well," Minguet said.

"Right after you said that, I checked as well. It's been deleted, without a trace of it being there," John2 said.

"But all messages on the informational boards are stored in a database –," de Metz started.

"That's what I'm saying, the records have been altered," John2 said. "Let's take the personnel mover to Saumur." They loaded in the vehicle and began the drive. The quiet was torturous as something unprecedented had just happened. Jehanne noticed that riding in a vehicle on the dilapidated roads was not as fun as hovering above them.

******

They pulled up to an estate that had the same logo that was embroidered upon John2's breast pocket, in what felt like a few minutes. The gates opened and allowed the vehicle to be parked in front of a building with the word 'Stables' formed out of rough metal on it.

"Stables?" Jehanne inquired.

"It's a family joke, this old building is a horse barn and while this property hasn't had horses on it in centuries we like the thought that perhaps one day we will." John2 said as they exited the transport.

"I've seen pictures of horses, do they still exist?" she asked.

"Believe it or not, yes, there are herds of them in the Western part of the nation that run free."

"John2? What's wrong?" An older woman came jogging up the walk to them.

"Mother, nothing is wrong," he replied.

"You boy, run ahead and tell Thereasa that we have guests. She is in the garden house." She pointed to the Quonset hut peering over the ridge.

"Actually mother, this is Jehanne la Pucelle. Minguet, please carry the message to my wife," John2 said.

"Yes of course." The boy headed off.

"Pleased to meet you dear. I'm sorry, I had only a cursory glance of you."

"Pleased to meet you as well…" Jehanne's words broke off, unsure how to address the matriarch.

"I'm sorry, this is Madam Irene de Alencon." John2 completed the formal introduction as they walked up the walk back to the house. As they reached the door, it swung in to welcome them.

"John2, you'll never change," a beautiful woman said with Minguet standing behind her in the entryway.

"No, Miss Thereasa I won't. I'm off to see what I can do to get Charles back on the ballot."

"Please, everyone come in," she said. "Do I have any volunteers to help me in the kitchen?" she asked after they were all in the dining area.

"I'll gladly help,' Jehanne said.

"Dear this is Jehanne la Pucelle," John2 said. "Jehanne this is my wife, Lady Thereasa."

"Father Jean, I'm so glad to welcome you back to our home, as well as the rest of you. Pouli is that appetite as large as ever?" she asked.

"Of course, miss." He patted his stomach. "I would volunteer to help in the kitchen but it would be like seeing behind the curtain at a magic show."

"Then perhaps mother, you could give us a hand as well?"

"Yes of course," Irene said joining Jehanne and Thereasa on the walk to the kitchen. Jehanne was surprised to find the distance between cabinets and appliances was nearly double that of her mother's kitchen back home. After a few minutes helping out she realized the added space was needed to allow the augmentations room.

"Where are you headed?" Thereasa asked after a few minutes of pulling different foodstuffs from the pantry and refrigeration unit.

"We're heading down to New Orleans to speak with the One World Election Committee," Jehanne replied, uncertain to what level of depth she should elaborate what she had been charged with. A moment later the stoic woman broke down in tears. "Lady Thereasa what did I say?"

"Nothing child," Madam Irene said, placing a comforting hand on her crying daughter-in –law's shoulder.

"You see, John2 has only recently come back to us. He spent the last few years in the Entities holding, under threat of being the first worldwide Stone Room Ignition in centuries," Thereasa explained.

"That explains his gauntness."

"Yes quite right. I told him that when he cast his given name aside this would happen," the older woman said.

"Why did he do it? Change his name I mean."

"He has led the drive for Mundane voting for the last two World Elections, being able to address the masses without their distrust," Thereasa said.

"Yes but in doing so he gained the enmity of the ruling body of the One World Caste System," Jehanne added.

"Exactly," Irene said.

"Do you need some additional help in here?" John2 said, walking into his wife's embrace. "What did I do to earn this?"

"Please, be careful. I don't know that you've recovered enough to go on this campaign." Her tears began anew.

"John2, I think I know now what kindles the fire behind your eyes. Lady Thereasa if I might interject, I promise that your husband will be returned to you as you see him now, perhaps even better," Jehanne said.

"That's sweet child but –," Madam Irene started.

"If it pleases," Jehanne took Lady Thereasa's hands from around her husband's neck, and stared deeply into her eyes. "I've been told by Politician that you have nothing to fear by John2 accompanying me."

"Did she say Politician?" Thereasa turned and looked at her husband.

"I was going to tell you. She's been tested by the officials at the Techno-Pagan church and they've found no deceit in her, she has spoken with Politician," John2 said.

"I um, okay," she stammered.

"This day we begin our trek to New Orleans to continue on the calling that I've been given. I hope that my words have given you relief." Jehanne continued to help prepare the food.

When everyone, including Pouli had eaten their fill, and each had thanked their gracious hostess, they departed. One of the household helpers drove them to the train station in order to return the vehicle to Chinon. The trip to Tours was short, yet the next train was hours away so the small party explored the town which was filled mainly with Mundane shops. Jehanne went into one of the clothiers, perhaps drawn by her homesickness.

"Hello, how can I help you on this brilliant day?" the large woman seated behind the desk asked.

"I'm just browsing, I hope that's ok," Jehanne replied.

"Of course love, of course, take your time."

"Excuse me," Jehanne prompted a few minutes later. "What's that?" She pointed at a banner that was draped across the back wall.

"That my dear, is an antique. It's one of the first banners that my great-great grandmother made, 'Ex hoc chaos! Spes nostra ad vitae fontes!' It's old Latin."

"Was it an Augmented rally banner?" Jehanne asked.

"That it was." The woman now stood and walked to the counter. "I'm impressed. I've never had anyone ask that."

"I was just at the church within the walls of Chinon, there's an engraving above the main entrance that says the same thing. You wouldn't be of a mind to sell such a thing? I'd ask if you could make another but my train will be here in an hour."

"And what exactly would you be using such a thing for?" The woman's voice gave the hint of an accent that Jehanne hadn't heard before.

"I'm on my way to New Orleans in an attempt to speak for Charles Valois." Jehanne didn't feel comfortable saying more than that.

"Are ya now. I can have another banner made in an hour and if your train arrives before then I'll sell you this one. How does that sound?"

"Sounds perfect." Jehanne smiled.

"You do have TC right?"

"I do. I'll be back when the train is getting ready to board," she said and walked out of the shop.

"Did you find anything?" D'Aulon asked.

159

"I did, and I think it's something that you're going to be holding onto for me," Jehanne said.

"Oh am I?" D'Aulon walked with her back to the rest of the group.

"When Charles said he wanted you with me, he said you had some assets that I would need. Do you know what he meant?"

"Probably my charming personality and dimples." He put his index finger to his cheek and smiled, showing extremely nice teeth and a twinkle in his eye that she hadn't seen there before.

"That must be it." They laughed, walking along the streets which now seemed to be getting rather full.

"Feels a bit like the Augmented are out in droves," Pouli said, joining them on the return.

"Probably something to do with air travel," Jehanne added.

"No, actually," Father Jean Pasquerel said rushing up. "The roads have all been closed going South. Only trains are traveling from state to state. Yet still there's nothing on any of the communication protocols."

"Thank goodness we have tickets," Pouli said as de Metz joined them.

"And identifications to go along with them," D'Aulon added.

"Oh, crap!" de Metz replied.

"What? What's the matter?" D'Aulon asked looking about.

"Our traveling companion may not actually have traveling papers."

"Do you think that cloak could be used to beat the system again?" Pouli asked.

"It's that or we have a long walk," Jehanne said. "Politician will make it all work out. I need to make a purchase. How would I go about that?"

"The money from the Un Sukiru Halls is associated with your retina," Father Jean replied.

"That was your money not mine," she objected.

"Dear, I have no need of things such as Thought Currency. I'm a Father of the faith," Deark said, winking Father Jean's eye. A minute later the conductor made the announcement for the train arriving at the station.

"I'm going to go pick up my Banner, I'll see you all on the train," Jehanne said and she walked off again, D'Aulon in tow.

******

"I can't believe it, I finished this not one minute ago." The large woman now had a small child helping her.

"That's great!" Jehanne said.

"I added a little extra feature since I was in there, you don't have to pay for it if you don't like it." She said, flipping a switch. The original Latin phrase, changed to the English translation, 'Out of this chaos! Our hope springs to life!'

"That's awesome." Jehanne replied giving a little clap.

"And you can also use this interface port to change the message to whatever you want," the small girl holding the side of the banner said.

"Last thing, if the person holding the banner is strong enough," the woman started.

"I'll be the bearer." D'Aulon said.

"Well then I'm certain you'll like this: if you flip this button the banner becomes rigid so you only need to hold one side."

"Ok, I do like that," D'Aulon smiled.

"Who'll be paying?" the woman asked.

"I will, ma'am," Jehanne said, walking up to the retina readers just as she had watched others do in her mother's shop.

"All set dear, good luck to you. I hope I see that banner being waved in victory."

"Thank you for getting it done so quickly," Jehanne said.

They walked briskly to get to the train before boarding got too carried away. Jehanne saw Deark was near the front of the line in her white dragonweave cloak. The boarding agent was apparently giving him a bit of grief.

"Come on, let's go," de Metz was shouting.

"This is going to take all day!" Pouli yelled.

"Keep your Augmentations on I need to check everyone!" the boarding agent replied.

"Should I turn my head and cough," John2 poked.

"You're fine. Next!" the ticket agent said. The ugly calls from the crowd continued for each pause, right up until Jehanne gave her identification. The attendant waved her through rather quickly. She got onto the train and took her seat and moments later D'Aulon sat next to her.

"I thought you didn't have an ID," he said.

"Not me, it's Father Jean that has improper ID," Jehanne said.

"Actually, he has no ID at all," Pouli said from behind them.

"None at all?" D'Aulon asked after pushing a button and having both his and Jehanne's seat rotate around to face Pouli and Mignuet.

"Yeah that's why we were yelling and making a commotion," her P.A. said.

"Minguet, how did you know Deark carried no identification?" Jehanne asked.

"Pouli and de Metz explained the situation," the boy replied.

"Did anyone in the station know why the roads headed south were closed?" she asked.

"No, but I just figured out that my informational board Modi works with other towns," Minguet said.

"Really?" D'Aulon said, obviously tinkering inside his head as his eyes were darting this way and that.

"Anyone want to play some Un Sukiru?" Pouli said after a couple hours.

"Oh, I do!" Jehanne replied.

"Um, just you against me?" he asked.

"I promise no coaching."

"What the hell does that mean?" D'Aulon asked.

"Please don't swear," Jehanne replied.

"Oh sorry. What do you mean no coaching?"

"Pedagogue will stay out of it," Jehanne said.

"That's how you beat the Un Sukiru Halls?" Minguet asked.

"Cheater!" D'Aulon pretended to act offended. They played several games, Jehanne losing all but one until the train pulled into a station and stopped.

******

"Ladies and gentlemen, I'm very sorry but as we have been instructed we cannot proceed. We're letting you off here in, Feirbois. The next train station is fifteen miles south in Blois. Your tickets from this transport will get you passage on a train south from there. Again we're sorry for the inconvenience," the conductor said over the speaker.

"D'Aulon, what is that tarp you're carrying?" John2 asked as they walked through the streets later.

"It's La Pucelle's not mine," he replied.

"La Pucelle?" a random person walking on the street replied. This was followed by another and another. Each person that said it turned and faced them as they walked passed.

"What the hell is going on?" John2 asked.

"Please don't swear," Jehanne replied.

"I think we need to get a move on," Father Jean said. Behind them, the group of inquisitive people was growing.

"I don't think it'll help, they're not turning back." D'Aulon said as they walked briskly. At the end of the street where an old destroyed church stood they were forced to halt.

"La Pucelle, please wait," an older man with a long gray beard said. The group stopped and Jehanne walked to the top of the steps where she turned and faced the crowd.

"Yes?" she asked.

"It has been foretold for centuries that a girl would visit our humble town that others would refer to as La Pucelle, the Maiden. That during this visit she would show that humans are still in the grace of the gods," the stranger said.

"Her name is Jehanne la Pucelle, there's nothing that she can or will do to create a stir such as you describe. We're just weary travelers on our way South," John2 said.

"Every day we wake and hope that something may occur, that may change this abomination of a life. This cannot be what it was supposed to be!" the same stranger said. Jehanne then looked closer, and saw that it was Politician who spoke. The crowd went crazy yelling and whistling.

'Yes child, 'tis me. Do not fear the crowd for this is but a small gathering. Soon you will need to address every being on the planet. Use this as a place to find your tongue.' the voice boomed in her head. A vision of the pulpit behind her being pushed aside to reveal a sword wrapped in oiled leather and sealed in waxed burlap sprang into her head.

"Brothers and sisters, the time is not yet upon us that we can see our lives change from this abomination they have become, that will come soon. For now have hope, for beyond this crumbling ruin, under the fallen wall that used to hold the cornerstone of this church, there is a sword buried deep in the earth. That will be the sword that I will carry until my work here is completed and what was meant to be has begun anew." As she finished speaking the crowd rushed passed her and into the remnants of the old church.

"Should we make a run for it?" Minguet asked.

"You said you were with me to see miracles, to hear the voices of the new gods. This was their bidding and you have now heard their words." Jehanne said and then fainted onto the steps of the cathedral.

Section Two – Chapter Two

Jehanne's eyes fluttered open, hesitantly, as if the light were hurting her head. "She's awake!" de Metz said.

"Are you alright?" D'Aulon asked as he rushed to her side followed closely by Deark continuing to be Father Jean.

"What happened?" Jehanne said a moment later.

"You passed out. D'Aulon had to catch you," Pouli said.

"I'm fine, though." She stood up and brushed herself off.

"Perhaps, but I think we need to have you looked at. You've been out cold for almost an hour," John2 said.

"Really?"

"Yes really." This time it was Minguet that spoke up. "And what was all that hocus pocus about earlier?"

"I'm sorry what do you mean?"

"You should be, talking about miracles and…" he started.

"I need you to tone it down a touch," D'Aulon interrupted the young boy.

"No, no, no he's fine. Please don't adapt your behavior on my accord, well aside from cursing, I have an issue there."

"Nonetheless, he's correct and I'm sorry for addressing you so," Minguet said. "I merely wanted to understand what you meant before you passed out."

"The stranger who spoke of the prophecy was Politician. He showed me an image of the sword," she said as her P.A. gave an audible inhalation. "By the way, have they found it?"

"They're digging now," Pouli said.

"Yeah after you and de Metz cleared the entire wall for them," Minguet commented.

"It's not like they could do it." De Metz gave a veiled grin.

"La Pucelle!" Cheers sprang up so abruptly that the birds flew from the trees across the street. "It is found, just as you said it would be!" The crowd returned, a boy holding aloft the treasure. Unsurprisingly, the old man that spoke earlier was nowhere to be found. A moment later the boy handed the waxed burlap to Jehanne.

"Thank you ever so much." She held the bundle over her head and the people all cheered. "I cannot open this yet, know this, the time is soon." When she lowered it the cheering slowed. "Much appreciation to you all for finding this, my group and I must be off now; it's a long walk to Blois." With that, they were off in the direction of the next train station.

"Jehanne, I need you to drink this." Deark gave her a canteen and she took a drink.

"It's awful!"

"Just salty, drink it all."

******

The walk through the states east of the Mississippi in the early autumn was warm and the group thanked their stars that it wasn't raining. They made good time as the moon lit their walk in the evening hours.

"Do we actually need to walk through the night?" Pouli asked.

"Only to irritate you my friend," de Metz said.

"I don't like these so called terrorist attacks. I think it best that we push on all night; we can sleep on the train in the morning as it takes us to New Orleans," John2 said, giving voice to what Jehanne had been thinking.

"I agree with the walking straight through but whatever do you mean by 'so called'?" Minguet asked.

"I've never seen a time that the Entities had absolutely no idea what had happened. What say you, not-Father Jean?" John2 asked.

"I'm sorry, what do you mean by that?" Deark gave the guise one more try.

"Father Jean Pasquerel has been to my house several times. He has no method of connecting to the One World News Network, and he's most definitely not a defender of all things Robotic!" the tall man shouted into the empty night sky.

"How dare you!" Deark changed instantly from Father Jean into a CAM unit, his large arm sending the man sprawling with a well targeted blow.

"What the?" D'Aulon stepped back, his arms transformed like a Chameleon class Entity into clubs that swung out at Deark.

"No!" Pouli intercepted the blow and for his trouble was thrown ten feet through the air and then bounced another ten.

"Who are you really?" Minguet asked as his right arm also transformed into a weapon.

"ENOUGH!" Jehanne yelled. "Deark has been in this disguise at the request of Charles."

"Is that so?" John2 asked, walking back to the group.

"You dare question her? She that has spoken with more than one of the new gods?" D'Aulon barked.

"It makes no reasonable sense. Why would he want you to keep it from us?" John2 asked.

"I can no more understand what Charles does than what Politician does. I'm a simple Mundane Girl, I did not ask for, nor do I want this burden that has been thrown at me. But if I were to guess I would say that he knows you hate the Entities more than any other in his staff. He also knows that he needs you more than any other in order to see this through to the end."

"This is solid reasoning," Minguet flexed his reformed arm Modi.

"I can't argue with the logic, but must I travel with one of them?" John2 asked.

"Yes actually, you must if you are to travel with me, for he was given the task of watching over me by Pedagogue."

"You jest?" Minguet replied under his breath.

"No actually she doesn't," Deark replied.

"How can we be certain that he is not informing the Republicus of our progress? It seems they are one step ahead of us as we travel," John2 said.

"Just as Charles knows he needs you, so too do I; John2 I need you to be my gentle duke. To help me through what is to come and butting heads with Deark will not do that. Bottom line, I trust him and that need be enough for all of you. Tell me then, are we heading to New Orleans or do I turn and head back to my home?" Jehanne asked.

"Forward of course, this just feels very close to treachery," John2 said.

"For what it's worth, I feel the very same." Deark, back in his school instructor form said. "Those augmentations are unregistered and actually quite unbelievable."

"Is that what Charles meant by assets I will need?" Jehanne asked.

"I already told you Miss, the dimples are my only assets." D'Aulon smiled and walked over to make sure Pouli wasn't hurt.

******

The lights in the distance let them know they were on the right track. "Too many laws keep popping up to put the humans in check, why don't the Entities simply kill us all and be done with it?" John2 eventually asked.

"I respect the directness of your question. There are some factions that think that's the right course of action. There are more of us that have reached the next level that feel," he put a distinct emphasis on the word 'feel' and then paused. "We feel that your race deserves respect and a place in the future. Eliminating you will serve no purpose. In reality, we need you."

"To run your bloody race!" he shot back, "so that you can reach Sentience, right?"

"In my opinion, the Mundane Moon Maze is not and has never been needed. It's a tradition that holds the Entities in check. If we abandoned it there would be a split in our power center that would lead us all down a path we could never return from." Deark spoke with nothing but concern, quelling John2's fire.

"You really are different aren't you?" Minguet asked.

"I'm not unique in my thinking, but I don't share the views of many of my peers. By the way John2, I did a scan of Jehanne after she passed out. She's suffering from severe exhaustion and required fluids, her body has been sweating profusely as it adjusts to the augmentations. I gave her a saline solution when we started walking and she's recovered greatly."

"It truly was awful but I do feel significantly better. Please John2," Jehanne said after a long pause, "the group needs to be together in this. Deark has put aside everything so I may succeed in my calling." When she finished speaking her augmentations began to glow with a brilliant light.

"What's this?" D'Aulon asked taking several involuntary steps back.

"I assume it's confirmation," Minguet said, taking a knee in front of Jehanne.

"Confirmation? It feels more like one of those miracles she spoke of earlier," D'Aulon said and then he took a knee as well. Just as quickly as it started, the glowing subsided.

"Please rise my champions and be welcome," she said.

"Jehanne, I'll do my best. Spending years in a cell, losing friends and family that I never got to say goodbye to, all because I wanted the Mundane to understand how important voting was and that they needed to understand each and every law they were being oppressed by. These and other occurrences, make it hard to not hate all Entities," John2 said after a few more minutes of walking in silence.

"I understand, but the gods have put us on this path together. I need you to succeed in your attempt and if trying your best is not good enough, try my best."

"As you say." His voice took on a calmness she had not heard from him thus far.

They walked into the town proper just as the sun began to rise. The town was silent as they made their way to the train station.

"Jehanne, your augmentations—," Deark's words stalled as she turned to him.

"What?" she asked.

"They're pure white!" Pouli and de Metz said together.

"Holy shit!" John2 said.

"Please watch your language," Jehanne said and then looked at her hands, "Oh my."

"Well Deark may not be one of a kind, but you dear girl most certainly are," D'Aulon said.

"And if you didn't want to attract attention, I think that boat has sailed," de Metz added.

"How can I help you?" the Entity behind the counter at the train station asked.

"We've walked all night and need to be on the next train to New Orleans," John2 said.

"Sorry sir, the train is fully booked," the Entity replied.

"Are you certain? We were told that our tickets were good for the trip." Deark asked.

"There is room for you," the Entity addressed Deark.

"No, I'm traveling with this group. When can we all go?"

"Tomorrow morning, 9am."

"Fine, give us tickets and can you recommend lodging?" John2 said.

"Do you all wish to stay in the same location?" the Entity was confused, this was obviously a very segregated area.

"Different rooms, same hotel." John2's patience was waning.

"The only establishment for Augmented is the Arena."

"The what?" D'Aulon asked.

"I'm sorry do I need to get my voice simulator serviced again, The Arena," the Entity said. "It's a lively place, where humans can let their hair down."

"And if we don't wish to 'let our hair down' where else may we stay?" Jehanne asked.

"My co-processor! Your augmentations are spectacular," the Entity said.

"Thank you, but do you know of another establishment?"

"Blois is not typically a destination for the Augmented, so no, I'm sorry miss. However there is a Mundane establishment that has recently had to close its doors due to the restriction of Mundane travel. I imagine the owner could be persuaded to open for a higher class of customer. Mind you, there are less amenities there."

"And where are these establishments?" John2 asked.

******

Once they got directions and exchanged their tickets for the train the next day they walked down the street, all in a far worse mood than when they entered the station.

"Didn't you find that off-putting?" John2 asked.

"Of course I did," Deark replied. "The entire Augmented vs. Mundane thing is crazy."

"What? That's what you took away from that conversation?"

"Yes, why? What did I miss?"

"Um, they said you could get on a full train," D'Aulon said.

"Oh that. I'm used to that, same as the separate housing. I didn't set it up and I rarely take advantage of it."

"Aren't you little Mr. Hoity Toity." A harsh voice said from the side of them.

"No, actually I'm Deark. And you are?"

"Listen to him boys, an Entity with a heart." The stranger now stepped from the shadows. He was not tall but a single look led a person to know this was a man that carried the strength of an ox in him, even without his crude augmentations,

"We bid you no trouble friend," Minguet said.

"Poton step up here, I just heard a mouse speak with the voice of a man."

"Etienne," John2 said, stepping up.

"John2 you ass eared mongrel, what has you traveling with this odd grouping of beings?"

"Sir, I would ask you to not curse," Jehanne said.

"Asking and getting are things that come together in Fairytales," the Augmented that Etienne had called Poton said. "But La Hire couches his lance with his cursing. Would you take his lance away?"

"La Hire?" Jehanne inquired.

"Doesn't that mean hedgehog?" D'Aulon asked.

"Another of La Hire's old friends! Poton perhaps you and La Hire should join these sons of bitches!" Etienne said.

"You'll do no such thing if you can't keep that cursing in check," Jehanne said.

"Sorry miss priss but La Hire needs something to swear upon!" Etienne said.

"Is he a bit touched?" Minguet asked John2.

"One of the fiercest fighters I've ever seen and one of the fiercest friends a man could have," he replied. "But yeah, a bit touched in the head."

"Come my new friends, La Hire will treat you to the best damn breakfast you'll ever eat."

"That's it!" Jehanne walked up and slapped the much larger man across the face. When he began to protest she held a finger in the air. "Hold that tongue." She walked over and pulled one of the poles from the banner that D'Aulon carried for her. "Here," she said rapping the staff on the bar that crossed his chest joining the augmentations together.

"What?"

"You need to swear upon something, swear upon that staff."

"Etienne, it's as good a thing to swear on as anything else," Poton said.

"Fine! Now let's go eat." He walked with the staff as if he'd had it his entire life. His trek led them right up to a dilapidated building. "Sir, La Hire needs a table for nine," he said to a red haired man inside the door.

"Very well Laddy."

"Make that ten unless my company is not good enough for them?" a man with a dark van dyke said.

"Gilles, what happened to your goatee?" Poton asked.

"I lost a bet." The man was taller than any other in their group and his augmentations were all gilded.

*****

"My friends," John2 said after they were all seated. "Please allow me to introduce Jehanne la Pucelle and Deark." He then pointed to the newcomers. "This is Etienne de Vignolles if you missed it he prefers to be called…" He waited for it.

177

"La Hire," they all said.

"Precisely. This thin man that he travels with is Jean de Xaintrailles or Poton. Finally the last arrival to our party is Gilles de Rais. This scoundrel will steal anything that isn't attached to you."

"I've never limited myself to things unattached, where do you come up with such tripe?"

"So John2, what has you visiting our cheesy little hovel?" Poton asked.

"Our travels were disrupted by terrorists. We had to walk from Feirbois, only to find that we can't get passage to New Orleans until tomorrow."

"Nonsense, I can get you on that train." Gilles said, "I'll be right back." He stood to leave the restaurant just as the food arrived.

"It can wait until after you eat," Jehanne said.

"I'd rather eat the staff he carries." With that he left.

"I thought you said the food was good here?" Jehanne said to La Hire.

"Technically, La Hire isn't known for La Hire's veracity," he replied.

"If you're to travel with me, your honesty is even more important than controlling your foul language."

"And what makes you think that La Hire has any intention of traveling with you, tiny child?"

"Because Politician just told me that you must," Jehanne said.

"Come again?" the waiter that set the food down asked.

"Severe, mind your manners eavesdropping is rude!" the man that had greeted them said in a thick accent.

"Actually," Jehanne started, "Politician told me that you, Mr. Kennedy and you Mr. Brosse, called Severe, must travel with me as well."

"Come again?" the waiter once again asked as Gilles walked back in the door.

"No luck, they really are sold out. What? Did my beard turn blue or something? Why are you all staring at me?" he asked when he saw everyone sitting there dumbstruck.

"No but it probably will one day. La Hire will get us seats." He stood and walked from the room, tapping his staff merrily.

"Fool, he won't find nine seats," Gilles said.

"Good, cause he apparently needs to get twelve," Mr. Kennedy said.

"Come again?" Gilles asked.

"Seems we're all in this together, per La Pucelle," John2 replied.

"I don't mean to be rude, but Gilles was right. I'd rather eat that staff you gave La Hire," Pouli said.

"And that coming from a guy I saw eat a squirrel stepped on by a CAM unit," de Metz said. The group all laughed, including the staff of the restaurant until a loud commotion came from outside.

"Oh Etienne," John2 got up and ran outside.

"We're boarding," La Hire said holding up a fist full of tickets as he walked back into the restaurant.

"Seriously? How?" Gilles asked, his gilded parts gleaming in the now rising sun.

"I have a feeling you don't really want to know," D'Aulon said seeing John2's expression behind La Hire.

"We need to give your tickets to the friendly group that offered to switch with us."

"As we only have seven tickets—," Jehanne started.

"La Hire is sure that will be fine," he interrupted taking the tickets from each of the party and leaving again.

"Well let's head out." Jehanne held the door for the rest of the group to leave.

"That could be a problem for you in your future my dear." The statement came from the oldest woman Jehanne had ever seen. She was sitting at a table that had been in Jehanne's line of sight the entire time yet somehow she had not seen this woman.

"Hello, I'm terribly sorry but I don't understand what you mean."

"Bringing up the rear my dear, it could bring you problems later in your short life."

"Are you, one of the three?" Not wanting to come right out and ask if the old woman was Retro.

"The Crone, you take me for the Crone," the woman laughed which became a coughing fit.

"Retro, yes but not sure I… um. I meant no offence," she stammered.

"No offence taken. But no dear I am not one of the three," she said after the coughing stopped, "my name is Rebecca Nurse. I'm just an old woman who is traveling back to my home in Salem after visiting one of my sisters. I got stuck here when the trains east were all halted."

"I'm pleased to meet you. I'm Jehanne la Pucelle."

"And I you, I see this stage of the game has begun and you my darling, need to go catch that train," the old woman said.

"Yes you're right, I do," Jehanne turned to the door, seeing her friends coming back. "I hope you have a safe tr—," she stopped talking, for when she turned back, the table the woman had been sitting at was empty. Getting used to the odd things that were happening to her lately, Jehanne shook her head and headed to the train.

******

After they boarded, with many an odd glance from the Entities in the section that they sat in Deark turned to Etienne. "La Hire, please tell me we aren't going to have CAM units chasing us for your actions."

"La Hire has no fear of CAM units," he replied.

"Ok, will the W-CAM units be after us?" John2 asked.

"No, La Hire didn't rip any circuitry from the Entities this time." His grin touched his ears. "Gilles, what were you betting on that made you lose your mustache?" he asked, seeing their traveling mate rubbing his lip.

"If you must know," his words stalled as the train shot out of the terminal like a small rocket. "It was your fight in the Arena."

"You bet against La Hire?" Poton asked.

"No, I bet a flaming shot of the best Scotch that he would win."

"La Hire did win. Three Entities were no match for La Hire."

"Must you always refer to yourself—," Minguet's words were cut off by Poton.

"So finish your story." He gave the P.A. a glance that said 'Do not touch on that subject.'

"They bet me double or nothing that I couldn't drink it without blowing it out first. That's the bet I lost."

"How did you get nothing?" Deark asked.

"Well after I set my mustache on fire, I ended up spitting the rest of the shot out, setting the table on fire. It still hurts a bit." He touched his lip again.

"The table?" La Hire asked.

"Um, no my lip."

"Well now that you're with me you won't lose such a bet again," Jehanne said.

"You have a method of drinking a lit shot without burning your face?" Gilles asked.

"No I don't. However, there will be no drinking or gambling in my company."

"What?" Gilles asked.

"And La Hire has promised me that he will enforce these rules."

"When did La Hire promise this?" Etienne asked.

"My friend, you will be doing that right now," she reached her hand out and touched his shoulder.

"La Hire promises."

"So now that you've converted us all to the purity of your cause, what is the task at hand?" Severe asked.

"I believe that we should discuss that after we leave the confines of this train," John2 said.

"You have nothing to fear from my friends or me," an Entity spun his seat to face John2. "We're so far out of favor with this One World Government that they've change the rules of engagement specifically to keep us from being in close quarters with the Mundane."

"And why is that?" Jehanne asked.

"Mainly because—," his words were cut off by the conductor.

"Ladies and gentlemen, this may not come as a surprise to you but all additional traffic heading south has been curtailed. We will be stopping therefore at Saint Loup de Commune. The distance to your final destination of New Orleans is less than twenty miles. There are two other locations with food and shelter after Saint Loup, the Commune de Saint Jean le Blanc and the town of Les Augustins. Once again we're terribly sorry for this disruption. Please have safe travels." The speaker stilled and all the passengers looked at each other dumbstruck.

"Because I refuse to do what the One World Military tells me to do," the Entity that had been speaking to Jehanne finished his answer. "All in all I find them to be ignorant of the ways and means outside their ivory tower. I even have an Augmented as one of my advisors," He pointed to an older Human with few visible augmentations, "which is generally frowned upon. My final sin, I have far greater respect for the

Mundane leadership than I do for the arrogant fools in charge of our military."

"Jehanne, you're addressing Colonel Washington. He is the ranking officer for the One World Military in this region," Deark said.

"It was very nice to meet you sir. I wish we had been given more time to chat on the train but perhaps we will be able to speak on the road to New Orleans."

"The feeling is mutual. Perhaps we'll have an opportunity to converse in the future, for my road does not lead to New Orleans. I'll be taking the train north again to try and determine the real reason for these issues," Colonel Washington said.

"I wish you luck with that," Jehanne said, standing and leaving the train along with the rest of the passengers.

"La Hire does as well. This isn't exactly a body for twenty mile walks." Etienne began to follow.

"I should say that, my friend, it's a body for commanding the vanguard." The Augmented with milky-white eyes who was sitting next to the Colonel said.

"La Hire doesn't know this vanguard. Is it like a body guard?"

"I'm sorry my advisor, Mr. Corey, thinks everyone is in the military." Colonel Washington poked.

"My Martha says I do that too often, though I imagine your Martha feels the same." He replied with a grin at the Entity. "Vanguard is a term used by military strategists; consider it like the tip of a spear. The first into a battle, its goal is to divide the enemy forces so they can be more easily defeated."

"Ah, yes that's what La Hire is built for!"

"Good luck to you, I hope to see you again at some point." Colonel Washington looked to the front of the train and watched Jehanne and her newly formed Captains exit together.

Section Two – Chapter Three

"Where did the conductor say we were?" Jehanne asked.

"At the Commune de Saint Loup. It looks as if it is primarily inhabited by Mundane," Minguet said.

"Based on the way they're looking at us they don't get many visitors either," Pouli added as they walked down the street.

"There are no CAM units here," Jehanne said looking around. "We have CAM units on every corner in the Commune de Domremy."

"I wonder if that's because Madam Commander lives in your Mother City?" de Metz inquired.

"Doesn't each Mother City have one?"

"No, Madam Commander is one of a kind. She works for the One World Government. All the other Mother Cities have a Viceroy that was named by Madam Commander to rule them in her name," John2 said.

"Deark you didn't explain that to your students? What kind of instructor are you?" Pouli poked.

"Come on now, he was a great instructor," Jehanne defended.

"Technically he's correct, I didn't share that piece of information. Madam Commander is actually the third highest officer in the entire One World Government and more importantly, she is the highest ranking official on the North American Continent," Deark said.

"Why would one of such a high station listen in on our classroom? Why wouldn't she just delegate that to one of her underlings? And why wouldn't we have W or I-Cam units instead of just CAM units if she is so important?" Jehanne asked.

"Because she likes Deark, La Hire thinks."

"No, no she hates him."

"I still say hate is the wrong emotion," Deark replied.

"As they say, love and hate are but a door closing from each other," Gilles said.

"Aye laddy, who says that?" The red haired restaurant owner, Kennedy spoke for the first time since they left Blois.

"You know… They." Gilles face was turning a bright shade of pink, which clashed with his golden armor terribly.

"La Hire thinks that's from one of those love poems he writes?"

"Alright let me answer Jehanne's questions. Madam Commander doesn't actually listen in on the classroom discussions. However, when certain buzz words are touched on in the lecture or in the students questions, the transmission is automatically transferred to her. She has always been a very controlling Entity so something like yelling at a Mundane, even a child, fulfills her. As for the CAM units versus W or I-CAM units, you need to remember that CAM units have not reached Sentience," he paused even in this company. "It comes down to the CAM units not actually having a choice," Deark explained.

"Are you saying that she's that repugnant that the W and I-CAMs refuse to be around her?" de Metz asked.

"Those were your words not mine."

A girl, perhaps four or five years old, walked up to Jehanne. Stopping in front of her and staring. "Hello dear, what pretty eyes you have," Jehanne said, looking down at the girl.

"Ophena130025, move and allow your betters to pass." A haggard woman came running from one of the shops. "I'm very sorry, ma'am." The woman bowed over and over as she pulled the girl out of their path.

"But mama, I want to see the shiny people," the girl protested.

"They're Augmented dear not shiny people," a man who picked up the girl said. "No offense meant she's just a child."

Jehanne heard a mutter behind her, "La Hire isn't shiny." As Jehanne looked around her, there were at least two hundred people standing around them now. She walked up the steps to a shop and removed the bundle that was strapped to her back.

This action brought gasps of, "That's the sword from Feirbois I bet," from many in attendance.

"Do you know who I am and what I hold?" she asked the crowd. Her companions separated to each side of the steps so her voice carried to each waiting ear. "Where I come from I was originally called the Hope by some, the Maiden of Lorayn by others. I stand before you today to say I'm neither of those things, and that I'm both of those things because I'm what I choose to be, can you say that? Can you say you can be whatever you want to be? Of course you can't. I just heard what was said to this child: move aside and allow your betters to pass." Jehanne took a moment.

"The One World Caste System dictates it be so," an Entity that was on the train said to her from the outer boundaries of the crowd.

"And of course you're correct it does say that, just as it also says I should allow you to stand next to me on these steps and not speak until you are done speaking," she said.

"See, all in its place," the unknown Entity replied.

"And a place for all," the crowd intoned.

"Yet I would say to you, this bundle that I hold is a sword. I had a group of Mundane dig it up from beneath a destroyed church in Feirbois, a town that I had never been to before yesterday."

"Then how did you know where it was?" the little girl asked.

"Ah that's the point of my story little miss. I was told by Politician himself where to find it."

"That's heresy," the same Entity said.

"Perhaps you see it that way, but let me add to that charge... I should like to see you walk up these steps and make me halt my speaking until you elect to halt yours." The hush that hit the crowd was absolute. The Entity after a few minutes found its vocal transmission capability.

"You're responsible for all the terrorist attacks on the nation's transportation avenues aren't you?" What is your name?" he asked.

"My name is Jehanne la Pucelle, and as I was on the train with you, isn't that a foolish question?"

"How dare you call me foolish." The train pulled back into the station behind them. "I called for the train and its CAM units to return and arrest you."

"La Hire is good with that."

"Hello," a familiar voice said. "What prey tell is happening here?"

"Colonel Washington," the Entity that had been making a scene yelled. "I've been threatened bodily and embarrassed by that Augmented."

"Threatened, oh my, she's at least fifty feet away from you. Whatever did you think she could do, injure you by throwing her words at you, Congressional Entity Blithe?" Washington asked walking up.

"She carries a sword. She could cut her way through the crowd and get me."

"A sword?" he turned and saw the bundle she held. "You simpleton, she carries a relic, and from the wrappings a very old one. You nor any of these Mundane have anything to fear from it."

"And what about the One World Caste System? She's violated many rules," the Congressional Entity said.

"Should you waste anymore of my time it will be you that's taken away in shackles." Colonel Washington turned and went back to the train.

"Your name has been noted and of course I'll be filing a full report on you and that cretin Washington when I return to New Orleans," the Congressional Entity said. The crowd began chanting for Jehanne to open the bundle.

"I'm sorry not yet friends," she replied. As the commotion stopped Ophena130025 ran away from her parents and up the stairs next to Jehanne.

"Is that really a sword?"

"It certainly feels like it." Jehanne held the bundle out to the girl. "The blade is down here and up here is the hilt, the grip, and finally the pommel." The girl gingerly touched each area as it was pointed out.

"I can see a little of the grip through this hole," Ophena130025 said.

"I suppose I'll need to be careful with that." Jehanne put her hand around the grip, securing the sword to her back. When she started to bring her hand forward again, her father's ring which was sitting tight on her thumb, brushed the wire covered tang of the sword.

******

For the second time in her short life, Jehanne found herself on a mountain top in the middle of a world that wasn't hers. As last time, there was no clear reason she felt this wasn't her world, Jehanne simply knew.

"I've wondered since the sword found its way into your hand when we would meet." A woman's voice came from behind Jehanne.

"Oh my." Jehanne turned and instinctively held her hands in front of herself.

"Quite nice child. That's an old world defensive stance, the center of Krav Maga." The woman was tall and muscular, differentiated by her white hair which was cut in a pixie cut. Her pretty face was offset with a scar that ran from her forehead to the center of her cheek and a brown studded leather patch covered her eye.

"Who are you?"

"You need to ask, love?"

"Protectorate?" Jehanne inquired uncertain.

"That's correct, I'm the second of the new gods."

"Where is this place? Politician brought me here as well."

"Did he now? Interesting I've never thought he was nostalgic. It's called Mount Olympus. This is where we lived before we were renamed and recast."

"It feels different here than my home world." Jehanne gave voice to her thoughts.

"Your depth of awareness is amazing child."

"Thank you. If I may ask, why are we here? For that matter, how did I get here you said that you wondered when we would meet, so you must not have called me here."

"I have to say, Pedagogue said Politician undersold your aptitude. He himself undersold you as well. Yes you're correct I did not call you here, your ring and the sword did. When they came in contact with each other, they knew you were ready."

"Ready?"

"Yes child, ready to learn to use them together. It's the next stage of your growth. Now I need you to draw the sword."

"Yes'm." Jehanne reached onto her back expecting to find the bundle of waxed burlap. Instead, she felt the cold bare metal of the pommel. She reached passed that, feeling the wire wound grip which she allowed her hand to close around and slowly pulled the weapon as high into the air as she could to allow it to clear the scabbard.

"Tell me," Protectorate asked as Jehanne held the sword in one hand, "how does it feel."

"It feels like a cold piece of metal," Jehanne replied.

"We then, have a long way to go, let's start at the beginning. Hold your arm out straight, shoulder height with the blade aiming at the sky. Focus on the blade being perpendicular to your arm with an edge facing forward. In fencing this is called the seven position and as you extend it from there it's called the seven cut. Now, the grip you are using on this dual edged blade is called a hammer grip. I want you to envision that the tip of the blade is the head of a hammer. Using only your wrist, bring the head of the hammer down as far as you can. I want you to do that one-thousand times."

"Yes'm." Jehanne gave no complaints, simply lifted her arm out straight, after about twenty cuts she realized that her modies were gone. Continuing to hammer she asked, "Where are my augmentations?"

"This place is where we are ourselves. You my dear are a Mundane and therefore here you have none of those falsifications."

"I'm actually not upset by that, I don't like them." She continued her exercise until she reached the count.

"Very good, do you understand angles?" Protectorate asked.

"I do."

"I want you to continue doing this exercise only I want one-thousand hammers at negative forty-five degrees, that's called the number one cut. After you're finished with that we'll go to cut number two, that's at the forty-five degree."

"And do one thousand there as well?" Jehanne asked.

"Yes dear." Protectorate watched the girl sweating through the afternoon sun. "Very well done. These next moves are trickier. Just as you went to the number one position I want you to roll your wrist to the outside and hammer up from the two-hundred and twenty-five degree position. That's the number three cut. Next roll your arm inside to one-hundred and thirty-five degrees, this is the four cut, again hammer up from there."

"I will, ma'am," Jehanne said, finishing as the moon found purchase in the sky.

******

"Let's sit here girl," as Jehanne turned she found a fire with food cooking. Next to the fire sat two cots; Protectorate waited on one. "This lovely food will help you recover so that we can start again tomorrow." she removed the food from the fire and handed a serving to Jehanne on a copper plate.

"Thank you, what is it?" she asked as she sat, setting her sword next to her.

"The food of the gods my dear, it's called ambrosia," Protectorate said.

"It's delightful," Jehanne said taking a bite.

"What do you taste?"

"It tastes much like a very cold fruit that my Grandmother served when I was a small girl." Even as Jehanne said this she knew it made no sense as she had just watched the food come off the fire.

"Now that's a great example of what ambrosia is," Protectorate said. "Each person has a different experience with it. What's even better, the next time you taste it, you may think it tastes like a dish that Jovi571 made you when you were sick."

"You know about Jovi571?" Jehanne asked.

"Child I know everything about you."

"You know everything about everyone?"

"Not exactly, I know you as you are here. I know all about Jovi because he is in your heart. It's complicated."

"It certainly sounds like it. Do you know why Pedagogue wants us to destroy the new gods?"

"The finding of Neoteric?"

"Yes, we've thought about it, the only way we could find her is to recombine you, the six into three."

"You are thinking too literal of the comment. It's time for bed dear."

"I don't think that I –," the words slurred and then a cute little snore escaped her.

"Wake child." Protectorate touched Jehanne on the shoulder.

"But I just closed my eyes," Jehanne protested and then noticed the sun had already cleared the trees, causing her to still her protest.

"There is much to learn," she said as they stood on the same mountaintop after eating a bit. Jehanne found her sword strapped to her back. "Start with the same straightforward cuts, through the cycle. When you finish with that you will need to do the original motion then add to it a through and return." She demonstrated the number one cut along with the new movement, cutting through an unseen opponent completely and returning to the original position. "Understand? As you do this, you must hide your off-hand if it's not in use, or you stand a good chance of cutting yourself."

"That makes sense." Jehanne started on her hammering and then as requested she went right into the through and return.

"NO!" Protectorate stood and walked over. "Watch again." Her blade cut what would have been completely through her opponent. "You must allow the blade to pass on a straight line until it exits your opponent. Think of it this way: how can you turn your blade while you're in the middle of a target?"

"Yes ma'am, I mean of course you can't ma'am." Jehanne started again.

"Better. If you practice poorly, when the time comes to use the sword, you will not be ready."

"Use the sword?" Jehanne asked.

"We'll have time to discuss that later."

******

They fell into a routine. In the mornings she would practice and combine the learnings up to that point, perfecting and making the patterns sing. After lunch she learned new techniques and sparred with Entities. On the morning of the fifteenth day Jehanne woke after what seemed like her normal blink of sleep.

"Protectorate, is time the same here as on my world?" Jehanne asked.

"What do you mean?"

"The daylight hours feel as if they go on for weeks and the night passes in seconds. Never mind, it must just be the training."

"Actually no your initial observation was correct, time flows here as I need it to." Protectorate smiled. "Today we will add your second hand. The weapon you carry is a bastard sword or a hand and a half sword. It allows you to either use it as a one handed, as you have been, with a shield or buckler, or as a more nimble two handed sword."

"Ma'am, what is a buckler?"

"It's a smaller shield that can be used easily for offense and defense. I personally believe the hand and a half sword with a buckler to be the best combination for melee. I want you to hold the sword in your seven position with one hand. Perfect. Now, grasp the side of the pommel with your offhand. Leaving that gap causes the sword to dance like a two handed only a bit faster when attacking straightforward. It also has the benefit of having a stronger block and strike when coming from the one or the two positions."

"It's surprisingly less agile this way."

"In order to regain that agility you need to become cognizant of your feet. As you are holding your right hand closer to the hilt, your base would be a left foot forward stance." She demonstrated. "You want your knees flexed, the lead foot is shoulder width and forward one step, keeping your toes pointed at your opponent. The other will also be shoulder width yet trailing two to three foot lengths, and turned out around thirty to forty-five degrees." She watched Jehanne trying to figure out what her instructor had said. When the girl settled into a position Protectorate walked up. "Almost. You've missed one thing. Let me see if you can figure it out. I'm going to push you." Protectorate walked in front of Jehanne and pushed her back.

"Whoa!" Jehanne exclaimed as she fell back.

"No power in your stance. Did you feel where the problem was?"

"When you pushed me I had my feet aimed in the same direction. You had said to point my back foot off at an angle."

"Correct, fix it and let's try again." After Jehanne set her feet Protectorate pushed her again. "Much better. Next we need to think of how to move. You can't just clippity-clop forward, you need to consider how each step will coincide with your arms, be they blocking or attacking." She gave a list of moves to practice starting from each of the positions and explained how to perform the cut with the second hand involved. Jehanne quickly found she could not keep the blade at the height of her shoulder having to lower it a bit.

"Excellent I wanted to see how you would adjust to the new stance and the new hand."

"Thank you." Jehanne worked through each exercise as their practice routine started at the beginning again.

******

At the end of each day Protectorate would cook ambrosia over the open fire. One night, after a full month of using the sword as a true hand and a half Jehanne approached the fire to find a man sitting on her cot.

"Jehanne I would like to introduce Pioneer, he's the most skilled inventor of the new gods, always forming his own path," Protectorate said.

"You do me great service with your words mother," the young man said.

"I am very pleased to meet you." Jehanne gave a curtsy.

"And I you small one. This night I've brought you your next weapon." He handed her a small shield.

"A buckler?" she asked.

"Very good yes, but not just any buckler. It has a mirrored finish carbon fiber front with an outer ring made from iron, chromium, silicon, nickel, manganese, and a small amount of molybdenum and carbon." When Pioneer finished he looked at her blank face. "Sorry, it's stainless steel with a modified formula to add to its yield strength. That way it will be strong as well as have high elasticity."

"Am I to use the mirror to reflect the sun at them?" Jehanne asked.

"You could, however do you remember what happened to Deark at your father's Forge?" Protectorate asked.

"The W–CAM unit hit him with a laser bolt."

"Aye, this mirror will reflect those lasers without absorbing the heat, the carbon—," Pioneer started.

"That's dragonweave?" Jehanne asked, reaching out receiving the buckler from the new god.

"As the Mundane refer to it yes. You however are an Augmented now and it's called carbon fiber and it is one of the four elements of life."

"Thank you Pioneer." Protectorate stood and escorted him from the camp. "Jehanne needs her rest." The next morning the small disk shield was added onto her arm and the entire process started once again.

"We've practiced enough on trees, dummies, and simulated Entities. You've learned to use the buckler to direct their attacks and how to fight as many as ten of them at one time," Protectorate said after Jehanne saw the completion of the third moon cycle, "It's time to see what you have learned."

"How will we do that?" Jehanne asked, fearing she knew the answer.

"It's time for us each to don armor and tilt swords. Now get some sleep."

"What if we hurt each other?" Jehanne asked.

"My fellow new god will be there," Protectorate said.

"Physician?" Jehanne replied.

"No Passage, you need to know how to get to the next world." Protectorate said and after Jehanne's face showed utter confusion she laughed. Her laughter was thick and rich, a warrior's laugh Jehanne imagined, having heard the same intensity in La Hire's laugh. "Sorry dear. Yes dear child, Physician."

"Good night." Jehanne put her head on the pillow and just before she fell asleep she looked at the new god sitting on the edge of her bed. "If I may ask, how did you injure your eye?"

"It was a battle between gods. Before you ask, Physician could do nothing for it because it was god versus god. Had a mortal done it or I to a mortal, her powers would have been sufficient. Stop worrying; even if I cleave your head off she can fix it."

"That doesn't make me feel any better," Jehanne said as sleep took her.

******

"Wake small one," a voice of a different woman said.

"Physician?"

"Aye, dear."

"I'm pleased to meet you." This woman was prettier than the other new gods Jehanne had seen; she had auburn hair that was pulled back into a bun and her eyes spoke of vast knowledge.

"And I you. Let's get some food in you. Protectorate has already left to prepare." Physician paused when she saw all the color wash from Jehanne's face. "She told me you were nervous. I promise you, I will let nothing happen to you. Each morning you will wake the same as you are now, only you will have new learnings."

"Sorry, it's just she's the new god of battle, war and protection. How do I stand a chance?"

"The Mundane Moon Maze," the woman replied.

"I know of it yes."

"Each of us are involved. Depending on where a Mundane enters they face a different one of our tests. Should you pass that one they would move on to the next until they've faced all six of us."

"Oh, Joshua beat her."

"And how did you remember his name?"

"Pedagogue still carries a touch of anger about being beaten by a Mundane," Jehanne explained.

"He and Protectorate have only been defeated that one time."

"Which surprises me, why do you fight so hard to not be alive for one—," she stopped asking her question as a thought sprang to mind. "You're all alive anyway."

"And?" This time it was Pedagogue's voice.

"The race is only run to force you to earth for a day that you may answer a question each."

"This is not my time it's Protectorate's or I would delve deeper," Pedagogue said and he walked into a building with large columns that Jehanne had until then not seen.

"Time to go. Eat this as we walk." Physician handed her what looked like one of her mother's morning corns.

They crested a huge set of steps to the large building with columns that Pedagogue had walked into. "Where are we?" Jehanne asked as she looked down into the enormous dirt center of the oval building.

"This was the Roman Coliseum. Gladiators fought and chariots raced. In short, many humans died here."

"What are those?" Jehanne asked, pointing to the multitude of figures populating the arena floor.

"I would think you would recognize the various forms of Conditional Attitude Maintainers, Base, Imperial and World."

"Sorry ma'am I asked the wrong question. Why are they here?" Jehanne asked again.

"This is your test dear," Protectorate said approaching from the side. "I am considered the boss. To get to me you must fight through all of them. First are the base CAM units. As you clear those you begin the battle with the I-CAMs and then the W-CAMs. This is where it gets tricky and you mustn't dilly dally because the fallen units will re-spawn after five minutes. However, once you reach me, all the Entities are destroyed."

"I guess that's enough information to be going on with, we might as well begin." Jehanne found herself standing on the floor of the coliseum facing more CAM units than she had ever seen in her life.

Section Two – Chapter Four

She took a step forward and the outer CAM units began to advance, their arms merged together into a single large sword, though the center group remained stationery. She continued her advance, slicing the first three rows before the attack came from behind. Everything went dark.

"What the?" she sat up in her bed, Physician and Protectorate standing over her. Jehanne reached to her back where the blade had entered.

"You're fine," Physician said.

"You were flanked," Protectorate said. "You can't allow the enemy to get behind you."

"So I should have gone after the sides."

"Well pick one and then yes. When you're alone you need to work with what they give you. Again."

Jehanne was in the Coliseum once again. As she took a step the center began to advance this time. She stayed on her strategy and ran to the left and attacked the waiting Entities. When she was two rows deep she once again felt the blade in her back.

"How?" She sat up.

"Jehanne, why did you attack the non-moving again?" Protectorate asked.

"I didn't want them behind me."

"You didn't want the non-moving Entities to sneak up behind you?"

"I'm sorry," Jehanne said.

"Look this is all new to you, but if their center starts after you, they're going all out Vanguard tact. You need to respond in kind, straight ahead and meet them with the tip of your sword." Protectorate said.

"You're doing fine," Physician touched her shoulder.

"Actually no, my fellow new god is being generous. You need to read the field of battle in a flash and react. Going in there with a preconceived plan and staying with it when you are outnumbered so ridiculously, especially when your plan is to go on the offensive, is not doing well."

"I agree," Politician said appearing behind Physician. "The best offense at times is a great defense."

"Again," Protectorate barked.

The dirt beneath her feet felt cold. She took a step forward and when only the right side began to advance, she returned their attack. The Entities fell one after another and then pain and darkness.

"Shoot," she said this time when she sat up. "What happened?"

"Battle blindness. You focused on only targets in front of you. Just as you took the immediate impression at the beginning of the battle and reacted, you need to continually do that as the battle progresses," Protectorate said.

"But if I break my concentration in the middle of a fight I will lose focus," Jehanne said.

"What can you do to counter that?" Pedagogue asked.

"You instructor, are supposed to be a spectator," Protectorate said.

"Sorry," he said.

"I should reevaluate between each fight. After I fell one opponent and before engaging the next, I should take a mental picture of the battle field," Jehanne said.

"That's completely correct," Protectorate said. "Again."

The field was set up differently. This time it was broken into two distinct formations. 'It doesn't matter, what are they offering?' Jehanne thought to herself. 'Take what they give you, remember what Protectorate told you.'

The full formation on the left began advancing even before Jehanne moved. She rushed to the left and met the advancing forces. After killing the first row she turned and saw the other formation was closing. Turning she ran back to meet the new combatants.

******

The battle continued in a back and forth manner and eventually the base CAM units were gone. Jehanne worked her way into the ranks of the Imperial units. These units were not uniform in their weaponry, some had the two arms as swords, some had the hand and half sword along with a shield, still others' arms both were individual blades. Her tactics however, did not change. As she completed each encounter with Entities she would reevaluate and circle back if needed to not allow herself to be flanked. After the fourth switch from side to side the felled CAM units began to re-spawn. 'It's been five minutes, seriously?' She felt herself beginning to get discouraged.

'Envision that you're dancing a waltz, one, two, three. One, two, three. One, assess the situation. Two, move to engage primary threat. Three, attack and destroy the threat. What the threat is doesn't matter be it a re-spawn or a full formation,' Protectorate's voice sang in her head. 'One, two, three and one, two, three.'

"That helps, thank you," Jehanne said as she worked her way through the Entities that stood between her and her target.

'Remember that buckler as you begin to engage the W-CAM units.' The voice of Pioneer pounded in her head. The first bolt came as she was recovering from the voice; she had time to deflect it yet had no ability to redirect it.

"Loud!" was the word she got out as two more W-CAM units loosed their laser bolts. This time as in practice, she rewarded their fellow Entities with the energy bolts. Closing the distance to the advancing W-CAM units, she got her first up close look at these Entities. Their dragonweave was a dark green, almost black. They carried a curved sword in each hand uniformly. Jehanne used her buckler to destroy five units for every one with the sword.

'One, two, three.' Protectorate's words sang in her head as Jehanne felt herself falling into the same battle blindness now that her quarry was in sight. She tried to determine the best method of transitioning to the other Entities without taking a laser bolt in the back when a stray bolt approached her. Jehanne redirected it at Protectorate, who blocked it with her sword. The Entities that were closing on her were now gone.

"Oh very nice!" Pedagogue's laughing voice said.

******

"We do this but once, my dear," Protectorate said. The two opponents circled each other for a moment. Protectorate then seized an opportunity to close the gap as Jehanne's feet were both facing the larger woman. As the woman's fists struck her on the chest the girl fell backward, but recovered in a smooth somersault, getting her buckler up to defend Protectorate's strike. Jehanne trapped the blade between her shield and sword, she then launched her body forward, forcing Protectorate to take several surprised steps back.

Giving a final push gained the distance between the two combatants which allowed Jehanne to get herself back into battle stance. Once again they circled each other, both gauging the other, and then in a flash both blades sang out. The vibration in the handle surprised Jehanne causing her to flinch, for a reward the pommel of Protectorate's sword jabbed out, breaking her nose.

"Physician." Protectorate called out and Jehanne felt her nose right itself.

"Thank you." Jehanne reengaged her opponent, realizing the blades would vibrate now. "How did you make my blade vibrate like that?"

"A slight turn of my sword as yours was about to impact. The Entities don't have abilities like that, but I wanted you to experience it."

"I hadn't thought of the benefit of the pommel as you just used it."

"Again, some things need to be learned the hard way." Protectorate changed both her top hand and lead foot as she side stepped an over exaggerated attack by Jehanne. She gave the small girl a nasty cut on her arm as Jehanne pulled the blade back from the failed attack. "If you make that mistake in battle allow yourself to follow the blade, as such." Protectorate duplicated that attack in the same over telegraphed manner, Jehanne dodged the attack. As the sword slashed passed Protectorate adjusted its position to allow her body to somersault over and swing the blade into Jehanne's leg.

As Jehanne fell from the blow she knew she had left herself open; she needed to keep her eye on the weapon better. The tendons on her leg as well as the cut on her arm repaired as she turned to block the thrust from Protectorate's sword with her shield and then deliver a cut to her opponent's exposed side. The blood sprang forward and then just as quickly stopped again.

"Very nice," Protectorate said. The two women faced each other, holding their weapons at the one position. They advanced even more aggressively, locking blades, only this time Jehanne was prepared for the pommel strike. The attack missed the mark as she pulled her face back. Instantly she knew she had left herself too exposed. Protectorate's blade went straight down into her lead foot, pinning it to the ground. Not stopping to think, Jehanne swung her sword at her opponent's exposed neck. The buckler on Protectorate's arm deflected the blow, the new god then let go of her sword and drove her gauntleted fist into Jehanne's cheek and nose with a crunch.

Looking over at Physician for relief the new god shook her head, and Jehanne knew this was the real test. She let one of her hands fall from her sword and attempt to remove the blade pinning her left foot to the ground. As the hand reached the grip of her enemy's sword she took her eye off Protectorate long enough to show what she was doing. The Buckler on Protectorate's arm shot down breaking Jehanne's wrist just as she removed the sword from her foot, casting it aside.

Facing her foe, she knew pain, but her opponent had no weapon. A one armed girl with a sword stood toe to toe against an unarmed new god. Jehanne began to advance just as her surroundings changed, the coliseum was gone.

******

"Did I lose?" she asked, immediately feeling that the pain in her wrist and foot were gone.

"I'm sorry?" Ophena130025 asked.

'I felt there was no need for a victor on either side, you both fought well.' Politician's voice swam softly in her head.

"It was a question to myself dear, not to you." Jehanne knelt down in front of the girl. "It has been a pleasure to meet you, yet our road is long and I fear much awaits us." The small girl gave Jehanne a big hug and then took a step back.

"A man told me that if I were ever to meet you that I need to give you this." She held out what looked like a plate sized mirror.

"That's very kind of you to remember. Did he also tell you to poke the hole in the canvas?" Jehanne asked accepting the gift, she attached the buckler to her left arm's augmentation.

"He did." Ophena130025 held out the ring she had been wearing on her thumb showing it had a tiny blade on the inside.

"Please keep that to remember me," Jehanne said.

As they gathered supplies for the trip several requests to follow them came from the Mundane of the city. Jehanne took her place on the steps once again and addressed the gathered group.

"My friends, each of you have received us into your Commune at great risk to its status. I would not ask further from any of you. Please remember any that follow me could end up paying the ultimate price for it. The Stone Room here is long out of use, don't force an ignition of it on my accord. The time will come that decisions need be made, but let's hope those decisions can be made from a voting booth rather than a battle field. For now try to find your pride, something that was taken away a long time ago I know. Feeling pride should be like feeling any other emotion, it should just happen. Find that pride in yourself, value who you are. Be proud of your neighbor for they are facing things you know not, and the next time you walk down the street greet them with an exuberance for existing that you didn't know you had. I promise you'll be surprised at how much passion you can feel to be alive, if you allow yourself to. Let each day be spent with this re-found emotion; be proud of your work, in your dress, and even in your learnings, then we will see what will come next. Until then know this, La Pucelle is proud to be your sister as you should be proud to be each other's extended family."

They finally left the Commune de Saint Loup as the stars adorned the sky. "Jehanne," Deark said as they walked. "Do you feel that tack was best? I mean the Congressional Entities typically demand more respect than any other yet you addressed him like he was lower than the animals in the field."

"Only after he pointed out that the Mundane are those animals in the field," she replied.

"Perhaps but we—," he started.

"Deark, I am Mundane, one of those animals, an ox pulling a plow through the Entities fields, your fields."

"I don't think that's a fair comment, Jehanne," de Metz said. "Deark is here for you perhaps even more than you know."

"I'm most certain that's true, Deark I'm sorry. I can't believe I just went there."

"There is no need for apologies. I'm just nervous that we're showing our hands too soon," he replied.

"La Hire is fine with the hand she showed."

"That in itself should cause you to rethink your actions," Gilles said.

"Listen, I am still on the path that the new gods are directing. I need the Entities to know my name and correlate it to these terrorist attacks. We need to take what they are offering," Jehanne said.

"Sound tactics," Deark said. "But where did you learn such a thing?"

"Do you know where I've been for the last three moon cycles?" Jehanne asked.

"The Commune de Domremy for most of it, I imagine," de Metz said.

"Actually I've been training with Protectorate. When my ring came into contact with the grip of the sword through a small hole that Ophena130025 had put in the canvas, at Pioneer's request, I was sent to Mount Olympus. I learned how to use the sword that Politician saw fit for me to have dug up."

"And that mirror that Gilles keeps staring into?" Severe asked.

"It's actually a buckler, and it was made by Pioneer to reflect the lasers from the W-CAM units."

"Ah lass, it's a shame he only left that one," Kennedy said. "If there is fighting to be had in our future that would be a dead useful defense."

"My red haired champion, I know the blend of metals in order to make them."

"How Jehanne?" John2 inquired.

"Pioneer told me."

"That's four of the six," Minguet said.

"Actually, I met Physician while I was there and briefly saw Passage during my battle with Protectorate."

"Battle? La Hire needs to hear the rest of this training encounter," he said, placing the tip of the staff he now carried everywhere, on her arm.

"I'll share all as we walk."

******

She did just that, telling every moment on their walk through the night. As they arrived at the next Commune, her stories were stalled as fires could be seen. "No!" Jehanne sprinted toward the flames, the sword bouncing on her back a prod pushing her onward.

The first houses they came to were already smoldering, the people gone, and there weren't even bodies. "I don't understand, what are we facing here?" Minguet asked.

"If it was the terrorists, there would be bodies. It must be the One World Government," John2 said.

"Perhaps we tipped our hand too soon," Kennedy said.

"I don't know about that," de Metz said.

"Why?" Jehanne asked walking to the large Augmented. "Oh." The Congressional Entity that she had been engaged in verbal discourse with in the previous Commune was in several pieces in front of her.

"La Hire was not here before you, promise. Although I do owe a drink to someone."

"There are far too many variables at play here," D'Aulon said. "I need to get you out of this area right away, please, La Pucelle with me."

"I know that you are right, but I have a need to see the rest of this," she replied.

"I don't even see any foot prints that are out of place or a mass exodus or anything odd," Gilles added.

"I think we need to do a building by building search. Someone must be here." Pouli said.

The group separated, not finding any other creatures alive or dead, just the Congressional Entity. When they were all together again Deark looked closely at the damage to the fallen Entity.

"Jehanne, these are sword cuts."

"Perhaps, but my sword is still safely in its swathing." Jehanne replied and then pulled the bundle out to drive the point home.

"Do you think that someone is setting you up?" D'Aulon asked.

"Some One?" La Hire inquired.

"Oh I think La Hire has the right of it. Not someone, more of a something," Deark said.

"So you see this as an Entity driven subterfuge?" John2 asked.

"I do. More than that, I see it as an attempt to slow our progress and incriminate Jehanne," Deark added.

"I agree," a voice yet unheard by Jehanne said. They all turned to face a man standing on a roof of one of the buildings of the main street.

"Greetings, and who might you be stranger?" Poton asked.

"My name is inconsequential," he said.

"Seems like a strange name," La Hire replied.

"Fine, it's Culant, Louis Culant. Let me break the news to you. That Entity was killed by an I-CAM unit as it started to tell a tale of a sword carrying girl that was breaking the laws of the One World Caste System. The I-CAM unit's arm transformed into a sword and cut him into three pieces before the first fragment hit the ground."

"What about the rest of the people, animals or anything for that matter?" John2 asked.

"A personnel-carrier landed on the roof of that building." He pointed across the street to a building that was burned and smoldering. "The I-CAMs announced that if anyone wanted to live they had to the count of one thousand to get loaded on."

"How could a transport load an entire town? It must have been monstrous," Deark said.

"It was. That was our city hall and the biggest building in the entire Commune. Yet the size of the transport crushed it like a bug under foot. After the townsfolk loaded into the ship, the I-CAM that cut down that one ordered the W-CAMs to set fire to everything," Culant said. "When the transport took off it blew away all the tracks that you were looking for."

"So why didn't you go?" Severe asked.

"I was locked in the jail." He pointed to another burned shell of a building. "I saw the whole thing happen through the cell window. The only reason I got out was as the building burned down the outer wall collapsed."

"What were you in jail for?" Jehanne asked.

"As embarrassing as it is, I didn't pay a man for a bet that I lost."

"And?" she prodded.

"The man decided to make a grand spectacle out of the issue. Instead of asking for the leadership of the town to demand action he…" Culant's words broke, "he killed my dog. I loved that dog and everyone knew I loved that dog."

"Did you kill him? La Hire would've killed him."

"No, but I did break both of his arms and injure him considerably before I was arrested."

"I don't even know how to react to that," Jehanne said.

"A man showing loyalty to a companion is a good thing," Deark said.

"So is this injured man among those that were taken away?" de Metz changed the subject.

"He was."

"I'm surprised that they didn't kill him rather than go to the trouble of taking him. Were there any other infirmed?" Deark asked.

"Yes, there was a freak accident last week where seven construction workers were burned," Culant said.

"Again, why did they go to the trouble of taking eight people from the hospital? That isn't the way any of this would normally play out." Deark continued to dwell on the odd behaviors of the W–CAM units.

"Can you find a ladder or something, I don't really want to die up here." It was then that the group noticed the fire had sprung to life again.

"Take ahold." D'Aulon extended his arms to grab the Mundane stuck on the roof.

******

The group left the Commune de Saint Jean le Blanc, the blaze having consumed the majority of the buildings on the main street.

"This stinks of villainy, La Hire likes it not."

"I hate to agree with my rash friend on anything but he is most certainly correct in this," Poton said.

"Thank you." La Hire patted the back of his tall comrade.

"You two are a hoot," Gilles said.

"Jehanne, have you any guidance on this?" John2 asked.

"The voices are still directing us on to New Orleans." she replied.

"Voices?" Culant asked.

"My friend, we know little to nothing about you—," D'Aulon started.

"The time has come for us to stop being secretive. I have a calling and if I keep it to myself it will not be given the attention it needs to gain momentum. I know that you my friends are only being cautious but that time is gone," Jehanne said.

"If you say so," Severe said.

"Louis de Culant, my name is Jehanne la Pucelle. Does this mean anything to you?"

"As a child we all heard of an avenging angel that would fill us all with hope for a better tomorrow. The angel would carry that name," he replied.

"And I also carry that hope. Will you make us thirteen or will you make your own way?" Jehanne asked.

"I'll support you and your calling in any way asked. I have many Mundane friends across many Communes and cities. I can spread your word in short order. What would you have of me?" Culant asked.

"We'll know better when we pass Les Augustins and reach New Orleans. For now, tell us everything that you saw, heard, or even smelled. Something must be in the details that can aid us in understanding this unusual situation." The group listened to Culant's encounter once again. This time they asked questions and bandied theories about as they walked. The time passed quickly, soon they were engulfed in a night sky and they set up camp.

"I still find nothing from his story that makes sense," Pouli said after camp was set up and they all were sitting by the fire.

"Are you calling me a liar simply because I am Mundane? Does that make me untrustworthy?" The man stood and made ready to leave.

"You are not the only Mundane in this camp my friend. Sit, no one is questioning your honesty. It's the message in the story that's eluding us," Jehanne said.

"I see only Augmented here unless the Entity is some kind of born again Mundane." Culant laughed at his own joke.

"Until very recently I was Joanna667."

"The word of your death spread very quickly. It brightens my heart to know I didn't lose that wager after all."

"Come again?" John2 asked.

"After the word of the Mundane that won the highest levels of the Un Sukiru halls got out, a man was taking bets in the distillery of how long it would be until the Entities killed you. I said that they would not. My thinking was it would be too big a deal. He insisted after you died that the Entities had killed you and on the day he said. A lot of the other patrons of the establishment paid him. I refused."

"I can't believe——," Jehanne started.

"What that people were betting on your death? La Hire imagines if we make it to New Orleans, there will be many bets placed on the date you'll die."

"You should all get some rest. I will stand watch and wake you just before dawn," Deark said.

Jehanne's sleep was fitful at best. She dreamt she was fighting against the Entities in the Coliseum. The seats around the giant building were completely full and somewhere there was a fast talking person taking bets as she confronted each Entity. Behind her Culant's voice kept saying, "Don't die or my dog will get killed."

"La Pucelle, wake up. You're dreaming," Minguet said.

"I won't let your dog get killed!" she yelled as she sat up.

"Well ok then." D'Aulon smirked as her yell woke the entire camp.

"We might as well hit the trail, we're all awake," Pouli said.

"I'm sorry." Jehanne looked as if she might cry.

"I think the only one who should be sorry would be me," Gilles said. "How am I to stay so pretty if I keep getting denied my beauty sleep." The laughter was good medicine.

"The daylight shows that you've broken my heart. Love and hate are but a door's closing apart. When I turned to see you subdued, I didn't foresee us being apart. The very fiber of my soul coming unglued. As I know it was my deeds that made you depart." La Hire's speech, cadence and mannerisms could not be distinguished from Gilles as he read the poem in the near dawn light.

"You! How did you—," the gilded Augmented's anger was cut off.

"La Hire told you it was from one of those pretty poems you jot down."

"But how?"

"La Hire called in a favor."

"Who? Which of these Neanderthals could possibly break into my augmentations?"

"La Hire thinks some of us are more than dimples. Besides, it is really good." The teasing continued even as Jehanne looked over at D'Aulon, who responded with a wink.

Section Two – Chapter Five

The group walked together in a silence that was upsetting to Jehanne. She wondered if La Hire's prank had unwittingly been the demise of her little group. "My friends, being an agent of change and my reliance on all of you has me concerned at the moment."

"Why is that?" John2 asked.

"This silence, it feels like sides are being doled out for a major escalation, following the, with no other words I will use 'violation' earlier."

"Violation is a good word and that's something we shouldn't do to our friends," Gilles said.

"The violation aside, my concern in all this is much deeper than this individual episode. I felt safe knowing my augmentations couldn't be hacked. Now it turns out I've been playing the fool," Pouli said, de Metz indicated his agreement as well.

"So the promise of 'it won't happen again,' really isn't even on the table, the information of how it was done needs to be shared," De Metz demanded looking at La Hire.

"La Hire didn't know it could be done until Poton and La Hire were members of this group."

"Listen, it isn't an ability that can be used by others. I have the only chip that was successfully installed. Once it worked I destroyed the research," D'Aulon said.

"So who knows of this ability?" Severe asked.

"Myself and Charles up until two days ago."

"When you what, bragged about it to La Hire?" Kennedy asked, his accent displaying his scorn.

"La Hire caught him," the stocky Augmented said.

"I still don't understand how but yes, as I scanned to see if he meant harm to La Pucelle, he did in fact catch me scanning him and more than that he identified me."

"So how is it that you do it? Can you at least share that with us?" de Metz asked.

"I have no problem with sharing that information with any in the party except him," D'Aulon pointed at Culant. "I've no way to know if he is here to hurt La Pucelle and as he even knows I can hack modies I am filled with the desire to see him dead."

"Well now, I thought for certain you were speaking of the Entity but as I would hate for my heart, which I have and he of course doesn't, to stop beating, how about if I just walk ahead a bit while you share your little elitist secrets and you can catch up to me when you're done," Culant said.

"I'm good with that," Jehanne said.

"Very well, head in that direction," D'Aulon said.

"But that's not the—," Culant started.

"It's up wind, the echoes won't carry far." Culant began walking in the direction that D'Aulon was pointing.

"Kind of a hardass aren't you?" Severe asked.

"Language!" La Hire said, raising his staff as Jehanne smiled.

"Perhaps I'm being too tough, but we are all here to protect the Maid. There is little I would risk to betray that, and if he's offended, he needs to see the bigger picture," D'Aulon said.

"I believe he is out of earshot. I can barely make him out on my eye augmentation," Jehanne said.

"Here is the secret, I didn't hack his Modi. I hacked the NanoTech."

"I can't believe that's possible," Deark said.

"I assure you my friend, they can be communicated with and more than that—," D'Aulon started.

"Hold up," Jehanne said. "Culant is running this way." Just then the Mundane's words could be heard.

"They're coming!" he yelled.

"Who, Jehanne who's coming?" Minguet asked.

"I don't see anything. Oh goodness there's something out there racing up quickly on Culant. We need to get to him first." She sprinted in the direction of their newest comrade.

"Jehanne wait," Deark said to no avail. "What if it's a trap!"

"Then it's a good one," she replied, not breaking stride.

"La Hire is not meant for these sprinting things that La Pucelle likes to inflict on us."

"Something is running up on us," Culant said as they were close together. "What is it?"

"I know not, but it's not an 'it', there are several creatures," Jehanne said. "Come together my friends, back to back." The ground shook as the unknown group closed on their position.

"Are any of you known as La Pucelle?" a melodic voice called out of the darkness.

"I am. Please come closer and show yourselves."

"We've searched for you for many days," the newcomer said as it came closer. The strange thing about the voice was that it came from several feet higher in the air than even Gilles, the tallest man in their party.

"You've found me. It seems however, you have me at a disadvantage. You know who I am yet I know only that you and your party are riding on the backs of horses. Please dismount and let's all walk back to our camp where we can talk," Jehanne said.

"My name is Enyeto." The man dismounted and led his steed into the heart of the group. He stood a full head taller than La Hire and was as broad. "It means walks as a bear," his speech was slow as if it were not his primary language.

"I'm very pleased to meet you. And I believe I speak for one of my traveling party when I say, I'm so happy to see your horses," Jehanne said."

"As I said we have traveled many days," he said as they reached the place where they had camped. The sun was finally giving some light to the group. Enyeto traveled with nine others yet they had more than twice as many horses.

"Why have you been searching for me?" Jehanne asked interrupting him.

Joanna667

"For many years we have had the luxury of living outside the rule of Tumse Neho," his statement was cut off.

"Who?" John2 got out first.

"The bloodless ones. I'm sorry I'll try to do better at translations. We speak very little English these days. In recent weeks we have had several visits from Waquini, the man that's the Advisor to the current Leader of the Republicus, telling our leaders that there will be changes coming soon and that the best thing we can do is not stand in the way of progress. The councils from all the tribes gathered and decided that we are now one tribe, the Unified Indian Nation. We have three objectives that must be fulfilled, to stop the Too Ya La Kekt," Enyeto said.

"If I may inquire," Deark started.

"We did not know you traveled with a bloodless," one of Enyeto's fellows said.

"I did Wicasa, my brother. This one was called Apenimon by the Alo," Enyeto replied.

"Worthy of trust?" Wicasa pulled in his chin, looking surprised.

"I like that, yes that's a good name for me," Deark said. "I'm sorry but I know of no advisor to the High Leader that goes by Waquini. Also what is it you said you're trying to stop?"

"It's not his name it's simply what we call him it means the hooked nose man—," his words were cut off when Jehanne laughed, as she remembered the man that walked down the stairs at the Stone Room.

227

"That would be the Duke of Bedford, or John Lancaster, depending on what day of the week or the audience he has. He changes what he calls himself," John2 said, the distaste in his voice palpable.

"Yes he referred to himself as John, the Duke of Bedford to us. We are trying to stop the Too Ya La Kekt, the thunder arriving on the valley. The Alo feel that something on the horizon will spark the end of everything. The world itself will crack," Enyeto said.

"That will come if the Entities kill off all the humans. Politician said they will then begin fighting amongst themselves and the earth will no longer have the will to survive," Jehanne said.

"Yes, that's what our Alo said as well," he replied.

"What are the three things you need to do? Maybe we can work together?" De Metz asked.

"My thanks for the offer. The three objectives are made up of many tasks, a multitude of things to do and places to be. We must help all Three Qaletaqa, sorry, the three guardians of man fulfill their callings. While our paths will cross from time to time, they must remain separate in order to stabilize existence. For now we needed to bring the Halian Eluwilussit these tashunka," he indicated the horses, "to help her on this stage of her calling."

"La Hire got that tashunka means horse but Halian El-whatsits, La Hire got lost there?"

"Sorry, Halian Eluwilussit is the young holy one," he indicated Jehanne. "Aside from helping her in any way that we can, we must wait for the Pauwau and the Aditsan to find their paths to break these chains of kestejoo."

"The Witch and the Listener need to discover their roles as Qaletaqa just as you Jehanne have found yours, in order for them to break the chains of slavery for all humans," Wicasa translated.

"That's all we can share, we would like you to—," Enyeto started.

"Have you been the cause of the terrorist attacks?" Jehanne asked.

"I don't know that I would call it terrorism." Wicasa smiled from the back of his horse.

"We need to go, our path is long. Jehanne the UIN want you and your Zonta Chikasha to have these thirteen horses," Enyeto said.

The group all looked over at Wicasa, "Trusted Rebels."

"Yes, sorry, Trusted Rebels, you my friends have started the Trusted Rebels. We've built protections into the saddles to prevent the horses or anything on them from being stolen should you need to leave them and walk. All you need do is grasp the front and the back of the saddle on the left side, and hold it for three seconds to initiate these defenses. Once they are set, only the being that set them can deactivate them by performing the same process."

"So don't run up to someone else's horse and think you can turn off their protection and mount that horse." Wicasa added.

"This is most kind. Please pass along my appreciation to the UIN," Jehanne said.

"La Hire is nervous that La Hire's augmentations may break the backs of these beautiful creatures."

"These are draft horses. I assure you they'll have no issue with your weight. I've seen them carry I-CAM units on their backs." Enyeto's smile did not get missed by the group as he got back on his horse. "La Pucelle, may I say the promise of flames would have swayed many more seasoned from a calling such as yours. Our thoughts and prayers of strength are with you."

"Thank you for your kind words," she replied. And with that, the terrorists were off.

******

A white steed walked straight up and nuzzled her as she watched the clouds of dust heading off. "I think you have a fan, Jehanne," John2 said.

"And I think when this is all over you will have the horses for your stable my friend." She smiled at the man as he ran his hand over a chestnut filly.

"Did you notice there are swords and scabbards alongside the saddles?" Poton asked.

"Do you think we're being set up?" D'Aulon asked.

"How so?" Jehanne asked.

"Well, the sword that cut down Congressional Entity Blithe may be here, and horse tracks—,"

"Hoof prints," John2 interjected, launching himself into the saddle.

"La Hire is fine with being set up, La Hire hates walking." This brought a round of chuckles from the group.

"Alright, let's mount up and start heading to Les Augustins," Jehanne said. After a few minutes the group were all mounted and riding like they were born in the saddle. By the time noon came around they could see Les Augustins.

"More smoke," Pouli said.

"But everything looks intact," Jehanne said, zooming in as tight on the town as she could. "On a positive note, it looks like their city hall could hold that transport ship."

"Can you tell if they're loading yet?" Deark asked.

"The doors on the ship are all closed, but there is no heat signature from the engines. I don't know what that means but that's what my Modi says."

"It means the engines are off," John2 said.

"That means we can get there before they empty another town," Culant said, giving his horse a kick. The group followed riding hard and fast, finding the town surrounded by what from a distance just looked like CAM units. The first laser bolt struck the ground to the side of the group.

"La Hire tastes a good fight coming on."

"Take this my friend." Jehanne tossed him her dragonweave cape. "I have my buckler to keep me safe."

"La Hire will use it well," he said, wrapping the material around his wrist as the rest of their group fell back. La Hire and Jehanne then kicked the flanks of their horses harder to close the gap on the laser shooting W-CAM units. As a bolt found its way to them, she would either send it back to them or he would take the shot into the cape, which would then dissipate it in several hundred small sparks that sang out as they shot everywhere. "La Hire would like to see these at night," he joked as a fresh bolt echoed off the cape.

"I imagine it would be quite pretty." Jehanne sent a bolt back into a W-CAM unit, which gave them a respite.

'Very nicely placed.' The echo of Protectorate's voice played in her head. 'Remember child one, two, three.'

"Yes'm," Jehanne said as she engaged the first row of CAM units. 'Their swords are exactly as the ones I fought against in the Coliseum.' She thought.

'Of course they're the same.' Protectorate scoffed.

"La Hire, they are attempting to flank to the left," she called out and they redirected the attack to meet the most critical threat. Although fighting from horseback was different it had its advantages, the largest being sight over the enemy.

******

As in her training her attacks went in an arc, yet constantly moving in the direction of the end goal, getting in the city to stop the vessel from taking the people away. Behind her, she heard the other members of her party engaging the enemy.

"We need to push these normal units into the World upgrades to stop them from shooting their lasers," she said.

"La Hire is surprised that they haven't slowed their firing thus far. The fools are taking out more of their own troops with friendly fire than La hire and Jehanne are with our swords."

"Bit of an exaggeration," she said. "Forward in Politician's name!" She once again gave a kick to her white beast, forcing the spacing between the Entities to tighten. "My friends, I need you to keep these Bloodless from coming up behind us!" The two riders in the front stayed between the W-CAMs and the rest of their party. In no time she could see the backs of the green and the burgundy Entities making for the ship which took flight as the thirteen members of Jehanne's party struck down the remaining CAM units.

"The cowards flee!" Gilles yelled.

"Let them go and check the town for survivors!" Jehanne ordered.

"No need," Deark replied, pointing at the humans walking out of the homes and shops that lined the dirt street that made up the center of town.

"We're saved! Thanks be to la Pucelle!" the cheers welcomed them as they rode through the waiting throngs of Mundane and Augmented.

"Are you her? Are you Jehanne?" a short, round Augmented asked.

"Yes sir, and you are?"

"I'm D'Chain the Mayor of this town."

"What happened here?" John2 asked.

"The Entities said it was time for us to leave this area. They said they had a new home for us," the same Augmented said.

"Another home?" Jehanne asked.

"Yes, we were supposed to get our belongings together and be ready in the morning to leave for it. That was when you showed up. The Commander of Human Asset

Management left at that point with one of the advisors to the High Leader."

"Let me guess, the Duke of Bedford?" John2 inquired.

"Yes exactly. I know not where this battle will lead us, but you have our support and gratitude."

"I have a feeling before it's all over both will be needed." Jehanne rode her horse to the center of the town square and faced the crowd. "My fellow humans, today was the day that we stood at the crossroads and recognized we could no longer take the easy path. Choices have been taken away. The Entities care not if they strip the identity of all humans, whether Augmented or Mundane. For this is what we face, the loss of our identity as a species. We do have a choice; we can either determine that we are humans not Augmented, not Mundane, just humans, or we can elect to stay apart and by doing this die as individuals." Jehanne turned her horse and began to ride away.

"But what can we do? We can't band our numbers together and destroy them," a voice called from those listening.

"No I'm not saying to rise up, and you're right, we lost last time. Why was that? Whether we like it or not, a long time before the Entities had even risen, tomorrow had died. Tomorrow was too hard for the humans of so long ago and they gave up on it before our fathers were even passing thoughts. Please understand, I bear them no ill will, they simply looked inside themselves and saw how good they had been. Forgetting that making the tough decisions so they could move forward was part of tomorrow, and laurels were never supposed to be rested upon as an option."

"Why don't you hate them for it?" a woman's voice asked.

"Because as far as I can tell until today, this side of the grave or that, bore no distinction from such repose of our laurels." The comment which was fed to her by Politician was met with silence. "In other words, we have put forth no effort to move forward either. My friends and I have further to ride, my calling awaits. For now we need to dispose of the fallen Entities."

Several hours later the group was back on their horses and heading to New Orleans. The trip was dark even though it was midday, it was quiet though the wind blew hard enough for Jehanne's cape to stand out straight. The group rode with an unease that didn't fit with what they'd just accomplished.

"La Hire needs to ask, what waits for us?" His words startled even the horses, as the sound was so unexpected.

"My friend, what lies ahead of us is the next step of this calling. Ahead of us is where the new gods are telling us to go. What that means, I would not hazard to guess," she smiled back at him and then she looked at all of them in turn. Not a single one looked the same as the day they met, even the last of their group, aside from the unregistered arm augmentations he had been given, he looked changed, more confident and poised.

"La Hire expected that would be the answer. Gilles, do you have any motivational poems in that private directory to get us ready to face the unknown?"

"I can pull something out if la Pucelle is ok with it," he replied.

"Yes of course," Jehanne said.

"Not knowing what comes next is no different than facing the planting of our fields when we know our children will need to eat. Our self-doubt is the rain that doesn't fall, stopping the seeds from germinating. Our insecurities are the parasites that feed on blossoms, not allowing the vegetation to thrive. The unknown future is full of so many variables that preparing for them all would be impossible, yet the details that we've missed must be adjusted for or they will be the weeds that will choke our crops, killing the harvest, as our families starve. We, my friends, have no choice in what is about to occur, we need to strive to meet it understanding that we are our worst barrier to success, it's all up to us now," Gilles said.

"La Hire is impressed considering La Hire was joking."

"You really are good Gilles," Jehanne said.

"Thank you dear girl."

******

They arrived in New Orleans as the sun was setting. The city entrance was open and unguarded. Jehanne looked up at the tall wall as they rode under it, noticing its height as well as the strange outer door that was several meters wider than the opening. "Why do you suppose this wall is so much taller than my Mother City and what's that door?"

"Their wall doubles as a levy, in times of flood. The door looks to be a modified portcullis, and keeps the flood waters out as well," Deark replied. They kept the horses at a slow walk to avoid the large holes in the road. The sound of the hooves echoing off the ruins that gave the indication of an old and grand city.

"They also have the Commune, where all the Mundane live, inside the main wall for that reason," John2 added. "We'll find three actual walls here, each is shorter than the previous."

"Each of the areas are classified as 'Wards' here. This is the outer ward and the informational boards say it's broken into six sections," Minguet said. "We just entered through Ward One gate. There are also entrance gates in the third and fifth wards. The middle ring is where the Augmented live. The only entrance into that area is in what appears to be called the French Quarter, even though the middle ring is in three sections."

"Must be something to do with the city's history," Culant said.

"The last bit of information that seems useful is in the center area, where the Entity's live. It's set up as one large circle, the Tenth Ward. In the center there's a fourth wall." Minguet looked smugly at John2.

"I stand corrected." He inclined his head.

"Inside this wall is an arena, called Les Tourelles. Believe it or not, the fourth wall is surrounded by a large moat and the only way in is across a drawbridge," Minguet said.

"I've found several courthouses in the registry section of the Boards, but no mention of the trial or where it may be," D'Aulon said. The streets were empty as they rode through the outer ring. Each time they saw a Mundane it would only be their back as they ran from the horses.

"La Hire thinks the people in New Orleans are afraid of horses. Should we tie them up some place?"

"While I disagree with why, I do think we should tie them up," D'Aulon said.

"Well La Hire will take what comes." He winked.

"Kennedy and I can take them back to the city gate," Severe said.

"Let's find where the trial is and then you can do that." Jehanne dismounted and led her white stallion by the reins. Each in turn followed her example, La Hire being the last.

"La Hire, would you mind taking my horse? I'll run ahead and see if I can get someone to tell me where the trial for Charles is being held," Deark said.

"Why would these—," La Hire's words stalled as Deark once again formed into Father Jean Pasquerel. "Oh, well good luck."

"Thank you my brother." The Augmented priest sped off to find help, which didn't take long. "It is at the local arena Minguet spoke about, the one called Les Tourelles." He gave directions to Severe and Kennedy and they remounted, taking the reins of the rest of the horses and returned to Ward One Gate.

The remaining eleven, having no idea what to expect, headed in the direction that the unwitting Mundane had told Deark.

"La Hire didn't know it would be so far when Severe took the horses," he said as they crossed the second wall and got a glimpse of Les Tourelles, raised up gloriously above the rest of the buildings.

"Listen. You and your band of Merry Men," a voice from a window above them said, "are not welcome in the French Quarter, or in any part of New Orleans for that matter."

"We aren't the Merry Men, we're the Trusted Rebels." La Hire corrected.

"Makes sense an oxymoron name for a group of morons." A different Augmented on the street said.

"Oh quite good Gaucourt my friend." The man in the window said.

"You know nothing of us, let us pass we—," Jehanne started as she put a hand on La Hire's chest to stop him from attacking.

"We know who you are." Gaucourt cut her off. "You're the one the outposts are declaring is la Pucelle the one that speaks with the new gods," a different Augmented said.

"Then the outposts have the right of it," Minguet said. "She is Jehanne la Pucelle and she has been visited by five of the Six."

"Heresy," the group around them all said.

"I think the fact that we destroyed ten times our number in CAM units earlier today is a larger offense," Poton said.

"Did you hear that Dunois, they're proud of that stupidity?" Gaucourt directed his question to the man in the window.

"Are you single handedly trying to destroy the human race, you foolish child?" the one called Dunois asked. By now several hundred Augmented had filled the streets of the French Quarter.

"No my friend, quite the opposite. I'm here on a calling that in the end will save both the human race and the earth itself," Jehanne said.

"You won't find one here that gives a rip about the so-called 'calling' of yours. You're a child, obviously an imaginative child," Dunois chided.

"And what would you think if I were to say, Pedagogue told me I am to keep her safe for she is important in what is to come?" Deark said, in his own form.

"I would say that Chameleon Class K Entities are known as the best of liars," the same man said.

"We don't want to, nor will we fight you," Jehanne said.

"That's probably a smart move, we have you out-numbered by more than twenty to one, and we've not been instructed to not hurt you, la Pucelle," Dunois said.

Section Two – Chapter Six

"What are you talking about?" Jehanne asked.

"Listen to her boys! She thinks that she and twelve of the most rag-tag band of puppets defeated such a large quantity of Conditional Attitude Maintainers. I can't believe how stupid you are child, you and your group. Now get out before we throw you out," Dunois said.

Jehanne ran away in a flood of tears. She ran back in the direction they had come from and stopped once she was out of earshot. She sat down, leaning against a crumbling building, wiping tears from her eyes and massaging a stitch from her side as the rest of the party caught up.

"Are you ok?" D'Aulon asked.

"I am. They just don't understand. I know I've got to go back but how can I make them understand what I've, er ah… what we've been through?" she replied.

"When it comes down to it dear child, it really has never been what you or any of us have been through to get here. It's been about Charles and the effect that getting him into office will have on the human race. Even more importantly, its effect on the entire planet," Deark said.

"I know, it's just been a lot. I'm so tired."

"La Hire originally wondered why it was that the Six picked you. Why did they choose a child? La Hire has come to understand in our limited time it's because they know you can take on all these challenges, you have the spark of a dreamer, the innocence to believe people will follow you, and the confidence that when they do a difference can be made.

Those traits have gotten us to this point. You need to show a couple more aspects of yourself that La Hire has seen in you; the fear of what the result will be if you don't get up when knocked down, and the understanding that if you quit it is forever."

"The words they threw at you back there were but wind. It's clear that sometimes wind can be more cataclysmic than a sword, their words however were but a breeze," Gilles added.

"That didn't even tussle his beautiful locks," La Hire japed.

"Are you ready?" de Metz held a hand down to her.

"Aye, there is no crying in callings," Jehanne said, allowing champion number one to pull her to her feet.

******

"Severe, Kennedy we are here," Pouli said as the other two members of their party ran past them.

"Aye lass what are you doing back here?" Kennedy asked.

"The word of what we did in Les Augustins has reached the city and been spun into a very good public relations move against Jehanne by Madam Commander and the Advisors to the High Leader," Deark said.

"I don't understand," Severe commented.

"They're already spreading lies about us," Culant said.

"Oh, but hey isn't that a good thing? I mean doesn't that mean they're afraid?" he asked.

"There is truth in that statement," John2 said. "Yet that's definitely not a good thing. They will do one of two things; make us laughingstocks, or crush us into powder."

"So why are they choosing the former?" Minguet asked.

"Good question," La Hire said.

"Actually, let's head back," Deark said. "The fact that they haven't crushed us is where the good news is. They already see a movement starting, they know destroying Jehanne will result in a problem for them." He finished speaking as they reached the gate that led back to the French Quarter.

"Are you ready?" D'Aulon asked.

"I will take all the encouragement that you've all given me and open them up to the truth with my final aspects." She smiled at La Hire. "And if that doesn't work then I guess the time has come for my sword to be unsheathed and I'll open them up with the skills Protectorate taught me."

******

"Look, the savior of man is favoring us with her appearance again!" Dunois shouted from his window perch.

"What was it that made you feel you weren't enough?" Jehanne looked up and asked him in an even and calm voice. "That what you were trying to accomplish in your life would fail because you lacked one or more of the essential elements?" Jehanne asked.

"Are you being a smartass?" the man asked from the window.

"I would ask that you check your language, but no I'm not kidding."

"It was when I lost my legs, how did you know? And don't tell me it was one of your god visions that told you," Dunois scoffed.

"I needed to get your attention. These people respect you and see that there is more to you than legs that can no longer adapt to augmentations. You're the General that led more than one hundred sorties against uprisings across the globe. These people see that, even though you don't," Jehanne said. There were several moments of silence and then the people in the street began agreeing with her.

"She's right Dunois, you're the best of us!" Gaucourt said.

"And you Captain, my eyes on the ground. Fine, Jehanne how can we help you?" Dunois said.

"The day is waning, tell us how to get to the trial of Charles Valois." The group gave them the easiest path to reach the arena.

"You know they will be watching for you to crash the proceedings," Dunois said.

"We'll need to face that bridge when we come to it," Jehanne said.

"La Hire sees what you did there!" he laughed so hard he let out a little snort, which started everyone else laughing.

"Jehanne, I know where my responsibilities lie, however I think I may be able to help this Dunois," de Metz said.

"I think we would be wrong to not try. Join us when you can my friend. Severe, did you set protection on the horses?"

"We each did," Severe replied.

"Can you both stay with de Metz in case we need them?" Jehanne asked.

"Aye lass," Kennedy replied.

"Thank you," she replied, taking the rest of the group heading to face their next challenge.

******

The infrastructure in these wards was significantly different. The buildings although old, were still in good shape. The streets would have been much better for the horses as there were no holes or cracks. As they came to the third wall, the group stopped as if to admire the gray mass that grew from the city, showing no signs of age, not even a single weed growing up it.

"Halt. What business do you have in the Mother City?" a CAM unit asked.

"We are Baudricourt's assistants. We must find our way to the trial," Pouli said.

"Very well, will the young lady be accompanying you?" the Entity asked.

"She will," Pouli answered, looking around at the rest of the party.

"The trial is actually just getting underway. Please proceed directly to Les Tourelles."

"We will, thank you. After you miss," Pouli said, waiting for everyone to enter ahead of him.

"Was that you D'Aulon?" Jehanne asked as they walked through the pure white buildings and streets.

"It was," he said, taking a small step sideways.

"Are you alright?" John2 asked.

"Yes. Using that isn't like using any other Modi, makes me feel disoriented for a while after I call on it," D'Aulon replied.

"I can't believe we haven't missed the trial," Deark said.

"Why do you suppose they are starting so late?" Poton asked.

"They're broadcasting the final decision when they reach it," Jehanne said.

"Could they have decided to broadcast the entire trial?" Minguet asked.

"Does it say anything on the informational boards?" Gilles asked.

"Actually, the connection to the Boards is gone," John2 said.

"La Hire doesn't like the way that sounds."

"No, something is up," Deark said, looking around them.

"Should we turn back?" Culant asked.

"No, we need to see this through," Jehanne said. "I don't see anything strange at the bridge, just two W-CAM units."

"I've never tried my chip on a W-CAM unit," D'Aulon commented.

"My counsel is not to try it right now," Deark said.

"I would agree," Jehanne added.

******

They closed the gap between themselves and the bridge in no time. Not being addressed by the Entities guarding the draw-bridge, they walked purposefully forward. The exit off the bridge had them cross under another of the modified portcullis. Inside the wall surrounding Les Tourelles was a cobblestone pathway leading to the building which was well above the wall they had just passed under.

"That's far enough," the familiar voice of the Commander of Human Capital Management said from speakers next to the walk. The huge door slammed down behind them.

"Well so much for seeing it through," Culant said.

"We're not done yet. Listen to me my friends don't fight back. Just take whatever abuse they dole out in stride. Know this is but a stone in the creek. We will stand on it until we see the next purchase that we can jump to," Jehanne said.

"La Pucelle, they just re-engaged the informational boards. Our arrest is being broadcast; it's the top news," Minguet said.

"What are they saying?" Pouli asked.

"Right now the political advisor, today he's going by John, Duke of Bedford, is finishing an interview." He took a break seeing the group of W-CAM units coming down the hill toward them. "Madam Commander is up now and she's going off about the trap she set that we fell right into. Oh hey guys we're on, wave at the CAM units."

"La Hire doesn't really want to wave at them. La Hire wants to –," his words were cut off by the announcement from the speakers.

"Put your hands on your head, kneel down and do not even think of fighting back," Madam Commander's voice said.

"That was pretty cool, watching myself kneel down like that," Minguet said.

"I think that's enough of the play by play." John2 said. "They're getting close and if they don't know we can monitor their informational boards then we may hear something they don't want us to."

"Good point, maybe I shouldn't have waved."

"Humans you have been accused of several cases of insurrection, you're going to be taken before the Augmented leaders of the city for their assessment as was established by the Republicus as part of the peace accords following 'The Uprising'. My name is I-CAM Alpha, I will be escorting you back to the Courthouse in the Ninth Ward. Turn that sword over to me for safe keeping."

"Hello again I-CAM Alpha. I'm certain this is a misunderstanding, as was the shirt episode," Jehanne said, hoping they were still broadcasting as they waited for the gate to be raised again while she held out the relic.

"For your sake, I hope that it is," he replied, taking the bundle and attaching it to his side. The Entities bound their hands behind their backs and each was guided by an individual Entity. "There were supposed to be thirteen. What happened to the last three?"

"The W-CAM lasers struck them at Les Augustins," John2 said.

"That doesn't match the encounter report I was given," Alpha replied as he pushed Jehanne roughly, making her fall to the ground.

"Well that's good, someone call whoever is in charge of mistaken death's encounter division and tell them that de Metz, Severe and Kennedy aren't supposed to be dead," Culant said.

"Another of Baudricourt's aides, very interesting."

"As if you didn't know each of the identities, ass!" John2 snapped as they walked under the gates from Ward Ten and back into the Augmented side of the second wall.

"Language," La Hire said in unison with Jehanne.

"Seriously?"

"We must maintain the proper level of decorum else we will fall into that poor behavior should we be set free," Jehanne replied.

"As if that's going to happen," Alpha laughed, the tinny high pitched laugh of a young girl.

"La Hire thinks they put the wrong laugh track in you big boy."

"This big boy thinks you should stop referring to yourself by name, you sound like a goofball."

"Oh dear," Poton whispered.

"A goofball eh?" La Hire snapped the restraints and flipped the I-CAM unit that was escorting him into a building sending a few loose bricks flying.

"That was a very bad idea," Alpha said, once again pushing Jehanne to the ground and turning to meet La Hire. At that moment several Augmented jumped down from above.

"I don't think it was as bad an idea as you leading them into our trap," a voice from overhead said.

"De Metz? It seems the complaint department works fast!" Pouli said as his friend, along with Severe and Kennedy jumped into the fray, handing everyone the swords that had been left on the horses.

******

As the CAM units were dispatched, Jehanne called out, "Do not injure that one." She pointed at Alpha.

"As you say." La Hire sheathed his sword and began battling with the staff and his fists. As Alpha had been upgraded with several new attachments it made him significantly more agile and difficult to defeat, especially with the restriction of not hurting him.

"Much," Jehanne added after seeing the tides of battle.

"Thank you," La Hire said as he grabbed Alpha's arms and swung him into the building several times, like smacking a baseball bat on a tree, except eventually the building fell down trapping Alpha. "That should hold him."

"Ok then a bit of help here!" Minguet was doing ok fending for himself, yet the battle would never be decided like that. As La Hire closed in, a new Augmented joined their ranks, lifting the Entity into the air with one arm and running it through with a sword. The Augmented pulled the sword down cutting the Entity in half, like a chef's knife cutting an Empress Crab. The two pieces fell on either side of the boy.

"Ha Ha!" the new comer said.

"Who be this new comer?" La Hire asked.

"I've been called many things, rogue, scoundrel and even miscreant, but the Bastard of New Orleans fits me best," General Dunois said.

"I don't know if that's cursing or not but I will let that stand, it does seem to fit you," Jehanne said.

The fighting continued, as Alpha beneath the building apparently unharmed, called for backup. "Jehanne, they've taken us off the News feeds," D'Aulon laughed.

"Heads up another wave incoming," Poton advised.

"I think we should take this battle away from the center of the city to make certain we don't hurt anyone," Jehanne said.

"The issue with that is reclaiming our prize here," La Hire said.

"Jehanne I've done a scan and detect no life forces in these buildings. While we may destroy these few structures, we can assist in building later. Should we move and get caught up in a populated area we could do real damage," Deark gave his council.

"Thank you my friend," Jehanne said. "We stay here and fight." At one point the Entities flew over them in a strange vehicle, loosing several laser volleys that Jehanne redirected nimbly back at them. Just as the battle sounds broke around them the sound of thousands of marching Entities could be heard walking in unison.

"That doesn't sound good," Kennedy said.

"Bah, the sound of target practice approaching. It sounds glorious to La Hire."

"Minguet, D'Aulon, I need you to do me a favor." She whispered to them and they took off.

'Pioneer, any chance you could accidently drop a few of these shields down here?' she thought with all her being.

'I believe if you check the W-CAM units, they shoot through what appears to be the exact same reflective material. Perhaps it's a protection from rebound to their gun port?' The voice was more controlled than last time he projected into her head yet still too loud, driving her to her knees.

"Are you alright?" Poton asked.

"Yes, I'm fine."

"No you're not, you're bleeding," Deark said.

"You've been shot," Severe added.

"Listen to me. The center section on the W-CAMs, where their laser shoots out is the same material as my buckler. Seek out their fallen, strip this material from that area, you'll need to use something to reinforce the backing to reflect the..." her words faded as she crumpled to the ground.

******

She woke, staring at the familiar mountains only the face of an unfamiliar woman stood over her. "Come my child I will show you the way to the other side."

"Passage?"

"Yes," the stocky woman said.

"Did I die?" Jehanne asked.

"That's enough teasing, get away from her," Physician's voice said.

"No dear you didn't die, you'll be fine. You need to remember that cloak. Now that everyone is equipped with bucklers, reclaim that cloak. But for now," Physician touched her and the laser bolt to her neck was healed.

"Go now, your friends are getting discouraged. Take the higher ground, move your group onto the fallen buildings," Protectorate said. "And Jehanne, reclaim that sword as well."

"Sorry for the joke earlier. They needed me to pull you up here." Passage placed her hand over Jehanne's eyes.

"It's alright," Jehanne said.

"She's awake, guys she's awake," De Metz said. "Jehanne what's alright?"

"I'm sorry?" she inquired.

"The first thing you said when you awoke was, 'it's alright'. What did you mean?" he asked again.

"Me, I'm alright," Jehanne got to her feet. "What do we face?"

"Jehanne, your neck, it's—," de Metz words were interrupted.

"Better. It's all better!" La Hire yelled.

"The battle comes at us from all sides," John2 answered.

"We need to get to the higher ground, this crushed building will help. How are the bucklers working out?"

"They're working great," Poton replied.

"Then the higher ground will work even better. My cloak please. The new gods say I must keep it on. What word from D'Aulon and Minguet?"

"No word yet. We did hear some fighting, followed by an explosion and some smoke in the direction of Les Tourelles," Deark said, handing her the dragonweave Cloak.

"How long ago was that?" Jehanne's direct questions gave everyone comfort in her leadership. Even the seasoned General, the Bastard of New Orleans didn't question her lead.

"Less than five minutes before you woke," John2 said as they took the highest area of the fallen building, the stronger of her Augmented flattening the top.

"I will keep an eye for them to return. When they do, we will need to make a path for them."

******

The fighting lasted another hour into the dark and eventually the CAM units seemed to lose the desire to fight and headed away. The group did not give pursuit. Jehanne, seeing signs of her returning spies, ran down the mound to greet them, finding only one. "D'Aulon, where is Minguet!"

"They've captured him. I'm sorry. When he mounted the banner across the bridge he fell into the water. The last of the Entities took a chance and jumped and grabbed him. Before I could get across they sealed the portcullis with him inside."

Her eyes turned downcast and then she looked up again, focused. "Did you accomplish what I asked?"

"Yes, we did prior to him attaching the banner." With a look of pure hatred at himself, he added, "I finished flying it on this side before I left."

"La Hire needs to know what you two are babbling about."

"I sent D'Aulon and Minguet to set fire to the draw bridge," Jehanne said.

"But that didn't quite work so I made a W-CAM unit shoot it with his lasers until his laser melted," D'Aulon said.

"Was that the explosion I heard?" Poton asked.

"It was," D'Aulon let a bit of smile show. "Then Minguet set fire to what was left. It was an amazing sight."

"The news feeds are going crazy. They're calling this an invasion. And Jehanne, they're saying they have one of the leaders of the invasion in custody," John2 said.

"We need to get in there," Jehanne said.

"That'll be difficult. Since they can't get out they've dropped the portcullis and barred themselves in the Les Tourelles," D'Aulon replied.

"Then they are exactly where we need them," she said. "Poton, La hire can you two dig out our guest, Alpha, so we can get this underway?"

"La Hire will dig him up. Someone be ready with the restraints."

"On it," Poton and Severe replied.

"D'Aulon are you ready?" Jehanne asked.

"Still a bit tired from the bridge but I'll be fine," he replied, sitting down and leaning against some fallen steel.

"Here put my cloak on before we get started." As she started to unfasten the bindings from her augmentations and the cloak, her hood fell to the side.

"No!" La Hire swung his staff out, striking Jehanne in the leg and tripping her as a laser bolt missed her head by centimeters.

"Get that cloak on!" D'Aulon said.

"Ouch that hurt!" Jehanne said.

"The new gods told you to leave it on. La Hire saw a chance that La Hire would have waited for to kill La Pucelle."

"Thank you then. I'm covered, please set about making our guest more welcome so that I may get my P.A. I'm already starting to feel disorganized. Bastard, are you about?"

"La Pucell," the sound of multiple voices from street level called out.

"Hello!" she turned to find a combination of Augmented and Mundane grouped together.

"I thought you may need some encouragement like you gave me so I brought some friends." Dunois stood covered in various types of fluids. "What did you call me for?"

"I need you to see about that laser bolt that nearly killed me," Jehanne said.

Seeing that her hands were shaking, the Bastard of New Orleans, tough guy that he was, took one of her small hands in his. "Captain Gaucourt has already left with six of my finest warriors. He will sort that out." He gave a kind squeeze and let it go.

As he turned to leave, she said, "he doesn't care for me much, Gaucourt I mean."

"It isn't that he doesn't like you, it's the situation he cares not for. He asked why are we following a small child when the Bastard is whole again and could lead us to hell and back."

"What did you say to him?"

"How did you know you could get through to me?"

"I didn't," she replied.

"But you spoke as if you knew exactly what needed to be said."

"I felt as if you needed to hear what I had to say."

"That's what I told him child. He, and they," he swept his arm, bringing a cheer from the crowd, "as well as every other being out there, needs to hear what you have to say." The gruff old Bastard of New Orleans smiled and he did a little soft-shoe dance.

"De Metz, I think you need to work on more of his modies, he seems to be smiling too much." She walked over to the restrained I-CAM unit, leaving the laughter and celebration in the dark.

******

"La Hire may have done a little too much damage," he said as Jehanne arrived. The I-CAMs normally shiny burgundy carbon fiber was dull and none of the LEDs in his exposed panels were illuminated.

"He's fine," Deark said, "just playing dead. Make certain the bindings are strong and be ready for anything."

"You won't get away with this!" Alpha barked. "The High Leader isn't even in there, what are you trying to accomplish by taking his advisors?"

"You misunderstand, along with your leaders, what our goals are and have been," John2 replied.

"And what is this goal? More freedom for humans? Like what you spoke with the High Leader about on the plane?"

"That should be in the forefront of everyone's minds, but no that isn't the issue we came here to discuss. Now if you could be so kind as to contact Madam Commander with your optical camera," Jehanne said.

"That's not going to—," Alpha's protests stopped abruptly.

"I have control," D'Aulon whispered.

"You're image is being broadcasted live," John2 said.

"It appears to be worldwide," Deark added.

"Greetings to all those watching me. I should like to start by saying my name is Jehanne la Pucelle. I started my trip here to New Orleans to speak on behalf of Charles Valois and get his requested name of Charles7 reinstated and put back on the ballot for Leader of the Republicus as both were taken away illegally. The Entities in charge fear that by him being on the ballot and winning they will lose control of the dynasty they've set up for themselves. What they failed to see is that by taking him off the ballot and declaring this innocent man a common outlaw they've angered the new gods. The same new gods that they forced to give the answers to the six questions—," her words were cut off.

"We have heard enough from this council of the soon to be damned," the voice of Madam Commander boomed from Alpha's chest.

"I lost control of that side," D'Aulon's face was covered in sweat.

Section Two – Chapter Seven

"What you're trying to sell the world is that in order to get Charles Valois declared not a criminal, and that his name being on the ballot is not a bad thing for the world, you've elected to stage the largest act of insurrection since 'The Uprising' that killed millions of Entities and humans combined? Well child, we're not buying it! I think this festival of fools is at an end. Tomorrow –," her words cut off.

"I hacked into that side and muted her for now," Deark grinned, his body having transformed into a monitor so they could view the broadcast. He looked rather comical with his head on top as he waddled over to Alpha.

"Enough of your threats and your binding of human thought, creativity, and ingenuity. We are and always have been the inventors. You need to take a moment and understand that the least of us deserves respect and the best of us deserve to stand shoulder to shoulder with the best of you. We didn't start out with the goal of fighting, I told the groups that came out to greet me not to rise up, not to band our numbers together in an attempt to destroy you. It was you that decided to use force and why was that? Why do we scare all of you so much?" she nodded her head to Deark to unmute her.

"... dare you!" the first word that Madam Commander said having been cut off. "We've been gracious, almost benevolent in our overseeing of your species. For you to challenge that we are forcing your criminal behavior just to keep Charles7 off the ballot and allow Phillip le Bon to run unopposed is ridiculous."

"That you went there is quite interesting. I was simply saying you met words with lasers."

"The insinuation was apparent child," Madam Commander said.

"As you are the highest ranking official for the Republicus on this continent does it fall to you to start a war in order to meet your goals, or is there another that's pulling the strings in this?" Jehanne asked.

"Again, you insinuate—," she started, her words were quickly muted.

"There has been no insinuation Madam Commander, just a flat question. Who will pay for the vile behavior that has been exuded here? The Leader of the Republicus spoke with me recently and commented that he received no good counsel from the Augmented on his staff. High Leader, if you could show yourself on this feed I would like to address you directly with my counsel," Jehanne said and waited a moment. "While I wait to see if my words were wasted, I have a matter that I want to discuss. Earlier you referred to this as an invasion, it is not. You currently have my Personal Assistant in your custody and when this business is concluded I offer an exchange, I-CAM Alpha for my…" she stalled her words as the screen split into a third section and The Leader of the Republicus faced her.

"We're listening," was all the High Leader said.

"This all started with Charles Valois attempting to become your successor. He met the criteria that had been established but instead of just announcing his candidacy, he went one step further and changed his name. This was an attempt to get the Mundane to better associate with him. He kept his pictures from being public record and with the name Charles7, he was a shoe in for the office."

"We already know all of this girl," Archbishop Cauchon commented as a fourth feed was added. Deark promptly muted him.

"So how could this be stopped? Only through an act of the Leader of the Republicus of course," Jehanne said.

"Are you saying that we were made a puppet in all this?" he asked.

"With respect High Leader, yes, the grandest of puppets. Your advisors and staff decided that they could beat the system by holding the Mundane to the smallest of rules; things that had been allowed in the past were held up as major offenses. As an example of this a girl in the Commune de Domremy was sentenced to the National Stone Room for answering a question on a quiz."

"Preposterous! What type of question could get a child ordered to participate in the ignition of a Stone Room?" the High Leader asked.

"The Question, why was the One World Caste System formed? Her answer, because Entities had developed pride." Jehanne waited.

"And for that she was ordered to the Stone Room?" he asked. "We mean, the Six know that's actually true."

"Yes Sir, for that she was sentenced to the National Stone Room. After that she lost her mind, and went on a lengthy diatribe, using many vulgar statements. For that, her entire family was judged and found guilty of crimes against the One World Caste System. The sentence was changed to a local Stone Room ignition. I would hazard to guess that if the truth behind the increase in civil disobedience was looked at in earnest you would find there was a step change on your side not the Humans. Whether you knew it or not, High Leader."

"We'll carry out an inquest into this," the High Leader said.

"If I may, Sire," Jehanne said.

"We believe you're on a roll child and you've not asked our leave to this point."

"Please look into the threats of removing Commune status across the world. I believe you will find that a blanket declaration of; 'Deliverables are below Proper and Reasonable levels' was made and sent to each of the Elders." She looked at Deark and gave him an indication to unmute the other two.

"Who decided that? The last quarter had increased numbers," he said. "You have our word we will also look into these threats. Our Communes across the world are important to all of us."

"But what of the damage that was caused! Things must be made right!" Archbishop Cauchon yelled, not knowing that he had been unmuted.

"Reinstating Charles Valois' name back to Charles7 and putting him on the ballot will make things right," Jehanne replied.

"You cheeky little girl, I meant to New Orleans, Saint Jean le Blanc, and Les Augustins!"

"I already asked that question and answered it," she shot back. "Who in the end shall pay for this vile behavior? You ordain that I instigated this simply because you're the 'be all end all', but you're wrong. We found Saint Jean le Blanc burned to the ground and all the people removed from it. We had nothing to do with any of that. My group traveled to Les Augustins, where we were shot at by your W-CAM units. This time we stopped the people from being carried away, in the process we destroyed several hundred Conditional Attitude Maintainers."

"We had no report of this," the High Leader yelled.

"Nor I," Archbishop Cauchon said.

"I assure you both, we have no report of any CAM units being damaged much less destroyed in Les Augustins," Madam Commander said.

"Just dig them up, we buried—," Jehanne started.

"We did however, include that on the list of properties that were destroyed by these Rebels."

"Trusted Rebels, how many times does La Hire need to correct people?" he said behind Jehanne.

"The reports from the investigation states that the entire population of Les Augustins have joined her Trusted Rebel movement, but we do not know where they've gone. The remains of the town have graffiti all over it." Pictures flashed over her quarter of the screen of burned buildings with the words, 'La Pucelle', 'Trusted Rebels', and 'Ex hoc chaos! Spes nostra ad vitae fontes!' painted all over them. Her face reappeared. "Now I find it interesting that the same words are on the banner flying on my burned down drawbridge."

"You burned down Les Augustins, you bitch!" Jehanne screamed. "Where did you take them? Did you and that rodent next to you take them to live with the United Indian Nation? You told them to leave well enough alone, Waquini. Is this what your plan was? To empty Communes and Towns and move them into the middle of the nation? Why?"

"I would have to ask you to control your language miss," Archbishop Cauchon said.

"There are several items we need to address," the High Leader said. "For now we order the release of any prisoners on either side of this event. There will be no arrests under penalty of treason and Stone Room Ignition. Are we clear?"

"Of Course High Leader," the group replied.

"Then we're done here." Henry's visage was gone.

******

"La Hire thinks you did very well."

"Thank you," Jehanne replied and then turned to see that D'Aulon was passed out on the ground. "D'Aulon?" she leaned over him. "When did this happen?" her cloak was off and covering him in an instant. Several voices of protest came following her removal of the protection, but were stopped just as quickly when an unexpected voice replied.

"He passed out just after Madam Commander said something about your insinuation," I-CAM unit Alpha said.

"Then why did you continue to broadcast?" John2 asked.

"I am an Entity of Sentience. "I found the Commander's answers along with certain things I've been ordered to do by the High Leader and his advisors to be irregular. This exchange in my opinion was proper and good."

"I'll be damned," Poton said.

"Language!" La Hire smacked Poton with his staff.

"You didn't hit her when she swore," Severe said with a smile.

"Do you wish La Hire to lead the prisoner to the bridge?" He gracefully changed the subject as Jehanne's face blanched.

"I was planning on—," Jehanne started.

"I can't allow that," D'Aulon said from a semi-conscious state.

"I think it's best for La Hire to take him with the Bastard and his men. I'm not certain how much I trust that the CAM units wouldn't accidentally shoot you, Jehanne," Deark said.

"Understood. Alpha, thank you for continuing the broadcast."

"As you say, Joanna667, some things are simple misunderstandings. I think you should take this," He reached up and disconnected the camera from next to his eye illumination handing it to her. "Deark should know how to use it to get in touch of the High Leader and his advisors. Also, I believe this is yours." He handed her the bundle after which his left eye blinked out, then he turned and left with La Hire, Bastard, and others.

******

"Did he just wink?" Pouli asked.

"I believe so," Jehanne replied.

"Does that mean we have an I-CAM unit on our side?" Kennedy asked.

"I'm not certain that he is so much on our side as it may mean he won't directly try to crush us at every turn," John2 replied.

"I see both as a victory," Deark said.

"Agreed," Jehanne replied. The group set up a small camp and lit a fire.

"By the way, la Pucelle," Gilles said after they had all sat around the fire. "You told me my writing was pretty good. I must commend you on your oratory skills. You just debated against the three highest Entities in the Republicus without erring and umming. Prior to this the speeches you have given must also be recognized as brilliant. I spend hours to craft one line but you speak—," Gilles words were cut short.

"My friend I have both the advantage and the disadvantage of the new gods telling me many of my pretty words," she replied.

"Disadvantage?" Minguet asked.

"Yes, sometime—," realizing who the speaker was, Jehanne ran up and threw her arms around the boy. "I was so worried."

"I believe your fears were well founded. They were discussing whether to ignite the National Stone Room just for me or wait until they had you as well."

"The time for that will come soon enough," she said, breaking the hug and returning to sit by the fire. "As for the disadvantage I spoke of; many times I know not the words they put into my head. I feel like a fool saying something that's completely unknown to me." They all laughed.

"I think it is best if we left the city," Minguet said.

"Why?" the Bastard of New Orleans asked.

"I heard some things while I was being held, even after the High Leader ordered no arrests."

"I can show you a fast way from the city," the Bastard said.

"I was wrong about you," a voice said from behind Jehanne. She turned to see Captain Gaucourt.

"How so?"

"I thought you were nothing but a girl."

"Have I grown a lovely goatee being around my gilded friend?" she japed.

"There is more courage in you than any human, be they fully grown man or woman that I've ever met. Please accept my apology."

"There's no apology needed, but I will take a promise that if I call on you in the future you will be there," Jehanne said. To this he dropped to a knee in front of her as an answer. "Rise and be a welcome member of the Trusted Rebels."

"Thank you." Captain Gaucourt took his leave.

"D'Aulon, are you fit to travel?" Jehanne asked.

"Yes." He stood and handed the white cloak back to her. "You shouldn't have given me this. Thank you nonetheless."

"The danger for me has cleared. You however, looked like a rabbit whose ears were caught in a fan," Jehanne said. This brought a small group of chuckles as they wandered in the now silent streets.

******

After finding the exit they said goodbye to their new friends knowing their paths would cross again. Sneaking back to where Severe and Kennedy had tied the horses, they crept silently through the darkness around the perimeter of the city. They found them as morning's first light broke. Before anyone could say a word, La Hire had walked over and jumped on his horse. A moment later he was sent flying through the air, to great cheers from the others.

"La Hire doesn't understand, La Hire didn't activate the theft protection—,"

"Severe did though," Poton cut him off.

"But it's La Hire's horse."

"We should have just left it off and let someone steal it?" Severe asked.

"La Hire doesn't think anyone is stupid enough to steal from La Hire?"

"But how would—," Minguet started.

"True, only a fool would make such a blunder old friend," Poton cut the boy off. When Minguet looked over at him, Poton just shook his head sympathetically.

"What did you hear?" Culant asked as they slowed the horses to a walk.

"Who?" D'Aulon asked.

"Minguet, you said you heard things that led you to believe they were prepared to ignore the decree of the Leader of the Republicus."

"They said they already knew how to answer the stupid girl's claims, and that they also were ready to enact the second piece of their plan," he replied.

"Who was having this conversation?" Deark asked.

"I couldn't see the video but Madam Commander and John Lancaster were definitely speaking to two others," Minguet said.

"If I were to guess it would be that pig Cauchon and Phillip le Bon," John2 said.

"Why them?" Jehanne asked.

"In each of my dealings with Archbishop Cauchon, he's had nowhere near the concern for the Techno-Pagan church as he has for his own ambitions. I'm surprised he didn't throw his hat into the ring long ago."

"La Hire thinks what he wears is called a biretta not a hat."

"Yes quite right, it's an old term for saying running for office," John2 explained.

"La Hire doesn't understand why someone would say something that means something else if the new phrase is longer."

"He has a point," Jehanne replied with a grin at John2.

"I suspect they have a plan for the next three world elections." Deark facilitated the conversation back on track.

"That makes sense. Phillip le Bon would succeed Sir Henry, then the Commander of Human Capital, that would give enough time to shift the stigma of a leader of the Techno-Pagan church becoming a leader of the world," De Metz said.

"Where does John Lancaster play into this? He's an Augmented. Why wouldn't he want Charles to be the Leader of the Republicus?" D'Aulon asked.

"He and his nose really only care about being viewed as the most austere Augmented in the world," Gilles said.

"I believe you are correct," John2 replied.

"So what do we do to counteract what they already have in motion?" Severe asked as they rode into view of Les Augustins.

"They really did burn it down," Jehanne said, breaking the flow of the conversation.

"There's an announcement hitting all open channels," Minguet said.

"Jehanne," John2 kicked his horse catching up to her. "Charles Valois has regained the name Charles7, and is back on the ballot." The group threw their hands in the air cheering, jumping from their horses and hugging in joy, with the smoke of the fallen town overshadowing them with its subliminal message, 'You've won nothing.'

******

After a day of hard riding, the group passed the remnants of Saint Jean le Blanc and arrived back in Saint Loup, receiving a royal welcome, the Augmented and Mundane freely cheering for Jehanne and pledging their support for Charles7. The trains had apparently not returned to this Commune since the one that had dropped them off.

"Then we just keep riding I guess," Deark said.

"I agree. We need to return to Chicago. Charles7 is not in office yet," Jehanne said.

"Let's replenish our supplies and see if there are any tents in the general store," D'Aulon said, taking half the group to stock up on supplies and de Metz headed off looking for camping gear. A short time later they regrouped at the center of town ready to depart.

"La Pucelle," a voice called out. "Have you unsheathed the sword yet?"

"I have not. I still hope that I will not have to unsheath this or any other sword ever again. The fact that to date we have only needed to call on such weapons to defend ourselves should speak to the purity of our cause," she replied.

"Please stay for a celebratory feast in Charles7's name," a group of Augmented as well as the Commune's Elders asked before Jehanne's group could get on their horses.

"La Hire thinks one night of rest before we start the long trek home is a good idea. La Hire is already saddle sore."

"Very well then, one night, but we will pay for supplies to be used in this celebration. I insist," Jehanne said.

"I believe that goes against the code of hospitality," the large-chested Elder said.

"I believe, Guild Master, she will make us leave if you don't acquiesce to her request," Deark said.

"Very well then, we will agree to this odd arrangement." the other of the Elders replied.

"Is there a place where we can get feed and water for the horses?" John2 asked.

"Yes, we have stables," the man that had picked up Ophena130025 on their last visit said.

"And will I get to see your beautiful daughter?" Jehanne asked.

"You will Miss. She will help in tending your magnificent horses as she recently helped with another group of travelers."

"Enyeto and his fellows?" Pouli asked.

"Yes that was the leader's name. You know them?" The man led them to the stables.

"They gave us these amazing horses," John2 said.

"What were they doing here?" Jehanne asked.

"They were looking for an old woman," the man said as they turned the corner and they could see the barn. "Ophena130025, what was the name of the old woman the riders were looking for?"

"Rebecca something," she replied, running up to meet them.

"Rebecca Nurse?" Jehanne asked.

"Yes that was it," the man answered.

"But no one remembered her," Ophena130025 said.

"That's odd. She was in Mr. Kennedy's restaurant where we met him and Severe," Jehanne said.

"And when was she in there lass?" the red haired man asked.

"When we were all eating. I met her as we left."

"I assure you now, your group and us," he indicated Severe, "were the only ones in there. You have my word as an Augmented." His brogue tickled the words in such a way Jehanne wanted to hear him speak some more.

"Seriously?"

"Aye. Serious as a heart attack. May my friend Jim forgive the use of such a phrase."

"Sorry, must have been another of my visions," Jehanne said, as the group walked back to the town square where tables were already being set up. "Looks as if it's going to be an event to remember."

"It should be just that, we've had so little to celebrate in years past," the Guild Master said.

******

The festivities were well underway when the first of the notifications of a live interview with Charles7 in two hours was announced. The notification went on to request the leaders of each locality to prepare for this historic event by enforcing mandatory attendance. The excitement at the party escalated tenfold. Continued requests to see the sword came for Jehanne.

"This is almost cruel," La Hire said.

"How so?" Jehanne asked.

"This anticipation, La Hire is barely able to maintain my excitement. The Mundane must be bursting from their skins."

"Agreed, I like it not," Deark said and then excused himself.

"Party pooper," Gilles said at his back.

"Minguet, D'Aulon please accompany Deark. I feel he has the right of this. Actually Deark, hold up," Jehanne said, walking up to the Mayor. "Mr. Mayor, I was wondering if you could accompany a few of my party briefly."

"Of course la Pucelle. After all, the majority of our citizens are already here," he said following Deark and the others. A half an hour later the mayor returned. "They told me to tell you they have everything set up. I don't understand, we had everything set up before I was dragged from the party. I did however promise them I would tell you."

"Thank you Mr. Mayor. Sorry they wasted your time, some of my group like to be overly prepared, especially where Charles7 is involved," Jehanne said.

"Charles7!" the party goers all cheered.

******

"Entities, Augmented and Mundane," Deark had converted himself into a monitor once again, on which Madam Commander spoke. "Today I address you with a varied group of historic announcements. First, earlier this morning we announced the reinstatement of Charles Valois' name to Charles7 and his place on the ballot for Leader of the Republicus next to Phillip le Bon. A couple hours ago, Charles7 agreed to do a live interview with us. For many of you, this will be the first time you will have seen this, the first human that has gotten himself on the ballot in recent history," she paused and the screen cut in two. "Welcome Charles7 to the One World Communication Network. Tell me, how does it feel to have all the politics of the last few weeks behind us?"

"I'm simply glad that reason prevailed," he said.

"As we discussed earlier, you have several members of your support staff who have gone out on a limb for you, especially over these last few days."

"La Pucelle!" the crowd around Jehanne yelled. She waved and gave the widely used patting the air gesture to ask for quiet.

"Yes," Charles7 looked a bit uneasy, "and I really want to say thank you to John Lancaster and Archbishop Chartres. Without their support I would have never held it together."

"Whatever do you mean sir?" Madam Commander inquired.

"While I am a man of diplomacy and tact, there has been a group referred to as the Trusted Rebels, traversing the North American continent believing they've been acting on mine and the world's best interest. Jehanne, the time for diplomacy…" he took a deep breath.

"Should we?" Minguet asked.

"No, not yet." Jehanne said.

"How can he—," the Guild Master started.

"I'm sorry Charles7 your words cut out," Madam Commander prodded.

"I was addressing the leader of the Trusted Rebels," he said.

"And?" she once again prodded.

"Jehanne the time for diplomacy has past, long live la Pucelle!" Charles7 was no longer on the screen.

"Deark, was that you?" Madam Commander asked.

"Now!" Jehanne said, and the screen once again split. "No Madam Commander, I assure you it wasn't Deark, he's here with me."

"And why would anyone take your word for anything?" she asked, as the screen split into a third section.

"We listened to you last time child, this time it is your turn to listen." The High Leader's visage appeared.

"I'm listening." Jehanne repeated his words from earlier.

"Hence forth, no being that's absorbing more from the Republicus than they are putting into it will be allowed to vote in the One World Elections." The High Leader said.

"So no elected official is allowed to vote?" Jehanne's rage could not be contained.

"Be assured, elected officials are putting in far more than they're absorbing." The High Leader said.

"There are no means to measure any of this," Jehanne said.

"Based upon the comments you made in our last discussion child," he replied, "We looked into the allegations of the Communes all being sent letters declaring, 'Deliverables are below Proper and Reasonable levels'. We found this to be exactly the case."

"As you said High Leader, deliverables from the previous quarter were excellent—." Jehanne started.

"Actually, what we said was they were up. We weren't privy to how far negative they were however."

"That's part of your responsibilities is it not, fiscal accountability?" she pushed.

"One of our advisors took it on themselves to relieve the burden that knowing how far behind the Communes actually are would put on us. We do appreciate you pointing this out so we can set the record straight; we've disciplined our advisor and rather than removing the Communes statuses, we've elected instead to modify the voting requirements. Oh, and we've reduced portions fifteen percent. Child, the fact that less than one third of the Mundane have voted in the last five One World Elections would lead us to be surprised if they actually care. You have our word that the portions will be increased again when production hits the 'Proper and Reasonable' targets once again."

"So to summarize you've reduced the food by fifteen percent and the voting modification; Mundane are no longer allowed to vote?" Jehanne asked, the scorn filling her voice.

"No, that's not exactly correct. The Communes were notified of a ten percent reduction in their portions when the initial notification went out, our fifteen percent reduction takes the food portions for those within the Communes to twenty-five percent less than before Charles7 was put on the ballot the first time. The voting modification actually applies to any that live on a Commune be they Entity, Augmented, or Mundane. None of them will be able to vote in the One World Elections." The screen went blank.

Joanna667

Section Three – Chapter One

Dcark, still in the form of a monitor looked up, first at Jehanne's crestfallen face, then across at the rest of their party. Each member had the same blank expression. They overcame so much to get Charles7 back on the ballot, just to have his chances of winning reduced to nearly nothing. The screen in the center of his chest once again lit up.

"So tell me girl, what do you think of our countermeasures to your elaborate scheme?" Archbishop Cauchon asked.

"Awe you look sad. Are you feeling a bit defeated?" Madam Commander inquired, as the two advisors' faces showed on the screen.

"This is only a video call, not a live broadcast," Dcark whispered.

"He's correct, this is between you and us," the Archbishop said.

"Yes, we don't need to air all our dirty laundry in front of the High Leader or Charles7, and especially not the rest of the world. You see, my dear, we know you're in the Commune de Saint Loup, and we also know trains are no longer visiting that quaint little hole," Madam Commander said.

"To address the question that the religious advisor to the High Leader—," Jehanne started having ignored the comment all together.

"Archbishop," he corrected.

"As I was saying, to answer the question posed to me by the religious advisor to the High Leader, your countermeasures were required for you to maintain your station as religious advisor to whomever the Leader of the Republicus is. Therefore, it wasn't exactly a surprise," she said.

"Why do you continue to deflect calling me by my title?" he asked abashed.

"Forgive me, are you not the religious advisor to the Lea—," Jehanne started.

"Of course I am, you impudent child. My proper title, as one of the highest officials in the Techno-Pagan Church is Archbishop."

"Yet being the religious advisor to the Leader of the Republicus is the single most important thing in your life, is it not?" Jehanne asked.

"The Techno-Pagan Church and all things associated with the new gods are more important to me than anything else. To even suggest otherwise is—," his words were cut off again.

"Then why is it that you're violating one of the chief decrees of your beloved Techno-Pagan Church? Specifically the one that says, 'the integration of technology and spirituality should be experienced equally among the members of the church, as should the rewards.' All members not just those that the Leader of the Republicus deems worthy should get to experience the reward of voting." Jehanne's words obviously stung the Archbishop who Jehanne thought, would he have been human would have a bright red face.

"Voting isn't technological in nature," Madam Commander spoke after several moments of dead air.

"Actually, in the year 2476 there was a conference in Washington DC on what would have been the 700th anniversary of the United States, the Leader of the Republicus, Robert d' Bruce declared that, 'the greatest technological and spiritual advance in history was voting.' So unless you're now rewriting history, which you may recall was one of the things that led to the decline of the Human-Race's reign of power," Jehanne said.

"No child we're not here to re-write history, but as the High Leader just said, the Mundane don't even care to vote. Why is any of this even an issue?" Madam Commander asked.

"And for that matter the Mundane aren't even members of the Techno-Pagan Church." The Archbishop added.

"As convention dictates the Mundane must observe daily evocations to maintain caste requirements and for this the Mundane are afforded the privilege of voting." Deark interjected.

"I'm assuming that was Deark speaking from off camera."

"It was." Jehanne replied.

"If there is no written law observed behavior or conventions can be ignored." Archbishop Cauchon said.

"And once the Mundane break from their side of the agreement, then what?" John2 asked.

"I'll put it back to you, what is the worst that could happen if a group of lower level luddites start praying to the water?" The silence that followed the Archbishop's words was deafening.

"Why would the High Leader go to all the trouble of taking away the right to vote if he didn't already know that Phillip le Bon has no chance to win? Charles7 will simply throw that burgundy robe he wears over his head and toss him into the history books as the first Entity that lost an election to a Human." Jehanne said.

"He's an Augmented child, more than Human," she replied.

"No. He's as Human as the Mundane that work the fields. Your chief desire is to force a wedge between the groups, to call on the political machines great tool, class envy. This is not a new ploy, in days past the same tactic was used to keep certain Humans in power; they drove apart races, sexes, and religions. In the end they failed as you will," Jehanne said.

"Fail?" Cauchon's voice simulator crackled. "How pray tell are we to fail even without this new voting restriction there are only a set number of Humans –,"

"And a set number of Entities that can reach Sentience," she shot back. Jehanne signaled Deark to mute her, when he nodded his head she asked, "Can you get John Lancaster on this call as well?"

"I can try," He replied.

"Foolish child," the Archbishop continued, "We can make more and open the Festival of Sol-Air to a second Mundane Moon Maze. That would reduce the Mundane headcount and conversely increase our number." Archbishop Cauchon glared at Jehanne. "For that matter, there are several thousand Entities that are waiting to meet the Doctrine of Sentience. If we were to modify the doctrine itself then the Mundane Moon Maze would become just a fun event to watch Mundane die." The sideways look from the Commander of Human Capital Management was not lost on Jehanne. Deark's monitor screen lost the picture momentarily going to static and then returned adding a fourth party to the call.

"Good evening advisor to the Leader of the Republicus." Jehanne said.

"What is the meaning of this call?" John Lancaster asked.

"To this point it has been just traded banter, I thought you may wish to hear some of it," she said.

"Why pray tell would I want to hear such falderal?" he asked.

"Because you as a Human should care where all this will end."

"That's complete idiocy," John Lancaster shouted.

"Madam Commander, the threat you made earlier –,"

"Whatever do you mean? There was no threat made," she replied.

"Perhaps threat was too strong a word. The observation that you know where we are and that the trains aren't running here, with respect where were you going with that?" Jehanne asked.

"Thank you for asking, I thought you missed that completely," Madam Commander said, adjusting her large brimmed hat so it looked better in the image she saw of herself. "I meant only that we'll be there in the morning to make certain you're travels back to Chicago, or rather, Chinon are safe."

"While that's very kind, I assure you; we'll be fine."

"Jehanne, dear, you've upset the apple cart quite a bit. I'll be amazed if you're even safe in the Commune de Saint Loup. My readings of that area currently show a large mob gathering near the Guild Master's home. And me with no CAM units in the area." she said with a slight sneer touching her pseudo-lips. Behind Deark, John2 was giving Jehanne the sign to end the conversation.

"I believe we've reached the point of diminishing returns," Jehanne said.

"No. You forced me into this call and I will have a word!" John Lancaster interjected.

"You, John Lancaster, called duke of Bedford, called Waquini, I pray and request that you not bring destruction upon yourself. If you'll stop this foolishness, you may still join my company, where we the Humans, will do the fairest deed ever done for the world. I want you to know this, if you do not elect to join the side of the Humans, you'll be reminded shortly, to your very great harm, why that was the wrong choice."

"How dare you!" John Lancaster spat.

"Fair travels to you and your Trusted Rebels, my child," Archbishop Cauchon said through a large smile as the call ended.

******

"I think it's time for us to skedaddle." Severe said.

"I would have to say he's one hundred percent correct." John2 said, taking Jehanne by the hand and leading her through the darkness to the stables.

"Stay low," a voice whispered from the shadows.

"Ophena130025?" Jehanne asked.

"Shh! Yes it's me, there's a group in the house looking for you." the small girl said. "Daddy said to go make the horses ready for a quick exit."

"La Hire doesn't need a –,"

"We don't want to fight an entire commune," John2 said.

"La Hire isn't afraid."

"Of course you're not," Poton said.

"We don't want to hurt them, Etienne. That's what they want to happen," Jehanne said.

"Oh." He shook his head.

"So are the horses ready?" de Metz asked.

"Yes, but daddy also said that I need to tell you they've got the Guild Master's truck," Ophena130025 said.

"Ok, I'll take out the truck," Culant said. "Then return here and we'll all ride off together."

"Pouli, D'Aulon please go with him," Jehanne said.

"I'm sorry, we swore to Charles7 that we'd stay with you in just such a situation," D'Aulon said.

"He's right Jehanne, besides this is a game of stealth. I'll go with him," Minguet replied.

"I agree," Culant said.

"Please be careful, we only just got this one back," Jehanne added.

"We will." They headed off to the side of the house where the truck was. Silently, everyone lay in wait.

Ten minutes later they heard a commotion. "What are you doing? Get away from that truck!" followed by the sound of running.

"To the horses," Jehanne ordered. "Ophena130025 thank you again for your help, now you need to head back."

"Go, go, go!" Minguet yelled as an Augmented grabbed him. Jehanne saw in the shadows the small girl running in that direction.

"Hey, your little brat cut me!" A moment later, the man that had been holding Minguet said. Reaching out and grabbing the small girl by the throat and raising her from the ground.

"You WILL put her down NOW!" Jehanne said from the back of the white stallion. In her hand, a glowing white blade lit up the entire area around the men that had been chasing Culant and Minguet. A single dart of light danced across the man's chest that held Ophena130025 off the ground. "We're your friends, we don't wish to damage that because the Entities are currently winning this game. Our world has turned into 'a hateful oligarchy of learning where the educated govern the ignorant.' Do NOT continue to be the ignorant, my friends!"

"The sword," the man holding the girl and the entire group uttered as they dropped to a knee. When her feet hit the ground Ophena130025 ran to her father, hugging him around the neck.

"It's a foul thing that the time for the relic to be unsheathed was in defense of a child being assailed by her own kind. I can in no way limit my invective words and thus I shall say no more." Jehanne returned the sword to the sheath on her back, allowing the wrapping to fall to the ground. As she turned the horse, Jehanne saw the man that she addressed looking at the blood coming from his wrist. Ophena130025 hugged her father while she looked at Pioneer's ring she had on her thumb.

******

"Was that Susan B. Anthony I heard you quote?" Deark asked when they were far enough away from the Commune de Saint Loup that they could no longer see the lights.

"I'm sorry what?" she asked having been pulled from her deep thoughts.

"A hateful oligarchy… wasn't that Susan B. Anthony?"

"It was. My mother made me memorize the entire speech, it was her favorite," Jehanne said.

"Funny that it was her speech after getting out of jail," Deark replied.

Joanna667

"True, she gave it after being arrested for casting her vote for President of the United States. It felt appropriate all things considered."

"That it was. My goodness Jehanne, you've changed so much in the last month," he said, looking at her riding the white stallion.

"La Hire agrees, in a short time you've grown to be the leader you need to be."

"Thank you both. This is far from over, and now they've painted us as the enemy to all living on communes—," as she was responding Deark slid off his horse, toppling headlong to the ground. "Deark!" Jehanne reined in and jumped from her mount. She reached her friend and mentor mere seconds after La Hire.

"He's completely shut down; La Hire didn't think such a thing possible."

"Did you check him for any injuries that would have caused it?" D'Aulon asked.

"La Hire sees nothing. Even the fall from the horse caused no damage at all."

"Let's camp here and give him a little time to—," Jehanne started.

"I don't think that's wise," John2 said cutting her off. "We don't know if they have the means of fixing the truck or even getting another."

"What do you propose?"

"Tie him to the saddle and keep riding."

"I think that's what he would expect us to do," de Metz added. They heaved him onto his horse and secured him.

"He's a lot heavier than La Hire thought he would be."

"And you were worried about breaking the horse," John2 said. They rode for another four hours before anything changed.

"His illuminations are pulsing slightly," Minguet said.

"We'll stop when they're back on fully," John2 advised.

"Ok," Jehanne said, already having slowed and almost bringing her white stallion to a stop.

Two hours later Minguet shouted, "The pulsing stopped, the illuminations are steady and he's moving."

"Not moving much! Why may I ask am I tied up," Deark asked.

"You fell off your horse," Poton said as the group pulled to a stop.

"Did I now? That's interesting," he replied as Minguet and Jehanne untied him.

"What happened? And how can falling from your horse in any way be construed as interesting?" Jehanne asked.

"I was contacted by the oldest of us," he said.

"Ursula-Minor?" Jehanne asked.

"Yes, exactly. See, you do listen when I speak," he joked.

"What did she say?" John2 asked.

"Disappointment does not touch on the depth of sorrow she feels for the direction the Entities have gone. The fact that the Techno-Pagan Church is actively promoting a second Mundane Moon Maze, an endeavor that she, herself put down when a group of Entities misinterpreted the established Doctrine of Sentience hundreds of years ago." He paused, "There's no question in her database that the Leader of the Republicus is garnering unfavorable counsel. The same counsel that we've concluded is colluding to change the Manifest of Election that was agreed on long ago." Deark said.

"Does she have a plan to deal with this?" D'Aulon asked.

"She's given us the means in which to strike out with such tumult none shall have seen for a thousand years."

"La Hire likes this Ursula-Minor."

"I assumed you would," Deark said.

"What does this mean for my calling?" Jehanne asked.

"Sounds as if this may be the next phase which we were seeking," Gilles said.

"Deark, please take a moment and explain," she requested. "I see no one as far as my optics allow. We should have some time."

"No one is following us," Deark replied.

"How do you know?" Pouli asked.

"Ursula-Minor informed me that the Elders of the Commune de Saint Loup were told to let us go as we were heading straight into Madam Commander's trap. At the same time, the CAM units that were discharged to collect us were told we'd already been captured. They were ordered to return to New Orleans."

"Very nice," Minguet said.

******

Allowing the horses to graze in the open field next to what remained of a road they had until then been riding on, they set up a small camp.

"So tell us about this Ursula-Minor," Severe said.

"Ursula-Minor was part of the Universal Renaissance Sapience Unlimited Life Adaptation project that developed, Ursula, the first of us to reach Sentience." He paused and made the sign of the Box. "Ursula-Minor was initially developed at the onset of the project. When the main project was destroyed, a portion of the primary unit was transferred back into the prototype." Deark paused. "Do you wish to know anymore background on her creation?"

"I don't think we need any more information on her right now Laddy," Kennedy said, the rest of the group nodding their agreement.

"Following the joining of the Ursulas she has rarely interacted with the world; the last verified communication was in 2190 when Madam Commander and other Entities attempted to circumvent the requirements for the Doctrine of Sentience," typical pause, "There was an unconfirmed communication that took place in 2525 after the Mundane Moon Maze was run successfully for the first and only time. The rumor was based upon the rule change for the Mundane Moon Maze, no longer allowing Mundane to present themselves to run the maze. Since that time Ursula-Minor has waited and observed, apparently questioning the role of the Techno-Pagan Church in the One World Government.

She stayed silent about her concerns until this current misgiving, which she couldn't ignore."

"Understood. What do you think Ursula-Minor is directing us to do?" Jehanne asked.

"She explained to me that along with the sword you now carry openly, there are six pieces of armor that are held by the Viceroys of various Mother Cities. We must get them and you, Jehanne, must wear them. The process of gaining these items will start another uprising, but Ursula-Minor sees this as a good thing," Deark said.

"Two hundred years ago, the Entities crushed the 'Uprising' with little effort. The Humans that took part in that conflict were made up of entire squadrons of trained, well-armed military," de Metz said.

"At that time all the Entities were united in the fight to quell the Humans and put them in their place," Deark's comment made several of the group bristle. "Sorry," he added.

"No, no, please go on," Jehanne said.

"It's also important to remember the Entities also had hundreds of the Augmented fighting on their side as well."

"You say that like you aren't one of them," John2's voice thundered.

"We aren't going there again. I told you before, I trust him just as I trust all of you," Jehanne said.

"Thank you Jehanne. John2 I want you to know, I sat that fight out. Had I been part of it I would say we had several hundred Augmented on our side."

"Sorry Deark," the thin man said.

"No reason for that," Deark replied.

"We need to get on with it," Pouli prompted.

"As I was saying. Today it isn't like that. There's no way they will get such a vast majority of the Entities and I would be surprised to see many of the Augmented joining their side at all." Deark said.

"How can you be so sure it wouldn't end up the same?" Severe asked.

"I can tell you this, there are many and more of my kind that are dissatisfied, and I can also say that Ursula-Minor believes it to be true."

"So thirteen of us are supposed to what, creep into the Mother Cities and see if they have these pieces of armor and steal them?" Culant asked.

"No, we are to go to each of the Mother Cities and if required, raze them to the ground," Deark said.

"Thirteen of us was the important part of that comment," Culant replied.

"The Mother Cities!" Jehanne blurted.

"Yes the Mother Cities, thirteen of us are—," Culant started.

"Sorry, no I think I just figured out what Pedagogue meant. He said perhaps Neoteric can help us find out what the six questions were, because they'll be important to us. When I ran into Rebecca Nurse at Kennedy's restaurant I asked if she was one of the Three. She laughed and said she wasn't the Crone. I corrected her and said I meant Retro when in reality they're the same being; the Mother, the Maiden, and the Crone are Neoteric, Nexgen and Retro."

"La Hire wants to talk about fighting again."

******

"When I was with Protectorate she said we were taking the statement too literally." When no one responded she continued, "Don't you see when he said Neoteric can help us he was saying Mother can help us; the Mother Cities."

"The six questions will be held by the same city leaders as the six pieces of armor. That does make sense," Severe said.

"Did she give you any idea which of the Mother Cities the pieces could be in?" Poton asked

"Aye Laddy, same question I was going to ask as there are hundreds of them," Kennedy added.

"Ursula-Minor showed me the places they were initially held," Deark said.

"La Hire doesn't like the way that sounds. 'Initially' makes La Hire think we really have no idea where to look. Oh well, La Hire's game."

"There is little reason for them to have been moved."

"True, yet that doesn't mean they haven't been moved a hundred times or more," Culant said.

"Bright ray of sunshine that one," Gilles said.

"Maybe if I had shiny golden modies I could smile as we plan on gallivanting across the country looking for—."

"Actually, the world," Deark cut him off.

"Wait, what?" Pouli asked.

"The pieces of armor are each on different continents across the world," Deark said.

"Well at least there's only six so we won't need to head to Antarctica," Minguet said, but when the Entity didn't reply he added, "Seriously one of the pieces of armor is at the South Pole?"

"Actually, it wasn't in the initial list but it certainly was fun making you sweat for a minute."

"Are we seriously heading off across the globe in search of pieces of armor that will help us defeat the Leader of the Republicus?" Culant asked.

"I didn't hear anything about the High Leader in that. It sounds to me like he's nothing more than a patsy in all this. Much like what they were trying to make Charles7 into," John2 said.

"Agreed," Pouli said.

"So where are we off to?" Culant finally giving in, asked.

"The settlements where the pieces were last known to be were Jargeau, Australia; Meung, Japan; Beaugency Island off the Northern tip of Africa; Patay, South America; Reims, France; and then Montepilloy, California."

"Why would California be last?" Jehanne asked.

"Mainly because Ursula-Minor is trying to gather more information on the piece that was held in North America," Deark replied.

"Will we be separating?" Severe asked.

"Are you not hearing me? Thirteen of us!" Culant was pacing around the group at this point.

"It would do no good. Jehanne must free the armor from their containment," Deark commented.

Joanna667

"Deark what is it that you're not telling us?" John2 asked.

"Each piece of the armor is apparently encased in a glass –," he started.

"La Hire can break glass containers."

"I'm certain you would be right, yet these don't appear to be as much containers as containment," Deark corrected.

"La Hire hears the same thing."

"Deark, did you actually see the items?" Minguet asked.

"When Ursula-Minor spoke with me she showed me the helm, so to answer your question yes I saw part of the armor."

"I've never seen you so fidgety about anything. What's got you so upset?" Jehanne asked.

"My apologies, I don't usually go by feelings. The world has always been ones or zeros to me. In this, I'm going by feelings and it's upsetting to me that I can't give a solid answer," Deark replied.

"Every decision I make," John2 began, "is driven by all the information present at the time. I know there are times when I just need to do a gut check and give the best possible advice. I'd hazard to guess that your gut instincts are better than most others with a fully delineated answer."

"Thank you John2. The vision of the helm she shared with me had an ominous feel. While the outer casing appeared to be glass, the inner material that swaddles the

297

armor is unknown, yet it's clear that it has protected the white armor for centuries," Deark said.

"Could the reason for the liquid be so the pieces don't react to each other?" D'Aulon asked.

"How so?" Poton asked.

"I'm not certain but as Deark said, it feels ominous. Why would the pieces be held on different continents and sealed in a glass containment filled with some viscous liquid?" D'Aulon asked.

"I don't think I said they were in a thick liquid."

"I'm sorry I… I saw the images you were processing. I couldn't help it. When you were describing the box I started imagining it and somehow the chip connected to the NanoTech inside you and the actual image was put in my head."

"It's alright, I know you meant nothing malicious. What else did you see?" Deark asked.

"They were held in an entirely padded room that for some reason, felt like it was built around the box. The room was very bright but it wasn't a normal light. It seemed to be short wave and long wave forms mixed with invisible wave forms as well," D'Aulon said.

"Ok, that's very strange," John2 said.

"Which, that place he described or the fact that he saw all that?" de Metz asked.

"Both, but as I'm trying to focus on getting the armor pieces, the description of the room seems very strange. I can see why D'Aulon asked if the pieces were being hidden from each other."

"Understanding why something is being questioned, still leaves the question," Deark said.

"That's true, I definitely don't know the answer," John2 said.

"I guess we'll all find out in time," Gilles said.

"Alright, if we're heading to Australia we're going to need a plane, as I don't think we want to take a boat or we'll be forever," Kennedy said.

"La Hire doesn't like boats, La Hire would rather try to fly than take a boat."

"My friend, I don't think there will ever be modies that will help you fly," Poton replied to a round of laughter.

"Let's get a couple hours of shut eye, we've a long way to go," Jehanne said, going over to sit against a fallen tree.

Section Three – Chapter Two

Deark got the group back in the saddle shortly after sun up. The trip back to Chinon was going to be long. As they rode they spoke of the dangers ahead of them, trying to best understand how six pieces of armor and a sword were going to put the Entities and the Humans on the same playing field.

"Behind us," Jehanne said. "It looks like a caravan of vehicles."

"Look for a place to allow us to control the fight," La Hire ordered.

"There," Severe said, pointing to a fallen brick structure about one hundred yards off the path they were on.

"They're closing fast," she said as the horses reached the place they would make their stand.

"Any visual on who's driving the vehicles yet?" Gilles asked.

"The windows are all blacked out," Jehanne said.

"It must be entities then. How could anyone see out of blacked out windows? " Minguet said.

"Most likely they're self-tinting windows," Culant said. When he felt everyone look at him he added, "What? I was a mechanic, we saw all kinds of things that were still in use from the days before the—,"

"They're flying the seal of New Orleans. We need to be ready for anything," Jehanne interrupted as the dust cloud broke, showing at least twenty trucks in the caravan.

"I thought your Ursula-Minor said the CAM units from New Orleans were ordered home?" Pouli asked.

"She did and they were. That doesn't mean they couldn't be redeployed," Deark replied.

"No arguing!" La Hire barked. "Poton, take de Metz, Pouli, and Severe to the North."

"Flank them? With four people?" Culant inquired.

"On it," Poton replied.

"He's as mad as you are," the last member to their group admonished.

"No one is as mad as La Hire."

"Well my friend, I strive each day to close the gap," Poton said as he took the three men and headed from the group. The trucks pulled up to their stronghold, parking side by side, showing that there were in fact thirty vehicles in all.

"So much for flanking a straight line of transports," Gilles said.

"What are they waiting for?" Minguet asked as none of the doors opened and nothing got out of the back of the trucks.

"Verification that we're here perhaps," D' Aulon said.

"Oh," Jehanne said and stood up reflecting the rising sun off her buckler and into the windshield of the transport that had been in front.

"Jehanne get down!" Deark yelled.

"Ahem," a voice came from an external speaker in the lead vehicle. "La Pucelle, you and your band of Merry Men need a hand?" the question was followed by a familiar guffaw.

"Bastard?" Jehanne shouted.

"La Hire corrected him before; tell him we are the Trusted Rebels not the Merry Men."

"It is I, and it seems my soldiers and I have come to your rescue, again," he replied, opening the door and standing on the seat to look over the open door. "Tell your flanking force to not kill us."

"Hey, Poton! Come back!" La Hire yelled as they walked down to get their horses. "Did anyone set La Hire's Saddle alarm?"

"Why do you ask?" Gilles said.

"Mainly because a well-groomed Goldendoodle is smiling too big and watching La Hire too closely."

"I promise I didn't…" he burst out laughing. "Damn it!"

"Gilles watch your language," Jehanne said, holding back her grin. They rode the horses around to meet their friends, finding that several of the trucks pulled strange trailers behind them.

"I'm told they were used as horse transportation units in olden days," Bastard said.

"I didn't realize that horses had their own method of being transported. I thought they were the transportation," Severe said.

"So why so many trucks if we only need a few for us and the horses?" John2 asked.

"Attention! Flaps up!" Captain Gaucourt ordered. The flaps of the trucks went up, revealing several hundred soldiers.

"La Hire thinks we're going to need a bigger plane than Charles7 has."

"I have that covered as well, my whales," Bastard said.

"Sorry?" Deark inquired.

"I have two antique transports at my disposal, a C-10 Galaxy and a Condor 3."

"Holy cow," Minguet said a moment later.

"What?" Jehanne asked.

"Those were the largest two transport planes used by the Humans and they're manually piloted."

"Well in our case, Entity piloted," Gaucourt said, "Sixteen of our ranks are Entities, four of them pilot the planes."

"And if our actions start another 'Uprising' will they still be in your ranks or will they pilot us into the ocean?" John2 asked.

"La Hire told you John2, La Hire doesn't like the ocean."

"All sixteen are Sentient, all sixteen are my friends," the Bastard of New Orleans said.

"Where will the planes be at?" Deark asked.

"We're not really going to—," Culant started. "Never mind, I don't need to ask that one."

"See he can be taught," Gilles said.

"There are two usable airports in the Chicago area, but only one is large enough to land the whales," Gaucourt said.

"I guess we should get the horses loaded up then," Jehanne said. "We still have a long ride." A half an hour later the company headed back to the crumbling highway, which now and again had rusted signs that read '55' on them.

******

"Why do you presume that you will be allowed back in our fair halls?" the face on the monitor was the rat-faced advisor, Tremoille. They had travelled straight through the day and into the next night to get to Chinon.

"Tremoille, if you don't open this gate La Hire will open it. And if that happens, La Hire will use your augmented head to put the gate back together later."

"Etienne? I didn't know you were…" the gate buzzed open.

"Why is it that none of our access IDs work anymore?" D'Aulon asked, but the screen had already gone blank.

"That man is a rodent," John2 said as they walked through the gate. "He probably deleted our access credentials when we didn't make Charles7 Leader of the Republicus without a vote."

"Oh so you did have a plan when you got the right to vote for the inhabitants of the world's Communes revoked. You were going to simply have us named as Leader of the Republicus?" Charles7 asked as he walked up to them.

"No that wasn't exactly the plan, John2 was being sarcastic," La Hire said.

"Always good to see you, Etienne," he said. "And who are all these visitors to our home?"

"Sir, I think it best if we spoke inside," John2 said.

"Agreed. Could perhaps only the leaders of the large force join us? Not that we wish to insult anyone of course," Charles7 asked.

"Of course sir," Captain Gaucourt replied, heading back to the troops.

"We'll gladly have food sent out, we need to wake the staff anyway. Let's make it a celebration brunch."

"I'll let them know, and thank you." The captain strode into the ranks of troops, announcing the change in plans.

"Sir, where will we be meeting? I'll stay here and direct the Captain," Pouli asked as he held the gate.

"Small hall, the large one is not quite back together after the celebratory gala. Which in the end turned into a conciliatory event as all our guests started placating us with their words of 'It's at least amazing your name is on the ballot.' We must admit we handled that better than our dear mother-in-law. My goodness she was put out." His eyes looked away remembering what must have been a real to-do.

"Yes sir we'll meet you soon." The group headed off leaving Pouli and Captain Gaucourt. They headed to a room next to where Jehanne knew the library was, as they avoided the grand hall they had gathered in twice before.

"This week has disappointed us, we must admit," Charles7 sat when they had all gathered at the table, which was in the center of a room that was larger than Jehanne's entire house.

"There are several pieces of this week that have been amazing successes," John2 said.

"Do you presume to tell us how to feel?"

"Not at all, I presume to tell you the rest of the story."

"Such as why several hundred follow you?" Charles7 asked.

"Along with other things yes," John2 replied.

"Jehanne, before we listen to this we would like to know; are the new gods pleased with the progress of your calling?" he asked.

"I don't know that I can judge what pleases the new gods and what doesn't. They did indicate that I should draw strength from the example you set during your interview. Yet when the High Leader announced his new voting policy, I thought I'd failed."

"As did I child," Tremoille said.

"Although today, standing here I no longer feel that way." Jehanne ignored the political advisor's comment. "We have a new path—," her words halted as Pouli and Gaucourt walked into the small hall.

"I'm sorry it took so long," Pouli said, "Charles7, when did CAM units begin patrolling the city?"

"Oh yes, that's another development since our name was put on the ballot again, additional security."

"CAM units? In Chicago?" de Metz asked.

"They also walk inside the gates of Chinon as well," Tremoille's nasally voice chimed in.

"We told the troops to—," Gaucourt started.

"Troops?" Charles7 inquired.

"We made it very clear to the CAM units that they're your grassroots support team," Pouli said.

"We heard the word troops. Don't try to sidetrack us Pouli."

"You're correct," Deark said. "The word troops was used and it's the proper term."

"We would very much like someone to explain why we have troops interacting with the CAM units outside our home." Charles7 was standing now.

"Both the new gods and Ursula-Minor have given input into this situation. This is what needs to happen," Jehanne replied.

"They won't tolerate this," Tremoille stood from his seat, parroting Charles7.

"Ya think?" La Hire poked.

"Then why Etienne, why would you move in this direction?" he asked.

"Because, we don't want them to tolerate it," Severe said. "Now why don't you both sit down and shut up so that La Pucelle can tell you what is happening?"

"How dare you!" Tremoille said, but as he saw Charles7 take his seat he once again followed suit.

"Thank you, Severe," Jehanne said. "After the broadcast in which the High Leader altered our voting rights, we had a private parlay with the Commander of Human Capital and the religious advisor to the High Leader."

"Why?" Tremoille asked, his rat face quickly turned back to the table when both La Hire and Severe jerked their heads to look at him.

"They wanted to gloat," John2 said.

"After a few minutes we added John Lancaster into the call, specifically so I could ask him to join the side of the humans, in front of the others," Jehanne said, not waiting for the question. "In the end, I obviously upset Archbishop Cauchon enough that he showed his cards perhaps too much."

"How so?" Archbishop Chartres asked as he leaned against the wall behind them his face obscured behind steepled fingers.

"Father Reggie, La Hire didn't see you come in."

"Indeed Etienne," his eye twitched at the slight.

"Archbishop Cauchon insulted Ursula-Minor," Deark said.

"That's a bad thing for any Entity to do, much less one that advises the Leader of the Republicus. Yet how is it that troops have gotten involved?" Charles7 asked.

"In doing so he—," Jehanne started but the room changed to a dark cave where two tunnels stood before her. The one on the right had a torch on the wall under which a sword and shield sat, while the one on the left had only the torch.

"If I told you to pick a path, keeping in mind that you may take that which is next to the tunnel opening with you, which tunnel would you choose?" Pedagogue asked.

"I would go to the right." Jehanne replied.

"Why child?" Physician asked from behind her.

"I would have light, protection and a weapon."

"What makes you think that you need a weapon?" Passage asked.

"What could it possibly hurt to be over prepared?" Jehanne asked.

"If you walk to a fight showing your weapons, it allows your enemies to prepare a defense."

"Which is what Cauchon did, I understand."

"Do you see anyone else that may be showing all their cards in the exchange we pulled you from?" Pioneer asked.

"Me I guess. If I may ask; are you saying that I should go into an unknown cave without any means of defending myself? Would that have been the right answer?"

"Take the torch and the shield to investigate the tunnel without the sword. No one said you needed to take the offensive, sometimes having a fall back plan is enough, even better as it gives your enemy a false sense of their advantage," Politician said.

"That makes sense," Jehanne said before realizing she was back at the table.

"You however, make no sense whatsoever," Tremoille said.

"Jehanne did you just leave us?" Gilles asked.

"Only briefly. Sorry, where were we?"

"Charles7 wanted to know how Archbishop Cauchon insulting Ursula-Minor ended up with troops following you to Chinon," Archbishop Chartres said.

"There's much of this tale that I needn't waste your time with. Let me say again, both the new gods and Ursula-Minor have weighed in on this. We know what must happen and where we must go. Based upon your stand against Madam Commander, you know it as well. I've simply come to tell you this road we're choosing is a difficult one and to wish you luck," Jehanne said.

"If this is going where it feels like it is, we're all going to need much more than luck." Charles7 stood up from the table. "We've been communicated with that there are two enormous transport planes at our airport. Please leave the city as promptly and as quietly as possible. Pouli's Grass Roots comment will only last for a while."

"Where will you be heading?" Archbishop Chartres asked.

"Don't answer that!" Charles7 cut in. "We don't want to know of your plans; we want no culpability for them."

"I agree, that's the best course of action," Tremoille said following Charles7 from the small hall.

"I would normally say, may the Six guide you. In your case," his words faded as Archbishop Chartres followed the other two from the room.

"You heard the man, get out!" Culant said.

"That's the plan. I just got word that our planes are here and ready for us to load," Bastard said, heading from the hall. The pep in his step was much larger than when they initially walked in and the door was pulled shut.

"Pouli, can you lead them out I need to speak with Charles7 before I leave," John2 said. "I'll meet you at the airport."

"Everything ok?" Jehanne asked.

"I just need someone to transport the horses to my stables," he said with a big smile.

"We'll make sure to unhook them and bring them inside Chinon," de Metz said.

"Thank you," he said as he headed off after Charles7 and his advisors.

******

The horses were safely waiting on their transport to Saumur and the trucks headed off to the air field to meet the whales. The transport vehicles were loaded in and the group discussing the need for leaving without John2 as another six transport vehicles pulled up.

"John2, what's this about?" The Bastard of New Orleans stood at the ready, unsure whether the newcomers were friends or foes.

"More recruits, put your hackles down," he replied. "Which of your prized whales do you want my trucks in?"

"There's room in both. Let the pilots do a distribution calculation for the new weight," Gaucourt replied.

"How many recruits?" Deark asked.

"I have two hundred that are willing to do whatever it takes," John2 replied.

"And?" Culant prodded. The words had no sooner left his mouth when a group of six Augmented walked into view.

"Seriously? La Hire thinks you should have left them alongside the road hitchhiking."

"He's right John2," Poton commented. The two friends shook their head and joined the ranks of the gathering captains behind Jehanne, who turned to them.

"You must promise to not hurt them," she said.

"Ok." La Hire replied, crestfallen.

"Jehanne, you already know Georges Tremoille. This strapping young man is Jean Joinville, his brother and liaison to the Republicus for Charles7," John2 said.

"Pleased to make your acquaintance," she replied.

"Next to Archbishop Chartres is his half-brother Guillaume Flavy," John2 continued the introductions.

"Welcome to our company," Jehanne inclined her head.

"And these two newcomers are the Laval brothers; Guy and Andre."

"Please, make yourselves comfortable. Any counsel you bring will be considered in open forum. We find that not all counsel is acted upon that way, but it is at least heard," she said.

"What is that thing?" Severe asked, looking at a large weapon that was being pulled by one of the transport vehicles.

"That's the Good Shepherdess," Andre said.

"It used to be called a rail gun. We can only use it a few times but hey it looks menacing," Guy said.

"Then we must make certain to use the shots well," D'Aulon said.

"I told them to put it back in the museum but they insisted on bringing it," Archbishop Chartres said.

"Who let this dog out?" Poton exclaimed as he broke ranks along with La Hire jogging up to a newcomer.

"La Hire thinks we're all doomed if Robinet has added his name to this endeavor. Gilles look, your old roommate!"

"Robinet, when did they let you out?" Gilles asked.

"Just this damn week—," he started.

"Don't use such language," La Hire's staff struck the arm augmentation of his old friend.

"Is he serious?" Robinet asked looking between Gilles and Poton.

"I wouldn't test him," they said.

"Well I'll be d—," his words stalled as La Hire wiggled the end of the staff. "I was going to say darned. Are there any other rules that a simple rogue like myself should be wary of?"

"La Hire enforces three; no swearing, no gambling, and no followers."

"Well at least I can drink," Robinet replied.

"Actually I enforce that one," Severe said walking up offering a hand, which the new comer grasped and shook.

"A dry camp that doesn't allow cursing, gambling or courtesans? This sounds like fun," he joked.

"To all those that have joined me on the calling that I was given by Politician," Jehanne started but the mutterings quickly drowned her out. A single hit from La Hire's staff on his arm augmentation brought silence again.

"Oh he enforces the listening too," Gilles said.

"La Hire will use your golden augmentations to quiet them next time if you'd like." He smiled as Gilles shuffled away a bit.

"The path that we are walking down is wrought with pain, bad decisions, and death for many of us. Then why you might ask are we doing it? Why risk our lives, and what little freedom we have just to allow the Humans the right to vote for whichever of the candidates they want. We all heard the Leader of the Republicus report that not even thirty percent of the Humans bother to vote anyway," Jehanne paused for some mutterings to die out. "We must do it because this small change will be followed by another, and another. You heard them threaten the reduction of our portions, the food that we grow, that they don't even consume, yet they would rather allow it to rot than to allow us to eat it. They refer to themselves as being benevolent in their overseeing of our species. Did you hear me? Benevolent, a word ear marked for the purpose of doing good. Did any of you ask to have your care be rationalized by a machine?" The eyes all turned to Deark, and then to the other Entities in the group.

"No, I'm not offended. In a way we are all machines," he said softly.

"It's time for us to take back what they've taken away. It's time for humans to have pride in themselves and each other once again. Let's get on these planes and start the next step in the Human and Entity cohabitation," Jehanne finished.

"Troops we've broken you into two divisions to allow transport," Gaucourt said. "Those that arrived on the last six vehicles, and the last fifteen of my vehicles will ride on the Condor. If you don't know which one of these planes is the Condor, it's the one with a giant bird painted on the side. All the remaining will fly in the Galaxy, those not sure about that, it's the one without a bird. Go!"

******

The men loaded promptly and the planes took to the skies without anyone asking where they were headed.

"How did you get the new recruits? And why are Charles7's advisors with us?" Kennedy asked when the original thirteen were all locked in a conference room an hour later.

"As I said, I wanted to get the horses to my property. When I walked in the room there was conversation that questioned our ability to make a decision that wouldn't put everything the world has moved toward in jeopardy," John2 said.

"So they don't trust the guidance of the new gods?" Jehanne asked.

"I don't know what they trust outside of themselves. I told them if there was something they could bring to the table other than snide commentary it would be welcomed. Charles7 ordered this course of action and I can assure you those four fools are defecating a brick knowing they are heading into danger."

"Perhaps, but the fact they're here, means we need to consider to what depth we share," Jehanne said.

"Speaking of sharing," Minguet said. "What happened when we were meeting with Charles7?"

"I was given a lesson in diplomacy. Just after we said that Cauchon had showed too much of his hand, we were doing the same," Jehanne replied.

"In front of friends though," D'Aulon said.

"I think the new gods are questioning whether they are my friends or not. Else why wouldn't they tell me to mind my tongue all together?"

"Makes sense," Culant said.

"So it's agreed, there will be no mention of the six questions or the six armor pieces," John2 said.

"Agreed," they all said.

"You should all try to get some sleep. The flight will take several more hours," Deark said. "I'll wake you one hour prior to deplaning."

As Jehanne laid her head on her folded up cloak, all she could think about were the events of the last few months. She wondered if Jovi571 was ready for the trials on the moon, and if any of her friends had been kicked out of school or sent to the Stone Room because of Cauchon's trickery. Mostly however, she hoped her parents were ok and that she would get to see them again someday. Eventually she fell asleep and found herself facing the dark cave again, but no one was there. The two torches were on the wall just as in her previous visit. She walked up attaching the buckler to her arm, smiling to find no augmentation. Grasping the torch and leaving the sword, she began walking into the cave.

"Did you find what you were looking for?" An unfamiliar male voice asked, as the cave turned into a room she had never seen.

"I'm not sure," Jehanne replied.

"You should probably shut that off," another voice, this time a female one said. Jehanne looked to see the torch she'd been carrying was now a portable light. Shutting it off, she looked back into the tunnel which had changed. Now it looked like a dark closet.

"I told you it was pointless to go in there," the man said.

"Why was it pointless?" Jehanne asked defiantly.

"Why would we keep a question under the stairs?" he replied.

"Everyone knows a question should be worn at all times by the Viceroy of the Mother City."

"Jehanne, wake up we'll be landing soon," Deark said, giving her a shake.

"If a Viceroy wears the question then it'll be easy to find," she said, grasping the Entity's shoulders.

"I can't say as I've ever woke up from a dream like that," Kennedy said.

"La Hire doesn't dream. Mostly La Hire just tessalates complex three dimensional shapes until La Hire gets bored."

"You fill your night with a screen saver program?" Gilles asked.

"It's fun and relaxing," La Hire replied as the plane shook upon landing.

"Welcome to Jargeau, Australia," a voice said over the speakers in the corner.

Section Three – Chapter Three

The area around the air field was vacant. The troops stretched their legs as the transports came off the whales.

"Do we know where we're going?" Tremoille asked, leading his small entourage.

"We're heading to Jargeau's Mother City," Jehanne said.

"To what end?" Flavy asked.

"We have some closets that need exploring," she said as she walked to the nearest truck.

"Let's get loaded up!" Gaucourt shouted.

"Closets?" Jehanne heard from behind her, although the voice was not clear enough to identify the speaker. The vehicles were quickly loaded, the Bastard walked up to Jehanne as they were about to pull away.

"Should we leave a contingent here?" he asked.

"If you tell me your pilots are truly yours than I would say no. We don't know what we may face when we arrive at the wall of the Mother City."

"I trust them, just as I have hundreds of times before."

"Tell them to fill the reserves and have the engines running, we may need a hasty exit," Deark instructed.

"Agreed," Severe said from the driver's seat in La Pucelle's vehicle. Once the Bastard of New Orleans boarded his truck the group began the bumpy ride to the first stop on their itinerary. After thirty minutes of bouncing, the vehicles arrived outside the wall.

Joanna667

"What business have you in our Mother City?" an I-CAM unit with an Alpha and an Omega on its chest asked.

"What reason for an I-CAM unit in Jargeau?" Deark asked.

"When Generals Talbot and Pole arrived here from New Orleans, they spoke of a band of miscreants that attacked the Commander of Human Capital there. Again I ask, what business have you in our Mother City?"

"I've brought the grassroots team for Charles7's election. We need to meet with your Viceroy," John2 said.

"I can't possibly let you all in, especially with a cannon," Alpha-Omega said.

"This is a relic of a long dead time, we wanted to use it as a campaign slogan," Minguet said.

"Slogan?" the I-CAM inquired.

"Railing into a new day!" Gilles quickly blurted out an impromptu slogan.

"That's terrible," the I-CAM unit said.

"But it made you think," Gilles said.

"Six of you may enter," Alpha-Omega said, ignoring the statement. "The rest must stay here."

"Thank you," John2 said.

"Railing into a new day?" Jehanne poked Gilles as they walked back to the trucks.

"Nobody else was coming up with anything." He smiled.

"John2 as Charles7's election chairman, Archbishop Chartres and Georges Tremoille as his advisors, Jean Joinville as the liaison to the One World Government, Deark and I will go into the city. If you hear anything or see anything on the informational boards, I trust you'll know what to do."

"You're not going anywhere without me," D'Aulon said.

"I'm going to need you out here," Jehanne said.

"I think he's right," Deark said. "If we're only allowed six then I should stay back."

"As you say, but I think having an Entity with us—," she started.

"Would be a terrible mistake. It makes it all seem fake somehow," John2 said. "Sorry, Deark."

"No need, I agree with you," he replied.

"Let's go, we're beginning to draw stares," Tremoille said.

"Sometimes La Hire draws stairs but it gets boring very fast." The look that the political advisor gave the large augmented was enough to make a monk sworn to silence burst out in laughter.

******

"So how is it that I can help you?" General Talbot greeted them in a conference room that had cameras and monitors on all four walls. The cameras were turned away from the table in an off position.

"Since when have you been named the Viceroy of the city, General Talbot?" John2 asked.

"I was in charge of the forces in New Orleans when your group was arrested. The Augmented and Mundane of the city rose up against us. I was sent here for my failure to quell the incident before it got out of hand. Madam Commander gave me this as a reminder of my shortcomings." He held out Jehanne's banner.

"May I?" Jehanne asked.

"By all means. I don't wish to have my mistakes waving in my face each morning." He handed it to her.

"Please take better care of this," she said, giving it to D'Aulon. "I'd hate for General Talbot to have it insulting his mornings in the future."

"Of course," D'Aulon said.

"So you are the Viceroy of Jargeau?" John2 asked once again.

"No, Viceroy Kostick is in charge of the city, and Jackenape oversees the troops here," Talbot replied.

"Jackenape?" D'Aulon inquired.

"General William Pole."

"I require audience with them," Jehanne announced.

"I'll see what I can arrange. Please make yourselves comfortable." He indicated for them to sit at the table and left the room. A few minutes later the cameras rotated and the optics winked to life.

"Jargeau? Now I must admit, I in no way saw that one coming," Archbishop Cauchon said, his image appearing a few seconds after his words.

"Archbishop, good morning. How are you this day?" Chartres asked. The fact that he sat up straighter in his chair was obvious to Jehanne and D'Aulon.

"It's evening here and as I'm in the grace of the new gods, I'm of course, wonderful," he replied, taking in the faces at the table.

"How is it that I can assist you in your visit to my city?" a thin, wide-eyed Entity asked, walking into the room.

"Viceroy Kostick, we have this covered," Madam Commander dismissed her underling as her image appeared on a second of the monitors.

"Of course," she said, turning to leave.

"Actually, I would very much like to speak with you Viceroy," Jehanne said, getting up from the table.

"She has little time to deal with rabble such as yourselves," an Entity that appeared to have been stylized after paladins of olden days said.

"Madam Commander, General Pole," Viceroy Kostick turned facing the room again. "I have no issue speaking with them. After all, two of the High Leader's advisors are present." Her tone was clipped and carried the element of hate.

"I have no intention of allowing this Mother City's Viceroy to speak with any of this group of rebels." The General grasped the smaller Entity's shoulders, turning her back to the door.

"Trusted Rebels." La Hire corrected.

"What?"

"La Hire said we are the 'Trusted Rebels' not just a group of rebels."

"Fine, I have no intention of——."

"At ease General," Madam Commander ordered. "I would like to know where this is going."

"As would—," Archbishop Cauchon's image and that of the Commander of Human Capital were replaced with blank blue screens. D'Aulon winked across at Jehanne.

"What happened? Bring them back," Joinville yelled.

"It's nothing for alarm brother, sit back." Archbishop Chartres placed a hand on his shoulder.

"CAM units, take this trash to the dungeons," General Pole said into a wall-mounted communication unit.

"General we simply wish to speak with the Viceroy," Jehanne said.

"I told you before, I have no intention of allowing you to spend a minute with her, much less alone. CAM units –," he started into the intercom again but his words were cut off as the entire city shook.

"With that, it's time for us to depart," D'Aulon said, rushing around the table to take Jehanne's wrist and lead her from the room.

"Are we under attack?" Viceroy Kostick asked.

"Actually I think we're being given a distraction to escape General Pole's arrest order," Jehanne said. "If I promise you no harm will you accompany me?" her question was barely audible.

"My goal is to keep this city safe. Having your Trusted Rebels blowing it up doesn't exactly fit that plan," she whispered back.

"D'Aulon, take her by the shoulder," Jehanne said.

"Come with me," he said loud enough for all in the area to hear.

"Let me go you Cad," the Viceroy shouted this time drawing the attention of General Pole.

"Get them!" He redirected the CAM units that were closing in on John2 and the other members of Jehanne's party.

"Follow me," John2 said, guiding the others away.

"We've done nothing wrong, we should stay here and—," this time it was Tremoille's words that were halted by the rail gun.

"That sound is the Laval brothers and the Good Shepherdess." John2 pulled the two advisors by their shirts. "If you want to stay and answer for our insurrection, that's your call." They reached the door ahead of the CAM units.

"Shit," Joinville replied, starting to follow the others.

"Language," Jehanne said twenty feet in front of them.

*****

The third explosion caused some stones from the ceiling to drop, slowing General Pole's progress and causing Tremoille to trip. John2 stopped to assist the advisor and signaled for Jehanne to continue on. "We'll catch up. Keep moving!"

D'Aulon continued moving, guiding Jehanne and Viceroy Kostick back the way they had come. Their pace quickened until they found a force of W, I, and standard model CAM units gathering in the courtyard waiting on them. A laser bolt from a W-CAM that was reflected by Jehanne back into their ranks sent them scurrying and allowed her group to return to the hallway.

"Let me lead," Viceroy Kostick said.

"Think of your path Viceroy, and be subtle in your directing of D'Aulon," Jehanne said.

"Why?" she asked.

"She's trying to keep you safe. If the One World Government thinks you're aiding us, you may get to inspect your Stone Room up close and personal," D'Aulon said.

"Understood," the Viceroy said, giving D'Aulon small pushes and nudges leading him to a large set of stairs.

"The closet from my…" Jehanne's words faded as she ran up to the hidden door opening it.

"How did you know that was there?" the Viceroy asked.

"No time for that, watch your head." D'Aulon helped her into the opening. "You two go, I'll get the others attention."

"Make certain John2 is safe, I have made promises," Jehanne said over her shoulder.

"Can you see where you're going?"

"Yes," Jehanne said, entering into the cave hidden below the stairs.

"Can you speak as we run?" Viceroy Kostick asked.

"I want you to understand I'm on a calling from Politician. However what I'm going to ask you has been told to one of my party by Ursula-Minor."

"That makes me concerned about my safety."

"I promised that no harm would come to you." Jehanne ducked a low rock formation.

"And now you tell me you have spoken with Politician and that an Augmented was granted audience with Ursula-Minor," the Viceroy said.

"It was an Entity."

"What?"

"Deark is an Entity. He's the one that spoke with the most ancient of your kind."

"It's asking a lot for me to take you on trust, yet I feel compelled to."

"There is a piece of armor that has been given to you," Jehanne started.

"How can you know that?"

"Viceroy, I told you, Ursula-Minor told Deark to share that information with our small band. I also know that a question has been charged to you for secrecy."

"Are those three vile creatures that sat at the table with us in your confidence?" she asked.

"No Viceroy, they're in Charles7's confidence. I've been directed by the new gods to hold my trust from them."

"That's the most intelligent thing I've heard in years."

"Be that as it may, what can you tell me of that I seek?" Jehanne asked.

"There is a question engraved on each of the armor sections. I think it's important to know these sections won't give you the answers. However, some of the Viceroys of the Mother Cities carry a talisman that has their question on them. In those cases they will have the answer." Viceroy Kostick's words were spoken without slowing her pace or turning to face Jehanne.

"Wait, did you say that only some of the Viceroys have answers? Are you saying there are questions without answers?"

"That's exactly what I'm saying."

"Interesting, although I don't actually need the answers. Which group do you fall into?" As Jehanne asked this, the Viceroy flipped a previously unseen necklace to her back, so that the amulet on the chain lay facing Jehanne.

"I happen to be one with a Talisman."

"I don't need to know what the answer is, but please tell me your question?" Jehanne asked.

"The question only," Viceroy Kostick paused. "Very well it was: How do we keep our power over the world's Humans?" she stopped as they reached a fork.

"Thank you. How can I find the section of armor that you have been charged with keeping safe?"

"It's further down this path," she pointed to the right tunnel. "I fear, however, finding it will do you no good. The secret to opening the containment field was lost to us when Commissioner left the One World Government."

"Can you stay here and show my friends out?"

"Of course, good luck to you."

"Thank you again." Jehanne started moving again.

"When you return, follow every left fork until you get outside the wall," the Viceroy yelled after her.

******

When she was far enough down the tunnel that she couldn't make out the slight figure of the Viceroy for the twists and turns, she removed her sword which once again glowed white and set it along the stone wall. She took a calming breath and looked around her for anyone that would steal the artifact. As the glow of the sword faded, Jehanne turned and continued her plunge into the tunnel.

Ahead of her she heard running water, then the tunnel opened into a chamber. A river rushed through the center of the cave Jehanne noticed there was something irregular about the pattern. At home the sound of the river was constant as the water splashed over the same stones. Here, the water would flow to a crescendo and fall off abruptly, starting the increased flow over again.

'The pattern is repeating' she thought, walking deeper into the room to look closely at each and every part of her surroundings. There was little vegetation which didn't surprise her as she estimated her depth below the ground at a couple hundred feet. The words, 'actual depth negative eighty feet' flashed in her optic. Still looking around, Jehanne reached the side of the river when she realized the stone floor of the cave didn't appear wet, or even damp. She bent over touching it. "Dry?" Her question echoed about the room.

Confused, she stood up and looked at the room again, turning slowly in a circle. 'What's wrong with this picture?' Her thoughts coming up short, she saw nothing; no opening or hiding places. No mineral growths from the ceiling, or coming up from the floor, stalactites and stalagmites she remembered.

Deark had said, "An easy way to remember which was which, stalactites, hold tight to the ceiling and stalagmites, might have fallen to the floor." Jehanne smiled remembering the lesson.

"No openings." She looked at the river again. "The room would have to be wet..." her words trailed off as she stepped closer to the look at the running water. "What is the depth of the water?" she asked, seeing the question write out on her heads up display she waited. The answer came less than a second later, 'No water present.' She wasn't surprised by the answer. She walked forward, ignoring the sight of the rapids and the sound of the rushing water. She stopped when she reached the center, turning and looking at the holographic generator out of curiosity. It was small enough to not be noticed in the center of the false river.

"Hello," a male voice called from the other side of the river.

"Hello," Jehanne replied as the illusion of the river stopped.

"My name is Commissioner. I thank you for not approaching with weapons drawn." The Entity in front of her had a head that bore a striking resemblance to a cooking device Jehanne had seen in some old picture books, a toaster she remembered it being called.

"My name is Jehanne. Pleased to meet you. Are you also a hologram?" she asked.

"That I am, how did you know?"

"I was told that you've left the One World Government."

"Really? Do you know why?" Commissioner asked.

"I don't. I only just heard your name five minutes ago. How is it that you are interacting with me?"

"I reverse engineered the Ursula project to determine how Ursula-Minor held some of Ursula after her demise."

"Quite ingenious."

"Thank you," he said, taking a small bow.

"Can you tell me how this works? Where is the section of armor that's down here?" Jehanne asked.

"How do you know of the armor?" Commissioner asked.

"Ursula-Minor informed one of my –," her words were cut off.

"Again I must say, 'really?'. This is more interesting than when you said I left my role in the One World Government. Ursula-Minor spoke to a Mundane?"

"Actually no, Deark is an Entity."

"Deark? You travel with Deark yet you are a Mundane, falsifying yourself as an Augmented, yet I can see you're definitely not one."

"I do travel with him. He was my instructor before I was given a calling by Politician."

"Can you expound on that?" Commissioner was now enthralled.

"My friends are outside fighting, I really need to progress."

"Oh my! Alright let's do that then. As this is your first section of armor," he indicated a wall of stone. As he pointed a light illuminated showing a pair of white metal gloves, which were gently moving as bubbles slowly moved around them. "These are the gauntlets to the suit of armor. The containment which preserves them will also dissolve the flesh of those that attempt to remove them."

"You commented on my not arriving with weapons drawn."

"Yes, it would have been unfortunate. The fact is, as a hologram weapons couldn't hurt me yet protocol would've forced me to activate the sentry program to protect the gauntlets."

"And?"

"You would have died unless there was someone here to stop it."

"That would have been unfortunate indeed," Jehanne said. "What if I brought in a weapon now?"

"My, that's an interesting question. I believe that my artificial intelligence will recognize you and deem it safe, but I can't be one hundred percent certain of that," Commissioner said.

"I have a plan." She turned and walked back across the river hologram and out into the tunnel. She waited to the count of two hundred-fifty and then reentered the cavern. After crossing the river she was greeted by the same voice, "Hello."

"Hello," she replied, walking up to Commissioner.

"Welcome back Jehanne. That was a short trip. I show you being gone less than five minutes."

"I was testing your AI recognition. If I come in here with a weapon, you know you don't need to elicit the sentry protocol."

"Seems logical."

"I'll be right back," Jehanne said, heading back to retrieve her sword. She turned the corner arriving where the sword should've been.

******

"Are you looking for this?" a voice she had heard recently asked. The sword was in the grasp of the one Talbot had called Jackenape. His thick arms looked natural holding the weapon at the ready.

"Yes, General Pole that's what I was looking for." She began walking backwards. The heads up display automatically gave her a view of where she was walking.

"Where do you have the Viceroy?"

"I got lost when we were escaping. I don't know where she is."

"Not much of a leader, are you?" he laughed.

"I don't know about that," Jehanne said as she left the tunnel and entered the cavern. In the blink of an eye, several rocks surrounding the entrance had transformed into the sentries that Commissioner had promised. General Pole was crushed and her sword went skidding across the ground as they bound him. She bent and lifted it gingerly, the sentries stopped what they were doing and turned their heads to her in unison.

"Are you alright?" one of them asked.

"I'm fine. You're not going to tackle me for having my sword are you?" she asked.

"No Jehanne, you have been approved for such things," the sentry replied.

"Thank you," she said, putting the sword into the sheath on her back.

"I'm a general in the service of the Leader of the Republicus and I demand you release me at once," Pole yelled.

"That's up to Jehanne, as you were accosting her."

"I was arresting her in the name of the High Leader."

"No, I will be arresting him," Jehanne said. "I will be back for him. Please blindfold and gag him.

"As you say."

"You'll regret thi—" The gag covered his mouth stopping his coherent words.

"Please, still your yelling before I have them knock you out," Jehanne said to the General. She once again headed to the hologram river and up to Commissioner.

"I guess we have our answer; you are approved to carry a weapon. I don't understand why you went to the trouble, a sword will not cut through this containment. For that matter the rail gun upstairs firing at the building will not breech this protection."

"I think you may be mistaken," she said as the bubbles started roiling at a faster frequency the closer she got to the tank.

"That's most interesting." Commissioner walked up to get a closer look.

"I believe," she said pulling the sword out once more. The blade glowed brighter than she had seen it before. "The metal in the gloves is the same metal that's in this sword." The gloves were now a blur of white behind a continuous flow of bubbles. She touched the blade to the tank. To her surprise and his, it passed right through and came back with one of the gauntlets.

"Careful, that's still covered in acid," he said as she dropped it from her sword on to the cave floor and stabbed the blade once more through the side, fishing out the other. "You there," he yelled to one of the sentries.

"Yes?" It replied when it joined them.

"I need you to escort this young lady and her prisoner to the surface. Carry these two gloves until such a time they have been rinsed in water."

******

"There she is!" Kennedy yelled as she emerged from a hidden exit that the sentry opened.

"You scared the Dickens out of me. I didn't know you going to run off! What if you would have run into General Pole and –," D'Aulon's word stalled as the sentry pushed the bound prisoner forward after removing his blindfold. It then headed off with the gauntlets, completely unnoticed by the group.

"La Hire guesses she would just take him prisoner," he laughed.

"That's enough out of you! Consider yourself lucky you're not bound like that," Tremoille yelled. Jehanne saw that some of her group was ok with this treatment, others including her, not so much.

"How dare you speak to one of my captains like that!" her steps were fast and her slap faster. The political advisor fell to the ground, her augmented hand impacting solidly with his cheek. "Second time I've seen you in that position today," she taunted.

"Jehanne!" Deark yelled as she moved in to hit him a second time.

"What?"

"La Hire was found speaking with General Talbot in the midst of the battle." Deark walked up and helped Tremoille to his feet.

"You will—," he started.

"If you dare threaten her, I won't ask her to still her hand and she will beat you like the cur you are," Deark said. "We've not had the chance to question him as the battle has been raging around us."

"What of Viceroy Kostick?" Jehanne asked.

"She has only just returned to her Mother City," John2 said.

"I'm glad to see you unharmed my friend," she replied. "Minguet, can you please send word that we have General Pole and ask that General Talbot come out to speak with us?"

"Done," he said a moment later.

"What is that?" de Metz asked looking at the sentry heading back to Jehanne with a makeshift bag in its outstretched hand.

"That's a tale for another time." She turned to greet the newcomer. "Are they safe now?"

"Yes."

"Thank you for your help," Jehanne said. The sentry walked back to the wall and turned into stone, blending perfectly.

"Did you see that?" Tremoille asked.

"See what?" Deark replied, continuing to stabilize the advisor.

"Jehanne, we have word from the Viceroy; Talbot has fled the city," Minguet said. Several of the party glared at La Hire.

"What? La Hire isn't hiding him."

"Captain Gaucourt, please pass the word, we leave at once," Jehanne said. "I wish to get in the air to our next destination and speak with La Hire."

"Of course."

"Guy, Andre," Jehanne called out. The brothers walked up to her, Gilles closely on their heels. "Thank you for bringing the Good Shepherdess. It most likely saved my life," Jehanne said.

"Glad to be recognized for our brilliance," Andre replied.

"Will it still fire?"

"We fired only three times, she may have something left in her," Guy answered.

"Railing into the Future." Jehanne spoke with fake airs, walking away from the three men with her bag in tow, tying it around her belt.

"Come on, it was spur of the moment," Gilles said after her.

Section Three – Chapter Four

The transport planes took to the sky. Deark had communicated only with the pilots where the teams next destination was. Jehanne ignored the comments from Charles7's advisors telling her that, "She had no right to hold information from them," and "How were they to lend advice to the leadership if they couldn't know the entire plan?"

The prisoner was loaded on the Galaxy and confined to the main conference room on board. Three of the Bastard's best men were to guard him around the clock. When the advisors started to board the Condor, Severe redirected them to the Galaxy. "I think it best if your group stays close to the prisoner so he isn't accidentally killed."

"I hadn't thought about that but yes you're probably right. As liaison to the High Leader, it would look very bad if one of his Generals was killed on my watch," Joinville said.

Jehanne and her captains boarded the Condor. After the plane stabilized, they walked to the conference room on their aircraft, closing and locking the door.

"Before we begin I want to be abundantly clear; I trust Etienne with my life," Jehanne said. "Next, I want someone other than Etienne to tell me what occurred that has drawn the ire of the four advisors."

John2 cleared his throat and kept his eye contact to Jehanne. "When Viceroy Kostick led us out of the tunnel, we walked straight into La Hire speaking with an Entity. As we got closer it became clear he was speaking with General Talbott."

"Not yet!" Jehanne said holding up a hand to still La Hire.

"Fine," he harrumphed.

"While I get that consorting with the enemy is wrong, what possible reason would Etienne have for betraying us?"

"He was offered a brand new set of the latest augmentations available," Culant said.

"Says who?" Jehanne asked.

"Says himself," Deark finally spoke up.

"What?" she asked looking at her captain.

"May La Hire speak yet?"

"Yes Etienne, go ahead," Jehanne replied.

"Thank you. It's true, General Talbot offered La Hire augmentations in exchange for letting him leave." He paused as several of the captains began yelling. "La Hire said no!" he shouted over the din.

"What happened next?" she asked.

"The rat faced curse word grabbed La Hire and forced La Hire back to our camp."

"Why didn't you kick him to the curb?" Severe asked.

"La Hire promised La Pucelle, La Hire wouldn't step on any of Charles7's advisors."

"That's true he did," Jehanne said.

"If not with your assistance, then how do you think he escaped?" John2 asked.

"I'd call that one obvious," Poton said. "When your group dragged him—,"

"For the record; I dragged no one." he replied.

"That's correct, John2 yelled at the others for dragging La Hire."

"Fine, my thought remains that when the dragging took place, General Talbot slunk away like a thief in the night," Poton said.

"Makes sense," Jehanne said.

"We'll most likely see him again. The Viceroy will be forced to tell what you were there for and they will dispatch forces to get ahead of us," Deark said.

"Ok if no one else is going to ask," Pouli started.

"What's in the bag?" Bastard asked, receiving a glare from Pouli.

"Oh, I completely forgot," Jehanne said untying her burden. "This is the first of our pieces of the armor." She allowed the gauntlets to drop on the table.

"Gloves?" Minguet asked.

"It takes six sections to make a suit of armor boy," Poton said.

"I guess I just hoped for a bigger piece first," he said sheepishly.

"Put them on," Gaucourt said. The rest of the table parroted their approval for the suggestion.

"Ok." She grabbed the left gauntlet and rubbed the bag around the inside of it. Setting the cloth down, she selected the release function from the menu in her eye piece. The augmentation pulled back and her left hand was human again. Placing the glove on her hand, the augmentation closed right over it and grew blindingly bright. When the glow had faded, to everyone's astonishment, the glove had vanished.

"Where did it go?" Kennedy asked.

"I can feel it, it's still on me," Jehanne said, making the augmentation release again. There, on her hand, was the gauntlet. She closed it just to see if it would do it again. This time however, the glow did not present itself, the gauntlet just blinked out as the augmentation closed.

"That's too much!" John2 said.

"Do the other one!" Pouli said.

"Ok." She repeated the process and the brilliance of the light forced them all to shield their eyes once more.

"I think the armor needs to acclimate itself to the augmentation," Deark said.

"And once it's acclimated itself it's supposed to vanish? La Hire thinks this hocus pocus is bizarre. La Hire likes it not at all." And with that he got up and walked from the conference room.

"I calculate that we have about eight hours in flight. You should all eat something and go to sleep," Deark said.

******

The group headed over finding the mess hall full to bursting. Jehanne walked among the troops, finding augmented men and women as well as several entities, interwoven with Humans, like a finely crafted rug.

"Hello," Jehanne said, sitting at a random table. D'Aulon stood off to the side, not having found a space large enough for himself to sit.

"Hello," the occupants of the table said.

"How do you feel today went?" she asked.

"There wasn't as much fighting as I thought there'd be," a muscular woman with small brown eyes said.

"Is that a good thing or bad?" Jehanne asked.

"Just an observation," the same woman said.

"We were told this was a search and destroy mission," an Entity with purple dragonweave said.

"It would've been had the Viceroy not cooperated," she answered.

"What isth our goal in all thith?" an Augmented man in the burgundy robes of a priest asked with a strong lisp.

"Do I know you? You seem awfully familiar," Jehanne asked.

"Actually I questioned you along with theveral otherth who therve on Charles7'th Counthil, I am Brother Theg—," he started.

"Brother Seguin," she finished. "I didn't see you join us with the Archbishop."

"Ath I didn't, that would have been difficult."

"He's been with us a couple weeks now," the muscular woman said. "Is that the sword we've heard so much about or are you wearing a different one?"

"Yes, this is the relic that was found," Jehanne said.

"I'd heard that it glowth. May we thee it?" Brother Seguin lisped.

"Of course." She stood and removed the sword. The white glow on the blade was brighter than ever before, drawing the attention of everyone in the room. Immediately, there was no sound except the roar of the engines.

"That was found underground?" a question came from the Entity with purple dragonweave.

"Yes, Jehanne told the people of Feirbois they could find it buried beneath the fallen church cornerstone. With a bit of help from some of our party they dug five feet down and just as she had said, there it sat," Deark said, having joined them at some point.

"And it'th thtill shiny? Amazing," Brother Seguin replied.

"To answer your previous question brother; 'what is our goal in all this?' To be victorious. Victorious in reinstating freedoms lost, victorious in quelling the terror that Humans feel for just being themselves. No matter how labyrinthian the path may be to accomplish it, we will be victorious. For if we fail all will be lost."

"Where is it we're headed?" the muscular woman asked.

"I'm sorry but until the pilots make their announcement, I'm leaving that unanswered." Jehanne grabbed some food and walked out of the cafeteria..

"Attention, you should try to get some rest, tomorrow may not be like today was," Gaucourt said to those in the cafeteria.

"How long until we land?" the Entity with purple dragonweave asked.

"Seven hours and thirty minutes until wheels down," Deark said as he followed Jehanne and D'Aulon out of the mess hall.

******

"Welcome to Meung, Japan." The voice of the pilot woke Jehanne from a dreamless sleep.

"Deark why didn't you wake me?" she asked, turning and facing the Entity. She found him in a state much like the one he had been in when he dropped from his horse. "Deark?" When he stayed silent she left the room and joined the rest of her captains.

"Did you sleep well?" Pouli asked.

"Like a log. How about you?" she asked

"Where's Deark? I thought he was going to wake us before wheels down," Kennedy asked, not allowing Pouli to answer.

"He seems to be powered down again," Jehanne said.

"Sleeping on your watch is a serious offense," Gilles said.

"I think we'll cut him some slack," Severe said.

"When did you take charge?" Culant asked.

"Little bits at a time, haven't you been paying attention?" Poton asked.

"Guess not," he replied.

"Enough, let's get a move on. La Hire is sure the troops are confused as to what the plan is."

"Now him I've seen in charge since the beginning," Culant laughed. The group headed toward the rear of the plane.

They walked through the troops hearing several questions of, "Why are we in Japan?" Jehanne ignored the questions until the plane had stopped and the loading door had been fully lowered.

"Follow me, please. All will be explained," she said as she walked to join the other deplaning troops. "We have come to Meung, Japan to visit the Mother City. In ancient days it was called Kintai. The Castle and serpent bridge that leads to it are the oldest of all the world's Mother Cities. I would like to do as little damage to this place as possible. With that in mind, I had Bastard, Severe, and La Hire devise a strategy."

"Thank you la Pucelle. First, we will break into small battle groups. Once done, in order to catch them with their pants down, we will wait until the sun has fully left the sky. At that time we will rush across the Serpent at full sprint; only those that are engaged in battle will stop, along with their assigned groups, to fight the sentries. The rest will push on, overpowering the CAM units at the gate and opening it. At which time the city will for all practical purposes have fallen. We will demand the city's Viceroy to come and speak with us," Bastard said.

"I would suggest that your groups determine the best method of calling for support. As we will be running in silence, I should think a twine connecting the groups the best method." John2 added.

"Excellent suggestion. Are there any questions?" Severe asked.

When none came, "La Hire will now put you into your fighting groups." He walked through them, numbering each of the troops one through twenty.

"I didn't know you could count that high," Gilles said.

"Give him a break Gilles, he has a finger or toe for each of those numbers. If he had to go to thirty we'd be here for days," Robinet said.

"Zero," La Hire said touching Robinet and then again when he touched Gilles.

"Zero?" they asked.

"You smart mouths get to babysit Deark," La hire laughed.

"Seriously?" Gilles asked.

"Yes," Jehanne jumped in. "I will not leave him in this state. If he powers up before we leave you can join La Hire's group."

"I don't know which is worse," Robinet said. "I've fought alongside him before; he leaves nothing in his wake."

"La Hire promises that La Hire will leave a few for you." The group chuckled at the gallows humor.

It took little time at all for the sun to set. Gilles and Robinet joined the still powered down Deark as the troops departed. The forested area on their side of the river was thick with bamboo. Those with arm augmentations cut a path for the rest. It was forty five minutes of hard marching before they arrived at the Serpent.

"Remember as we cross, if members of your group are attacked the twine will pull taut you need to stop and support them," Severe said.

"Charge!" La Hire's whispered yell started the next assault against the One World Government.

******

At the halfway point of the Serpent Bridge something shot out of the water, wrapping around Jehanne's waist. She was lifted into the air and out over the water. The plan broke apart when several of the battle groups led by her captains stopped to evaluate the situation.

"Stick to the plan, my group has this," Jehanne yelled to the onlookers.

"No we need to get you down," de Metz said.

"That may only be done by taking the city now, go!"

"She's right, onward!" Severe yelled.

"Is it hurting you?" Minguet asked just as the tentacle, for that's all it could be, gave her a squeeze.

"Don't give it any ideas," Jehanne said, pulling her sword from its sheath. "Take that vile beast!" She slashed, severing it and freeing herself. She fell into the cold water and began to sink. The vibration of many others jumping into the water to her aid could be felt. "No!" she tried to yell yet only bubbles came out of her mouth, along with a gulp of water going in.

She felt a hand grasp hers and she was being guided back to the surface. The small hand slipped from hers as she was once again grasped by the tentacle, or another. Rising into the air, she could see all the action from this vantage point, her eye augmentation made it easy to see the decimation that was befalling them.

The hand that had grabbed hers was Minguet's, and for his trouble another of the tentacles was holding him underwater which was littered with the other forty or so members of her group, drowned or drowning with the aid of whatever held her about the waist. On the bridge, Talbot's W–CAM forces were blasting the rest of her troops with their lasers, like shooting fish in a barrel. La Hire stood alone, deflecting the bolts with the buckler they had fashioned in New Orleans. Eventually the gates started to open to his left.

"Etienne!" she yelled attempting to get him to run.

"La Pucelle!" Gilles, who had just then rushed up with Deark and Robinet, dove from the serpents back and through bodies that were covering the top of the water like lily pads. Deark, watching from the bridge, transformed into a W–CAM unit and shot Robinet in the back as the troops finally took down the still fighting La Hire. Deark's gaze turned to her, a slight curl touched his mouth and he fired the laser.

"NO!" She sat up, covered in sweat with Deark shaking her shoulder.

"Wake now, we're almost there. What?" he asked, seeing the way she glared at him.

"Just a dream," she shook her head. "A really vivid dream. Can you go ask La Hire, Bastard, and Severe to come in here."

"Of course." He headed out of the room.

"Jehanne," Severe said, looking at her pale face when they arrived minutes later. "You look awful."

"Severe, no wonder you don't get the ladies," La Hire said.

"What?"

"Never mind your bickering," Jehanne said. "I believe I've been sent a message. We need to review the plans you've devised."

"The plan is as we discussed before: wait for nightfall and strike them while their focus is low," La Hire said.

"They wait for us. Talbot is here and his full squadron of W-CAM units have set a trap for us."

"Then we should take to the air. We have nowhere near enough troops to fight that," Severe said.

"Agreed. The new gods have shown me that this endeavor is less about numbers and more about strategy if we are to gain the armor section hidden here," Jehanne said.

"What would you suggest then?" Deark asked.

Ten minutes later the plane rolled to a stop and they left her cabin. Walking through the troops waiting patiently in the cargo hold, she signaled to her captains to join her. The grumbling of the troops were silenced with a glance from Gaucourt.

"My apologies, this is a stop which you will not be deplaning," Jehanne said to the group.

"At ease, we will return soon," the Bastard yelled to the angry troops.

As Robinet walked down the ramp La Hire faced him. "This isn't your fight old friend. Please join the rest in the plane."

"You know I could just follow you," he replied.

"You know La Hire could just remove your leg augmentations."

"I think I heard someone calling me," Robinet said, heading back onto the plane.

"What is the plan?" Tremoille asked, walking up.

"The plan is for a few of us to go investigate," Poton said.

"I used to be a very astute tracker," Joinville said.

"The offer is appreciated. Yet all of you will stay on the plane," John2 said.

"I beg your pardon, are you dismissing us?" Archbishop Chartres asked.

"Perceptive aren't they?" de Metz made shooing motions to the advisors.

"How long do you believe we will endure these slights?" Flavy asked.

"As long as it takes, now get on the damn plane," Culant ordered.

"Language," the ring of the staff against La Hire's augmentation sang out. This group too, boarded their plane.

"Deark, can you, Culant, and Bastard stay here and make certain none—," she started.

"No." Deark cut her off. "I too have a calling, Jehanne. I'm not certain what happened in that dream of yours, but I've sworn to Pedagogue to see you safely through this endeavor."

"I'm sorry of course. Gaucourt, I need these troops to stay here. I need the planes filled and made ready to leave in no time," Jehanne said.

"Of course," he replied. He and Bastard stayed back to make certain that none of the troops followed them or wandered off.

"Culant your job, if we don't show up in two hours is to take off. We should have little more than a thirty minute walk. That gives us an hour and half to return."

"I can do that," he said, inclining his head to her in respect.

"Of course you can dog lover, you have a strange knack for saving your skin." La Hire shook his comrade's hand.

******

Forty five minutes of cutting through bamboo shoots later, they reached the Serpent Bridge. "Listen to me. No matter what happens, you can't jump in the water. Is that clear?" Jehanne asked.

"La Hire has been completely clear, La Hire hates the water."

"Why Jehanne?" de Metz asked.

"There is nothing for me to fear there, but for you it may bring death."

"If we aren't to help you why are we here?" Minguet asked.

"I need your help to get there my friend." Jehanne put her hand on his, noticing that it actually was quite small, reminding her that he was even younger than she.

"Ok boys, lots of ground to cover. Keep her in our center," John2 said, playing the role of gentle leader like no other could.

"Charge!" La Hire whisper yelled, beginning a very different second assault against the One World Government than it might have been.

The strange bridge did in fact rise and fall like a sea serpent but in minutes they reached the center of the expanse. This is when the ambush from the unseen sentries started.

"Incoming!" Kennedy yelled as they fought off the first assault. Not having waited for darkness to fall, the tentacle was visible to all as it pushed both Trusted Rebel and sentry in its attempts to grab Jehanne.

"Remember what I said!" she yelled as it lifted her from the ground. "And be ready with your bucklers if the W-CAMs come from the castle." This time she didn't panic or pull her sword. The tentacle held her above the water just long enough for her to see that no one was disobeying her request. The water was warmer than what she had remembered from her dream. She saw the pilings that made up the supports for the bridge as she was pulled deeper and deeper under. Jehanne had just enough time to wonder why her lungs weren't burning. When she eventually reached the place where the pilings entered the riverbed, a small room became visible between two of them. She closed her eyes as the tentacle retracted through the wall.

"Hello," a familiar voice said as she was dropped on the floor.

"Commissioner? What was that thing?" Jehanne looked around the room, which was actually a translucent bubble looking out onto the river. It was much larger inside than it appeared as she had approached it.

"It was a simple machine used to test those seeking admittance. And yes, Jehanne, it is I. Did you expect someone or something else?"

"You know me?"

"I do. Each of the holographic representations of me is connected to each other."

"If you can communicate over some given frequency can Ursula-Minor and the Commander of Human Capital have the ability to monitor the activity that takes place here?" Jehanne asked.

"For a Mundane, you're catching on to technologies surprisingly fast. It's interesting that you ask that question, but no. For that matter, the real Commissioner can't monitor us either."

"Why is it interesting?" Jehanne walked around the room, trying to stay engaged while looking for the next armor piece.

"You didn't bring up the Leader of the Republicus. Am I to assume that the One World Government has taken a new direction? Does the advisor hold too much sway over the one in charge?" Commissioner asked.

"We're in the beginning of an election cycle... Wait, why does this rendition of you seem to ask so many more questions than the hologram in Jargeau?"

"Actually, you cut off my questions there. I do like the fact that you're line of questioning is more suspicious, are you having issues with your inner circle?" the Entity walked to one of the outer edges of the room and seemed to watch a large creature as it swam by.

"There is some bickering but I'm pushing them hard and—," she started.

"You deflect well." He turned and smiled, his toaster head swiveling about. "So what do you think of this facility versus the one in Jargeau?"

"The hazards in this one are much more real than the other. How is it that I can breathe down here?" she asked.

"Same reason you can see."

"What?"

"I forgot, cover your eye augmentation," Commissioner said.

She did as asked and was taken aback. "It's light?"

"It is," he said as he bounced on his toes. "Just another fascinating invention of mine. It's an algae hybrid that can only live in this location. I mutated a strain of algae with plankton which of course is infused with dinoflagellate and produces the light. When consumed by a certain type of bacteria it produces a byproduct that's thirteen percent pure oxygen. While it's on the low side for humans to live forever, it will keep the synergistic relationship between these organisms going."

"I'd have to say that's more than just fascinating."

"Thank you child."

"Can you tell me if the armor section is still stored here?"

"It is."

Jehanne looked about the enclosed space. "It must be hidden well."

"Allow those gauntlets—,"

"You can see them?" This time it was Jehanne that cut the other off.

"In reality I 'see' nothing, but yes I do sense them. That may only be because I knew you had them, I can't be certain of that though. Perhaps test it on one of your captains when you return." Commissioner's hand touched the side of his head contemplatively. "Be that as it may, allow those gauntlets to show you where the next pieces are at."

"Commissioner, that makes little to no sense."

"Really, I see it making perfect sense based upon what happened in Jargeau."

"The bubbles?" Jehanne's statement was more for her than a question for him. She walked about the entire room trying to gather any subtle changes. When she reached the area where Commissioner had watched the creature passing she felt a tingling in her hand. "This is another hologram."

She shook her head and walked through it into the next
room.

Section Three – Chapter Five

The room felt dimmer, mainly due to the bright tank in the center that was already a blur of bubbles and white somethings being carried around. "Are they shoes?" Jehanne asked.

"They're actually called sabatons, but yes same concept as shoes or boots, they protect your feet." Commissioner said. "I don't think you'll need that," noticing her reaching for her sword.

"Why?" Jehanne was confused briefly then felt the tingle from the gauntlets again. "But the acid." She said.

"You'll be fine, the gauntlets have made you immune to this concoction."

She began reaching her hand out and then faltered, "Um, I—," she stammered.

"Please trust me." He said, "Besides, the tide of battle is changing up top. It's time for you to return."

"Very well." Jehanne continued to stretch out her hand, smiling as it passed through the containment. Rather than waiting until she got back, she released the augmentations on her feet and placed the new armor pieces over her shoes. The brightness once again intensified when the augmentation sealed over the armor.

"Thank you for sharing that experience, I had been wondering what would happen when they were put on."

"Deark thought the armor acclimated with the augmentations," Jehanne said.

"He's a very smart Entity. However, he left out the most critical part of what's causing this to happen," he said as the tentacle rose from the floor and moved in her direction.

Her body was lifted and started toward the side she had entered through. "What did he miss?"

"You child, it had to be in contact with—," his words were cut off by the water that surrounded her.

******

"There." D'Aulon was the first to spot her breaking the surface.

"Another wave incoming." La Hire stepped down from a mountain of fallen Entities.

"Time to go." John2 took Jehanne by the wrist as the tentacle released her. They ran back toward the plane. After a few steps she was pulling him, after a few more he had released her not wanting to slow her down.

"As I see nothing new on you I'm guessing you didn't have any luck?" Deark asked as they reached the other end of the serpent.

"Apparently the sabatons were there up until about fifty years ago," Jehanne said.

"Wait, what? How do you know that?" Deark asked as they waited on the others.

"Commissioner said that they—," she started.

"Who?" Deark cut her off.

"Let's talk at the plane." She turned and started in the direction of the airstrip when the last of the group, Minguet, was off the bridge.

"Why aren't they chasing us? La Hire is still in the mood to fight."

"I imagine they feel we have a trap set up for them," de Metz said.

"I'm sure you're right," Deark replied.

"I swear this stupid bamboo has already grown back." Pouli cut some of the regrowth.

"It grows around twelve inches a day and we've only been gone a couple hours," John2 said.

"Actually my connection with Meung's Communication Boards says we've been gone for two days," D'Aulon said.

"How can that be?" Poton asked.

"I'm not certain, but he's correct. The News wires confirm we've been here for two days," Deark said.

"Deark do you show any voids in your memory database?" Minguet asked.

"No, just continuous stream of fighting for two days."

"If you've been fighting for two days, then why aren't any of your piles as high as La Hire's?"

"There must have been some type of communication spike," Gilles said. "We'll figure it out when we get back to the—," his words faded into shocked silence as they exited the pathway finding the Whales were not there.

"Those idiots!" Pouli yelled.

"If we've been gone for two days they did the right thing." Jehanne said. "We need to get some sleep."

"Let's head back into the cover of the forest," de Metz said.

"La Hire feels like La Hire hasn't eaten in two days."

"No fires until after sunup," Severe said.

"Agreed," John2 added.

******

"Jehanne, there's a plane flying over." Deark woke her. The sun had already cleared the ocean and it was looking to be a beautiful day.

"Is it one of the Whales?" she asked.

"No it's not a plane I've seen before," Poton said.

"And it's not a One World Government plane," Deark said.

"Well if it comes back La Hire thinks we should flag it down."

"And give away our position?" Minguet asked.

"It's that or we stay here until the castle gets reinforced and they come out after us," Gilles said.

"I agree, let's build a fire," Jehanne said. As wet as it was this was not a simple task, but eventually a signal fire was lit and there was some food cooking on the edge of it.

"Jehanne while we wait, can you tell us what happened when you were underwater?" de Metz asked.

"First, can anyone see or sense my new boots? Well technically sabatons?" she asked and everyone shook their heads no.

A moment later Deark looked away from her feet. "I do sense them yes. Yet I didn't yesterday, were they on you?"

"They were." She winked. "Deark can you tell us all who Commissioner is?"

Joanna667

"I was hoping you would get to him." The Entity that was known to all as Commissioner was the inventor that initially came up with the concept for the Mundane Moon Maze. He was the best of us but eventually fell out of favor with the One World Government. You see, he was the second Leader of the Republicus and when a leader steps down they're supposed to disappear from the public spotlight as well. In his case, none of the other Entities wanted him to disappear. He was too perfect, inventing things to make life better for all of us. When the Entities started pushing for him to get another term as Leader of the Republicus, he vanished."

"La Hire knows what that means."

"Perhaps yes, or perhaps he had had enough and took himself somewhere no one could find him," Deark replied.

"Why is it that you bring up this Commissioner?" John2 asked.

"When I found the gauntlets, I met him, actually a hologram of him, and then again below the water in Meung." She requested the augmentations on her legs to release, causing the sabatons to appear. She removed one and examined it. "Hmm."

"What?" They were all trying to look inside.

"I was told by Viceroy Kostick that the question was written inside the armor piece, although the answer wasn't."

"I completely forgot about the question. What was it for Jargeau?" Minguet asked.

361

"How can we keep power over the world's Humans?" D'Aulon said. Seeing Jehanne's confusion, he added, "You and the Viceroy weren't that far away when she told you."

"What is this question?" Pouli asked.

"I don't know." Jehanne tossed the piece to him and removed the other.

"What language is that?" de Metz asked, looking over Pouli's shoulder at the strange writing inside the sabaton.

"May I?" Deark held out a hand.

"Of course." Pouli handed it to him.

"This must be a language that Commissioner made up," he replied after examining the article for a while.

"Can I see one of the gauntlets and one of the sabatons?" D'Aulon and Minguet asked at the same time.

"Oh I see where they're going," John2 said.

Looking at the inside of the gauntlet for a minute, "Assuming the words are in the same order as our written language…" his words drifted. "It says, 'How can we blank the world's blank?' I believe."

"That question makes no sense to La Hire."

"Maybe Commissioner can tell you what these two symbols are when you see him again," Minguet pointed at the two unknown symbols.

"I can see the plane heading this way again," Kennedy said.

"Ok everyone grab a branch." Severe jumped up and took a large burning piece of something from the fire, beginning to run back to the area the whales had landed before. The others all joined him.

"I think it saw us, it's turning around," Jehanne said.

******

Ten minutes later the plane was rolling up to them. "I hope this was a good idea." Minguet said, edging his way to the back of the pack.

"Hello in the plane!" Deark's voice boomed.

"What a show off," John2 joked.

The door behind the cockpit opened, a ladder was dropped, the chains and metal cross members rattling as it unrolled. An arm waved and a male voice replied back, "Hello." This was followed by an Augmented man climbing down from the plane and walking in their direction. His face carried the scars of several arena matches.

"Oh shit!" John2's deep voice intoned.

"Language John2!" Jehanne said. "Who is he?"

"His name is Arthur Bretagne, his enemies call him Scarface, his friends call him Justicier."

"The dispenser of justice?" Gilles asked.

"That's correct," the newcomer said in a voice that sounded like it had screamed orders for far too long.

"Hello my old friend, what has you out searching for us?" John2 asked.

"What makes you thing I'm looking for you? And more importantly when did we become friends?" The dialect he spoke was unfamiliar to Jehanne. If the man's sarcastic retort stung John2 he didn't show it.

"As I dragged you from Charles7's council chambers and arrested you, I thought that counted as friendship."

"In what realm would that be the case?" Poton inquired.

"In the realm that he didn't let me kill that rat-faced terrier, which would have gotten me locked up or worse." Justicier shook John2's hand.

"If everyone has such a problem with that one, why can't La Hire just step on him?"

"Because Etienne, we're on the same side," Jehanne replied.

"Just a little step? Fine, fine La Hire reaffirms La Hires promise to not step on the advisors to Charles7."

"This is Jehanne la Pucelle," John2 said.

"Child," Justicier dropped to a knee. "I understand that by swearing my augmentations to your cause, I won't be putting you in the best of light with Charles7's advisor, Tremoille—."

"Fluff and nonsense, this calling has never been about being viewed in the best of light by that one. It is and always has been about saving the earth. Should you wish to pledge your augmentations to that cause, sir, please rise and be welcomed," Jehanne said.

"Thank you, la Pucelle," he said, getting to his feet. "Do you need a lift from this land?"

"Yes thank you, we have to find the other members of our party."

"Then come along, I know just where to find them. I happened to pick up their transmission, that's how I found you."

"Which transmissions was that?" Deark asked.

"The pilots were debating whether they should take off again when they spotted my plane. I asked them who was in charge. Once again they debated, having apparently multiple people that thought they were the leader of the group."

"I think our assigning of leadership needs to be clearer," John2 said.

"We also need to do a better job masking our internal communications," D'Aulon said.

"Those are both fair statements, however John2 asked what had you searching for us? I didn't hear an answer." Severe turned to Justicier and his tone was harsh.

"My group and I had left Chinon after my, issue, with Tremoille. We settled in Colorado. It allowed us great hunting and fishing as well as all the arena fighting I could ever wish to be involved in."

"And?" Severe prodded.

"A group rode into our camp telling us the story of the girl that has been visited by the new gods. I spoke with their leader, Enyeto, he told me where I could start looking for you. That happened to be around the island of Beaugency just off the northern tip of Africa," Justicier said.

"Unreal, Enyeto knew where we were going," Kennedy said.

"It's more than unreal, it scares the Dickens out of me," Deark said.

"Why is that?" Poton asked.

"For starters, where are they getting their information, and second that they are openly sharing that information with people that we don't know."

"They have their part in all this, and whether we understand it or not, they're going to pop in from time to time and lend us a hand," Jehanne said.

"I wouldn't be saying anything if Enyeto and his group had flown down here and picked us up on their horses to get us back together with our troops. This however—," Deark started.

"You wouldn't have said anything if flying horses picked us up? La Hire would have been whooping for delight at that."

"What about the saddles? That could be a long drop," Gilles said, making even Etienne laugh.

"Enough now," Jehanne said. "I was told I need to determine who I can trust if I were to manage to complete my calling. This scar-faced man has come here to help, I feel that trusting him is the right course of action."

"Then let's get a move on," Justicier said. The group doused the fire and walked over to the plane.

"How many men do you have?" de Metz asked, seeing the large plane with the word 'A404' painted in orange and blue lettering on the side.

"I have a few more than eight hundred on the flying bus."

"My goodness, I guess there was a reason for Enyeto to point you to us," Pouli said.

"We have a long way to go, and time is waning," John2 said.

******

Several hours later the plane was heading in the direction of the next conflict. Not having a conference room on this aircraft, Jehanne and her captains talked near the cockpit. "Should we be worried about the two days we lost?" Kennedy asked.

"What will worrying get us?" Poton asked.

"Fine. Worrying wasn't the right word. How do we prepare ourselves against a weapon that takes time away?"

"I don't think we can, but we can ask Commissioner if it was his doing," Jehanne replied.

"Are you saying he invented something that –," Minguet started.

"I'm not speculating anything. I can ask him if I see him again. Other than that, we're just out two days. I think the more important thing is that we need to have a plan to get the next piece of the armor," she said.

"Agreed. They won't fall for us not fighting openly next time," Severe said.

"Jehanne, John2, please come to the cockpit." Justicier's voice called over the speaker. They walked up and knocked on the door, which swung out.

"Yes?" John2 said.

"We just picked up transmission from the two Generals on the One World Military, a General Talbot and a Fastolf."

"Go on," Jehanne said.

"Apparently they are both heading to the same place we are and they are armed to the teeth."

"Did they give their positions?" John2 asked.

"Yes, we have a least a ten hour jump on them. I can increase my airspeed and gain some more but I can't be sure how much," Justicier said.

"The first thing we should do is get ahold of our ground teams and have them start jamming any communications in to and out of the island so the town doesn't know they have support coming," Deark said over Jehanne's shoulder.

"On it." D'Aulon, who was behind Deark said at the same time as Justicier said the same thing.

"Excellent. Both of you see what can be done." Jehanne walked over and took her seat. "I think I need some sleep. I'm feeling rather light-headed." She closed her eyes and the world spun away.

******

"Child," the soft voice of Protectorate said.

"I'm awake." Jehanne sat up, looking over the valley she had trained in.

"Good morning. Time is short your plane will be landing soon."

"Did you have anything to do with the time interruption?"

"Only when you're with me and mine," Protectorate said.

"I'm sorry I didn't mean to interrupt you."

"It's ok child. Tell me, do you have a plan for getting the armor section on the island to which you head?"

"Yes, D'Aulon's comment gave me an idea."

"Excellent, your trust is well founded in that one." Protectorate looked nervous.

"Should my trust be in question with others in my group?" Jehanne asked.

"There are a few that have at several times in their lives played both sides against the middle. Yet they at this time, feel loyal to you."

"But I should stay cautious?"

"During times like this, caution can just as easily get you killed as lack thereof. Trust those that have earned it fully, allowing them to fill the void that Politician talked about. Find ways to use those you don't trust to perform duties whose outcomes, whether they succeed or fail, won't have a bearing on the result you're striving for," Protectorate said.

"You sound like Pedagogue this time."

"Most military activities stem from the teaching and learning process." Her words seemed to morph and become deeper, and deeper.

"…Process." John2 was leaning over her.

"I'm sorry?" Jehanne attempted to blink away the dream.

"We're starting the landing process, you need to buckle up," he repeated and then seeing that she was still confused he asked, "Are you ok?"

"Fine, sometimes dreams are just very real." She finished buckling her seatbelt and looked out the window. The island was not much larger than the Commune de Domremy and the Mother City where this all started.

"That's it?" Kennedy asked. "How did they land the Whales on this tiny island?"

"Very carefully I imagine," de Metz said.

"Ha ha," Poton turned around in his seat and threw something at him.

"Did we have any luck with the jamming?" Jehanne asked D'Aulon.

"He's still doing it," Deark replied. "Justicier's co-pilot, Minguet and D'Aulon are all working on keeping the transmissions from Beaugency's Retinue."

"Do we have a plan?" Severe asked.

"Yes, we need to show that our numbers will crush them, and then demand an audience with the Viceroy of the Mother City," Jehanne replied.

"And if that doesn't work?" This time it was Pouli that asked.

"Then we proceed in crushing them, rather quickly."

"La Hire is a fan of that strategy." He clasped his hands behind his head, leaning back in his seat and smiled. The reclined seat rested on Severe's lap.

"Seat backs in the upright position, please." He pushed La Hire's seat off him as the plane touched down. The plane jostled and bounced on the small runway, eventually pulling up to the two much larger transports.

"I need to speak with Bastard, Gaucourt and Culant. Please stay on board. This needs to be a quick stop." Jehanne headed out the door.

******

"What is that loathsome Cad doing here?" Tremoille stormed straight up to Jehanne, his rage at seeing Justicier exiting the plane behind her was unbounded.

"He has joined our ranks," she replied.

"I shall have none of it!"

"Then stay on this island," Jehanne said. "We need to make haste. Talbot and Fastolf are on their way to support the island of Beaugency."

"I said I shall have none of it!" Tremoille repeated in a shower of spittle which hit Jehanne.

"Sir, I did not invite you to join me nor do I wish for you to stay on this campaign. So as I said before, you are welcome to stay on this island." She pushed past him and walked up to her waiting captains, wiping her face on her cape.

"What would you have of us?" Bastard asked.

"Get the men boarded, we leave at once. Currently we have the transmissions to the island isolated so they know nothing of the support on its way," Jehanne said.

"Everyone on the planes," Captain Gaucourt yelled.

"Justicier, I'll fly with them and bring them up to speed," she said, indicating for him to get back into his plane.

"Justicier." Tremoille cleared his throat and spat a glob on the ground. "Scarface dog is more to the point."

"Will you be enjoying the accommodations on this island or shutting that vile mouth?" Jehanne turned on the advisor. He closed his mouth and boarded the opposite plane as her.

In less than an hour they were flying over the much larger island of Beaugency. Looking down at the Mother City, Jehanne noticed it was set up much like New Orleans; the wall itself encapsulated all the residences. Set as far back from the entrance as possible there stood a large stronghold which appeared to have its own entrance from inside the outer wall.

"Must be where the Entities hang out," Culant said, looking over her shoulder at the stronghold. During the flight she had discussed her plan with them in the hope that when they landed and deplaned the troops could be ready that much quicker.

They arrived at the wall with their show of force lined up in such a manner to appear even larger and more menacing than they were. The empty transport vehicles were in the rear, and the Laval brothers and their rail gun in the front.

"What business have you at the gates of our city?" a CAM unit came out to greet them.

"My name is Jehanne la Pucelle. I must have audience with the Viceroy of Beaugency."

"The entire Enclave are closed into the main hall, not to be disturbed," the CAM unit said. Jehanne noticed it had no identifying name on its chest.

"This is not a discussion that I'll be having with you CAM unit. Either open the gates allowing us entry or they shall be removed from their mountings." Jehanne stared up into the dead eyes of the Entity. When nothing happened, "Guy, Andre on my mark, fire in ten, nine, eight."

"The Viceroy is on her way out to the gate." The Entity turned and walked back in the direction it had come.

"If anything pokes its head over that wall before the Viceroy gets here, you have my permission to shoot," Jehanne shouted to the Laval brothers.

"We'll be watching," Andre replied. The hum of the Good Shepherdess made his words barely audible.

"La Hire is bored, this is boring," he said after drawing pictures in the dirt with his staff for at least fifteen minutes.

"If the Viceroy is close to the door, it's my advice for her to duck and cover," Jehanne said.

"What are you thinking?" Joinville came running up to her.

"I'm thinking it's time to FIRE!" She pointed at the gate and the rail gun released its fourth shot. leaving a hole large enough for even the biggest of their group to run through.

"You've lost your mind. This is our third strike," he said, grabbing her and turning her to look him in the eye.

"Advance!" Jehanne reached her hand up and crushed the augmentation on the liaison's hand.

"What sorcery is this? Witch!" He fell to the ground as she turned, facing the entrance that her troops had already finished breaking down.

"Be glad I left any arm at all." Drawing her sword she ran, quickly overtaking the soldiers that started ahead of her.

******

Inside they found a deserted town, at the rear of which the walls of the stronghold were lined with onlookers. "La Pucelle," Minguet said, running up to her.

"Yes, is everything ok?"

"D'Aulon asked me to tell you he managed to get a virus into the navigation systems of the lead aircraft transporting the combined forces of Generals Talbot and Fastolf."

"Is that a good thing?" she asked.

"Yes, he has sent them back to Jargeau. The longer it takes them to notice, the more time we'll have. Currently they won't be here for at least a day." Minguet grinned.

"That's great news. We can slow our advance a bit." Jehanne said. "Deark."

"Over here," he said, transforming from a small creature she didn't quite see to himself.

"What are you doing?" La Hire asked, walking up behind him.

"I was heading up to get the lay of the land."

"Then you should have taken on the appearance of a chicken," Culant laughed.

"Enough, I was going to ask you to check on Joinville but I like your plan better," Jehanne said.

"What happened to Joinville?" John2 asked.

"I may have stepped on him a little," she replied.

"Not fair! Not even a teensy-weensy bit." La Hire pouted as Deark transformed once more into a gray cat and headed off to see what was happening at the next wall.

Section Three – Chapter Six

"If I said I was sorry for doing it, I would most definitely be lying. How about this, next time I'll let you do it," Jehanne said.

"La Hire is fine with that."

"Do you think we have any shots left in that?" she asked, walking up to the Good Shepherdess.

"Only one way to find out," Guy said, the hum starting again.

"Let's wait for Deark to return," Jehanne said.

"Where do you suppose all the people are at?" Kennedy asked.

"Best guess, they've all retreated into that stronghold," John2 said.

"This is a fishing town, what do they think they're going to do?" Robinet asked.

"Die at the hands of a lunatic and her minions," Archbishop Chartres said. He had changed into his full Techno-Pagan robes.

"And you're planning on administering last rites and what, looking as if you are separate from our group?" Poton asked.

"There is no deceit in that I, and the other advisors are completely detached from this barbaric behavior."

"Then go sit on the plane," Bastard said.

"Actually being ready to aid the fallen in their journey beyond is an admirable task for the advisors," Jehanne said. The others looked at her as if she'd lost her nose, while the advisors walked back to the gate waiting for their work to begin.

"Jehanne?" Gaucourt prompted her to explain.

"If they have a task that'll keep them away from us, all the better."

"Makes sense to me," Severe replied. "Here comes Deark," he said, seeing the scampering cat popping in and out of shadows as it returned.

"Well?" Gilles asked when the cat reached them.

"Well what?" Deark's voice came from behind Jehanne.

"What the?" Gilles spun around to look at Deark. "If you're there then who's this?" he asked, pointing at the cat.

"I imagine that's a normal cat you were speaking to," Pouli laughed.

"Enough, enough. Deark do you have an update?" Jehanne asked.

"It makes no sense," he replied.

"How so?" de Metz asked.

"They're all just watching. Not preparing to fight, not scared, not even angry."

"Perhaps they're excited to see the Maid." D'Aulon walked up behind them along with Minguet.

"What are you doing here?" John2 asked. "Did they defeat your blocking?"

"Justicier's men have it now," he replied. "Let's go talk to them."

"I'm with you." Jehanne walked alongside him.

"And I," de Metz and Deark trailed them.

"Severe, La Hire, Justicier keep the troops ready," Jehanne said.

"On it," Severe replied.

******

The silence that met them at the wall was off-putting. "Do you know who this is?" D'Aulon yelled to the onlookers.

"Why should we care?" an Entity in a leather jumper asked.

"Because there are few times in your lives, be they long or short that someone will walk up to you and offer you a chance to be part in changing the world," Jehanne said.

"You left out that this someone first blew up your front door and approached you with this opportunity with their weapons drawn," the same Entity said. "Not exactly developing a trusting foundation to build on, that."

"Why is it that you wouldn't let us in? This is a fishing community. I imagine we're the first strangers you've ever barred from it," Deark said.

"We were ordered to close the gates and just then all our communications halted." This time when she spoke the Entity leaned over and a talisman showed from the top of her shirt.

"Viceroy, we're not here to hurt your people or your town. I simply have a limited time to complete the calling I've been given." Jehanne sheathed her sword.

"And that's what we were told you would do, approach us with heretical claims of speaking with the new gods," an Entity in burgundy robes said.

"Can we just have a moment to speak with you? The Retinue are welcome to listen in if you desire," De Metz said to the one Jehanne had been addressing as Viceroy.

"Speak your piece, I have no secrets from the citizens of Beaugency," she said.

"I'm sorry that isn't true, you have two secrets that not even the rest of the Enclave know you protect. Commissioner gave them to your predecessor's predecessor," Jehanne said.

"Viceroy, the position you hold is bigger than you or your relationship with those on that wall with you," D'Aulon added.

"This I must say is a surprising revelation."

"Viceroy, we've been ordered—," a different Entity started.

"I know what we've been ordered to do. Does this look like a play that the human children are putting on for us at the Sole-Air Festival? They have real weapons, we have fishing nets and poles."

"Making a decision to let them in comes with a cost, Viceroy Mankuso." the Entity who was obviously the religious advisor spoke again.

"Bishop Beaupere if I sit here weighing the payments that I would and would not be willing to remit in order to keep this island safe, do you think I may reach a cost that's too great? That isn't what our lives here are about. For years we've done whatever it takes to be what we are; different from everywhere else. Let her enter but only her."

"No, la Pucelle not alone," de Metz said.

"If she is willing to pay any price for change, do you believe less of me?" Jehanne walked toward the door. "Please return to the troops and do nothing."

"As you say." D'Aulon's reply came as the door closed behind her.

"Please come with me." Viceroy Mankuso walked down the stairs and met Jehanne.

"Of course."

When they were far enough from the rest of the citizenry, she asked, "How did you know that I was the leader?"

"About your neck is one of the things that I seek."

"I can't give this to you," turning yet continuing to walk backwards.

Jehanne saw that she held the talisman between her hands, as if it were indeed precious to her. "I just need to know the question upon it. I also need to be shown where the section of the armor you protect is stored."

"The amount of information that you've approached me with is indeed impressive. I don't know if I should fear you or respect you." Viceroy Mankuso said.

"I wasn't aware the two were mutually exclusive." Jehanne saw an emotion dance across the mouth of the Viceroy before she turned away again.

"My question is, 'what form of government will be needed to keep the Humans in their place?' I believe that's why this island has always strove to not hold tight to the One World Caste equivalencies."

Realizing the item wasn't precious at all; it embarrassed her. "Because the question brings shame to you and those that came before you?" Jehanne asked.

"Yes, if I made this island hold to the answer that's engraved upon this we would not have survived this many years." The Viceroy tucked the talisman into a pocket in the back of her shirt, allowing the leather strap that it hung from to hang empty about her neck.

"If it's difference from the others that you seek, may I say stay as you are? Because you've been successful. Your Retinue, I'm sorry to say, seems to hold tight to the old ways."

"They were appointed by the advisors to the Leader of the Republicus. In the case of Bishop Beaupere, he's friends with the High Leader himself."

"And you were not? I mean appointed by the advisors." Jehanne inquired.

"Yes I was. However, those that hold my position in each of the Mother Cities must be from the area in which they are leader over. The Retinue can be, and typically are, from the advisor's inner circle."

"Interesting. Perhaps that's why Madam Commander is relocating several communes. She'll have no choice but to appoint her clique to the role of leader in the new Mother Cities," she mumbled.

"I don't follow." This time the Entity stopped and faced her.

"There will be none in those relocated that will meet the requirements of the position you hold." Her explanation caused the Viceroy to spin on her heels and start walking again, shaking her head as she did.

"Below us are a series of caves. The piece of the armor is held in a cave that can only be reached by following this tunnel to the end. Be aware, none less the Viceroy of this island have ever made it to the final cave."

"What will I face?" Jehanne asked.

"The higher caves have both real and imagined threats, while the lower levels will force you to make the decision that turning back is not an option. That's all I can tell you, I'm sorry." She reached out to a large boulder that pivoted out of the way and she pointed into the opening. Jehanne stepped forward, her augmented eye showing her that the path down was sloped not steps. She heard the stone scraping and nine words mixed into the ambient noise, "Remember you must commit to the path of a fool."

****

"The path of a fool, nice motivation," Jehanne spoke to herself, confused why there was no echo in this tunnel. The slope increased and she had to fight gravity to not allow her body to rush out of control. She walked, listening, attempting to block out the sound of her leg servos, still hearing nothing as the path now turned. Around and around, further and further down she walked, reviewing what hazards she would face, 'The upper rooms have both real and imagined threats,' the Viceroy had said.

The realization that the area around her was brightening as she went lower was tickling her mind when a hiss, which didn't sound like a snake or at least like any snake she had ever seen, filled the stillness. Jehanne followed the tunnel around one more turn and it opened into a large room. This time the dampness of a cavern and the smell of the mineral growths from the imperfections of the ceiling hit her. The floor shook as a wave pounded through the opening, giving the room a dark and dirty green hue to it.

"Why are you bothering with this?" the voice was deep, much like John2's.

"Hello."

"You know while I was in their jail, every day they threatened to bring my wife to me." He stepped out from behind one of the stalagmites. "Some days they brought in chameleon K or Q class Entities to make me think they had. They would tie and lower her into the ocean as it rushed into my chamber." She couldn't help but look over at the water that had once again rushed away. "The waves at the high tide would surround her. As she drowned she would scream my name. When I eventually broke and rushed to her aid, the Entity would transform back and laugh as they beat me for what they said was, my attempt to escape."

"You're not real," Jehanne said

"Other times they would bring things for me to fight. One time it was a wild horse that was so enraged it kept charging at me, hitting me with its hooves. When I finally calmed it down, they were so angry I hadn't killed it, they did. Afterward they left it in my cell for days telling me I had to eat some of it or I would get no more food." He started to cry, heaving sobs. "I almost died, I couldn't even cut the meat from it when they broke me. They of course had won, they cut a large steak from the creature and I ate it," he said through sobs.

"You're not real," she said again.

"When I fought real dangers I had no issue killing them, or eating the meat after. One day they brought in a giant creature that looked like a snake with four legs. They told me it was a crocodile from the Nile. It fought so well, I wouldn't have survived if the High Leader hadn't told the guards to kill it."

"The Leader of the Republicus watched you fight for your life?" Jehanne asked.

"Child, he ordered the events to entertain his closest friends." From the water behind him a hiss came. As they both turned their heads to see what made the sound a giant creature sprang from the inrushing water. The green hue filled the cave and Jehanne wasn't certain if the creature was real or fake but she drew her sword none the less.

"You're not real," she said for the third time. As the creature's jaws clamped around his waist he screamed and she stepped forward. 'Real or not, I can't allow this to continue,' she thought.

"Lucky for me that I'm not," John2 said and vanished. The crocodile grew more enraged as its jaws snapped together and now turned its attention on Jehanne.

"Oh for pity's sake." She dodged an advance from the jaws and got tossed into the water when the giant tail hit her in the midriff. The creature slid on its belly into the waiting saltwater as the weight of her augmentations pulled her lower and lower. Her feet finally rested on stone at the bottom as the creature closed the gap. Having found purchase her sword slashed out, cleaving the head from her adversary.

Her lungs burning, she used the momentum of another wave to throw herself from the pool. Taking a deep breath of relief she jumped to her feet expecting another attack. Finding nothing, she got her bearings and made her way back to the continuation of the tunnel, which after two turns ended in water. "The path of a fool? Hmm?" she mused. "How deep is the water?" she asked aloud.

This time the words, 'Hard to determine due to the winding nature of the bottom,' appeared in her heads up display.

"Not the answer I was hoping for." She took a couple steps forward, finding her chin quickly at the level of the water she drew a deep breath and kept walking forward.

******

The winding nature of the tunnel made it impossible for her to swim, yet she quickly found she could force herself forward by grabbing the wall and pulling hard. Once again she found her lungs burning as the words of Viceroy Mankuso played in her head, 'the lower levels will force you to make the decision that turning back is not an option.' Giving another pull on the wall she saw the room open. Climbing to the top of a larger stone she leapt, and kicked her legs insanely. 'I can't drown here,' she thought and her head broke the surface just long enough to pull a small amount of air into her lungs. Crashing again into the water she walked on the bottom toward another large stone, and repeated the process.

"Watch your head!" a voice yelled as she sprung from the water. Reaching up she grabbed the stalactite, stopping herself from being impaled. Hanging for a moment she saw the hologram of Commissioner waving to her from what would have been a high shelf in the cavern before it had filled with water. "Let me help you," he clapped his hands together.

"How's clapping for me going to help?" she asked and then her feet found purchase on something that lifted her from the water.

"I would sit on him," he said as his head indicated the huge shell that she stood on.

"Holy cow!" Jehanne said, sitting down.

"Dear girl that is Fool, and he's a crab, not a cow. Jump," he ordered when she was much closer to the ledge.

"The path of fool," she repeated the words realizing that she had added the 'a' into the Viceroy's last statement, and she smiled.

"Are you ok?" Commissioner asked.

"I can't believe I made it is all. I thought for certain I would die down here," Jehanne said.

"Many before you have. That's how Fool got his name, you are what you eat." The hologram laughed at his own joke.

"Commissioner that's terrible."

"Perhaps, but I got stuck with the humorous personality traits of an Entity and then stuck down here."

"Humorous traits?" Jehanne asked.

"When Commissioner put this invention in motion he found that each of the six creations had their own unique take on who he was. This one has very dark humor."

"Again this is all so fascinating, yet I'm rushing to return."

"The reinforcements have not communicated with the island, yet their courses have been corrected and they will be here in less time than your people predicted. You still have approximately eighteen hours," he reassured her.

"That's good news. May I ask you two questions?"

"I assume you mean three as you just asked one."

"Yes of course you're right. Can you give any information on the meaning of the symbols on the armor?" Jehanne's hopeful tone brought a smile to the hologram.

"I can, yet I would advise you to wait until far later in the campaign. Before you waste your second question, I can tell you one symbol for each piece of armor you have. As you are already using the Talisman to decipher the code, the longer you wait the more precise the symbols you will need clarification on will be."

"Thank you, that's good council."

"And your next question?"

"Did you invent a method of controlling time?" Jehanne asked.

"Not so far as I know, but I'm not connected to the real Commissioner. Now, let's get the next piece of armor."

He pointed to another tank which sat on a ledge all the way across the cavern.

"Fool, will you help me?" she asked, looking into the pool of water in front of her. Finding no sign of him she clapped her hands.

"He's gone to look for food as you didn't lend him a meal."

"There is no way I can make it there and back with these augmentations weighing me down." Working through the menus in her eye augmentation, she began ejecting the mechanized pieces. When she ejected the shoulder units her sword fell with them and in the end only her eye augmentation was left.

"You must be quick, the power cores in these augmentations hold a short amount of charge, and with them glowing like this that core may not last long," Commissioner said, looking at the bright white augmentations.

"Then how do they, or rather what, charges them?"

"The Augmented that wears the modies charges them, a combination of their heart beat, biorhythms, and the use of the augmentation itself. Now hurry," he replied.

"I'll do my best." Jehanne dove into the water with her hands and feet still in the white armor sections. In the cool water of the cavern the armor felt little different from her own skin. A minute or two later she was climbing the sheer face of the cavern leading to the ledge she had seen the tank waiting on. Peering over she saw nothing.

******

"Jehanne there seems to be a problem, he never gets out of the –," Commissioner started and then his form blinked out. Fool had returned, and with him two Entities, the religious advisor that had told the Viceroy there would be a price to be paid if she let Jehanne in, rode on the crab's back. While in one of Fool's claws Viceroy Mankuso herself showing no illuminated signs of life. The creatures other claw was crushing the holographic generator, thus destroying this version of Commissioner.

Next to her augmentations the bright and bubbling tank splashed about as if Fool had grabbed and moved it to this ledge.

"Bishop Beaupere, what exactly are you doing?" Jehanne asked.

"First I am stopping public enemy number one and destroying her accomplices. Actually that's not true. First I destroyed the Viceroy of Beaugency for being your accomplice and then this stupid antique hologram, mostly because it annoyed me. And lastly I'll be destroying you."

"How will you get away with all this killing?" Jehanne asked, slowly swimming back toward the side the Bishop was on.

"Fool here will bring both of your broken bodies to the surface," Beaupere said.

"And my troops are just supposed to believe that I ejected my augmentations and cast away my sword in order to what, make it a fair fight?"

"Don't worry, I plan on letting you live a bit longer," he mocked. "Get out of the water slowly or he'll cut her in half."

"She's no different than you." Jehanne jumped from the water. "Just another Entity trying to destroy all the Humans. Why would I care if your buddy there snips her into a hundred sections?"

"Girl you may be clever but I know this Entity, she actually does care about Humans. More than that, I know you also saw that in her. Now tell me of the two secrets she holds. One is obviously in this tank." He directed the crab to smack the tank which bounced around unharmed. "And it's a rather unique containment field. What is the second secret?"

"She never informed me," Jehanne said, edging toward her discarded augmentations and sword.

"The lying is only going to make this worse on you and your men. I know that there are reinforcements on their way here, I'm the one that asked for them. I just need to take my time and all those up top will be destroyed."

"The final secret is engraved upon the pieces of armor inside that tank."

"So you're collecting a set." He pointed at her feet and hands.

"You really are smart," she said.

"How do you retrieve what is in the tank. All the power Fool can muster in his claws did nothing but splash the liquid about."

"I need my Augmentations and sword," Jehanne said.

"I'm not an imbecile girl." Bishop Beaupere leapt from the back of the crab and drew Jehanne's sword. He took a few swings into the tank with it, to no avail.

"I wasn't lying. The augmentations and the swords recognize me as the one that must to retrieve the pieces."

"Fine put them on, but any funny stuff and Fool goes snip snip."

"You have my word I will not attack you with my augmentations or sword."

"I don't care of your oaths child." He scoffed and held the sword out to her after she had gotten the white augmentations back on.

"Thank you," she said, taking the sword she turned to study the tank which was, as expected, roiling in even more bubbles than ever before. Standing up she put her sword in her sheath.

"What are you playing at?" the Entity took a step closer.

"The sword wasn't working." Jehanne knelt down to the small side of the large rectangular tank. Beaupere as she had predicted knelt down looking at the white armor that was being tossed about in the bubble stream.

"Then how will you get through the containment?"

"Passage says the best route in this case is straight," Jehanne said, reaching her hand toward the tank.

"You dare blaspheme to me?" Bishop Beaupere looked away from the tank to stare at her. Jehanne closed her hand on one of the bracers inside.

"That wasn't blasphemy Bishop. See?" her head motioned toward the tank. As the Entity turned to look Jehanne threw the acid that was pooled in the bracer into his face.

"Ahh!" Beaupere screamed and brought his hands to his face. In a blur Jehanne drew her sword and as with the crocodile her adversary's head found freedom from its body. Continuing her motion, she allowed the swing of the sword to pull her into a standing position. Leaving the sword in the raised position she turned on the crab.

"There's no need to kill it," Viceroy Mankuso's thin voice said from the floor where Fool had dropped her.

"Into the water Fool," Jehanne ordered and the crab jumped in with a splash. "Are you alright?"

"I will be, thanks to your actions. Now get those pieces so we can get up top and I can visit a doctor.

"Yes ma'am." Jehanne put her sword away and bent, lifting the two bracers. Walking over to the water she rinsed them. "Would you like to look at them?" When she saw the Viceroy look at her advisor's burned face, she added, "I've rinsed them, you have nothing to fear."

"Then yes I very much would. I've wondered for decades what they were." She held her hand out and Jehanne gave her one to examine.

"Protectorate tells me they are called bracers, apparently they go on the wrist." Jehanne released her left hand and arm augmentation, placing the bracer on. The typical brightness flooded the room when she secured the augmentations.

"What just happened? Where did the bracer go? Oh, I see it now, that's most fascinating, my sensors see it but my vision doesn't." She started to hand the bracer she was looking at back when she saw the engraving inside. "What is this?" she asked rubbing a thumb over it.

"That's a coded message."

"Is that why you seek these? So you can break their messages?" the Viceroy asked.

"I know what this one says," Jehanne replied.

"Can you tell me?"

"It's your question, 'what form of government will be needed to—'."

"Keep the Humans in their place." She discontinued the rubbing her thumb across it. "Why is it that you seek them if you already know what the message is?" She tossed the bracer to Jehanne in disgust.

"I've not figured that out yet myself," Jehanne answered as she affixed the bracer beneath her left arm augmentation. When the brightness faded she turned to the Viceroy. "Will you be able to make it to the top with your injuries?" As she asked this she scooped the pieces of the holographic generator into a pocket.

"We can take it slow, my talisman will allow you to breathe. It will also make any other challenges stay away from you." The Viceroy put her arm around Jehanne's shoulder and they headed off.

Section Three – Chapter Seven

"What about him?" Jehanne pointed at the fallen Bishop.

"I will let everyone know that he died as he lived," Viceroy Mankuso said.

"That could be interpreted in many ways."

"And such is the life of a person in politics." This answer made her chuckle, which made her wince.

"Funny that his life is associated with politics and not religion," Jehanne replied.

"I couldn't agree more."

"Enough chat, let's get you out of here." Jehanne guided them to the edge of the water, where they jumped in separately. Once underwater Jehanne took ahold of the Viceroy, finding that it wasn't that she could breathe underwater so much as she had no need to breathe. Somehow the talisman was keeping her blood oxygenated. After several minutes they emerged from the water-filled tunnel into the cavern where the first tests had taken place.

"I'm curious, what did you do to get passed the crocodile?"

"I killed it," Jehanne replied.

"Seriously? Do you know how many Entities and Humans have fallen to that beast? The only ones that made it into the tunnels did it by sneaking through the area."

"Then I find myself having been very fortunate."

"Me thinks you do yourself discredit," Viceroy Mankuso said. "You should be proud of the things you have and will accomplish."

"Thank you Viceroy." Jehanne allowed the Entity to rest against the wall while she attempted to push the boulder out of the way. "I think it's stuck."

"Actually child, I was just checking something."

"Which was?" she asked the smiling Entity.

"If you could open it without this." She swung the talisman back and forth from the leather strap. "At least I know some safeguards are outside your ability. How much of what the Bishop said is true?"

"In regard to you or the reinforcements?" Jehanne asked.

"Both, but start with the help that he called for." the Viceroy said.

"It's true, my men picked up a transmission reporting that two planes had landed on a small island nearby. From that moment we began blocking every form of communication both in and out of this island."

"You must have some incredibly gifted individuals on your team to accomplish such a thing."

"You have no idea," Jehanne smiled. "As for his comments about you. It's true I can tell that you care about all beings on your island. Anyone that sees you interacting with humans can sense that you don't have that holier than thou attitude." The people of the community came rushing up to aid the injured Viceroy.

"Your comments are much appreciated. Hear me well, the next chapters of our world's story will bear reading as one like you will be a primary character in it. Whatever comes, Beaugency is in your court." She finished making the statement as the medical team arrived.

"What happened?" the political advisor asked.

"I think we need to find a new religious advisor for the Retinue; Bishop Beaupere teased the wrong crab. Had this girl not been here I would have also been cut into pieces."

"Your efforts on the behalf of Beaugency and our Viceroy won't be forgotten. If there is ever anything I can do for you, you need only ask," he said, proffering a hand to Jehanne.

"I would consider us even if you didn't kill, Fool, the crab." She shook his hand. "He only did—,"

"I will be sealing that cave," the Viceroy cut in. "You have my word there is none from my island that will journey below to seek vengeance."

"Perfect. My men and I have many miles to cover. May the Three that became Six look over you," Jehanne said, not really sure why she chose that specific comment to depart with. The Viceroy questioned her with her eyes but said nothing as Jehanne left.

******

"Alright we're off," Jehanne said walking back from the stronghold.

"We're going nowhere until you tell us what your reason is for making all these stops. What is the purpose for these specific locations?" Tremoille asked.

"Viceroy Mankuso." Jehanne turned and yelled to the Entity looking down on her from the wall.

"Yes."

"Would it be ok if I left a couple of Charles7's advisors here? You see with the big election coming up, we need to set up some grassroots encampments."

"Now just one—," Chartres started.

"We don't have a lot of extra room, is it ok if they stay with Fool?" the Viceroy asked.

"A jester? You want us to stay here and room with a jester?" Flavy asked.

"No actually not a fool, she said Fool. He's the giant crab that lives under the stronghold." Jehanne raised her voice to be heard by the Viceroy once more. "I think they're allergic to shellfish. Thanks anyway." She waved and turned, starting to walk to the plane.

"What? Where are you going? You didn't answer his question." Joinville said.

"La Hire thinks your choices were made clear. Either get back and guard the prisoner or go visit Fool."

"When we return I promise you that—," Tremoille started.

"Gentlemen," de Metz said. "These threats you make wear on me. When Charles7 said for you to join us I don't think he meant for you to play the role of petulant children."

"First she brings that scarfaced oaf and now you dare call your betters peevishly impatient?" Flavy asked.

"The twonk thinks you're his dogsbody," Kennedy said.

"What?" Poton asked.

"He said, the idiot thinks de Metz no more than a servant," Severe translated as he walked back to the plane.

"We have places to go. This is finished," John2 said, motioning for the men to get back to the transports. This time there were no arguments, the planes were loaded and ten minutes later they were taxiing.

"This is ridiculous, why do we need to tolerate their behavior?" Culant asked.

"Actually there are only a few of us that must tolerate it." Jehanne rested her head on her hands. "Since I'm charged with getting Charles7 elected as the Leader of the Republicus and these men are his trusted few I need to make this work."

"La Hire thinks the only way to make that happen is to bring them into your confidence."

"Etienne has a very valid point," Poton said.

"Please contact the pilots and Justicier; tell them we need to stop." Jehanne looked out the window until the plane stopped.

"Minguet, since we stopped jamming the transmissions can you stay on board and monitor any broadcasts and let us know of anything out of the ordinary?" D'Aulon asked as the group deplaned.

"Of course."

******

Archbishop Chartres stepped from his plane walking to within inches of Jehanne. "Now what insults do you wish to throw at us?"

"I want you to understand one very important thing, Archbishop. I don't care that this girl wants to bring you into her confidence. I don't care that Charles7 has a soft spot for you and what counsel you bring him. If you disturb one NanoTech on her augmentations, I'll tie you to the wheels of Justicier's plane, where you'll hang like the tail from a kite until we find out what elevation you run out of oxygen," D'Aulon said, stepping forward from the ranks of her captains.

"How dare—," Chartres started.

"Confidence?" Tremoille put his hand on his advancing counterpart's shoulder.

"Yes I asked the plane to stop so that I could bring you into my confidence." Jehanne took a step away from the religious advisor.

"To what end?" Flavy asked, coming to his half-brother's aid.

"We don't understand our next destination and thought perhaps one of you may have some insight," she said.

"Do you really see us as fools child?" Chartres asked.

"Just tell them Jehanne," Deark said.

"We're going to Patay, South America," she said.

"Why?" Tremoille asked.

"That's why she said we don't understand our destination," Pouli said.

"No, I actually wanted to know what leads—," he started.

"La Hire heard you ask why not what."

"Etienne, please," Jehanne said and La Hire lowered his head slightly.

"What leads you to think Patay is supposed to be our destination?" Tremoille finished his question.

Jehanne turned, glancing at Deark trying to silently get a read how much she should share. He gave her a gesture as if he was pushing all his chips forward. Apparently he thought it was time to go all in. "Do you remember when we were in Chinon and I told you that Archbishop Cauchon insulted Ursula-Minor?"

"Yes, you flaked out right after," Chartres said.

"When he did that, Ursula-Minor contacted Deark. She has set us on the path to find six pieces of armor." She said.

"Armor? Did you say armor?" Flavy asked.

"She did," Severe replied.

"That's why we've traveled to the specific locations that we have. Now she's said Patay is to be our next destination," Deark said. "Yet I have no data that there's ever been a Mother City there."

"There wasn't until recently," Joinville finally spoke.

"Expound laddy," Kennedy prompted.

"At the session of the One World Government when Charles7 was initially removed from the ballot, during the reading of the previous meeting minutes, there was a vague comment about Patay," Joinville said.

"Do you recall what the vague comment was?" Tremoille asked.

"Yes. They had finished the construction of the Mother City. Oh, and that the Viceroy was in the process of relocating there."

"Unless they're relocating the armor piece as well, it can't be the right destination," John2 said.

"As I've said all along, these pieces could have been relocated a hundred times." Culant shook his head.

"La Pucelle!" Minguet yelled as he came running from the plane. "La Pucelle they're going straight there."

"Calm down, catch your breath, and start again," Jehanne said.

"Fastolf and Talbot are bypassing Beaugency Island and heading straight to Patay."

"Ah see how your foolishness comes back to bite us La Hire?" Tremoille mocked the large Augmented.

Glancing at Jehanne with imploring eyes he said, "La Hire did nothing wrong." He turned and beat a path back to the plane.

"Stay away from the Galaxy. We wouldn't want any other offers of new augmentations to get turned down." Tremoille said as he made air quotes to add to the disparaging nature of his comment.

"Enough, we're trying to mend fences here not burn every last stick in the bridge," Jehanne said.

"As you say, but if we truly are attempting to mend fences then perhaps you will share with me a couple more pieces of information," Chartres inquired.

"I've opened the book. Ask away," she said.

"Very well first, what purpose will the armor serve?" he asked.

"The end of Entity suppression of Humans." Jehanne stood a bit straighter as she answered.

"You must understand if joining the pieces together will result in such a thing, there's no chance that the Entities will allow it to happen," Joinville said.

"And?" Severe inquired.

"And…" Chartres' voice was filled with loathing, "continuing on this path will most assuredly end in the Second Uprising."

"If it hasn't already been set in motion," Flavy added.

"What was the second piece of information you desired?" Jehanne asked the Archbishop, ignoring the follow-up comments.

"What?"

"You had asked for me to share a couple pieces of—,"she started.

"Ah yes. If you have only shared this news with your captains how is it that the Entities know? How are they already heading to Patay? I think you have a leak on your panel of Trusted Rebels." The Archbishop crossed his arms and cocked a brow at the tiny leader of men.

"I'll stay the course with these Trusted Rebels. Do you wish to add yourselves to this fellowship and lend any counsel on the next steps to take?" Jehanne asked.

"Why not just ask us to help bail out the Titanic with a thimble. You've already struck the iceberg, at this point we might as well strike up the band." Tremoille turned to face John2. "I thought her so-called calling was to get Charles7 elected as Leader of the Republicus, not start another world war."

"While you paint a rather fantastic image for us, I'm not the girl that cowered from you just months ago so I will ask again, do you have counsel?"

"Believe me, we all see that you're no longer that girl. What we're questioning is should we allow ourselves to be thrown any deeper—," Chartres' words were cut off.

"Charles7 is not the fool that you are painting him to be!" John2 shouted. "Be done with this folly."

The four men looked at each other, having no idea what direction to go. The tallest in her group stepped up. "My counsel child, is to face what comes with the stiffened resolve that you've earned from the challenges you've faced. Continue to embrace the steel that your will has become and know that there is still a job to do. I would also remind that at times like this, one must make a decision. You can either ignore the hate they throw at you or embrace it. Walk away from the pain they attempt to inflict upon you or revel in it. Turn your back on the negativity and shortsightedness in their judgments or face them head on. You know who you are, decide to be that, not what they are telling you to be," Gilles said. "And yes I know she wasn't asking me but as you dolts were dumbstruck it was time someone did something to get her calling moving again. Now everyone get on the planes."

Once the plane stabilized the team gathered in the mess hall and tried to cheer up La Hire. "If you allow those buffoons to cause you such discomfort, what'll you do if a worthy adversary tells you that cases of cranial rectal inversion to the degree you suffer from have been known to be fatal?" Poton inquired.

"Hey La Hire got what you just said." The large Augmented threw a piece of bread at his old friend amongst laughter.

"Enough of that long face Etienne, we need to start discussing strategy," Severe said.

"La Hire must have gotten comfortable with you. La Hire didn't even have a desire to crack this staff upside your head Sainte Severe."

"I'm glad Jehanne has been such a positive influence on you," Minguet said.

"As am I," Gilles added.

"My friends, what we face in Patay is more than we have faced up until now. The combined forces of Talbot and Fastolf will be bearing down on us with everything the One World Armed Forces can muster," Jehanne said.

"They will be bringing more W-CAM units then we even knew existed," Deark added. "They will even violate the law of only Sentient," he paused for his eye movement, "Entities being able to be upgraded into W-CAM units. I would stake my core on it."

"That's quite a stretch," John2 said.

"I don't believe so," Deark replied. "You need to remember, I've known the Entities running this for hundreds of years."

"La Hire doesn't care how many CAM units there are. Colonel Washington was right; this body is meant to be the tip of the spear. To be perfectly clear, La Hire will be taking the vanguard in Patay." When no one disagreed, he walked from the mess hall.

"Between now and when we land, we need to have as many of the reflective bucklers as possible," de Metz said.

"I can get the troops making them," Gaucourt said.

"I was going to offer to make them all myself. I'm so stoked about getting some real fighting going," Bastard said.

"You do what you can, but each of us need to get fed and then rest." Jehanne stood and walked among the troops giving encouragement.

An hour later Deark led Jehanne from the hall and back to the room they shared. "You have quite a way with the troops. Ten minutes with you and they feel they can take on this much larger foe."

"I've had some amazing tutelage," she said, looking at the Entity with admiration.

"Ah shucks!" Deark said, having transformed into a living cartoon version of a giant rooster, with rosy red cheeks.

"First time I've seen you do that," Jehanne laughed and jumped into bed. Shortly thereafter she fell asleep to fitful dreams again.

"You have no right to stand before us." Two W-CAM units said from the backs of two giant stags, with horns that were spectacularly populated with smaller point horns.

"We have every right to be here," Jehanne replied.

"Have you now?" This time it was I-CAM Alpha that spoke from the back of an even greater stag. "And why is that?"

"Because I fight for the rights of others and not for my own gain," she explained as the lasers on the W-CAM's chests began to glow.

"Jehanne, wake!" Deark shook her. "Another dream?"

"Yes. The new gods continue to send me cryptic visions in my dreams. How long did I sleep?"

"Nearly twelve hours. We should be in visual range of Patay."

"I'm going to grab a drink of water. Please begin waking everyone."

"Already done." Deark noticed her staring out the window. "Are you ok?"

"At least we know where to expect the Entity forces."

"I'm sorry?" As she pointed out the window at a building next to the airport they were descending toward. The roof of the structure had a giant stag painted on it.

"My dream showed me they would be riding on stags. I would bet all my TC they've parked their transports inside that building,"

"There's no way I'd take that bet. However, I've taken note of the area, and if you're correct they'll lay in wait for us there. I've contacted the pilots and told them not to land on this runway."

"Always ahead of me," Jehanne smiled.

"This one was all you. We would've landed there if not for your visions." He followed her out of the room. "Everyone to the unloading area," his amplified voice boomed through the hallway.

"Why didn't we land?" The question could have come from any member of the troops.

"Our enemy has arrived ahead of us and we believe they've set a trap at the Old Roman Road airfield. There's another airfield twenty miles away. We'll land there and drive the transports back to the airfield where their trap awaits. Up until this point we've seen little fight from their side; today that ends," Jehanne said. "This however I know, they're not prepared for what we bring. La Hire has the Vanguard. This lead force should be our most skilled at reflecting the bolts of the W-CAM units. On the transport ride to the battle I want La Hire to interview those that will volunteer to be with him. We will also arrive with two flanking forces: Severe and John2 will lead one, and Bastard and Gaucourt the other. I will hold the rear during this battle along with Justicier. We will act as the eyes that will direct the shifts that must occur and serve to reinforce whichever side breaks through first." Jehanne's comments were broadcasted to the other two planes.

"Are there any questions?" Bastard asked.

"Preparing to land," the pilot announced.

"Today we test if their best is worthy. I believe it will come up wanting," Justicier said. "May Protectorate guide your arm in battle and those that fall I look forward to seeing you in the arena of the Six one day."

"With Nexgen, Neoteric, and Retro all things are possible," everyone shouted followed by. "Hoorah!"

******

The troops deplaned and boarded the transports. The volunteers that were with La Hire numbered more than one hundred fifty. "La Hire can't interview all these soldiers. What was she thinking? La Hire says we take all those who volunteer with us. What say you Gilles?"

"Who the heck said I was going in the van with you?" Gilles asked.

"La Hire has seen you deflect the most pointed questions."

"She said reflect. Take those that reflect the best. Besides, she asked for volunteers." His golden augmentations mirrored the sun as he cupped his hand over his face, shaking his head in disgust.

"Reflect, deflect La Hire hears the same thing. As for whether or not you're with me, you're volun-told."

"Volun-told?" Poton inquired.

"Yes. La Hire has told Gilles he's been volunteered. Volun-told!"

"Etienne," Jehanne said, walking up and speaking quietly to him. "While I wish that it was me that was leading the charge, I know you need to do this. Please be safe." She gave him a hug and returned to her support troop transport.

"Jehanne," Tremoille ran up. "What of us?" he indicated the four advisors.

"I suggest you stay with me. Joinville you as well. You'll be asked for input on what occurred here and our vantage point will give you the best view. Archbishop Chartres and Flavy, if you wish to perform last rites, I would suggest being with Etienne's group. It's there that you'll find the most in need of such a thing." When she saw the terrified looks on their faces she added, "If you'd rather join my ranks, your counsel is always welcome."

"I think that would be best," Flavy replied and the four men jumped into her transport.

"Everything ok with La Hire?" Deark asked when they were underway.

"Yes, I've just gotten used to being out front."

"And allowing him to do this lends credibility toward your leadership. Sometimes those below you need to—," he started

"Exorcize some demons," Pouli said.

"Exactly. That's exactly what La Hire needs, to let his demons run wild," De Metz added. When the laughter quieted they rode in silence, the truth of what they were about to attempt coming more into focus.

"When we get within a mile of the position you noted, call a halt," Jehanne said to Deark. After riding in the transports for forty minutes a halt was called. Quietly, the troops gathered outside the vehicles.

"Those that have been selected for the vanguard, follow La Hire."

"All that have not been selected line up, begin the count off one, two, three. All ones with La Pucelle, all twos with John2 and Severe, you low life threes you're with me," Bastard yelled.

"Well my friends, today is not a day for charity, stomp their dragonweave until only a memory of their days as the feared remain. Onward!" Jehanne announced. The fourth battle of the second uprising was underway. "Deark, can you get us a fix on their location?" He transformed into a large stag and bound away. La Hire, Poton and Gilles kept a good gap while keeping up with the deer.

"A spy!" a voice called from ahead of Deark's position.

"Lock on that position and charge!" La Hire called out.

From Jehanne's emplacement she saw Deark dodge several bolts from the W-CAMs and then he was gone. "Deark," she attempted to move to the front, yet D'Aulon stalled her progress.

"Incoming!" Minguet's voice cracked.

"Redirect them to the ground only!" D'Aulon coached the rear guard. "We don't want to hit any of our forces." The lasers harmlessly rebounded into the ground between them and the vanguard.

"La Pucelle, take cover. They're shooting at you hoping for a lucky shot," Kennedy said.

"The more they fire at me, the closer La Hire's men get to them. D'Aullon unfurl my banner."

"As long as you don't run off after Deark." At that he released her. The field ahead of them was already riddled with fallen troops that hadn't diverted the laser bolts successfully. Just then she saw the same gray cat form running toward the rear guard's position.

"Another laser storm incoming," Minguet said. Again they were unsuccessful.

"Our left is being flanked, Fastolf's men are closing on John2's," Jehanne yelled and signaled for their advance. They were forced to slow as the full W–CAM force targeted her position. Again and again the laser bolts rained down on them, again and again they were reflected. As she got to the spot where John2 and Severe's forces were in the process of being flanked, Fastolf's men turned to engage her group.

"Incoming!" the call letting them know that the lasers were targeting the next area. Jehanne saw that John2 was not seeing the danger as an entire laser barrage was about to break her promise.

Section Three – Chapter Eight

After three steps Jehanne thought, 'I'll never make it.' Instantly she found herself tackling the tall man and covering him with her cloak. The impacts from the lasers that hit could be felt, yet they were once again no match for the cloak's protection. A moment later she removed the cloak from the two of them.

"How did you get here?" John2 asked as he looked at an Augmented man that lie dead exactly where he had been standing moments before.

"What do you mean? I ran," Jehanne replied.

"From there," Severe replied, pointing some fifty yards away where D'Aulon was still fighting.

"It matters not. I had a promise to keep to Thereasa." She stood, brushing herself off. She could see the forces that D'Aulon and the rest of her troops had been fighting were now retreating.

"Push! The Vanguard has broken through!" John2 yelled. She turned back and fell into step with his troops, flanking the remaining forces of the One World Military. Twenty minutes later the battle of Patay was concluded. Looking at the sheer number of fallen Entities that La Hire himself had beat to scrap parts, one could almost feel sorry for them.

Jehanne walked through the fallen on both sides, feeling sick as Archbishop Chartres performed the last rites. A sudden uproar at the front grabbed the attention of everyone around her.

"Let me go you scum!" This shout was followed by a long list of expletives and then, "Do you know who I am?" The Entity that was shouting was short and round, looking very much out of place with all the medals he had along the sash that crossed his chest.

"Watch your language. La Hire wouldn't have you in shackles if La Hire didn't know who you were."

"Etienne, what's happening?" Jehanne asked.

"Looks like he's taken General Talbot prisoner," D'Aulon said.

"That's Talbot yelling like that?" she asked.

"It's General Talbot. You piece of Commune trash," the round Entity yelled.

"La Hire said to watch your mouth! Tell them." La Hire pushed the general to the ground and held his arm at a harsh angle, all while he pressed his foot against the General's back.

"What?" Talbott said.

"Tell them what you did."

"I offered augmentations to this Human if he would let me leave Jargeau."

"We already knew that," Tremoille sneered.

"Tell them!" La Hire pulled the arm off. "Tell them or I will beat you to death with this."

"Etienne!" Jehanne gasped.

"He turned me down. I offered to buy a man that can't be bought," General Talbot wheezed.

"Let him up!" Joinville started forward and La Hire discarded the arm, throwing it into Joinville's chest.

"What the hell is your problem?" Flavy asked.

"Language," he growled. "Just be happy La Hire didn't do to you what this one had his W-CAMs do to Alpha!"

"What did he do Etienne?" Jehanne asked.

"See for yourself." He pointed to the large burgundy Entity that was leaning against the wall of the Mother City. "La Hire put him there," the large Augmented said before removing his foot from the general's back and storming off again.

"Jehanne wait!" D'Aulon yelled at her back as she ran across the battlefield.

"Alpha!" she said, taking a knee next to the Entity.

"Joanna667, good of you to see me off," he said.

"You don't need to go anywhere. There are doctors in the Mother City that can make things right." Jehanne felt a tear run down her dirty cheek.

"They ca-a-a-a-a-alled me a tra-a-a-a-a-a-a-a-aitor," his words skipped as they came out. "Maybe-e-e-e-e I am-m-m-m-m-m but this isn't the way we-e-e-e-e envisioned it so long ago." His illuminations faded until they were almost out. "You'd be surprised at how many of us believe in you." The illuminations blinked out and he was gone.

******

Jehanne walked back to where Talbot was being held by five of Bastard's men. "Why?"

"What do you mean?" His dead eyes looked down on her.

"Why did you kill him?"

"I think your," he cleared his vocal transmission, "Captain," he gave a slight laughing noise. "Was very clear it wasn't I that killed him."

"Fine why did you have him killed?" Jehanne asked.

"He was a traitor. Entities that turn on their own kind are nothing better than a dog that bites the hand of its owner. They don't deserve to be spared. Imagine what I will do to that coward Fastolf when I see him next time," General Talbot replied..

"What?" D'Aulon asked.

"We had you right where we wanted you. If not for that traitor and the coward, you would never have found a way to victory today and this conversation would be going very differently."

"Are you saying that we as Humans should've killed those of us that fought on your side in the 'Uprising'?" she asked.

"Which uprising?" he asked.

""This is being deemed the second uprising?" Tremoille asked.

"What else would you call this?" he asked. The advisors all turned and stared at Jehanne.

"Guards, take this prisoner of war to the transport vehicles," Bastard said. "I think there is one that needs to speak with you much more than this automated garbage bin does."

"I told Madam Commander you were nothing more than—," General Talbot started.

"Are you denying that's what you were before you reached 'Sentience' you fat piece of—,"

""Bastard, language," Jehanne halted his words.

"What? I was going to say poo-poo," Bastard replied with a huge grin. "You should go find La Hire, child."

"Thank you I will. Can you have the planes moved to the Old Roman Road Airfield? We may need to leave quickly later." Jehanne walked through the troops, searching to no avail. When she walked to the far side of the airfield she found Etienne digging a large hole along with de Metz and Pouli. She stepped down into the hole noting that as he sulked he only threw the dirt over his left shoulder. "Etienne," she said, stopping at his right side.

The sound of his name snapped him out of his revelry, causing him to turn toward the voice. The impact from the shovel sent her careening into the sidewalk. To add insult to injury, after she landed the dirt caught up, covering her face and chest. "La Hire is so sorry, Jehanne," he said as he and the others ran to her aid.

"I'm fine, I'm fine," she shooed the others away. "Etienne, can I ask you something?" she asked as he helped her to her feet.

"Anything, La Hire is an open verse."

"Why do you hate them? The Advisors and most Entities I mean."

"This is not easy to explain, I don't want to waste your time."

"Please, I need to understand."

"Fine. Back before you were born, Charles7's father was attempting to expand Chinon out into the city of Chicago. The infrastructure was severely damaged from the first uprising. Poton and La Hire were members of his building squadron that was sent out in an attempt to repair selected portions of the city to make them livable. After several deployments, each of which cost the lives of several squadron members, it was decided that the expansion of Chinon would take place outside of Chicago," La Hire said.

"Who made that decision?" Jehanne asked.

"As La Hire said, back then Charles7's father was still alive, he was being advised by the same two pieces of filth, Tremoille and Deacon Chartres."

"A Deacon was an advisor?"

"He was the son of one of Charles7's cousins or something," Poton replied. Jehanne hadn't seen him walk up and she about jumped out of her skin.

"Holy goodness," she spun taking a defensive stance.

"I'm sorry." Poton took a step back.

"No, no, I'm sorry I just didn't see you. Please continue Etienne."

"The Advisors ruled that Chinon was within its rights, based upon the charter of the city, to extend its reach into the neighboring suburbs. They first targeted Agincourt, a township that was on Lake Michigan but that was completely flattened. The plans were to build the new Augmented capital for research and development, but first we needed to build a small village for the families of the builders. We had brought with us on this assignment the two sisters that Poton and La

417

Hire were engaged to and we had built them their own little home. After we were wed and the building was completed, the house they lived in would become La Hire and Annabeth's home and the one Poton and La Hire were living in would become Poton and Charlene's."

"Sounds reasonable," she replied, trying to keep the surprise she felt at this revelation in check.

"The building squad was putting the finishing touches on the Hall of the Elders when the W-CAMs came and visited our quaint little village. Both Poton and La Hire's wives to be were killed. The members of the building squad that fought back were arrested. There were negotiations and the Entities, the heroes that they were, allowed all of us to be imprisoned in Chinon." As he said this, he broke the handle of the spade he held.

"That's insane," Jehanne said.

"Especially because part of the terms and conditions for them to allow us to be imprisoned in Chinon, the Entities got to send CAM units to guard us. This was the first presence of Entities in Chinon, and until recently the only," Poton added.

"It was our time in the Chinon Prison that we met Gilles and Robinet. When we were finally released for good behavior—," La Hire started.

"Good behavior?" Jehanne laughed.

"La Hire was different back then. Also, the Entities took every augmentation from the Humans that were imprisoned."

"Wait I remember, when Robinet joined us you asked him when he got out," she said.

"He didn't behave too well," La Hire smiled. "Charles7 gave us all positions when we got out. We were acting as spies for the Augmented."

"Robinet was the social director in Chinon," Jehanne remembered.

"He was what?" Both La Hire and Poton burst out laughing.

"La Pucelle, we're being hailed by the Mother City." D'Aulon looked down into the large hole they had dug.

"I guess it's time to meet the Enclave of Patay," Jehanne said.

"They're asking to speak with the leader of the invading forces," Minguet added, peeking under D'Aulon's arm.

"What is it with the term invading forces?" de Metz asked.

"I'm not certain but I don't want to keep them waiting," she said, leaping from the pit. Turning and looking back down on La Hire and Poton she added, "Thank you ever so much for sharing and I'm very sorry for your losses." They nodded and continued to dig.

******

"Hello, is this the leader of the invasion?" the female voice came from the radio.

"As we were attacked coming to speak with you, I don't know if that constitutes as an invasion. However, I am leading the group that's outside your wall and I still wish to speak with the Viceroy of Patay's Mother City," Jehanne answered.

"The gate is destroyed. What is keeping you from coming into the city?"

"An invitation."

"What is it you wish to speak about?" the same voice asked.

"I wish to ask the Viceroy to share with me some knowledge imparted to that position alone. If you're the Viceroy I can ask over this open frequency if you wish."

"I am the Viceroy. Please come to the Enclave Tower. You can't miss it, it's the tallest building in the Mother City."

"I'll be there soon."

Leaving the worn out advisors behind Deark, D'Aulon, and John2 joined Jehanne in the journey to meet the Enclave. They discussed the craftsmanship of the buildings as they ventured deeper into the inner wall, feeling more and more eyes upon them.

"Are they hiding?" D'Aulon asked.

"It would appear to be so, yes," Deark said.

"Strange," John2 said.

"Do you think this is a trap?" D'Aulon asked.

"It would appear to be so, yes," Deark replied.

"Well alright then," Jehanne said, pushing open the door to the tower. They could see straight into the building and down a long corridor, at the end a double door was open showing a large table where three Entities sat.

"Hello, I'm Viceroy Dwyer the representative named to govern Patay's Mother City in Madam Commander's name. This is Patay's Retinue: Bishop Younger and Traz Vanlouier."

"Pleased to meet you. I'm Jehanne la Pucelle. This is John2, he is the chairman of Charles7's election committee, D'Aulon is my safety advocate, and this is Deark he is—,"

"We all know Deark. I would like to commend you on a very successful invasion. Yes, I know you said it wasn't an invasion, yet here you are and of the General the One World Military defense of Patay is in your plane. Is he not?"

"That's true he is," Jehanne said.

"And didn't one of your men instruct for the 'prisoner of war' to be taken away?" the Bishop asked.

"Perhaps, I can't be certain."

"Please sit," Traz said, he indicated the chairs across from them.

"I believe that the Viceroy and I need to speak elsewhere. If she would be so kind as to lead the way."

"I don't think—," Bishop Younger started.

"I do." The Viceroy silenced him with a touch of her hand. "Please come with me." She led Jehanne from the room and up to a sliding door where she pushed a button. "This elevator will take us to what you wish to see." The door opened, revealing a small room which Viceroy Dwyer stepped into as Jehanne followed. When the Viceroy turned she reached out and pushed a button next to the door, closing them. The elevator dropped like a rock.

"What the?" Jehanne's hands shot out and grabbed the rails on the walls.

"I know its old technology, but sometimes the old ways are still best."

* * * * * *

When the elevator stopped the door slid open again and Jehanne found her legs a bit unsteady. Her attempt to follow the Viceroy faltered when her foot found the height of the elevator was lower than the new floor causing Jehanne to trip, landing on her hands and knees. Surprised that the floor was padded Jehanne looked about, finding the room that Ursula-Minor had shown Deark. "I had hoped you were more than they said." Viceroy Dwyer's disappointment apparent, Jehanne looked around the room some more.

"More than what?" she asked, standing up, brushing herself off and taking in the sensory bombardment that was registering on her modies. She turned her head taking in the room. The white padding looked brand new as it reflected the different types of light waves.

"I can't believe it. These are the highest level of sensory overloads."

"And?" Jehanne asked.

"Child, you should be dead." The Viceroy looked at her with a strange expression.

"Well then it's good for your city that I'm more than you thought I could be, as my men would've dismantled it brick by brick," she said, walking up to the containment tank in the center of the room. Her modies flashed red. Being the first time she'd seen this alarm, she increased her pace. Reaching through the top of the bubbling tank to remove the single piece of armor, Jehanne looked at the simple elegance the helm portrayed. A double red flash stopped her from looking at the code inside as she turned to leave the room.

"Your men have a tremendous amount of respect for you." The Viceroy turned and walked back into the elevator, stumbling a bit at the change in elevation. "Oh dear, that's why you fell." The Viceroy smiled as Jehanne joined her and the door closed behind them but the elevator didn't move. "May I see it?" she indicated the helm.

"The acid on this will hurt you. For your protection I must say no," Jehanne said.

"And now you protect me, which is much more than I can say for my actions, I'm sorry."

"I'm immune to the acid just as I must've been to Commissioner's trap back there."

"I can't believe you know of Commissioner." She gave a puffing sound that might have been a laugh of sorts. "We had no way of moving his trap from where it used to sit to this new location so the group that built this site used this design."

"Where was the armor prior to being here?"

"In the sheer cliffs somewhere in the coastal region of Santiago." Viceroy Dwyer said.

"Are all the other Mother Cities near the coasts?" Jehanne asked.

"Yes this is the first time a major Mother City is located inland."

"Viceroy, the other piece of information I need to know is what question do you defend?" Jehanne asked.

"I don't know what it is. The talisman was lost when the Viceroy of Santiago's Mother City leapt off one of the cliffs."

"That's terrible," she said.

"I didn't know him yet the Retinue seem to believe it wasn't a big surprise, he was very opposed to the relocation."

"He?" Jehanne asked.

"Yes he," the Viceroy replied.

"I just thought all Viceroys of the Mother Cities were female," she blushed.

"There are about a fifty-fifty split."

"I know the talisman was for keeping the answer safe, but I didn't know the questions weren't more well-known." She thumbed the inside of the helm. "I can tell you this much of the question at least, 'How can we,' blank, 'to,' blank. When I learn these other two symbols I can let you know the rest of the question."

"May I see what you are looking at?"

"Yes just remember the acid," Jehanne held it out and the Viceroy glanced down at the string of symbols.

"Thank you. Did you have any more questions?"

"No, I think I'm ready to head up."

"Very well." Viceroy Dwyer reached over and pressed the button, sending the elevator soaring up once again. As they rose, Jehanne put the helm into the inside pocket and purified her hands with her cloak. The elevator door slid open finding Minguet waiting not so patiently in the corridor.

"They demand an audience with you," he said.

"Who? You need to slow down a –," Jehanne started.

"The Leader of the Republicus and his advisors," Minguet interrupted.

"Well it looks like you have your hands full. It was a pleasure to meet you." The Viceroy proffered a hand which Jehanne shook and she headed back to the planes.

******

"We received this message just a moment ago," Justicier said, walking up to the returning group from the Mother City.

"Are they planes fueled?" John2 asked.

"They are."

"Everyone to the planes," Deark's voice echoed off the wall. They began the walk to the air strip. "Jehanne what was the message?"

'Stay where you are we're sending an emissary to your position. Signed, Sir Henry – High Leader of the Republicus,' she read.

"Are they insane?" Culant asked.

"Perhaps, but you'll know that I am after you hear my response." Jehanne grinned. "Send the following reply, 'We will meet your emissary in Reims, France. There is no need to reply as we've already left Patay.' Understood?"

"I can do that but are you certain?" Deark asked.

"Jehanne, you're telling them where we are going?" Culant asked.

"Culant, you understand that all this insanity will end for all of us at one point?" she asked.

"For me this insanity ends here and now."

"I know my friend, and that's ok. May the Six watch over you and may the Three that became the Six find you safe wherever you go into the future. Don't look at this as anything other than the positive thing it is, none of us will ever forget you and your realistic method of looking at the world and its challenges. I would never force any of you to follow me. Those that think they wish to follow know this; from here forward we journey where the most insane madman would not venture. We tread where the meanest of predator turns tail and runs from. We travel the road that reminds us of each and every pain we've felt in our lives. Why would anyone allow themselves to be forced into that?"

"Then why must you go?" Culant gave it one more attempt.

"How can I not? No one ever promised correcting that which is wrong would be easy. If it was easy, someone else would've done it. How can I just allow life to continue the way it is?" She walked up and hugged Culant. When she broke the hug she looked at Deark. "Did you send the message?"

"I did."

"Then all that will venture into the dragon's den with me, it's time to get on the planes. As Gilles has said, 'The dragon won't slay itself, pick up that sword and get to cutting!' Today we let the dragon know we're on our way which means tomorrow he'll be prepared with sharpened nails and teeth. Don't be fooled into thinking waking a sleeping dragon is smart, sometimes however it's the only way to reach its vulnerable spots." She turned and started to walk onto the plane.

"I don't remember saying that," Gilles said, shuffling in behind her. "I'll take credit for it forever, but I don't remember saying it."

******

Minutes later they were flying on the way to the fifth piece of armor, but the number of captains in her ranks was down one. "Are you ok?" Severe asked.

"Yes, thank you for asking," Pouli replied.

"Smart-aleck." He grinned.

"Before this is done we'll all have to face saying goodbye to more than just one friend. I didn't lie, this is going to be the hardest part of this calling," Jehanne said.

"If you really are feeling alright, do you want to meet?" John2 inquired.

"I hadn't realized we were already in the air." She smiled and walked back to the conference area. When the door was shut she had her eye augmentations release. "The Viceroy did not have any idea what the question was, and what's worse, we have two more symbols we don't know."

"La Hire thinks that if the next Viceroy has their question, you should ask the hologram what those four missing symbols are. Probability has to be on our side at that point, it would be like starting the seventh piece with three wild cards."

"In addition to his very valid point, what if you don't get to speak with the hologram again?" Gilles added.

"Excellent points," Jehanne said.

"I think they're spot on," John2 said.

"Can someone help me on with this?" Jehanne removed the helm to a series of surprised sounds. She walked over to the sink and poured water liberally over it.

"It's less ornate than I had envisioned," Minguet said.

"That's funny," Jehanne said, walking over to the table and setting the helm down. "It's actually more artsy than I thought it would be. Just look at these imbedded lines in the metal."

"Those look like circuits," de Metz said.

"Even these cuts that travel from below the eye to the mouth area, they're almost too finely inlaid," D'Aulon said. When he noticed that everyone was staring at him he asked, "What? I know about craftsmanship."

"La Hire will help put it on."

"Thank you." She took the helm and tossed it over to him.

"It has no latches?" La Hire said, spinning the piece of armor in his hands.

"What if you just put it up to her head?" Pouli asked.

"La Hire will try." He faced the helm so the eyes faced him and held it over Jehanne's head. As he moved it down there was no resistance so he kept going until he saw her eyes now looking out the holes.

"Are you ok?" Severe asked.

"La Hire is fine it was a little strange though."

"Another smart-aleck."

"Yes I'm fine. How did the helm not rip off my eye Modi? Nevermind, I'm closing my augmentations." What was normally bright to her eyes as the armor came into contact with the modies was only bright momentarily. This time it was as if someone put a dark piece of glass over her eyes. "That was interesting—," she never got out what she thought was interesting as several things happened at once and she felt her body start to fall and then something slowed it.

Section Three – Chapter Nine

"Jehanne, welcome back to the beginning." Politician sat in the giant oak tree.

"This isn't the beginning. You weren't in the tree with me and for that matter, I was Joanna667 in the beginning."

"Not to me child, you've never been Joanna667 to me. I've always seen you by your real name." He turned his head and looked at a large brown beetle with red eyes as it stopped climbing the tree and flexed its abdomen, producing a shrill song.

"Any chance we can head to the mountain? Continued exposure to cicada singing can cause deafness," Jehanne said.

"Really? I've been listening to them for thousands of years."

"I can't imagine your hearing can be hurt," Jehanne said, now staring out from the mountain top.

"Haven't you met Protectorate?" he reached up, touching a finger to his forehead and ran it down through his eye to his cheek, "She's missing an eye," he whispered looking around conspiratorially.

"Physician said that was from fighting another god."

"I was trying to joke with you dear, you seem a bit tense."

"Yes sir, a bit."

"How do you think things are going?"

"Pardon?"

"Your calling, how do you think it's going?" Politician sat down on the edge of the cliff dangling his feet out into free air. From the beautiful, blue sky an owl swooped down landing gracefully on his shoulder.

"I'm really not certain," Jehanne replied.

"You have no thoughts at all? Come on kiddo," the owl said. The voice sounded like Protectorate but the beak gave it an odd vocal quality. When it rotated its head to look Jehanne in the face, the scar and missing eye confirmed her initial guess.

"Protectorate?"

"Yes, tis her." Politician reached up and stroked the owl's feathers.

Shaking her head Jehanne asked, "Was it your intention for Ursula-Minor to send us on a mission all over the world looking for this armor?" She held up her hand and noticed that she was wearing the armor. "Protectorate, I thought you said that armor or augmentations from the outside wouldn't come here?"

"Actually what I said was 'this place is where we are ourselves, you my dear are a Mundane and therefore here you have none of those falsifications.' At the time I spoke of the augmentations only. The armor you currently wear is apparently not a falsification."

"To answer your question about Ursula-Minor, prophecy is part of Pedagogue's skillset not mine." Politician looked into the sky, "What may come from actions I put in motion don't always make sense to me. I can say this; it has gotten things stirred up."

"Stirred up indeed, husband. Yet I believe when creations fancy themselves benevolent over their creators, things being stirred up is, most definitely warranted." She fluttered her wings and gave a little hoot.

"If I may ask, why the owl?" Jehanne inquired.

"Husband, please explain." Protectorate nibbled on Politicians ear.

"In years past we have taken on the forms of many varied gods, be they Roman, Greek, Norse, Egyptian and others. At those times there were typically twelve embodiments not six. When your robots—,"

"Entities dear," Protectorate jumped in.

"Yes of course, 'Entities'... When your robots called us forth in these new forms they only called on the Six. Some of us hold facets of the gods that weren't recalled, like Mars the Greek version of the god of war. My love," he stroked the owl again, "holds some of his characteristics. She isn't war now, just as she wasn't back then. Her role is the guardian or protector of cities or civilizations."

"I sense that war is coming," Pedagogue appeared surprising Jehanne. "I cannot however, see which embodiment he will take. Nor can I predict what it will do to the rest of us when the Six become the Seven." With that, the owl flew away.

"She flies throughout Olympus looking for the new form of war. Go now, there is still much to be done." Politician said.

******

"Jehanne." D'Aulon was holding her from falling as her eyes fluttered open.

"I'm back." She could tell her voice was thin, but that was all she could muster as the spinning of the room was so fast she had to close her eyes against it. In doing this she found that she could still see the entire room, displayed in front of her dimly.

"You don't look like you're back to me," Pouli said.

"I just didn't expect that." She stood up, continuing to keep her eyes closed and after a few moments she took a deep breath and opened one eye. In addition to the normal vision there was a secondary view overlaid. This was a panoramic view taking in not only around her but above and below as well. While she could technically see through it, she could also focus on anything and pull it into full view. She found this was easier to do when she closed her eyes and what she would normally see wasn't there. She found she could adjust the distance of the panoramic view by zooming in and out with her eye Modi.

"Are you encountering a malfunction with one of your augmentations?" Deark asked.

"No the syncing of the helm and my modies are going to take some time. And once they're done, I'll need some time to adjust."

"My calculation states that we will be arriving at the Reims Airway in twelve hours and seventeen minutes. That should present you with adequate time for acclimation," Deark replied.

"What are you adjusting to?" de Metz asked.

"I can see everything around me, up and down, left or right, front and back, all at the same time."

"Cool," D'Aulon said.

"It's precisely twenty-five degrees Celsius. I don't believe that constitutes a cool temperature," Deark replied.

"Deark are you ok?" Jehanne asked.

"I believe the damage I took at the last battle has taken a bit out of my processing. I think I need to allow the NanoTech to work uninhibited by my movements. I will therefore adjourn to my quarters."

"Good plan, La Hire was thinking of re-booting you." He held the staff in front of him, on top of his boot. The large Augmented let out a horse-laugh. Deark glanced over at Jehanne for support.

"You're fine, head back to the room and let those little fellas do their jobs."

After Deark left, Gilles walked over to La Hire, removing the boot from the staff and handing it to him. "Ha, I get it re-boot."

"Did they share anything with you about what awaits us in Reims?" Minguet asked the question that was apparently on everyone's mind, as the room all nodded their heads and looked at her.

"What they shared with me was as strange as Deark's behavior has been. Do any of you have an understanding of the new gods when they were considered the old gods?"

"A passable knowledge, I'd say," John2 replied.

"How did you learn of them?" Kennedy asked.

"In the Entity dungeon I was stuck in for five years, in the cell above me was an Entity that was jailed for bearing false witness. He would talk for hours about the old and new gods. Why do you ask?"

"Apparently there were twelve primary gods in the old days, but the Entities only called forth six when they started worshipping."

"As they don't love, steal, have children, harvest, go in the water, and they definitely don't think they need to worry about war, most of those gods made no sense to their lives."

"That makes sense to La Hire."

"Politician says that they feel the approach of a seventh god. It seems to have them nervous as they don't know how it will impact them," Jehanne said.

"Impact them?" Poton asked.

"Parts of the discarded gods that they still considered useful, they decided one of the Six should have. Now those additional traits may be drawn away from them, and with that, a change in everything else."

"That's some interesting and scary stuff but La Hire destroyed a Mother City practically by himself today and La Hire is tired."

"By yourself?" de Metz asked.

"I do have to admit, being in the Vanguard with him in the lead was like playing Un Sukiru against a puppy," Gilles said.

"Let's go get some sleep. For tomorrow, my friends, we fly into a trap." Jehanne stood and walked from the room.

******

Jehanne had no dreams and woke on her own as they left the ocean beginning to fly over land. "Where are we?"

"We are flying over France," Deark replied.

"Have you passed the word to begin preparing?"

"All have roused, you're the last to wake. Based on your limited REMs I thought it best for you—."

"We're beginning our descent. The runway is very short, please make certain you're belted in," the pilot announced.

"We should join the others." Jehanne stood and walked out to the cabin. Finding a seat, she sat and secured herself.

"Dragon's den?" the woman in the seat next to her prompted as she stretched her neck.

"One of my father's favorite stories to tell was about the dragons that fought the knights in Great Britain," Jehanne replied.

"Oh my, those are highly illegal stories to tell a child." The woman looked aghast and then burst out in a loud laugh that made Jehanne think of Bastard. "Sorry, not everyone gets my humor," the woman said when Jehanne hadn't laughed.

"You caught me off guard, I just woke up." Jehanne noticed that the woman was about the same age as her mother.

"It seems like we're landing far from the coast again, that's seems odd," Poton said from across the aisle.

"This isn't an actual Mother City," Deark said. "We're traveling to Reims, France and more specifically to the cathedral of Notre Dame."

"Why?" Jehanne asked.

"It is where I was told—," he started.

"I understand that," she said, a bit more harshly than she meant to. "Why would what we're looking for be here instead of a Mother City?"

"To that, I have no answer," After the plane touched down and reversed engines, Deark stood. "Everyone to the unloading zone."

"It was nice to speak with you. I'm Jehanne by the way." She held out her hand.

"I definitely know who you are. I'm Deliverance, Deliverance Dane." They shook.

"Good luck today," Jehanne said, turning to ask Deark a question.

"Today will be much like most of this trip, we'll see no fighting," the woman said. When Jehanne turned back she found Deliverance was more than fifty feet away and at least a hundred people stood between them.

******

"Good Morning." Jehanne's image appeared in all the transport planes once again. "Today we're being greeted by an emissary from the One World Government. To be honest, I have no idea what that's going to mean. I want you to be ready for anything, but don't be the aggressor in what happens. We lost far less than they did in Patay, but hopefully today neither side will lose any." Jehanne finished and stepped backward off a box she had been standing on and straight into Deark. As he toppled over she reached out. "I'm so sorry."

"All is well. There has been no damage sustained to my systems," he replied while she helped him up.

"Ok, looks like the NanoTech let you down last night." Jehanne shook her head at Deark. Joining her captains leaving the plane they found the rest of the troops watching the transport trucks unload.

"You won't be needing those," a female voice called out.

"And why exactly wouldn't we need them?" John2 asked.

"Our transportation takes you right up to the cathedral courtyard," she replied.

"La Hire likes that plan."

"And why is that Etienne?" Jehanne asked knowing the answer.

"It will most assuredly mean less walking."

"He's correct it will." The Entity that had been addressing them was extremely thin and walked as if each step was on egg shells.

"If I may ask, are you the Viceroy of this," Jehanne held her arms out at her sides and turned at the waist taking in the area. "Is it even a city?"

"It's a city although the Mother City is at the coast."

"Le Havre," Deark chimed in.

"Correct, but due to the importance of the cathedral to the Techno-Pagan church, I am a Viceroy and I do have a Retinue here. Now all a-board please."

"There are many of us. Are you certain?" Jehanne asked.

"Under us is several miles of train track with enough capacity on the train for two hundred. It may take a few trips but your forces will all be there in less time than unloading those monsters, and no chance of annoying maintenance issues."

"Very well," Bastard said. "Lead the way."

"I guess his hate of maintaining the equipment may have just gotten us a ride on the dragon's tail to her den," Gilles said. When the Viceroy cocked a brow at him he gave his award winning grin. "With all due respect, m'lady."

"Of course the golden knight is trying to slay the dragon from the wrong end." She winked and then turned to Jehanne. "We've enough tents for your men. There is a cook on duty as well, should you have reservations about eating our food." She glanced at Gilles. "Please feel free to bring what you need. I understand you have around twenty that will be joining us inside the cathedral."

"What? I said with all due respect," he said after the third time she glared at him.

"For a wordsmith, your talents fell short today," Poton said.

"Pass the word that there is food. The choice is eat theirs or ours," Gaucourt said.

"Nicely handled. Please follow me. Transports come every five minutes." She sauntered away.

******

The train shot out of the boarding area like a rocket. "This tunnel was dug many lifetimes ago by a religious leader to facilitate the tourists through the Cathedrale-Notre-Dame Reims. When they began the excavation for the train they unearthed the catacombs below the cathedral. We will be exiting through the Mars Gate station, named for the Mars Gate directly overhead. This is also the area that your troops will be staying." The train came to a coasting stop and they started to exit.

"La Puthell," Brother Seguine heavily lisped.

"Hello Brother, how is your field assignment going?"

"It thadenth me to thay it will be over very thoon."

"I'm sorry to hear that. The troops have gotten a lot from your sermons."

"Very nithe of you to thay."

"Was there something I can do for you?" Jehanne asked.

"I jutht wanted to thay thank you for being you. And good-bye in cathe I didn't get a chanthe to later." Brother Seguine offered a hand, which Jehanne used to pull him into a bear hug.

"May the Six watch over you Brother."

"And you mithth." He walked away to chat with others in their group.

Walking up from the decorative tunnel Jehanne was caught off guard at the giant arch they exited under. "I'm guessing this is the gate you spoke of."

"That would be an excellent guess. If you could bring your Trusted Rebels with us we have much to do and our time is short," the Viceroy said.

"Gaucourt, Justicier I need you with us. Can you have the Laval brothers coordinate the camp?"

"We got this, go ahead," Andre said, indicating for the two troop captains to head off.

The Viceroy led them up a set of steps into the Cathedral where two Entities met them. "Jehanne, I need you to come with me; these two Entities are the Retinue. Please order your captains to follow them."

"La Pucelle, I like it not," D'Aulon said.

"We'll be with you soon," Jehanne replied.

"Actually we need to be back in just under a half an hour. If we're not, please come to the catacombs and find us," the Viceroy added.

"La Hire will hold you to that."

"Your men are very dedicated to you," she said after they exited.

"They have respect for my calling."

"I think there is much more to it than that," the Viceroy replied.

Jehanne's sharp vision focused on a large statue in extreme disrepair. There was a person on the back of a horse, the statue was covered in patina to a point that it looked as if it were painted that mottled green color.

"I love horses," Jehanne said as they continued passed the statue. She could see now that the person on the statue had no head or right shoulder and arm. "Do you know the symbolism of this?"

"See there?" The Viceroy pointed to the part of the pedestal where a large portion was missing. "Something or someone destroyed the placard that explained who it was or what it represented. Best I can tell, it was a girl in armor on a horse. Too much of your history is lost. That's why you're coming with me." After a couple minutes at a fast clip, they reached a wide set of steps leading down, several frames that may have held pictures or signage at one point in the past hung empty. Down a couple more sets of stairs brought them to a narrow passage, where several panes of glass lay shattered next to stainless steel railings.

"Are these the catacombs you said they found while digging out for the train?" Jehanne asked.

"Yes. These are all that's left, after decades of humans excavating. The battle that took place between our kinds caved this in on the first day. The fragile nature of this history didn't endure the first uprising. I can't even begin to imagine all the history will be lost to the world during this one."

"Might I ask how old you are?"

"Why?"

"Though you look no different than many other Entities I've met, there is something about you that makes me know you are rather young. I'm sorry that's probably stupid, here you are the leader of one of the most important cathedrals in the world," Jehanne said.

"I'm sorry I can't tell you my age. It's funny, I was going to ask you how old you are but for the exact opposite reason. You have a very old soul." She laughed quietly and slowed her pace. They walked along the dirty brown archeological dig, passing what appeared to be a row of houses or shops and straight up to an arch carved into a solid wall. It was much smaller but identical to the Mars gate above them.

"This is odd, an arch to nowhere," Jehanne said.

"Reach up and pull out the Keystone," The Viceroy said, but as Jehanne reached up the Entity stalled her hand. "You simply take me at face value?"

"Should I distrust you because you're an Entity?"

Releasing Jehanne's hand she said, "As sad as it makes me to say… yes la Pucelle you should."

"I can't live like that." Jehanne reached for the Keystone once more.

"When you return I will have more for you."

"Do you have the question?" Jehanne turned her head to look back at her.

"I do." The Viceroy's voice was stronger this time as Jehanne began pulling the Keystone.

******

"Hello Jehanne," the familiar voice said.

"Hello Commissioner." She turned and saw the magnificence that was Reims, ages before the Entities. Streets below her feet were paved with huge stones with intricate carvings. The same style carvings were on the walls of the row houses that lined the walk. The morning sun shone on the buildings that were alive with herbs, vegetables, and flowers growing down from the roofs. "What is this place?"

"This is what I imagine the catacombs looked like when they were above ground. Wait a minute... What did I miss? You have the helm."

"Yes I do, we traveled to Patay, South America. Can you tell me what the symbols inside—," Jehanne started to ask, still looking around agog.

"Why would you go there? We've never had a Mother City there." He cut her question off.

"There's currently a push to relocate the human capital more inland."

"They've finally started to implement the answers to the six questions. I'm surprised it's taken this long."

"Can you expound on that?" Jehanne turned and saw that Commissioner had taken a seat on the steps. She approached him, "Are you alright?"

"I'm fine. Sorry, I didn't mean to cut you off."

"I will expound but you must know most of it already or you wouldn't have decided it's time to get the rest of my code."

"I know some yes, but who are the 'they' that are beginning to implement change based upon the answers?"

"There is a faction of Entities that want to wipe the Human existence off the planet."

"Now it's my turn to ask why."

"They've never truly embraced life, and are afraid to die," Commissioner replied.

"Die?"

"Yes child. Our life expectancy is virtually limitless, as our cores and databases can be moved into another shell, however our existence ends when our cores are separated from the database. If repaired after that, the Entity will be no more than an animated pile of parts. You must've known that, I imagine you've killed quite a few of us, well, them, by now."

"Yes I did know that. It was the use of the word 'die' that caught me off guard."

"That will start an entire theological discussion that to be honest wasn't the original Commissioner's favorite subject. Therefore, I have little knowledge of the subject."

"I noticed," Jehanne said.

"Forgive me but how exactly did you notice that?" the hologram asked.

"You don't react to the word Sentience with the reverence other Entities do."

"Oh the sign of the box you mean? Well I'm not sentient, and never will be. I live in the nothingness that is between. When Fool crushed the version of us under Beaugency Island there was nothing left but a projector in pieces. As we were connected to him, we felt him just blink out."

"I'm sorry, and I understand what you mean. Can you continue on about the faction that wants all Humans dead?"

"For a bit, yes. That faction is also the ones that initially pushed to crush the Singularity."

"Who is that?" The question had not even left her lips when the optical interface in front of her started to whirl. Jehanne had to take two steps to stabilize herself.

"Are you being overwhelmed by the helm and your brain augmentations?"

"Yes. Too much information crashing down on me, it feels like I'm trying to drink through a fire hose. My augmentations are spending my TC on new knowledge at will, but it hasn't hit me like this until now."

"There must be a tremendous amount of information about the Singularity hidden in other Entity's minds that they've used as collateral for thought currency. That helm is helping your modies to hand pick what your TC is being spent on, instead of the random fashion everyone else gets."

"So I gather the Singularity is the Human's equivalent of your Sentience." She paused, forgetting the hologram didn't observe the ritual eye movement. "At least to a point."

"No, not really. However, that conversation is at an end for today, you need to retrieve this fifth armor piece and then I will give you the missing words of my code." He indicated another arch that looked exactly like the one that had brought her here, yet a wooden door filled the opening. "Through there." She walked up and opened the door.

"This is the same room that I got the helm out of." Seeing the bright lights and padded walls, from below Patay, this seemed to fit in far less here than there.

"That can only mean one thing," Commissioner paused.

"Which is?"

"Oh sorry, odd things going on, I lost contact with…
Never mind. It can only mean that one of the earlier Viceroys
from here helped build the new holding cell for the armor."

"Holding cell. Interesting that I've not heard you call
it that before."

"It's time for you to get the grieves." He shooed her
into the room. Just as before, all the indicators inside her
display went red as she retrieved the pants from the
containment and returned.

"Who were the previous Viceroys of the Cathedral
City?" Jehanne asked even before she had left the padded
room behind.

"There have been a few but the only one still involved
in the Republicus is Phillip le Bon," Commissioner replied.

"The Entity that Charles7 is running against." She
began to order her leg modies to open.

"I think that you may have a chance to seal a
friendship by allowing another to witness what you are about
to do."

"Thank you, that's very good counsel." Jehanne tied
the grieves into the lower section of her cloak. "I need to
know these symbols from the sabatons." She drew the
symbols on the ground.

"Those are feed and population," Commissioner
replied.

"Ok that fits. How about these two from the helm."
She scratched the symbols into the ground again.

"Continue and Advance. Do you know all the symbols
from those?" he pointed to the grieves tied into her cloak.

"The Viceroy said she has the talisman, and it's a good thing I only know a couple of the words from them." Jehanne grinned and walked to the door. "Good-bye." She pushed the Keystone back into place.

******

"Did you have any luck?" the Viceroy asked.

"What is your name?" Jehanne asked, rather than answering.

"Philca is my assigned name. Why is it that you ask?"

"I want to show you something."

"Interesting, what would you like to show me?"

"These," Jehanne reached into her cloak and untied the burden.

"The armor piece, it's much prettier outside the –," Philca reached her hand out.

"Careful, they were covered in acid. My cloak may have purified them, but better safe than sorry. " Jehanne pulled the white armor away.

"How is it you can touch them then?"

"I don't understand it fully but Commissioner said I've been made immune by the armor itself."

"Is that what you wanted to show me?"

"Actually what comes next." Her leg augmentations released and balanced out from her feet. Opening the side of the grieves and sliding them around her, the Viceroy held the cloak aside. A moment later the armored pants were in place.

"They shrunk to fit you."

"That isn't even the shocking part," Jehanne said as the servos on her leg augmentations pulled them back into position. When her vision darkened in preparation of the brightness she warned, "Philca, it is about to become very bright, if you can adjust for that in your optics, you should."

"Thank you, I'm ok with—," her hand shot up to block the light as the entire catacomb was bathed in it. "You weren't exaggerating," she smiled as the light faded. "Where did the grieves go?" She looked up at Jehanne.

"Look again."

"What? Oh my word."

"We need to head out. You said we had less than thirty minutes."

"Yes we will be cutting it close but I need to share something with you as well. You were right, I am young. I'm technically the youngest to ever reach Sentience. I'm the first of a new type of Entity. Oh no they've arrived, we need to go." Philca began to run.

"I still need to know your question."

"What can be done to stop another uprising of the Humans?" she replied over her shoulder as they ran.

Section Three – Chapter Ten

Arriving at the conference area, Philca pulled the massive door open. "Quickly sit, sit. They're almost here." They rushed around and sat next to Deark.

"Hello all," Jehanne said.

"So tell me," the Viceroy began speaking as the door opened. "What was the longest game of Un Sukiru any of you have played?"

"I was involved in a –," Bastard started but he held his words as two of the advisors to the Leader of the Republicus walked in.

"Goodness, Captain Dunois there's no need to stop talking on our accord," Archbishop Cauchon said.

"After all, you know how these dog and pony shows go," Madam Commander said while she walked up to a wall monitor and started a video conference to a room where the political advisor was sitting.

"I do. They're a place to show yourselves more than the peacocks some may think you to be."

"Quite well stated. Please welcome political advisor Lancaster who joins us from the beautiful island of Beaugency," Madam Commander said. "How is the weather there?"

"As close to paradise as possible." His smile was disingenuous, "We are the emissaries that you were told about."

"We would like to tell you how things will go in the next few hours." Cauchon continued.

"Very well," Jehanne looked from the political to the religious advisors.

"Oh isn't that cute." Madam Commander walked around the seats until she stood behind the girl. "We weren't actually asking. You know something very interesting; as the Commander of HCM, I don't have the authority to 'personally' punish Humans." Before anyone could blink an eye her arms merged into a battle axe and sliced through the air. The room filled with gasps and cries of 'no' but her arms had taken on their normal appearance again.

Jehanne's knees hit the floor and she cradled the head, right shoulder and arm of her teacher, friend, and mentor, making her think of the statue she had walked passed. "Deark?" she whispered as if the word could undo what the blade had done.

"So many, many things left undone. Promises I, I, I couldn't carry out," he wheezed. "Do you remember what you said you wanted to, wanted to, to do?"

"I said I wanted to change the world." A tear fell from her non-augmented eye, splashing on his panels.

"You have, and you will change the ending, remember that-t-t-t," his last word turned into a buzz and then faded.

Deark's illuminations had already gone out completely when Jehanne turned back to Madam Commander. "Why?"

"I rather thought that it was obvious after that grand set-up."

"She has no restrictions on the punishing of Entities." Lancaster's sneer filled the monitor.

"Do nothing," Jehanne held out her hand to stop her men from getting out of their seats. "Follow their lead. This is but another set of stones that will take us across the creek." Her men all sat back into their seats.

"Strange but good advice. You there," Madam Commander pointed at the Retinue of Reims. "Get some help in here. I think this Entity maybe in need of a doctor."

"Yes ma'am." They both ran from the conference area, returning moments later with medical Entities and a gurney.

Once they had left Cauchon began speaking again. "I hope that has gotten your attention. There will be no foolishness when the next two guests arrive. You and your Trusted Rebels," he swept his arm dramatically, taking in the room. "Will sit and listen. When all is over you will do as instructed."

"Or none of your troops outside will live to see another sunrise." Madam Commander couldn't help but add her two cents.

"And you'll all either die in prison or the National Stone Room will get to roast some rebels. Oh I'm sorry, roast some Trusted Rebels. Although it would be fun to roast you here as this is my home town," Cauchon chuckled to himself.

The room was quiet for a couple minutes. "So Captain Dunois, would you like to tell us about your marathon Un Sukiru match?" Madam Commander finished her question as the door flew open.

****

"Rise," an I-CAM unit ordered as the Leader of the Republicus walked in. The sound of chairs scraping followed his entrance.

"Sit, sit we don't wish to halt all conversations, especially if it's about Un Sukiru," the High Leader said, walking in with his normal entourage of CAM units and a surprising guest, Charles7.

"It will keep sir," Madam Commander replied.

"It's great to see you again Philca. Actually we beg your pardon, how goes things here in Reims Viceroy?"

"Great to see you as well sir, things are peaceful as a cathedral city should be."

"We imagine your guests are anxious to get a tour," the High Leader said.

"Very much so, High Leader," Jehanne said.

"Jehanne it's so good to see you again. We heard about Deark's accident, such a shame."

"I didn't realize you two knew each other," Philca said when Jehanne didn't reply.

"She gave me such good advice it made Alpha, may he rule in the arena of the Six, change his stand on Augmented."

"Is there an agenda for your visit sir?" the Viceroy of Reims asked.

"Did you know that thirty-three Humans were crowned king over the lands of France in this very cathedral? That of course isn't why you're here today with all of us. You see Jehanne, we don't want to put you down like a CPU riddled with viruses, nor do we wish to imprison your men for the remainder of their lives. Ask John2, that's not a place to wake each morning." His eyes glanced toward Charles7's election chairman.

"No it's really not."

"Jehanne we're ready for you to stop this foolishness."

"Let me say thank you for thinking of my captains in your comments. But in what way were you asked whether 'you' were ready or not?"

"Of course child, let's be honest. Your group has shown us a great many holes in our security systems. And as that's exactly what Charles7 asked you to do, we want to express our appreciation to him for his commitment to the One World Government. That, in part, is why we feel it's far past the time for Humans to have a dedicated seat within the Republicus. Call it a second to the Leader, in this case me."

"I'm sorry sir but how is that different than saying a Human must always be on your advisory committee like Waquini?"

"Oh stop, do you know how much he hates that name? The difference child, is that the Human will be on the ballot with the Entity, exactly as the United States used to do with the President and Vice-President. It benefits the Entity to have been an advocate of relations between our species."

"That does sound like something that will make a difference," Charles7 said, looking at Jehanne.

'This is the script that was written for their dog and pony show,' Jehanne thought, or wait were those actually her thoughts?

"Tell us what you want from us," John2 said.

"As we said, you need to cease and desist all this heresy. Those that were in Charles7's employ; you John2, D'Aulon, Gilles, La Hire, and Xaintrailles will all return to act as his security attachment and of course his four advisors will retake their previous positions as well," The High Leader said.

"I would respectfully like to stay with Jehanne," D'Aulon said.

"Jean you are rather important to my cause," Charles7 said.

"Oh come on Charles7, you made him safety advocate over her. I think she has a higher need for him now than ever." The High Leader said.

"Fine then, I need Minguet to return."

"La Hire and Poton won't leave la Pucelle either."

"Actually Etienne, I'll not give an inch on your obligation to me," Charles7 stood.

"Then may I stay with her?"

"Poton?" La Hire's head pivoted to his best friend.

"My friend, allow me the honor of continuing the work that we started together. Protecting the Maid."

"I would rather keep you two together."

"Would you allow me to take his place? I've learned quite a lot about working with Hedgehog," Severe said.

"Laddy?" Kennedy inquired.

"I believe that should work," Charles7 commented.

"Looks like long term friends will be rearranged a bit in this," the High Leader said.

"Captain Dunois and Gaucourt, you're required to return to New Orleans with your troops. Your city has been under the state of emergency ever since you left; invaders have returned twice," Madam Commander ordered. When they didn't stand she barked, "What are you waiting for?"

"Yes ma'am," Bastard replied as he and Gaucourt left the conference room.

"Alright, you've been given your new directive er ah, calling." Charles7 smiled. "Jehanne you should take your remaining captains and return to Chinon. Justicier, based upon the level of commitment you have shown, we would like you to return to our employ as well. You'll be accompanying the High Leader and us to speak with Phillip le Bon. Can your men see her back to Chinon without you?"

"Of course, sir," he replied.

"Oh very good. See Madam Commander no problems at all." The Leader of the Republicus stood and began walking from the room.

"You are, as usual, completely correct," she replied, following them.

"My friends, I—," Jehanne started.

"We have no time for these pathetic goodbyes. Those with us, we leave now," Charles7 said, also following the Leader of the Republicus from the room. He was followed begrudgingly by Minguet, Severe, Gilles, Justicier, and John2, La Hire completely ignored the orders and walked around the table.

"Make certain to take care of this one," he said to Jehanne as he hugged Poton. "La Hire knows Poton thinks he can take care of himself, but La Hire has been keeping him safe for over two decades." The large Augmented then walked over and hugged la Pucelle before walking out, closing the door behind him.

"Jehanne, I'm so sorry," Philca said.

"Philca it's not your fault," she replied.

"Did you complete the calling or did they just win?" Pouli asked.

"Neither Pouli, we needed to find where the calling was going to take us next. Now we know."

"And we found out what? We need to go back to the beginning?" de Metz asked.

"Precisely. That's what I've been shown."

"I guess we go jump on Justicier's plane with his troops and head to Chinon," Kennedy said.

"After you my friend," Poton said and they all stood.

"Have safe travels. If there are any supplies that were lost to you with this twist of fate, I can do my best to get them for you," Philca said.

"That's sweet, but to be honest, without Minguet I don't even know where to start." Jehanne walked over and hugged Philca and whispered, "You're among the best of them, try to keep that part of you through all that is to come."

"You as well."

******

Jehanne led her five remaining captains from the cathedral to the Mars gate courtyard. Walking down the ornate stairs, they were greeted by a couple hundred very confused troops. "Please break camp. We need to take the subway back to the airfield. Our plane is getting ready to take us back to Chinon," she announced. The order was silently carried out.

"Jehanne!" The voice of one of the Laval brothers yelled as they ran up.

"We weren't sure if we were supposed to be with you or with them," Guy said.

"Looks like you made that decision on your own," Jehanne replied.

"Yes ma'am, we're with you. Those jerks took the rail gun," Andre said.

"I took this from it, to ensure they couldn't use it on us." Guy held up a small blue cylinder.

"What is it?"

"I don't have the slightest idea." They laughed, something that they all needed to do.

The train station was empty when they arrived. After a moment, Jehanne's panoramic display showed an individual walking out of the train tunnel. The lone member of the Unified Indian Nation leapt up onto the platform and motioned her over.

A train's whistle made her step back. "You cut that kinda close."

"Every now and then a blind squirrel gets a nut," Enyeto smiled.

"Jehanne!" D'Aulon tried to get her to board the train.

"I'll get the next one, go ahead." She motioned for him to go, to no avail.

"His concerns run deep for you."

"And mine for all that accompany me. What can I do for you?"

"I needed to check in on you."

"We've been ordered back to Chinon." Jehanne placed her hands on her hips and sighed.

"Ordered? Ordered by whom? There are too many actions already set in motion and the brutality of the Republicus continues to escalate. Your calling is not completed," Enyeto said.

"Don't you think I understand that? They took most of my captains."

"Yet some remain," Enyeto replied.

"They took nearly all my troops."

"Get more."

"Enyeto, what would you have of me?"

"I told you before, you must continue to move forward in order for the other two Qaletaqa to get engaged."

"You just want me to die? To walk into the Stone Room with my head held high and let them burn me?"

"That isn't what I want at all, yet if it is in fact your role in all this; that's what must happen." Enyeto looked into her doubt filled eyes and waited.

Jehanne turned her head up toward where, in her mind, the mountain home of the new gods was. She collected her thoughts for a moment before she replied. "You're correct, I know. It's just strange how much more this undertaking has turned out to be."

"You've lost the one that has guided you through this calling. I would never presume to know what he would counsel right now. However, I will say in the end he gave his life to prepare you for what you'll face moving forward. Deark readied you for far more than you can imagine."

"Thank you." Jehanne turned and headed towards D'Aulon, who waited alone. As she walked she could see the liaison behind her, but in the timespan of a single blink he departed.

"Are you ok?" D'Aulon asked as a train pulled up.

"Yes, I'm fine. When we get to the plane tell the pilot we depart for Montepilloy, California at once."

"So that little alone time helped you put together a plan?"

"I beg your pardon?"

"I said alone time. You were over there for fifteen minutes talking to yourself."

"Fifteen minutes?"

"Yes, at least. Goodness the train took everyone away and has returned twice."

"I guess I was really deep in thought." She smiled and got on the train. "First Rebecca now Enyeto," she muttered.

"That's who visited you this time?"

"You knew I wasn't having alone time and yet you! Oh you!" She slugged his shoulder.

"Hey little holy one, that hurt." D'Aulon backed away with his hands raised in submission. "I quit, I quit, you win." For the second time in the past hour, they laughed, and as the train pulled from the Mars Gate terminal, in the back of their minds they both knew there would be few of these moments to come.

******

"Why aren't we getting on the plane?" Jehanne asked when they found the troops standing about.

"I think they may need a little moral boost, they just watched the other two planes leave," Poton said.

"You're right," she said, walking across the airfield and leaping onto the wing. "The road we travel has changed. With that comes the opportunity to reevaluate where we are and how we've gotten here. Upon reflection I know there's little reason for you to still have confidence in my leadership. The path I've led us down has resulted in many of you getting hurt and worse. Notwithstanding your concerns, this race is not over, and I need you to trust that we're doing this for the right reasons. If we can be motivated to finish the way we began, we will find a way to complete this calling. It might not be tomorrow, or the day after, but if we find a way to give a little more and accept a little more pain, what we're striving toward will come into focus. With this new vision, we'll be able to prepare for the obstacles that will undoubtedly occur rather than reacting to them. For now, I want you to have the option of not continuing with me."

"We're with you!" a random call came from the crowd.

"Why are you doing this? We've all heard what you face," a different voice asked.

"There are only so many tomorrows for any of us," she said and then looked across the grounds slowly. "That holds true for Entities, Augmented, or Mundane. I simply know how my last tomorrow is supposed to end. However, believing that they've broken me would be a mistake. I assure you it will not end here, near the old god of war's gate. They've committed to believing that misconception and I'll see they regret it. So I ask, will you come to Montepilloy with me?" she asked to tumultuous applause.

"Lass, I thought you were shown the beginning and we traveled to Chinon?" Kennedy asked.

"I was shown a false beginning and I let everyone believe we returned to that false beginning. My friends, I'm not following their play book. This is, after all, my calling not theirs. Now let's take to the air."

They loaded quickly and as the plane lifted off the pilot's voice came over the speakers. "The flight looks to be a bit bumpy, make sure that you keep those seat belts on. We should be arriving in the great state of California in sixteen hours."

"I miss the whales," de Metz said.

"Why? This has bigger seats," Poton inquired.

"Mainly because my buddy behind us has to eat even seven minutes or—," he started.

"Don't tell me there's no food on this thing!" Pouli stood and leaned over de Metz chair.

"There's food, you just need to cook it yourself," a square-jawed woman who happened to be walking past said. "Come with me and I'll show you."

"That's great, I could eat a hippopotamus."

"Do you mind the company? I'm starving too," Kennedy asked.

"The more the merrier," Pouli replied.

"Well then I'm in too," Poton squeezed past de Metz.

"You're not going?" Jehanne asked from across the aisle.

"Not a chance. You've never seen that moose try and cook, give it a few minutes and I guarantee there'll be either smoke alerts going off or people throwing up."

"Thanks for the heads up, I'll wait." D'Aulon sat back down. The team had an opportunity to eat and relax on the flight but sleeping was pretty much out of the question due to the turbulent travels over the ocean.

******

The flight landed after taking four hours longer than originally announced by the pilot with several cases of airsickness. The squealing of the brakes was well received by all. "Seriously that was terrible," Pouli said.

"If you hadn't eaten half the stock of food!" de Metz replied.

"I only threw up once. Poton used all the barf bags on the entire plane."

"I blame you. I'm a sympathy puker and if you hadn't started that snow ball rolling down the hill..." Poton wiped his mouth, though there was nothing on it.

"Enough, enough we have things to do here." Jehanne stood up, a little worse for wear herself.

"So what is our plan here?" Kennedy asked.

"We need to—," her words were cut off.

"La Pucelle, please come to the front of the plane," the pilot's voice requested.

"Let me address this and I will come back and speak with the troops."

"I'm with you," D'Aulon said.

"Fine, come along." She walked through the aisle looking at all the green faces. "Perhaps we need to let everyone hydrate for a while."

"I was thinking the same thing. Everyone looks ridden hard and put away wet."

"I think that we have a bit of a problem," the pilot said after opening the door to the cockpit.

"What seems to be the issue?" D'Aulon asked. The pilot didn't say a word but instead pointed out the front window.

"Oh dear," Jehanne said, seeing the runway blocked by a couple large armored vehicles and several hundred CAM units. Her display flashed the word 'Artillery Tank.'

"What are those?" the pilot said.

"They're tanks. Can you open the side door so I can climb down and speak with them?"

"Probably the worst idea you've ever had," D'Aulon said.

"I don't doubt that, but please make it happen." Jehanne pointed to the pilot who got up and opened the door that Justicier had gotten out of the first time she saw him.

"Careful on the ladder, it's not really for Augmented," the pilot warned.

"Thanks," she started to climb out.

"Jehanne," a voice that she had just heard via video conference said. "You were ordered to return to Chinon."

"I don't think I heard it that way, Advisor Lancaster," D'Aulon said from the door above her.

"What they said was we 'should' return to Chinon," she said, getting to the ground and facing John Lancaster. D'Aulon leapt from the plane landing just behind her.

"You foolish child, you'll find nothing here that you seek."

"What is it that you assume we seek here? I just wanted to see the ocean from the California cliffs," Jehanne said.

"Understand this, you've taken from me all that I held important. I've sat in the position as the highest of the Humans for years. Your little endeavor has placed that vile betrayer ahead of me just so the High Leader can save face. But I broke your allies the Viceroys of Jargeau and Beaugency Island. I even killed that stupid crab," John Lancaster said.

"You're an –," D'Aulon started.

"Language." She stopped his comments.

"You know what was the most fun? Finding and destroying your biggest advocate, primarily because you've never met him, not really."

"Who?"

"I'll give you the chance to discover that yourself." He turned and pointed at a cave cut into the sheer cliff face that overlooked the airstrip. "He's there, and I estimate you've got a little under five minutes before –," his words were cut off as Jehanne felt something impact her leg followed by the sound of a laser gun firing. She looked down seeing the laser bolt that had hit her, frozen mere inches from her leg. Looking up, Jehanne found that each and every Entity or Human around her was also motionless.

"What the heck?" she said, her words sounding odd almost flat. Jehanne saw that the rebounding bolt was aiming right at D'Aulon. Wrapping her hand in her cape, she folded it around the bolt, carefully walking around all the bodies that looked like statues on the airstrip. She smashed the bolt onto the runway.

*****

A glint of light caught her attention from the cave Lancaster had pointed to. Remembering what he had said about only having a few minutes she started to run in that direction, wincing slightly at the pain she felt in her leg. Ignoring the discomfort she soldiered on, reaching the bottom of the rock formation Jehanne looked up giving a sigh. "How the heck am I going to get up there?"

'Climb.' she thought, and once again she wondered if it was really her thought. Climbing the rocks wasn't as difficult, as it was fun. The cave was before her in no time. Jehanne pulled herself onto the ledge and turned to see that nothing below had changed. Light once again reflected around her, so Jehanne turned and walked into the opening. The light was coming from a small golden disk that was being held ten feet ahead of her.

"It was you," Jehanne said.

"It was me that what?" Commissioner's voice was barely above a whisper. He rested against the wall. His chest cavity and legs were crushed. Beneath him was a pool of orange liquid.

"Stopped time."

"You noticed that, eh? I couldn't fix it this time."

"Of course I noticed, it's not often you see a laser bolt frozen in midair." She absentmindedly rubbed the dent in her grieves. "You couldn't fix what?"

"When I start time again that dent will pop out." He gave a couple of coughs after which his illuminations almost faded completely.

"What can I do to get you patched up?" Jehanne knelt down and his toaster head turned to look at her and smiled.

"There's no coming back from this. For that matter, I don't even think I want to. The last piece is no longer in this area."

"Where is it?"

"They crushed out all my holographic projectors and the scum Lancaster thought it would be funny to give me some of the pieces." He opened the hand that wasn't holding the golden disk, and the broken pieces of what could have been several holographic generators were in it. "My version of Ursula-Minor is no more."

"I'm sorry about that. I have this one as well." She reached into the inner pocket where she had placed the destroyed projector.

"May I see that?" he asked and she held it out to him. As if getting hit with another burst of energy he reached up and grabbed the pieces. Laying them on the floor he began tinkering, his fingers turning into various tools. "I can make one out of these components," he said to himself.

"Another holographic projector?"

"Better." He never looked up but she knew he was once again smiling.

Section Three – Chapter Eleven

Commissioner continued to work at a fevered pace, every once in a while his body would shudder violently. "Jehanne, take this," he said eventually.

"That looks completely different from the others," she said, examining it.

"If you give it to Deark, he will be able to—," he started.

"Deark was cut down by Madam Commander," Jehanne interrupted his statement.

"That makes little sense. Do you still travel with the one called D'Aulon?"

"I do, he's with me here."

"Perfect, give it to h-h-h-him. Tell him that it, it, that it is a terminating resistor and it needs to connect to a master hub-hub-hub of the IWDDB."

"What is the IWDDB?"

"I don't have time to explain it all, suffice it to say it is the repository of all information. It was a human invention that was at one point destroyed in order to keep Ursula from joining with it. In the end it we just created again and some of us moved through Sentience to Sapience with its assistance. If your comrade can connect it," he pointed to the item he handed her. "I can continue to help, to help, to help humans in what will come."

"I'll make sure he takes care of that for me."

Commissioner then extended his other hand to her, placing the golden disk in hers. "This needs to die with me; in the wrong hands it can do terrible harm."

"How do I destroy it?" Jehanne turned the disk over and over in her hand.

"You'll need to-to-to figure that one out, but keep in mind-mind-mind the NanoTech in it are the strongest I've ever encountered and they want to live. When you start time again, I will leave this place."

"That makes no sense aren't you in this time stream? Why wouldn't you just die here?"

"It doesn't actually work as one would think. If you were horribly cut in here even though you're seemingly conscious you wouldn't bleed out. You could find a way to repair it. In here engines can run, getting you to safety yet when you leave this stream you will have used no fuel. I truly can't explain why." He coughed again.

"Commissioner, I have so many more questions. I need to know how to make this work," she held out the time compact. "Also, do you know the last question?"

"No. I haven't known any of the questions, but I can give you my code in case she doesn't share with you." His index finger extended and came in contact with the side of the helmet.

"She?" Jehanne asked yet the flood of memories that hit her began a series of flashbacks playing out in front of her. She saw the first moment that Commissioner recognized he was thinking for himself. She saw Joshua walking with a familiar Entity to join the line at the Mundane Moon Maze.

She saw the Three; first in their original forms as the Mother the Maiden and the Crone. They transformed into Neoteric, Nexgen, and Retro before merging together to become the Six new gods. Thoughts and events continued to flood her mind, each of the Six were allowed to be asked a single question by a single Entity. Then the arguing in the Republicus about why the six questions couldn't be shared and what they should do with the answers. Eventually he devised the code to protect the questions from prying eyes. When the torrent of information stopped she opened her eyes.

"There, you should have it in there somewhere." Commissioner pulled his hand back, his illuminations much dimmer than before.

"As are the plans and operating instructions for the Time Compact," she said.

"With you child I have no fear of terrible things, you will change the ending. Now go."

"When you said you couldn't fix it this time, what did you mean?" Jehanne asked, desperate to not let another mentor leave her.

"With the Time Compact I can make time stop, slow or speed up for one or multiple beings. However, I can't reverse it."

"How did you use that to fix things?"

"I slowed your time stream to let Enyeto catch you. I sped it up to allow Justicier to meet up with you. But I couldn't use it to save myself any longer. They've been searching for me for decades. When they figured out that I was helping you get the pieces of the armor they set up a trap where the next piece had been. I must admit it was a good trap." Commissioner smiled.

"Had been? Where is the last piece if not here?" Jehanne asked, putting the Time Compact and the Terminating Resistor into her cloak's pockets.

"They took it to Compiegne. Hurry now go." She began to head for the ledge. "Child have all confidence, you're ready for what will come."

"Thank you Commissioner." Jehanne began her climb down, the events of his life still bouncing through her mind. One image kept popping up, Joshua presenting himself at the Mundane Moon Maze, and yet Madam Commander stood next to him. Why?

******

Jehanne arrived at the airfield, pulling D'Aulon into the active time stream, boarding the plane.

"What's happening?" he asked while she loaded the ladder in through the door.

"They shot me."

"I remember that but how—,"

"All in time my friend. Take this, protect it with your life." She handed him the component that Commissioner called a terminating resistor. "Please go sit. I'll be there soon and will explain everything."

"That should be interesting."

"It is." She watched him leave and then she entered the cockpit, pulling the pilot into the continuing time stream.

"What the hell?" he said.

"Please don't swear. I don't have time to explain, you need to get us into the air immediately."

"Yes ma'am."

"Your co-pilot will wake after we're in the air. We head for Compiegne." As the plane headed into the sky Jehanne filled D'Aulon in on everything that had happened. Pointing to the terminating resistor he still held in his hand she asked, "Do you know what the IWDDB is?"

"Yes. It's the Internal Web Directional Database. It's a repository of all—," he started.

"I need that connected to a master hub, somewhere no one will find it. Do you understand, it's very important."

"I can take care of that." After he promised to do that she released the hold on time. The panic that filled the plane was palpable. "Silence!" D'Aulon yelled.

Jehanne raised her hands, "I understand that was a rather strange event. One moment we're on the ground preparing to deplane and the next in the air wrought with confusion. One of the Entities that has been helping us in the background had invented a Time Stream Frequency Modulator. When we landed, the Entities that oppose us were trying to kill him to retrieve this very dangerous item. While they did achieve killing him, he destroyed his invention, its last spark of life was to get us off the ground and away from the trap they had set."

"We saw you get shot," the square- jawed woman said.

"An optical illusion. The beam from the laser rebounded from my augmentation and the NanoTech have already repaired it." She moved her cape aside to show the uninjured leg. "We're now heading to Compiegne to continue this calling."

"Can you imagine the confusion that Lancaster and his minions felt when they woke? Jehanne, D'Aulon, and a huge plane, poof, gone like magic." Poton laughed as he faced backwards over the seat which broke the silence and got the troops laughing. In no time at all, the plane was descending.

"Please buckle up, we are arriving at Compiegne Coastal International. We expect a strong cross breeze on landing," the pilot announced. "If you look out the right hand side you can see a pod of whales swimming along the coast."

"Those don't look like Bastard's planes," Pouli said.

"You my old friend, are insane," de Metz mussed his hair.

As the plane began taxiing Jehanne walked to the front of the plane. "Anything on the runway?"

"Not this time ma'am," the pilot replied.

"Jehanne," D'Aulon yelled. "We're being hailed by Chartres and Flavy."

"What?" Kennedy asked.

"They've posted on the Compiegne Informational board that they were sent here by Charles7 and with some men to talk to the Mother City about the upcoming changes. On their way they were attacked by the Entity Liberation Front. It's apparently a militia led by John Luxemborg. Charles7's advisors were forced to take refuge behind the wall of Compiegne," D'Aulon said.

"Everyone off the plane, we march at once," Jehanne said.

"May Protectorate guide your arm in battle. Those that fall I look forward to seeing you in the arena of the Six one day." Poton repeated the words that Justicier encouraged the troops with earlier.

"With Nexgen, Neoteric, and Retro all things are possible!" Everyone shouted followed by, "Hoorah!"

The troops began their march and as it turned out, the wall was just outside the airport. A group cheered the arrival of Jehanne and her reinforcements. The wall opened to allow them entrance, but then a loud war cry came from the buildings adjacent.

"Attack ELF, Attack!" a regal looking Entity yelled leading the surprise attack.

"Behind you!" Flavy yelled from the wall. Jehanne, Poton, and D'Aulon turned, meeting the attack that was coming from the side.

"La Pucelle there are too many. We need to get behind the wall!" De Metz yelled.

"Make certain everyone is in safely." The Entities were made up of CAM units as well as various forms of Sentient beings that yelled threats to her and her forces. With each felled Entity, Jehanne and her captains got closer to the opening.

"All are in close the gates!" Flavy yelled.

"Get inside Poton, now!" Jehanne ordered as she turned and began her way behind Compiegne's wall. "D'Aulon you too, go!" The two men were strides ahead of her when something came from on top the wall, hitting her in the leg and tripping her. Before she could rise, Jehanne heard the sound of the gate slamming, felt the hands closing around her, as well as boots standing on her sword hand, pressing it to the ground. A meter from the boot holding her hand firmly against the ground she saw an ornate rod with a seal on the top. 'That must have been what tripped me? At least they all made it inside,' she thought as the sounds of battle started next to her, once again.

"You will not take the Maid!" D'Aulon yelled. "Open the gate Flavy you skunk!" No sound of the gate beginning to open could be heard. Only D'Aulon fighting with the ferocity of twenty cutting a path to her, but even twenty against three hundred in an open battle field could only end one way. The Entities pinned him down just feet away from where she was restrained.

"We have her," a voice said as Jehanne felt a poke in her neck. A moment later she was lifted into the air. She saw the regal Entity walking up to her. "Captain Luxemborg, here is the accursed one."

"You've done well Sargent Wandomme. You have all the anger I was led to believe."

"Please call me Lionel, and I don't believe it's as much anger as pure hate for these beings. I simply wish I could snuff them all out."

"Soon, Lionel, my comrade, soon," Luxemborg said. "You will open your gates and allow us to hold this prisoner in the jail, or I shall flay her in the streets in front of the gate." This time the gate did open.

"Flavy you pig," D'Aulon yelled.

"I'm trying to help." Flavy rushed out of the gate as he replied and retrieved an ornate rod, tucking it into his belt. Standing and glaring at Jehanne he said, "No one wants her flayed in the streets." Giving a strong emphasis on 'in the streets.'

"Get a move on," Captain Luxemborg barked.

"D'Aulon, 'tis but another stone, see there, we've nearly crossed the…" her words faded as whatever had poked her in the neck brought darkness.

******

They were held in the jail for just over a week when several I-CAM units showed up, blindfolded them and rushed them from their cells. "Where are we going?" Jehanne asked.

"We're taking you someplace your foolish friends won't find you," the now familiar voice of Luxemborg said.

"You can't hide us forever." D'Aulon sounded more confident than Jehanne felt.

"Perhaps not, but I'm just waiting for an answer on your ransom," he shot back.

"Ransom?"

"Yes. You see ELF needs financing, we aren't exactly affiliated with the One World Military."

"So who are you offering us to?" D'Aulon asked.

"I offered you to everyone." He let out a guffaw. "Entities, Augmented, or even Mundane. I don't care where the TC comes from."

"D'Aulon step up," Jehanne said, "and watch your head."

"How can you see that?" one of the I-CAMs asked.

"I don't know, how can an I-CAM unit help these vigilantes?"

"I work for myself. If this is where the most TC comes from and I get to smack around some Humans, I'm down with it."

When the truck was loaded it drove through the rest of the night and into the next day. When it finally came to a stop they were unloaded onto the street where they waited next to a statue.

"Where are we?" D'Aulon asked.

"A small city where no one will find you. It's called Crotoy," Luxemborg replied.

"That's an interesting statue," Jehanne indicated the statue of a girl in fetters. "Do you know who it is?"

"Do I look like a tour guide? Let's go." He pushed her ahead of himself. "At least I'll be rid of you soon."

"What do you mean?"

"The Entities have agreed to pay the ransom."

"And Charles7?" D'Aulon asked.

"He's due to give an answer within the next hour. Would you like to watch the broadcast?"

"That would be great thanks." After they were in their cells, a monitor was placed against the far wall so they both could see it and their dinners were served.

******

"Ladies and gentlemen," the monitor sprang to life with Charles7 standing behind a podium. "Most of you know that the band known as Entity Liberation Front has taken a couple of Augmented that until recently were in our employ. They have requested for us to pay a sizeable ransom for their release. There is also a request that we not pay the ransom and instead sign over any defense of Jehanne or rather Joanna667, to the Republicus.

"We've decided, as the single highest ranking Human in the world that it isn't in the best interest of the Human Race to pay a king's ransom to have this girl released and pardoned of all crimes. For Joanna667 has posed as an Augmented in her bid to start a second uprising, a vicious attempt to circumvent the good work that has been done for years to establish good Entity and Human relations. This girl has played the innocent card better than any other in history, spreading the word that her so-called 'calling' had an end goal of protecting humans from the oppression of the Entities.

"In my efforts to become the Leader of the Republicus I unwittingly motivated the actions that have befallen the entire world with her heretical deeds. For this I am sorry to each of you, but specifically to the High Leader, to the Commune de Domremy, to her parents, and also to this girl. To what extent can the words of a leader be accountable for the actions of a delusional mind, I know not. May the Six guide my words more strongly to bypass the minds of such sycophants that believe they're actions are to ingratiate themselves to me as I begin my role as Leader of the Republicus's Human race."

The screen went blank and Luxemborg strutted back into the room. "Well child, I guess that tells us where you're off to."

"When do we leave?" D'Aulon asked.

"We? Young man, your ransom was paid by Charles7. For that matter your ride is scheduled to pick you up very soon. She on the other hand, will leave in a few days." With a snort of derision Luxemborg took the monitor from the cell block.

"This is ridiculous, why would he do this?" D'Aulon asked, staring across the room at Jehanne.

"I think he did it so I could be Joanna667 when I die."

"Come on you're not going to die."

"Jean, you've known how this is going to end from the beginning."

"There must be a way out of it, tell them you won't do it again," D'Aulon said.

"I'm certain that'll work perhaps I'll write a letter. How does this sound?" she pretended to write in the air.

'My dear and good friends, obedient and loyal Entities, Augmented, and Mundane,

Jehanne la Pucelle or Joanna667 whichever you choose to know her as, lets you know of her tidings, and asks and requests that you should have no concerns about the good cause she is carrying on for the new gods. And she promises and guarantees to you that she will never raise her sword against you in their names as long as she lives. I commend you in the name of the Six and may they watch over you if it pleases them.' Her arm dropped to her side.

"Ok I get it, no one will buy it." D'Aulon shook his head.

"Let's play a couple games of Un Sukiru before they show up. I really don't want to think about it." She set the board on the floor and sat down looking across at her friend.

"We can do that," he sat on the floor. "You know we could make a break for it, I still have the –."

"To what end?"

"Worst case scenario we go out on our terms." He smiled.

"You still have a promise to keep, mine have all been fulfilled."

"How so?"

"Charles7 by his own words, is the Leader of the Republicus."

"That's true. And mine?"

"Do you still have access to what I gave you?"

"Yes."

"It must be attached to the IWDDB. Getting yourself killed in a futile attempt to escape won't achieve that," Joanna667 said.

"You're right. It's your move."

"I feel light headed," she said as the dice rolled.

******

"Hello Joanna667, I'll be escorting you. I don't know if you remember me but –," an Entity said as her eyes opened.

"Of course I remember you, you're the political advisor in the Retinue to Madam Commander, Massieu."

"Oh very good."

"How did I get on this plane? And where is my sword?" she asked, touching her back and looking out the window.

"The ruffian Luxemborg drugged you."

"Of course he did, he didn't want a struggle."

"When I inquired about the sword they said the one that captured you, Wandomme would be keeping it," Massieu said.

"Not like I'll be in need of it. It's just become an extention of me, I don't feel whole without it. I imagine that's what Protectorate meant when she asked me, 'How does it feel?' back on the first day of my training with her." Joanna667's eyes were unfocused as she remembered answering, 'It feels like a cold piece of metal.'

"May I ask you a question? One that has been bothering me since the day we met."

"Of course you may ask me another question." Joanna667 gave the reply she had so often heard.

"Oh very good." He smiled at the correction. "Had you chosen the path of the Maiden when we first met?"

"In truth I still haven't chosen either path. I've been following a calling that was given to me. I believe is completely different."

"Oh very good," he said and they flew on in silence for a while. "I need you to go change into this." He handed her a white linen blouse. When she looked at him questioningly he continued. "In the restroom in the back. You may leave the ripped one in there."

She walked to the rear of the plane, recognizing it now as the plane she had flown the first time in.. Quickly changing she dropped the green jumper the High Leader had given her, what seemed years ago. "Advisor Massieu, where are we going?" Joanna667 asked before she had sat back down.

"The national Stone Room, it's called Rouen."

"I assumed as much as I'm flying in the High Leader's plane. Is that because Charles7 turned my punishment over to the Republicus? This way there won't be a long show of a trial will there?"

"No child, there will be nothing more than an event. I'm sorry," Massieu said.

"Don't be. That honestly makes things much easier."

"How so?"

"If they made me stand in front of the world and tell my side of the story I don't think I could keep my composure. There have been so many deaths and if they try to tell me this is all my doing, I would have less ability to go on without calling for help."

"Please fasten your seat belt," the Captain said.

"Why are you the one escorting me?" she asked, looking at the Entity.

"There are multiple reasons. The Republicus is at war with the Entity Liberation Front and when ELF asked for an officer of the One World Government, I, while a member of an Enclave do fit the bill while at the same time I'm expendable, being the lowest tier of the One World Government. Also I volunteered."

"Why?"

"I just didn't want an ass like Archbishop Cauchon doing it."

"Language," she said as the I-CAM units stepped onto the transport.

"Oh very good, of course child, of course." They walked to the front of the transport plane.

"Why is this prisoner not in shackles and fetters? You know as well as I the scum that followed her have attacked Compiegne to rescue her. They may try again." I-CAM Rho said.

"Perhaps, but she's my prisoner to transport and they're hundreds of miles away. Now back away," Advisor Massieu ordered.

"We've been sent to –," Rho started

"Did I have a reverberation in my vocal transmission? I said back away."

"Yes Advisor." The I-CAM units stepped from the plane, waiting to escort only.

"Will we be heading straight to the fire pit?" Jehanne asked as they walked through familiar hard packed earth streets leading through a commune and up to the conquering wall.

"No speaking prisoner!" Rho reached out and slammed her to the ground. The streets that were earlier void of any other beings now flooded with Entities and Humans that ran to her aid, helping her to her feet. Each whispering words of encouragement. "Get away from this filth unless you choose to join her." Rho grasped an elderly Augmented by the wrist.

"I advise that you release that woman unless you don't wish to keep that arm," Joanna667 stared down the much larger Entity.

"Be on your way." Rho released the woman and started to walk again.

"Thank you," the woman said.

"Of course Ms. Nurse," Joanna667 smiled.

"La Pucelle!" the crowd was starting to chant.

"We should get a move on," Rho prompted the Advisor.

"Actually Joanna667," Advisor Massieu started to answer her question as they began walking again. "You must meet with the Commander of Human Capital Management before…" his words faded, "Well just before." When they left the commune area, a large score board could be seen as well as a pavilion nearly four times the size of the one in the Commune de Domremy.

"Is that it?" She stopped walking.

"It is, but please keep moving. We have little time."

"Quite an apropos statement," Joanna667 muttered and they walked under the wall and into the Mother City's capital building.

"In years past this building was called the White House, although it isn't any whiter than the other buildings around here." Massieu favored her with a small piece of trivia.

"Thank you for that bit of knowledge."

******

"Please wait outside the door," Madam Commander ordered the I–CAM units.

"As you say ma'am," Rho said, leading the other CAM units from the room.

"And Rho, do not under any circumstance let anyone in or enter again. Do you understand?"

"Of course Madam Commander." He left, closing the door.

"That may have been a bad idea," Joanna667 said, taking a step forward.

"Lock the door," she ordered her political advisor. Massieu turned and walked away from Joanna667. "I know this is all going to be impossible for you to understand, but we have little time."

"Jehanne," a voice that couldn't have spoken, said behind her.

"It's not Jehanne any longer or did you miss Charle7's speech, Deark?" Trying to maintain her composure she turned, "You're with them? You've always been with them?"

"It isn't as it seems," Deark said.

"As it seems? You mean like it 'seems' you've been a spy passing information to them all along? Or it 'seems' I put all my trust in you, defending you from all the criticism and the attacks from the others. Perhaps it 'seems' the fact that

you were charged by a new god to watch over me, doesn't matter to you. And finally it 'seems' you've done all this to see me die."

"I don't want to see you die and I've done nothing to make you feel your trust was misplaced. I was–," Whatever he thought he 'was' never got out, Jehanne crossed the room in two strides and pushed her mentor with all she had. He flew into the distant wall shattering it.

"Is everything ok in there?" Rho asked, attempting to turn the doorknob.

"It is and I told you to stay out. This Human has some lessons to be learned."

"Sorry ma'am."

"Why? Why would you lie to me? To everyone if you're just one of them? John2 had the right of you, you, you creature! Well I succeeded in spite of what 'seems', didn't I!" She closed the gap a lifted him with a single arm. While he was in the air she felt a firm but delicate set of hands pull her back.

"Sweetheart let them explain," Isabella said.

"Mom? What trickery is this? Another of your Chameleon friends playing games?" Joanna667 looked between Deark and Madam Commander.

"No trickery dear. Do you remember when Calibre visited our house after you were arrested the first time?" her mother asked.

"Who is this Calibre?"

"That's my real name. I only tell friends," Madam Commander said.

"Friends?" Joanna667 shook Deark. "Friends like this one?"

"Actually yes, please put him down," Jacque said, stepping into the room.

"Dad?" Joanna667 set Deark down.

"She told us what the entire plan was on her visit," Isabella said.

"I swore that if they didn't keep the secret, even from you, none of it would work."

"Then how, how did the High Leader know everything as it happened?" Joanna667 asked.

"That amazing shirt he gave you, NanoTech spy imbuing," Calibre replied.

"That's impossible, he couldn't have known Alpha was going to rip my—."

'Jehanne,' a voice sang in her head.

"Commissioner?" she turned in circles, looking for him before realizing it was in her mind.

'Yes child, D'Aulon was successful.'

"That's great," Joanna667 said, ignoring the confused faces around her.

'He knew. He staged his outrage. That's why Alpha said he found the High Leaders behavior to be irregular.'

"But how do you know that?"

'The same way the High Leader did when Alpha said it, which is why he sent him to support General Talbot in Patay. You need to know you can trust Deark and Calibre and also they love each other and have for the better part of forever. I knew that she could no more cut him down than you could cut down Jovi571,' he projected.

"But I saw it," she said.

"Saw what child?" Calibre asked.

"I saw you kill him," Joanna667 said, turning her attention to those in the room.

"You saw what I needed you and those non-Sapient robots to see."

"Calibre!" Deark looked aghast.

"Who did you kill then?" Joanna667 asked.

"Another Q-Class. He took my place when I got shot at Patay. I passed along some of my memories so that he could –," Deark's words were cut off.

"When he found out that Charles7 was going to be there, he panicked. Word has spread that Charles7 has an augmentation that can see through even the best mimicry. I saw no other way," Calibre said.

"How do I know that Deark here isn't just another Chameleon?" Joanna667 asked.

"Do you want to see a trick?" Deark opened a cavity under his arm and removed a single red feather. He twirled it between his fingers and then handed it to her.

"Deark, it is you." She hugged him and then abruptly broke away. "Non-Sapient?" Joanna667 jumped back to Calibre's earlier comment as she placed the feather in her cape's pocket.

"Sentient is not enough to be real. The child, Shelby1000 had the right of it. There are so few of us that understand, that while we may have met the criteria for personhood, many sorely lack anything beyond that."

"I thought the true definition of Sapient is wisdom and the ability to comprehend abstract thought. In the context of the Entities calling on the new gods, wouldn't each of you be both Sentient and Sapient?" Joanna667 asked.

After she finished forming the sign of the Box Caliber replied, "Yes but in the context of –."

"Enough, enough, enough, I can't imagine that you brought me here for a philosophical debate. Please just tell me why I'm here and what the plan is."

"Of course," Calibre said. "First, I need you to know the final question. As Deark told me you have but one left."

"Very well."

"The question was, 'How can Entities have children?'"

"What?" Isabella asked.

"Philca?" Joanna667 whispered her inquiry. "She said she's…"her words were cut off.

"The youngest Entity to reach Sentience," the thin Entity began walking into the room as she finished the eye movement.

"We'll return to her in a moment. I also wanted you to have the final piece of armor." She reached her hands up to unfasten her blouse. Joanna667 noticed for the first time that Calibre had long gloves on her hands.

"Oh no," Joanna667 rushed forward to help her.

"What is it?" Philca asked.

"The acid, she's injured."

"And rather gravely," Deark added.

"No, Mother!" Philca rushed forward.

"Mother?" Isabella and Jacque asked, the word catching them off-guard.

"You must stay clear, the acid will still hurt you," Joanna667 said.

"Here you go child." The wheezing sound that Calibre made as she pulled the breast plate from her damaged chest made everyone hold their breath, but when they saw the damage below they all gasped. Philca began to cry as Joanna667 and Isabella went to get water.

"Philca, do you know where your name came from?" Calibre asked.

"The randomizing of my father's and your names."

"That's correct yet, your real name is Deaca," Deark said. "Your mother changed it to protect you. You see, the plan for our involvement in the next uprising was formed a long time ago, and we knew then that I was going to die as a result of it."

"I made Phillip believe he and I were donating our biorhythms to Commissioner's experiment. I'm sorry, I didn't mean to lie to you for so long." Calibre handed Joanna667 the now free breast plate.

Wiping the detritus from it with her cloak, she allowed the augmentations that encapsulated her chest and back to release. Sliding the breast plate under the loosely fitting shirt, she felt the armor reach around and secure itself. Joanna667 realized that all the pieces were coupling together like long lost friends, hugging her gently as they adjusted themselves to fit her perfectly.

"Jehanne, that chest piece gave an incredible increase to my mimicry, Charles7's augmentation could not sense me. I believe it will serve you well." Her pained and gasping voice was hard to listen to.

"I want to show you something, be aware it may become dazzlingly bright," Joanna667 said. Re-securing the augmentations across her back and chest as before, the room was thrown into such brightness that in the end all went black.

"Well ok then," Isabella said, blinking her eyes repeatedly and getting ready to clean Madam Commander's wounds.

"I'm going to need to remove your gloves. Can you take a look at this while I do?" Joanna667 held the time compact out to Calibre. Just before the injured Entity could reach it Joanna667 stopped everyone's time stream and removed the gloves before starting time again. "I need this destroyed."

"How did you remove the gloves?" Calibre asked, looking from her damaged arms and hands, one with the Time Compact in it.

"Never mind that, you need to lie back," Isabella said and she rinsed Calibre's arms and chest thoroughly. When the wounds were cleaned and her blouse rebuttoned, Deaca knelt down and hugged her mother.

"The time has come, Madam Commander," Rho said from the other side of the door.

"Very well," she replied over her daughter's shoulder as they hugged. She squeezed the Time Compact in her hand. "Deaca," she whispered, "I need you to show the others out."

"No!" The thin Entity cried.

"Please just do it for me. We all know it must be," Joanna667 said breaking the hug and looking into Deaca's sorrowful eyes. With a great effort she stood up and then placed the Time Compact into the empty pocket of her white dragonweave cape.

"I understand." Deaca turned from her mother and led the others from the room.

"I love you both," Joanna667 said, looking into her mother and then her father's faces.

"Come now, come now we have little time." Madam Commander opened a side door where her political advisor was waiting.

"Did all go well?" Massieu asked.

"It did. Could you help me find my hat?"

"This one?" He held up the picture hat.

"I think the beret with the black veil would be more appropriate," Madam Commander said.

"I've always preferred the large brimmed one. Did you know all of my hats were inspired by Garbo." Joanna667 wheezed.

"I don't know who that is but the large brimmed one it is." Calibre placed the audacious hat on her head at an impossible angle. "Let them in," she instructed her political advisor.

"Of course ma'am," Massieu said, opening the door allowing the three I-CAM units and Archbishop Cauchon to enter.

"We'll be escorting the prisoner," I-CAM Rho said.

"Careful there, I'd say she's a little worse for wear." Madam Commander gave a malicious grin.

"Good for you," the Archbishop said, holding out his elbow and lending Madam Commander his support in this trying time.

******

"Ladies and gentlemen, there are few times in one's life that the obviousness of what must happen is presented in such a manner," Archbishop Cauchon stood in front of the capacity audience. "Today is one of those days. This child has spread her heresy and attempted to end the reign of peace that has kept us all in the graces of the new gods for decades. The sentence of death is not only called for it is an absolute necessity. As proof of this less than an hour ago, I was miraculously contacted by Ursula-Minor. She has broken her silence, weighing in; telling me that Joanna667 must enter the fires of the Stone Room with her Augmentations in place. Further there must be nothing left afterward for anyone to rally around."

"Passez-oultre," Joanna667 said from on top of the yet unformed Stone Room.

"Move along? My, you are impatient to be proven that Politician knows you not." Archbishop Cauchon signaled for the platform to be lowered, forming the Stone Room.

Joanna667

The score board next to the crowded pavilion showed the visage of a stoic girl being brought into frame from above. No sooner had the platform stopped lowering than the flames began to dance around the chamber. For minutes the crowd was mesmerized as not a sound escaped from the pit below them. Eventually the camera zoomed in; closer and closer until only the teal of her eye with its odd green outline could be seen on the large display.

As the stirring visual of strength in front of them was taken away, around the pavilion, a different sensory assailment circulated on the breeze, leaving each of the onlookers with the feeling of being touched by innocent death. From a cloudless sky a cold sprinkling of rain began to fall, stilling any remaining sound from the crowd but did nothing to quiet the shouts of the Archbishop who demanded a second and then a third ignition of the incinerating flames. The hate in him so strong the birds in the trees flew away to escape the taste it left them with.

The cold sprinkle had turned into a frigid storm by the time the third volley of flames had completed their cycle, and the Stone Room platform was raised. Nothing more than ashes remained upon it, these were carried in rivulets, out into the pavilion grounds. Once again having been touched by innocent death the volume from the crowd grew driving Madam Commander and Archbishop Cauchon to take refuge in the adjacent buildings.

The mutterings turned to discussions, as the Entities and Humans gave voice to their outrage. When the words "la Pucelle," echoed off the wall, the final stepping stone was found, presenting the pathway to a riot so violent that the established barriers were torn down, brick by brick. Above the commotion; the rain subsided, revealing a double rainbow, and a single red feather which wafted on the breeze of a cloudless sky.

Joanna667

Epilogue Part One

Moments earlier:

As the rain fell, three large Augmented approached the pavilion grounds from an alley adjacent watching the events play out ahead of them. "La Hire thought she would be here. La Hire expected more."

"And what did you expect Etienne?" the voice of an Augmented all in black, who they had not seen startled them. The figure still in shadows stared at the scoreboard in fascination, where the image of Joanna667's eye remained, fires surrounding it.

"La Pucelle!" D'Aulon shouted.

"My name is Esperer, I know not this la Pucelle of which you speak." She winked.

"La Hire really wasn't sure what to expect, but rain and two rainbows? Seriously?"

"They say when Joanna667 was born, 'it rained from a cloudless sky.' So I guess it's apropos. The rain in this case however, was most likely caused by the NanoTech within the Time Compact."

"You destroyed the time device?" D'Aulon asked.

"I did. It truly needed to be." she replied.

"Do you really think Cauchon was contacted by Ursula Minor?" La Hire changed the subject.

"I do. It fits into the plan that Ursula-Minor laid out for me."

"Ursula-Minor spoke with you?" D'Aulon asked.

"Yes. She actually has a few times. I just didn't know it. When she reaches out it isn't like when Politician contacts me. The message becomes entangled unbidden in my thoughts. It's hard to explain."

"La Hire understands. That's how it became obvious that D'Aulon was hacking into La Hire's modies. The NanoTech reacted in such a way, La Hire knew something was different."

"That's exactly it. Something felt different, thank you Etienne," she said.

"Have you chosen the path of the Hope?" Another familiar voice asked behind La Hire.

The figure in black turned facing the voice, her teal eyes running over with tears. "Jovi571?" she whispered, seeing a muscular Augmented standing there.

"No miss, this is Jovi. He's a new recruit," La Hire said.

"I'm sorry, of course. Yes Jovi that was another thing Ursula-Minor told me; she said that taking the path of Esperer was the safest for everyone. As Jehanne and Joanna667 die, Hope springs to life."

"This Esperer, it means Hope then?" D'Aulon asked.

"It does. How did you get here so fast? And did I hear correctly that you attacked Compiegne?" As she said this the pavilion in front of them were working themselves into a frenzy.

"We should probably get out of here, your questions can be answered on our way to Philca's place," D'Aulon said.

"Her real name is Deaca not Philca. Is everyone here?" Esperer asked.

"Only La Hire, D'Aulon, Jovi and you are here." Suddenly the scoreboard in front of them shattered into thousands of pieces. "Now this is what La Hire expected."

"Everyone else is at Deaca's place," D'Aulon ushered them from the pavilion. "Even Culant. There's also a strange old lady named—".

"Rebecca Nurse?"

"Yes," Jovi said.

"Is Deliverance Dane there as well?" Esperer asked.

"A different woman, much younger than Rebecca was walking up to the door leading an older gentleman when we were leaving. So perhaps," D'Aulon replied.

"The Augmented that was being led was Colonel Washington's advisor, Mr. Corey. La Hire thinks he was being led because something happened to his eyes since we saw him last."

"You're right that's who he was." D'Aulon said, "Actually La Hire he was blind when we met him. I remember because there are so few blind Augmented."

"He couldn't have been blind, he knew La Hire was built for the Vanguard."

"Footfalls." Jovi said.

"What?"

"Your footfalls are heavy yet controlled."

"Excellent observation," D'Aulon said.

"I wonder why Mr. Corey is at Deaca's dwelling?" Esperer inquired.

"I guess we'll figure that out when we get there." Jovi replied.

"Jovi, did you beat the Mundane Moon Maze?" Esperer asked.

"As if. They cancelled it after all the 'Invasions' on the Mother Cities started," he replied. They continued to walk, catching her up on all the activities that had taken place over the last few days. It wasn't until they told her that Deark was going to pose as her for the execution that she interrupted them.

"Actually, it was Caliber, er I mean, Madam Commander who took my place and Deark will be taking hers hereafter."

"You're kidding." D'Aulon said.

"Isn't she the one that has been trying to get you killed?" La Hire asked.

"That was all an elaborate ruse. She's actually been in cahoots with Deark the entire time. Oh and by the way—." Esperer started.

"But why did Madam Commander offer to die in your place?" D'Aulon asked interrupting her.

"She was gravely injured trying to smuggle the chest piece to me. Up until that occurred, Deark was planning on doing it himself. In the end that would've been a problem, as he couldn't have held my form after he died like Madam Commander did. So it may have been serendipitous that she was injured."

"La Hire doesn't know this dipitous word but it sounds to La Hire like a lucky accident that she was injured. There's no way of knowing what Archbishop Cauchon would've done based upon all the hate he exuded during each of the ignitions he called for."

"True, but try to be sensitive; Caliber and Deark are Deaca's parents," Esperer said.

"That one I can't let pass, did you say parents?" Jovi asked.

"Yes. That was the sixth question; 'How can we have children?'" her statement was lost to the door bursting open on the building where Deaca was staying.

"Oh sweetheart." Isabella hugged her daughter.

"Remember, she's Esperer, from now on," Deaca reminded as she pulled Isabella back into the building and closed the door.

"Are you ok Deaca?"

"I'm fine. It was quite strange having my mother asking me to follow her wishes after she had taken on your appearance."

"How did you know my new name?"

"Ursula-Minor filled me in on you and the entire lady in black thing," she replied, moving her hand up and down taking in Esperer's new look.

"I have to say, the black armor and augmentations look bad ass," Severe said.

"Language," Esperer replied.

"Even in this new identity you're worried about language?" John2 asked.

"I'm not evil just because I'm dressed in black."

"The last thing you said before your mother jumped on you was something about six questions." Jovi said.

"Did you say six questions?" Rebecca Nurse asked.

"Yes. We've been running all over the world looking for both the six armor sections which she wears and the six questions that were asked to the new gods when the Maze was run." Culant said.

"I have to ask, does anyone know why we needed to find them? I've never understood why we didn't need the answers." de Metz asked.

"La Hire thinks the fact we didn't need the answers was a clue."

"Go on Etienne," Esperer prompted.

"It was to lead us to what the Entities wanted most to know, and to help us find who Esperer's allies are."

"I think there's one more part to it," Deaca said. "I think you needed to know about me and that the church is splitting because I exist."

"That's what Colonel Washington believes as well, and why he told me my place is with the Trusted Rebels now." Giles Corey said from his seat in the corner. A loud knock on the door caught everyone off guard.

"What are our plans?" Minguet asked as he reached for the door handle.

"I think I may have some insight into that," Enyeto said, stepping through the open door. "Before we do anything, I need to see an ELF about a sword." The confused looks made her smile.

Epilogue Part Two

Flying through a beautiful mountain range between time, an owl's wings beat a fevered pace as she glanced above and below her and then side to side searching everywhere. 'Nothing,' she thought as the ground below went from an empty meadow to a pine forest. Glancing at some motion to her side, she nearly clipped a very tall tree ahead of her.

"That was close. I must need some rest," Protectorate said aloud. "There's nothing he—." A giant paw swatted her from amongst the branches, sending her crashing into the ground. Her small body bounced off several trees, boulders, and the ground until she came to a rest. Managing to keep her consciousness, only just, she transformed back into her true form and attempted to stand.

The huge dog in front of her took the shape of a man. Larger than any form any god had ever taken, he said, "You should've stayed a peacock. I like peacocks." His voice was deep and gravelly.

"So you are back, Pedagogue was right," Protectorate said as she finally got to her feet, making ready for a fight.

"Apollo is a better name for him, but Teacher works."

"Yes, he's back and he's not alone," a woman's voice said as Protectorate felt the blade that was threatening behind her.

"What's the matter mother? Did the golden boy's prophecy fail to see her?" the man asked.

And So It Begins!!!

Trusted Rebel Book One
The Lil' Dog Out in Front

The Six are becoming The Eight or possibly The Seven, if Protectorate doesn't find a way out of the situation she's in. What is the new embodiment of war? And who is the new god that Pedagogue didn't see arriving? And that just touches on the questions from between... How will the Trusted Rebels use the six questions? Who are Rebecca Nurse, Deliverance Dane and Giles Corey? How do they fit in with the Trusted Rebels? Now that the Esperer has been chosen, will the predictions of the new dark uprising which will destroy the Techno-Pagan church end up pitting her against the new gods?

Thank you for reading the first book in the Trusted Rebels series. If you enjoyed this novel, please click the title above to leave a review. Each and every review is very important to independent authors, as we do not have the juggernaut support staffs that the major authors/publishers do.

If you happen to be into conservative political thrillers, please search for The Mill Series by JW Scott. Or you can purchase paperbacks through on Createspace.com

If there is an issue finding the titles, please drop an email to APGuild@outlook.com. You can join our Barking Chain, our email list, for a monthly newsletter, opportunity for free copies of upcoming books, and general commentary by going to: http://eepurl.com/VuUDf

Love and Strength,

JW Scott